Günter Grass

CAT AND MOUSE
and Other Writings

The German Library: Volume 93

Volkmar Sander, General Editor

Günter Grass

CAT AND MOUSE
and Other Writings

Edited by A. Leslie Willson

Foreword by John Irving

CONTINUUM · NEW YORK

833.914
Gra

1994
The Continuum Publishing Company
370 Lexington Avenue, New York, NY 10017

The German Library
is published in cooperation with Deutsches Haus,
New York University.
This volume has been supported by Inter Nationes,
and a grant from Robert Bosch Jubiläumsstiftung.

Printed in the United States of America

Library of Congress Cataloging-in-Publication Data

Grass, Günter, 1927–
    [Selections. English. 1994]
    Cat and mouse and other writings / Günter Grass ; edited by A.
Leslie Willson ; foreword by John Irving.
        p.   cm. — (The German library ; v. 93)
    ISBN 0-8264-0732-3 (alk. paper). — ISBN 0-8264-0733-1 (pbk. :
alk. paper)
    I. Willson, A. Leslie (Amos Leslie), 1923–   . II. Title.
III. Series.
PT2613.R338A28   1994
833'.914—dc20   94-12221
                                                            CIP

Acknowledgments will be found on page 295,
which constitutes an extension of the copyright page.

Contents

SPEECHES

Foreword

I t is important to realize that Günter Grass has a long-standing reputation of telling Germans what they don't want to hear. Against the authoritative landscape of history, Grass's characters are at once larger than life and vividly real; yet they confront the authority of history with an even larger authority — Grass's relentless imagination. Günter Grass does not distort history; he out-imagines it.

When Grass made very serious fun of the Germany of the Third Reich, many Germans laughed with him. When Grass makes very serious fun of the Germany of today, fewer Germans are laughing. Quite the opposite of trivializing the past, Grass has always said that it is impossible to maximize the Holocaust — that too much could never be made of it. And as for his predictions regarding a reunified Germany, he has been largely right, and to be right about such horrors as now befall the new Germany does not make Grass any happier.

Günter Grass, both in his fiction and in his courageous, often unpopular politics has consistently spoken out against the "many-faceted moral bankruptcy of the Christian West." He has not limited his speaking out to the repression of the West *and* the East, nor to the insidious fear-mongering of the right wing; he has also bashed the irresponsibility of the New Left. Consistently, he voices tolerance, good humor, and good sense. It is not surprising that he has made many enemies among those literati who are merely fashionable, among polemicists, among the politically cynical and the politically impatient. Predictably, Grass's critics have complained that his novels have become deliberately terrifying and apocalyptic.

No wonder. He has never been a writer who seeks to be *liked*. As a novelist, he is a wide-ranging moral authority; he's *not supposed to be* "polite." In fact he's often at his best when he's a little *im*polite.

That was what my former landlady in Vienna said about him. This was 1962, when I was a student at the University of Vienna. I was carrying around the German edition of *Die Blechtrommel*, pretending my German was good enough that I could read Grass in the original. I knew the book was good, but unfortunately I couldn't read it without a dictionary — or without one or two Austrian students sitting beside me. Nevertheless, I carried the book around with me; it was a great way to meet girls. And one day my landlady saw me carrying the book around and she asked me what was taking me so long, or was I reading *Die Blechtrommel* twice? Well, I was surprised that a woman of my landlady's generation was also reading Günter Grass — in those days, I preferred to think of Grass as exclusively student property — and so I asked her what she thought of Grass, and (proper Viennese that she was) she said only: "Er ist ein bißchen unhöflich." ("He is a little impolite.") Of course, it was clear that she *loved* him.

In his novel *The Call of the Toad* he is even a little impolite about such a revered subject as death, and especially concerning where we want to be buried. If Grass once described a writer's gradual progress as "the diary of a snail," now the writer has swallowed a toad and it is this creature (within him) that compels him to speak. Günter Grass's toads have a way of speaking to us even after they've been flattened on the highway. This is an exquisite novel, both political and a love story; it is as bitterly comic and ironic a short novel as Grass's *Cat and Mouse;* it is as moving and touching a love story as García Márquez's *Love in the Time of Cholera,* but it doesn't drift so far into fantasy as that novel. Indeed, as in the very best of his novels, Grass is Dickensian... in the sense that he combines darkly comic satire with the most earthly love, the most positively domestic affection.

And just as Günter Grass is capable of out-imagining history, he will long outlast his critics... just as snails make their own progress and toads go on crossing the road.

In 1962, I was proceeding at less than a snail's pace through *Die Blechtrommel;* it was embarrassing — but I couldn't read German as complex as the German of Günter Grass. Finally, a friend from the States saved me; he sent me the English translation of *The Tin Drum,* and from that moment I knew that all I ever wanted to do was write novels, and read them; was to be funny and to be angry; was to stay funny and to stay angry.

Then one night — this was maybe eleven years ago — Günter and I had dinner in New York, and as we were saying good-bye, I thought he looked a little worried. Well, Grass often looks worried, but what he said surprised me because I realized that he was worried about *me.* He said, "You don't seem quite as angry as you used to be." This was a good warning; I've never forgotten it.

After leaving Günter in Frankfurt in October of 1990, the day after reunification, I traveled to several German cities. I was reading largely to university students — in Bonn, in Hamburg, in Munich, in Stuttgart. About a hundred times, students asked me if I had given Owen Meany the same initials as Oskar Matzerath as a gesture of homage to Günter Grass — a kind of tipping the hat — and I said Yes, Yes, Yes (of course, of course, of course)...about a hundred times. But I had also been quoted in the press as agreeing with Grass about the problems of reunifying Germany too quickly, and everywhere I went, although the audiences at my readings were generally friendly, there was always at least one *un*friendly question from the audience — and it always concerned the matter of my agreeing with Grass. It was Grass they were angry with. As for me, they thought I was just some fool foreigner who was going along with what Grass had said. And all *I* did was *repeat* what he had said, and repeat that Günter Grass had *always* made good sense to me. But this answer was unsatisfying to the students, for they had already embraced the future, and they did not want to be reminded of the past. To them, there was comfort in a mob, for a mob can drown out any single voice.

It is inevitable that we writers take no comfort from a mob. *Our* method is speaking slowly and carefully and at length, like snails and toads. A mob always wants to go too fast.

As so often, *The Tin Drum* returns to mind. I am thinking of the part when the Nazis force the Jewish toy merchant, Sigismund Markus, to kill himself. At that moment, little Oskar Matzerath knows that he has seen his last tin drum. For poor Markus, for himself and for a Germany forever guilty for its Jews — little Oskar mourns. "There was once a toy merchant, his name was Markus, and he took all the toys in the world away with him out of this world."

Günter Grass is the greatest living novelist today.

JOHN IRVING

(Excerpted from an introduction by John Irving to a reading by Günter Grass on December 14, 1992, at the 92nd Street Y in New York City. Printed with the permission of John Irving.)

Introduction

G ünter Grass is a born everything: an orator with a voice that
ripples with the tides of the Baltic Sea, a consummate artist
whose hands mold and draw a bewitching metaphorical world,
and a writer whose like has seldom been seen, who seems to have
been imbued from birth with an uncanny control of every figure of
speech ever to come from the pens of generations of writers. Readers of Günter Grass who have thrilled to the pyrotechnics of his
great novels know only a small part of the author, whose poems
are songs of enthrallment and whose plays are serious frolics. He
is a political man of unusual courage who knows the power of
a single word. Had he been born in the seventeenth century he
might have been doomed as a heretic. As a twentieth-century man
headed for the millennium, Günter Grass reflects the worries and
concerns of billions of his fellows on this earth: the ghastly face
of hunger appalls him; the wretched homeless engage his sympathy; the horror of war and mankind's merciless onslaught on one
another and on Nature anger him. He is incomparably articulate.
He can be wrathful. An encyclopedia of history, he knows that
rats may have a better chance than we to inherit the earth. But
he knows, too, that hope hunches down in squalor and endures
in human eyes. He's a born everything, maybe every man, woman,
and child, every dog and doll and scarecrow, every snail and toad,
not to mention fish and fowl. No other author can cook up a nasty
brew or prepare a feast unequaled as can Günter Grass.

In 1956, Günter Grass published his first book, a slim volume
of poetry with the title *Die Vorzüge der Windhühner* (The Ad-
vantages of Wind Chickens), with ink drawings by the author.
That first book, a paperback whose title poem was lost when li-

braries threw away the integral dust jacket and bound the book for its shelves, established full blown the distinctive literary voice of the author and linked drawings to words, an inseparable amalgamation of his unique artistic instincts. In later years he was to explain that he tests his metaphors with that merciless instrument, the drawing pen — if the metaphors work graphically, then they are valid as literary devices. His graphic work has graced the dust jackets his books (and illustrated his volumes of poetry and some of his plays) ever since. With the publication of his first massive novel, *Die Blechtrommel* (*The Tin Drum*) in 1959, Grass became an overnight sensation throughout the world, a reputation that he has maintained to this day as Germany's most versatile author in the twentieth century.

Born in Danzig in 1927, Günter Grass added the Polish free city (now Gdansk) to the world's famous literary cities: Dublin, Berlin, Paris, San Francisco, and Oxford (Mississippi) among others. An exuberant reader Grass has sprinkled literary, historical, fairy-tale, ethnic, political, and religious allusions through all his work, which is written in an inimitable style that is instantly recognizable by virtue of an amazing array of figures of speech and inventive turns of phrase. The public readings he has given of his work are legendary, since he is blessed with a vigorous and vivid baritone instrument: his voice. When he met with translators at work on his novel *Der Butt* (*The Flounder*) to answer their queries, they discovered that his mere reading of poems from the novel cleared up all the interpolative questions they had.

The German political and social character — particularly the guilt felt by many after the events of World War II and their burdensome Nazi heritage — is a theme that runs through much of his work, as it does in the novella *Katz und Maus* (*Cat and Mouse*), a work published in 1961 that was reviled and praised. After the publication of the novel *Hundejahre* (*Dog Years*) in 1963, critics eventually realized how the three works (*The Tin Drum, Cat and Mouse,* and *Dog Years*) were connected in theme and character and dubbed the three the *Danzig Trilogy,* a designation that remains.

Grass became involved in political battles in Germany during the sixties, adding his voice in political essays and speeches in support of Willi Brandt and the SPD (Socialist Party of Germany): a crowing rooster sketched by Grass became the Party symbol. His play *Die Plebejer proben den Aufstand* (*The Plebians Rehearse the Uprising*) — with an uncomplimentary portrait of Bertolt Brecht, in the view of many critics — became a sensation in 1966. The novel *Örtlich betäubt* of 1969 (*Local Anaesthetic*) comes to grips with the restless political age, particularly the unrest of German youth. The 1972 volume *Aus dem Tagebuch einer Schnecke* (*From the Diary of a Snail*) is a semi-autobiographical narrative that elaborates on his political views and involvements.

Grass, the author of plays and ballets, after little success on the German stage finally stopped writing plays, blaming the interpretation of poor directors for the lack of stage triumphs. His play *Davor* (*Uptight* on the stage in America, *Max* in published form in English) of 1970 enjoyed its best success in Washington, D.C., in a production directed by Alan Schneider in the spring of 1971.

Grass received the Prize of the Group 47 in 1958 (for a reading of a chapter from *The Tin Drum*) and remained through the years a devoted and supportive member of the Group. His accolade to founder Hans Werner Richter and the authors of the Group was made in 1979 in the novella *Das Treffen in Telgte* (*The Meeting at Telgte*), which — though not a true key novel — memorializes the postwar twentieth-century renaissance of German writing in an exuberant tale about poets of the flourishing baroque period in Germany, who meet toward the end of the horrendous Thirty Years' War in 1647.

The concern Grass has expressed in all his writings — in poems, plays, novels, and essays, as well as in his many sculptured and graphic works — about the human condition, about the welfare of humankind, is exemplified in other novels: *Der Butt* (*The Flounder*), published in 1979, riled many feminists with its account of the battle of the sexes, which has been waged since time immemorial. *Kopfgeburten oder die Deutschen sterben aus* (*Head-births; or, the Germans Are Dying Out*) of 1980 is the first of a series of novels on apocalyptic themes, in this instance the increasing population of the earth. *Die Rättin* (*The Rat*) brought the hero of *The Tin Drum*, Oskar Matzerath, up to date and continued the view of the future in 1986; and the journal of his sojourn in India, *Zunge Zeigen* (*Show Your Tongue*) in 1988 is a desperate description of hunger and poverty in the world on the example of India. The most recent novel by Grass, *Unkenrufe* (*The Call of the Toad*), 1992, returns to Gdansk with a German widower who meets a Polish widow and embarks on a capitalistic enterprise ad absurdum, the return of dead Germans (former residents of Danzig) to the city of their birth for burial.

Günter Grass is irresistible to readers, who delight in his literary antics and pyrotechnics while being entertained, horrified, scandalized, amazed, and enthralled. The work of Grass is a catalogue not only of German peccadilloes and escapades in the twentieth century, but the work as well of an indefatigable latter-day prophet who warns humankind of the perilous present (the result of a ponderous and wicked past) in a world where fear is still omnipresent, mayhem is rampant, and trees turn brown and wither, but the human spirit remains undaunted.

A. L. W.

Part One

CAT AND MOUSE

Chapter 1

...and one day, after Mahlke had learned to swim, we were lying in the grass, in the Schlagball field. I ought to have gone to
the dentist, but they wouldn't let me because I was hard to replace
on the team. My tooth was howling. A cat sauntered diagonally
across the field and no one threw anything at it. A few of the boys
were chewing or plucking at blades of grass. The cat belonged to
the caretaker and was black. Hotten Sonntag rubbed his bat with
a woolen stocking. My tooth marked time. The tournament had
been going on for two hours. We had lost hands down and were
waiting for the return game. It was a young cat, but no kitten.
In the stadium, handball goals were being made thick and fast on
both sides. My tooth kept saying one word, over and over again.
On the cinder track the sprinters were practicing starts or limber-
ing up. The cat meandered about. A trimotored plane crept across
the sky, slow and loud, but couldn't drown out my tooth. Through
the stalks of grass the caretaker's black cat showed a white bib.
Mahlke was asleep. The wind was from the east, and the crema-
torium between the United Cemeteries and the Engineering School
was operating. Mr. Mallenbrandt, the gym teacher, blew his whistle: Change sides. The cat practiced. Mahlke was asleep or seemed
to be. I was next to him with my toothache. Still practicing, the cat
came closer. Mahlke's Adam's apple attracted attention because it
was large, always in motion, and threw a shadow. Between me
and Mahlke the caretaker's black cat tensed for a leap. We formed
a triangle. My tooth was silent and stopped marking time: for
Mahlke's Adam's apple had become the cat's mouse. It was so
young a cat, and Mahlke's whatsis was so active — in any case
the cat leaped at Mahlke's throat; or one of us caught the cat and

held it up to Mahlke's neck; or I, with or without my toothache, seized the cat and showed it Mahlke's mouse: and Joachim Mahlke let out a yell, but suffered only slight scratches.

And now it is up to me, who called your mouse to the attention of this cat and all cats, to write. Even if we were both invented, I should have to write. Over and over again the fellow who invented us because it's his business to invent people obliges me to take your Adam's apple in my hand and carry it to the spot that saw it win or lose. And so, to begin with, I make the mouse bob up and down above the screwdriver, I fling a multitude of replete sea gulls into the fitful northeast wind, high over Mahlke's head, call the weather summery and persistently fair, assume that the wreck was a former mine sweeper of the *Czaika* class, and give the Baltic the color of thick-glass seltzer bottles. Now that the scene of action has been identified as a point southeast of the Neufahrwasser harbor buoy, I make Mahlke's skin, from which water is still running in rivulets, take on a texture somewhere between fine and coarse-grained. It was not fear, however, that roughened Mahlke's skin, but the shivers customary after long immersion in the sea that seized hold of Mahlke and took the smoothness from his skin.

And yet none of us, as we huddled lean and long-armed between our upthrust knees on the remains of the bridge, had asked Mahlke to dive down again into the fo'c'sle of the sunken mine sweeper and the adjoining engine room amidships, and work something loose with his screwdriver, a screw, a little wheel, or something really special: a brass plate inscribed with the directions in Polish and English for operating some machine. We were sitting on the superstructure, or as much of it as remained above the water, of a former Polish mine sweeper of the *Czaika* class, built in Gdynia and launched in Modlin, which had been sunk the year before southeast of the harbor buoy, well outside the channel so that it did not interfere with shipping.

Since then gull droppings had dried on the rust. In all kinds of weather the gulls flew sleek and smooth, with eyes like glass beads on the sides of their heads, grazing the remains of the pilothouse, then wildly up again, according to some indecipherable plan, squirting their slimy droppings in full flight—and they never fell into the soft sea but always on the rusty superstructure. Hard, dense, calcareous, the droppings clung fast, side by side in innumerable spots, or heaped up in mounds. And always when we sat on the barge, fingernails and toenails tried to chip off the droppings. That's why our nails cracked and not because we bit our fingernails — except for Schilling, who was always chewing at them and had nails like rivets. Only Mahlke had long nails, though they were yellow from all his diving, and he kept them long by neither biting them nor scratching at the gull droppings. And he was the only one who never ate the chips we broke loose — the rest of us, because it was there, chewed the stony, shell-like mess into a foaming slime, which we spat overboard. The stuff tasted like nothing at all or like plaster or like fish meal or like everything imaginable: happiness, girls, God in His heaven. "Do you realize," said Winter, who sang very nicely, "that tenors eat gull droppings every day?" Often the gulls caught our calcareous spittle in full flight, apparently suspecting nothing.

When shortly after the outbreak of the war Joachim Mahlke turned fourteen, he could neither swim nor ride a bicycle; there was nothing striking about his appearance and he lacked the Adam's apple that was later to lure the cat. He had been excused from gymnastics and swimming, because he had presented certificates showing him to be sickly. Even before he learned to ride a bicycle — a ludicrous figure with his deep-red, protuberant ears and his knees thrust sideways as he pedaled — he reported for swimming in the winter season, at the Niederstadt pool, but at first he was admitted only to the "dry swimming" class for eight-to-ten-year-olds. Nor did he make much progress the following summer. The swimming teacher at Brösen Beach, a typical swimming teacher with a torso like a life buoy and thin hairless legs, had to put Mahlke through his paces in the sand and then hold him by a life line. But after we had swum away from him several afternoons in a row and come back telling fantastic stories about the sunken mine sweeper, he was mightily inspired and in less than two weeks he was swimming.

Earnestly and conscientiously he swam back and forth between the pier, the big diving tower, and the bathing beach, and he had no doubt achieved a certain endurance by the time he began to practice diving off the little breakwater outside the pier, first bringing up some common Baltic mussels, then diving for a beer bottle filled with sand, which he threw out pretty far. My guess is that Mahlke soon succeeded in recovering the bottle quite regularly, for when he began to dive with us on the mine sweeper, he was no longer a beginner.

He pleaded with us to let him come along. Six or seven of us were getting ready for our daily swim, elaborately moistening our skins in the shallow water of the family pool, as a precaution against sudden chill. And there was Mahlke on the plank walk: "Please take me with you. I'll make it, I'm positive."

A screwdriver hung around his neck, distracting attention from his Adam's apple.

"OK!" And Mahlke came along. Between the first and second sandbank he passed us, and we didn't bother to catch up with him. "Let him knock himself out."

When Mahlke swam breaststroke, the screwdriver bobbed visibly up and down between his shoulder blades, for it had a wooden handle. When he swam on his back, the wooden handle danced about on his chest, but never entirely covered the horrid piece of cartilage between chin and collarbone, which cut through the water like a dorsal fin, leaving a wake behind it.

And then Mahlke showed us. He dove several times in quick succession with his screwdriver and brought up whatever he was able to unscrew: lids, pieces of sheathing, a part of the generator; he found a rope, and with the help of the decrepit winch hoisted up a genuine fire extinguisher from the fo'c'sle. The thing — made in Germany, I might add — still worked; Mahlke proved it, squirting streams of foam to show us how you extinguish with foam, extinguishing the glass-green sea — from the very first day he was tops.

The flakes still lay in islands and long streaks on the flat, even swell, attracting a few gulls which were soon repelled, settled, and like a big mess of whipped cream turned sour drifted off toward the beach. Then Mahlke called it a day and sat down in the shadow of the pilothouse; and even before the stray tatters of foam on the bridge had time to lose their stiffness and start trembling in the breeze, his skin had taken on that shriveled, coarse-grained look.

Mahlke shivered and his Adam's apple jogged up and down; his screwdriver did dance steps over his quaking collarbones. His back, white in spots, burned lobster-red from the shoulders down, forever peeling with fresh sunburn on both sides of his prominent spinal column, was also covered with gooseflesh and shaken with fitful shudders. His yellowish lips, blue at the edges, bared his chattering teeth. But he tried to bring his body — and his teeth — under control by clasping his knees, which he had bruised on the barnacle-covered bulkheads, with his big waterlogged hands.

Hotten Sonntag — or was it I? — rubbed Mahlke down. "Lord, man, don't go catching something. We've still got to get back." The screwdriver began to calm down.

The way out took us twenty-five minutes from the breakwater, thirty-five from the beach. We needed a good three quarters of an hour to get back. No matter how exhausted he was, he was always standing on the breakwater a good minute ahead of us. He never lost the lead he had taken the first day. Before we reached the barge — as we called the mine sweeper — Mahlke had already been under once, and as soon as we reached out our washerwoman's hands, all of us pretty much at once, for the rust and gull droppings of the bridge or the jutting gun mounts, he silently exhibited a hinge or something or other that had come off easily, and already he was shivering, though after the second or third time he covered himself with a thick, extravagant coat of Nivea cream; for Mahlke had plenty of pocket money.

Mahlke was an only child.

Mahlke was half an orphan.

Mahlke's father was dead.

Winter and summer Mahlke wore old-fashioned high shoes which he must have inherited from his father.

He carried the screwdriver around his neck on a shoelace for high black shoes.

It occurs to me only now that, in addition to the screwdriver, Mahlke, for certain reasons, wore something else around his neck; but the screwdriver was more conspicuous.

He wore a little silver chain, from which hung something silver and Catholic: the Blessed Virgin; most likely he had always worn it, but we had never noticed; he certainly had it on ever since the day when he had started to swim in harness and to make figures in the sand while practicing his kick.

Never, not even in gym class, did Mahlke remove the medal from his neck; for no sooner had he taken up dry swimming and swimming in harness in the winter swimming pool at Niederstadt than he turned up in our gymnasium, and never again did he produce any doctor's certificates. Either the silver Virgin disappeared under his white gym shirt or lay just over the red stripe that ran around it at chest level.

Even the parallel bars held no horrors for Mahlke. Only three or four of the best members of the first squad were equal to the horse exercises, but Mahlke was right with them, leaping from the springboard, sailing over the long leather horse, and landing on the mat with Virgin awry, sending up clouds of dust. When he did knee-swings on the horizontal bar — his form was miserable, but later he succeeded in doing two more than Hotten Sonntag, our gymnastics champion — well, when Mahlke ground out his thirty-seven knee-swings, the medal tugged out of his gym shirt, and hustled thirty-seven times around the squeaking horizontal bar, always in advance of his medium-brown hair. But it never came free from his neck, for the wildly agitated chain was held in place not only by his jutting Adam's apple but also by his protuberant occiput, with its thick growth of hair.

The screwdriver lay over the medal, and in places the shoelace covered the chain. However, the screwdriver did not outshine the medal, especially as the object with the wooden handle was not allowed in the gymnasium. Our gym teacher, a Mr. Mallenbrandt who was also assistant principal and was well known in sports circles because he had written a rulebook to end all rulebooks for the game of Schlagball, forbade Mahlke to wear the screwdriver around his neck in gym class. Mallenbrandt never found any fault with the medal on Mahlke's neck, because in addition to physical culture and geography, he taught religion, and up to the second year of the war guided the remnants of a Catholic workers' gymnastic society over and under the horizontal and parallel bars.

And so the screwdriver had to wait in the dressing room, over his shirt on the hook, while the slightly worn silver Virgin was privileged to hang from Mahlke's neck and succor him amid gymnastic perils.

A common screwdriver it was, cheap and sturdy. Often Mahlke, in order to detach a small plaque no larger than the name plate beside an apartment door, had to dive five or six times, especially when the plate was affixed to metal and the screws were rusted. On the other hand, he sometimes managed, after only two dives, to bring up larger plaques with long texts inscribed on them by using his screwdriver as a jimmy and prying screws and all from the waterlogged wooden sheathing. He was no great collector; he gave many of his plaques to Winter and Jürgen Kupka, who fanatically collected everything removable, including street markers and the signs in public toilets; for himself he took only the few items that particularly struck his fancy.

Mahlke didn't make things easy for himself; while we dozed on the barge, he worked under water. We scratched at the gull droppings and turned brown as cigars; those of us who had blond hair were transformed into towheads. Mahlke at most took on fresh lobster tones. While we followed the ships north of the beacon, he looked unswervingly downward: reddened, slightly inflamed lids with sparse lashes, I think; light-blue eyes which filled with curiosity only under water. Sometimes Mahlke came up without any plaques or other spoils, but with a broken or hopelessly bent screwdriver. That too he would exhibit, and always got an effect. The gesture with which he tossed it over his shoulder into the water, exasperating the gulls, was commanded neither by resigned disappointment nor by aimless rage. Never did Mahlke throw away a broken tool with indifference, real or affected. Even this act of tossing away signified: I'll soon have something more to show you.

...and once—a hospital ship with two smokestacks had put into port, and after a brief discussion we had identified it as the *Kaiser* of the East Prussian Maritime Service — Joachim Mahlke went down into the fo'c'sle without a screwdriver and, holding his nose with two fingers, vanished in the open, slate-green, slightly submerged forward hatchway. He went in headfirst — his hair was plastered flat and parted from swimming and diving; he pulled in his back and hips, kicked once at the empty air, but then, bracing both feet against the edge of the hatch, pushed down into the dusky cool aquarium, flood-lighted through open portholes: nervous sticklebacks, an immobile school of lampreys, swaying hammocks, still firmly attached at the ends, overgrown with seaweed, a playhouse for baby herring. Rarely a stray cod. Only rumors of eels. We never once saw a flounder.

We clasped our slightly trembling knees, chewed gull droppings into a sludge; half weary, half fascinated, we counted a formation of Navy cutters, followed the stacks of the hospital ship, whence smoke was still rising vertically, exchanged sidelong glances. He stayed down a long while — gulls circled, the swell gurgled over the bow, broke against the forward gun mount — the gun itself had been removed. A splashing as the water flowed back between the ventilators behind the bridge, licking always at the same rivets; lime under fingernails; itching on dry skin, shimmering light, chugging of motors in the wind, private parts half stiff, seventeen poplars between Brösen and Glettkau — and then he came shooting upward: bluish-red around the chin, yellowish over the cheekbones. His hair parted exactly in the middle, he rose like a fountain from the hatch, staggered over the bow through water up to his knees, reached for the jutting gun mount, and fell watery-goggle-eyed to his knees; we had to pull him up on the bridge. But before the water had stopped flowing from his nose and the corner of his mouth, he showed us his find, a steel screwdriver in one piece. Made in England. Stamped on the metal: Sheffield. No scars, no rust, still coated with grease. The water formed into beads and rolled off.

Every day for over a year Mahlke wore this heavy, to all intents and purposes unbreakable screwdriver on a shoelace, even after we had stopped or almost stopped swimming out to the barge. Though he was a good Catholic, it became a kind of cult with him. Before gym class, for instance, he would give the thing to Mr. Mallenbrandt for safekeeping; he was dreadfully afraid it might be stolen, and even took it with him to St. Mary's Chapel; for not only on Sunday, but also on weekdays, he went to early Mass on Marineweg, not far from the Neuschottland co-operative housing development.

He and his English screwdriver didn't have far to go — out of Osterzeile and down Bärenweg. Quantities of two-story houses, villas with gable roofs, porticoes, and espaliered fruit trees. Then two rows of housing developments, plain drab walls ornamented only with water spots. To the right the streetcar line turned off and with it the overhead wires, mostly against a partly cloudy sky. To the left, the sandy, sorry-looking kitchen gardens of the railroad workers: bowers and rabbit hutches built with the black and red boards of abandoned freight cars. Behind the gardens the signals of the railway leading to the Free Port. Silos, movable and stationary cranes. The strange full-colored superstructures of the freighters. The two gray battleships with their old-fashioned turrets were still there, the swimming dock, the Germania bread factory; and silvery sleek, at medium height, a few captive balloons, lurching and bobbing. In the right background, the Gudrun School (the Helen Lange School of former years) blocking out the iron hodgepodge of the Schichau Dockyards as far as the big hammer crane. To this side of it, well-tended athletic fields, freshly painted goal posts, foul lines marked in lime on the short grass: next Sunday Blue-and-Yellow versus Schellmühl 98 — no grandstand, but a modern, tall-windowed gymnasium painted in light ocher. The fresh red roof of this edifice, oddly enough, was topped with a tarred wooden cross; for St. Mary's Chapel had formerly been a gymnasium belonging to the Neuschottland Sports Club. It had been found necessary to transform it into an emergency church, because the Church of the Sacred Heart was too far away; for years the people of Neuschottland, Schellmühl, and the housing development between Osterzeile and Westerzeile, mostly shipyard, railroad, or post-office workers, had sent petitions to the bishop in Oliva until, still during the Free State period, this gymnasium had been purchased, remodeled, and consecrated.

Despite the tortuous and colorful pictures and ornaments, some privately donated but for the most part deriving from the cellars and storerooms of just about every church in the diocese, there was no denying or concealing the gymnasium quality of this church — no amount of incense or wax candles could drown out the aroma of the chalk, leather, and sweat of former years and former handball matches. And the chapel never lost a certain air of Protestant parsimony, the fanatical sobriety of a meetinghouse.

In the Neo-Gothic Church of the Sacred Heart, built of bricks at the end of the nineteenth century, not far from the suburban railway station, Joachim Mahlke's steel screwdriver would have seemed strange, ugly, and sacrilegious. In St. Mary's Chapel, on the other hand, he might perfectly well have worn it openly: the little chapel with its well-kept linoleum floor, its rectangular frosted glass windowpanes starting just under the ceiling, the neat iron fixtures that had formerly served to hold the horizontal bar firmly in place, the planking in the coarse-grained concrete ceiling, and beneath it the iron (though whitewashed) crossbeams to which the rings, the trapeze, and half a dozen climbing ropes had formerly been affixed, was so modern, so coldly functional a chapel, despite the painted and gilded plaster which bestowed blessing and consecration on all sides, that the steel screwdriver which Mahlke, in prayer and then in communion, felt it necessary to have dangling from his neck, would never have attracted the attention either of the few devotees of early Mass, or of Father Gusewski and his sleepy altar boy — who often enough was myself.

No, there I'm going too far. It would certainly not have escaped me. As often as I served at the altar, even during the gradual prayers I did my best, for various reasons, to keep an eye on you. And you played safe; you kept your treasure under your shirt, and that was why your shirt had those grease spots vaguely indicating the shape of the screwdriver. Seen from the altar, he knelt in the second pew of the left-hand row, aiming his prayer with open eyes — light gray they were, I think, and usually inflamed from all his swimming and diving — in the direction of the Virgin.

...and once — I don't remember which summer it was — was it during the first summer vacation on the barge, shortly after the row in France, or was it the following summer? — hot and misty day, enormous crowd on the family beach, sagging pennants, overripe flesh, big rush at the refreshments stands, on burning feet over the fiber runners, past locked cabins full of tittering, through a turbulent mob of children engaged in slobbering, tumbling, and cutting their feet; and in the midst of this spawn which would now be twenty-three years old, beneath the solicitous eyes of the grownups, a little brat, who must have been about three, pounded monotonously on a child's tin drum, turning the afternoon into an infernal smithy — whereupon we took to the water and swam out to our barge; from the beach, in the lifeguard's binoculars for instance, we were six diminishing heads in motion; one head in advance of the rest and first to reach the goal.

We threw ourselves on burning though wind-cooled rust and gull droppings and lay motionless. Mahlke had already been under twice. He came up with something in his left hand. He had searched the crew's quarters, in and under the half-rotted hammocks, some tossing limply, others still lashed fast, amid swarms of iridescent sticklebacks, through forests of seaweed where lampreys darted in and out, and in a matted mound, once the sea kit of Seaman Duszynski or Liszinski, he had found a bronze medallion the size of a hand, bearing on one side, below a small embossed Polish eagle, the name of the owner and the date on which it had been conferred, and on the other a relief of a mustachioed general. After a certain amount of rubbing with sand and powdered gull droppings the circular inscription told us that Mahlke had brought to light the portrait of Marshal Pilsudski.

For two weeks Mahlke concentrated on medallions; he also found a kind of tin plate commemorating a regatta in the Gdynia roadstead and amidships, between fo'c'sle and engine room, in the cramped, almost inaccessible officers' mess, a silver medal the size of a mark piece, with a silver ring to pass a chain through; the reverse was flat, worn, and anonymous, but the face, amid a profusion of ornament, bore the Virgin and Child in sharp relief.

A raised inscription identified her as the famous Matka Boska Czestochowska; and when Mahlke on the bridge saw what he had found, we offered him sand, but he did not polish his medal; he preferred the black patina.

The rest of us wanted to see shining silver. But before we had finished arguing, he had knelt down on his knobby knees in the shadow of the pilothouse, shifting his treasure about until it was at the right angle for his gaze, lowered in devotion. We laughed as, bluish and shivering, he crossed himself with his waterlogged fingertips, attempted to move his lips in prayer, and produced a bit of Latin between chattering teeth. I still think it was even then something from his favorite sequence, which normally was spoken only on the Friday before Palm Sunday: *"Virgo virginum praeclara, Mihi iam non sis amara..."*

Later, after Dr. Klohse, our principal, had forbidden Mahlke to wear this Polish article openly on his neck during classes — Klohse was a high party official, though he seldom wore his uniform at school — Joachim Mahlke contented himself with wearing his usual little amulet and the steel screwdriver beneath the Adam's apple which a cat had taken for a mouse.

He hung the blackened silver Virgin between Pilsudski's bronze profile and the postcard-size photo of Commodore Bonte, the hero of Narvik.

Chapter 2

Was all this praying and worshiping in jest? Your house was on Westerzeile. You had a strange sense of humor, if any. No, your house was on Osterzeile. All the streets in the housing development looked alike. And yet you had only to eat a sandwich and we would laugh, each infecting the other. Every time we had to laugh at you, it came as a surprise to us. But when Dr. Brunies, one of our teachers, asked the boys of our class what profession they were planning to take up and you — you already knew how to swim — said: "I'm going to be a clown and make people laugh," no one laughed in the classroom — and I myself was frightened. For while Mahlke firmly and candidly stated his intention of becoming a clown in a circus or somewhere else, he made so solemn a face that it was really to be feared that he would one day make people laugh themselves sick, if only by publicly praying to the Virgin between the lion tamer and the trapeze act; but that prayer of yours on the barge must have been in earnest — or wasn't it?

He lived on Osterzeile and not on Westerzeile. The one-family house stood beside, between, and opposite similar one-family houses which could be distinguished perhaps by different patterns or folds in the curtains, but hardly by the vegetation of the little gardens out in front. And each garden had its little birdhouse on a pole and its glazed garden ornaments: frogs, mushrooms, or dwarfs. In front of Mahlke's house sat a ceramic frog. But in front of the next house and the next, there were also green ceramic frogs.

In short, it was number twenty-four, and when you approached from Wolfsweg, Mahlke lived in the fourth house on the left side of the street. Like Westerzeile, which ran parallel to it, Osterzeile was perpendicular to Bärenweg, which ran parallel to Wolfsweg. When you went down Westerzeile from Wolfsweg and looked to the left and westward over the red tiled roofs, you saw the west side and front of a tower with a tarnished bulbiform steeple. If you went down Osterzeile in the same direction, you saw over the rooftops the east side and front of the same belfry; for Christ Church lay on the far side of Bärenweg, exactly halfway between Osterzeile and Westerzeile, and with its four dials beneath the green, bulbiform roof, provided the whole neighborhood, from Max-Halbe-Platz to the Catholic and clockless St. Mary's Chapel, from Magdeburger Strasse to Posadowskiweg near Schellmühl, with the time of day, enabling Protestant as well as Catholic factory workers and office workers, salesgirls and schoolboys to reach their schools or places of work with interdenominational punctuality.

From his window Mahlke could see the dial of the east face of the tower. He had his room in the attic; the walls were slightly on a slant, and the rain and hail beat down directly over his head: an attic room full of the usual juvenile bric-a-brac, from the butterfly collection to the postcard photos of movie stars, lavishly decorated pursuit pilots and Panzer generals; but in the midst of all this, an unframed color print of the Sistine Madonna with the two chubby-cheeked angels at the lower edge, the Pilsudski medal, already mentioned, and the consecrated amulet from Czestochowa beside a photograph of the commander of the Narvik destroyers.

The very first time I went to see him, I noticed the stuffed snowy owl. I lived not far away, on Westerzeile; but I'm not going to speak of myself, my story is about Mahlke, or Mahlke and me, but always with the emphasis on Mahlke, for his hair was parted in the middle, he wore high shoes, he always had something or other dangling from his neck to distract the eternal cat from the eternal mouse, he knelt at the altar of the Virgin, he was the diver with the fresh sunburn; though he was always tied up in knots and his form was bad, he always had a bit of a lead on the rest of us, and no sooner had he learned to swim than he made up his mind that someday, after finishing school and all that, he would be a clown in the circus and make people laugh.

The snowy owl had Mahlke's solemn part in the middle and the same suffering, meekly resolute look, as of a redeemer plagued by inner toothache. It was well prepared, only discreetly retouched, and held a birch branch in its claws. The owl had been left him by his father.

I did my best to ignore the snowy owl, the color print of the Madonna, and the silver piece from Czestochowa; for me the center of the room was the phonograph that Mahlke had painstakingly raised from the barge. He had found no records; they must have dissolved. It was a relatively modern contrivance with a crank and a player arm. He had found it in the same officers' mess that had already yielded his silver medal and several other items. The cabin was amidships, hence inaccessible to the rest of us, even Hotten Sonntag. For we went only as far as the fo'c'sle and never ventured through the dark bulkhead, which even the fishes seldom visited, into the engine room and the cramped adjoining cabins.

Shortly before the end of our first summer vacation on the barge, Mahlke brought up the phonograph — German-made it was, like the fire extinguisher — after perhaps a dozen dives. Inch by inch he had moved it forward to the foot of the hatch and finally hoisted it up to us on the bridge with the help of the same rope that had served for the fire extinguisher.

We had to improvise a raft of driftwood and cork to haul the thing ashore; the crank was frozen with rust. We took turns in towing the raft, all of us except Mahlke.

A week later the phonograph was in his room, repaired, oiled, the metal parts freshly plated. The turntable was covered with fresh felt. After winding it in my presence, he set the rich-green turntable to revolving empty. Mahlke stood behind it with folded arms, beside the snowy owl on its birch branch. His mouse was quiet. I stood with my back to the Sistine color print, gazing either at the empty, slightly wobbling turntable, or out the mansard window, over the raw-red roof tiles, at Christ Church, one dial on the front, another on the east side of the bulbiform tower. Before the clock struck six, the phonograph droned to a stop. Mahlke wound the thing up again, demanding that I give his new rite my unflagging attention: I listened to the assortment of soft and medium sounds characteristic of an antique phonograph left to its own devices. Mahlke had as yet no records.

There were books on a long sagging shelf. He read a good deal, including religious works. In addition to the cactuses on the window sill, to models of a torpedo boat of the *Wolf* class and the dispatch boat *Cricket,* I must also mention a glass of water that always stood on the washstand beside the bowl; the water was cloudy and there was an inch-thick layer of sugar at the bottom. In this glass Mahlke each morning, with sugar and care, stirred up the milky solution designed to hold his thin, limp hair in place; he never removed the sediment of the previous day. Once he offered me the preparation and I combed the sugar water into my hair; it must be admitted that thanks to his fixative, my hairdo preserved a vitreous rigidity until evening: my scalp itched, my hands were sticky, like Mahlke's hands, from passing them over my hair to see how it was doing — but maybe the stickiness of my hands is only an idea that came to me later, maybe they were not sticky at all.

Below him, in three rooms only two of which were used, lived his mother and her elder sister. Both of them quiet as mice when he was there, always worried and proud of the boy, for to judge by his report cards Mahlke was a good student, though not at the head of the class. He was — and this detracted slightly from the merit of his performance — a year older than the rest of us, because his mother and aunt had sent the frail, or as they put it sickly, lad to grade school a year later than usual.

But he was no grind, he studied with moderation, let everyone copy from him, never snitched, showed no particular zeal except in gym class, and had a conspicuous horror of the nasty practical jokes customary in Third. He interfered, for instance, when Hotten Sonntag, having found a condom in Steffenspark, brought it to class mounted on a branch, and stretched it over our classroom doorknob. The intended victim was Dr. Treuge, a dottering half-blind pedant, who ought to have been pensioned years before. A voice called from the corridor: "He's coming," whereupon Mahlke arose, strode without haste to the door, and removed the loathsome object with a sandwich paper.

No one said a word. Once more he had shown us; and today I can say that in everything he did or did not do — in not being a grind, in studying with moderation, in allowing all and sundry to copy from him, in showing no particular zeal except in gym class, in shunning nasty practical jokes — he was always that very special, individual Mahlke, always, with or without effort, gathering applause. After all he was planning to go into the circus later or maybe on the stage; to remove loathsome objects from

doorknobs was to practice his clowning; he received murmurs of
approval and was almost a clown when he did his knee-swings on
the horizontal bar, whirling his silver Virgin through the fetid vapors of the gymnasium. But Mahlke piled up the most applause in
summer vacation on the sunken barge, although it would scarcely
have occurred to us to consider his frantic diving a circus act.
And we never laughed when Mahlke, time and time again, climbed
blue and shivering onto the barge, bringing up something or other
in order to show us what he had brought up. At most we said
with thoughtful admiration: "Man, that's great. I wish I had your
nerves. You're a cool dog all right. How'd you ever get ahold
of that?"

Applause did him good and quieted the jumping mouse on his
neck; applause also embarrassed him and started the selfsame
mouse up again. Usually he made a disparaging gesture, which
brought him new applause. He wasn't one to brag; never once did
you say: "You try it." Or: "I dare one of you guys to try." Or:
"Remember the day before yesterday, the way I went down four
times in a row, the way I went in amidships as far as the galley
and brought up that famous can. . . . None of you ever did that. I
bet it came from France, there were frogs' legs in it, tasted something like veal, but you were yellow, you wouldn't even try it after
I'd eaten half the can. And damned if I didn't raise a second can,
hell, I even found a can opener, but the second can stank, rotten
corned beef."

No, Mahlke never spoke like that. He did extraordinary things.
One day, for instance, he crawled into the barge's one-time galley
and brought up several cans of preserves, which according to the
inscriptions stamped in the metal were of English or French origin; he even located an almost serviceable can opener. Without a
word he ripped the cans open before our eyes, devoured the alleged
frogs' legs, his Adam's apple doing push-ups as he chewed — I forgot to say that Mahlke was by nature an eater — and when the
can was half empty, he held out the can to us, invitingly but not
overbearingly. We said no thank you, because just from watching,
Winter had to crawl between the empty gun mounts and retch at
length but in vain in the direction of the harbor mouth.

After this bit of conspicuous consumption, Mahlke naturally received his portion of applause; waving it aside, he fed the putrid

corned beef and what was left of the frogs' legs to the gulls, which had been coming steadily closer during his banquet. Finally he bowled the can and shooed the gulls overboard, and scoured the can opener, which alone struck him as worth keeping. From then on he wore the can opener suspended from his neck by a string like the English screwdriver and his various amulets, but not regularly, only when he was planning to look for canned goods in the galley of a former Polish mine sweeper — his stomach never seemed to mind. On such days he came to school with the can opener under his shirt beside the rest of his hardware; he even wore it to early Mass in St. Mary's Chapel; for whenever Mahlke knelt at the altar rail, tilting his head back and sticking out his tongue for Father Gusewski to lay the host on, the altar boy by the priest's side would peer into Mahlke's shirt collar: and there, dangling from your neck was the can opener, side by side with the Madonna and the grease-coated screwdriver; and I admired you, though you were not trying to arouse my admiration. No, Mahlke was never an eager beaver.

In the autumn of the same year in which he had learned to swim, they threw him out of the Young Folk and into the Hitler Youth, because several Sundays in a row he had refused to lead his squad — he was a squad leader in the Young Folk — to the morning meet in Jeschkental Forest. That too, in our class at least, brought him outspoken admiration. He received our enthusiasm with the usual mixture of coolness and embarrassment and continued, now as a rank-and-file member of the Hitler Youth, to shirk his duty on Sunday mornings; but in this organization, which embraced the whole male population from fourteen to twenty, his remissness attracted less attention, for the Hitler Youth was not as strict as the Young Folk, it was a big, sprawling organization in which fellows like Mahlke could blend with their surroundings. Besides, he wasn't insubordinate in the usual sense; he regularly attended the training sessions during the week, made himself useful in the "special activities" that were scheduled more and more frequently, and was glad to help with the junk collections or stand on street corners with a Winter Aid can, as long as it didn't interfere with his early Mass on Sunday. There was nothing unusual about being transferred from the Young Folk to the Hitler Youth, and Member Mahlke remained a colorless unknown quantity in the official youth organization, while in our school, after the first summer on the barge, his reputation, though neither good nor bad, became legendary.

There is no doubt that unlike the Hitler Youth our gymnasium became for you, in the long run, a source of high hopes which no common gymnasium, with its traditional mixture of rigor and good-fellowship, with its colored school caps and its often invoked school spirit, could possibly fulfill.

"What's the matter with him?"
"I say he's got a tic."
"Maybe it's got something to do with his father's death."
"And what about all that hardware on his neck?"
"And he's always running off to pray."
"And he don't believe in nothing if you ask me."
"Hell no, he's too realistic."
"And what about that thing on his neck?"
"You ask him, you're the one that sicked the cat on him. . . . "

We racked our brains and we couldn't understand you. Before you could swim, you were a nobody, who was called on now and then, usually gave correct answers, and was named Joachim Mahlke. And yet I believe that in Sixth or maybe it was later, certainly before your first attempts at swimming, we sat on the same bench; or you sat behind me or in the same row in the middle section, while I sat behind Schilling near the window. Later somebody recollected that you had worn glasses up to Fifth; I never noticed them. I didn't even notice those eternal laced shoes of yours until you had made the grade with your swimming and begun to wear a shoelace for high shoes around your neck. Great events were shaking the world just then, but Mahlke's time reckoning was Before learning to swim and After learning to swim; for when the war broke out all over the place, not all at once but little by little, first on the Westerplatte, then on the radio, then in the newspapers, this schoolboy who could neither swim nor ride a bicycle didn't amount to much; but the mine sweeper of the *Czaika* class, which was later to provide him with his first chance to perform, was already, if only for a few weeks, playing its military role in the Pitziger Wiek, in the Gulf, and in the fishing port of Hela.

The Polish fleet was small but ambitious. We knew its modern ships, for the most part built in England or France, by heart, and could reel off their guns, tonnage, and speed in knots with never a mistake, just as we could recite the names of all Italian light cruisers, or of all the obsolete Brazilian battleships and monitors.

Later Mahlke took the lead also in this branch of knowledge; he learned to pronounce fluently and without hesitation the names of the Japanese destroyers from the modern *Kasumi* class, built in '38, to the slower craft of the *Asagao* class, modernized in '23: *"Fumizuki, Satsuki, Yuuzuki, Hokaze, Nadakaze,* and *Oite."*

It didn't take very long to rattle off the units of the Polish fleet. There were the two destroyers, the *Blyskawica* and the *Grom,* two thousand tons, thirty-eight knots, but they decommissioned themselves two days before the outbreak of the war, put into English ports, and were incorporated into the British Navy. The *Blyskawica* is still in existence. She has been converted into a floating naval museum in Gdynia and schoolteachers take their classes to see it.

The destroyer *Burza,* fifteen hundred tons, thirty-three knots, took the same trip to England. Of the five Polish submarines, only the *Wilk* and, after an adventurous journey without maps or captain, the eleven-hundred-ton *Orzel* succeeded in reaching English ports. The *Rys, Zbik,* and *Semp* allowed themselves to be interned in Sweden.

By the time the war broke out, the ports of Gdynia, Putzig, Heisternest, and Hela were bereft of naval vessels except for an obsolete former French cruiser that served as a training ship and dormitory, the mine layer *Gryf* built in the Norman dockyards of Le Havre, a heavily armed vessel of two thousand tons, carrying three hundred mines. Otherwise there were a lone destroyer, the *Wicher,* a few former German torpedo boats, and the six mine sweepers of the *Czaika* class, which also laid mines. These last had a speed of eighteen knots; their armament consisted of a 75-millimeter forward gun and four machine guns on revolving mounts; they carried, so the official handbooks say, a complement of twenty mines.

And one of these one-hundred-and-eighty-five-ton vessels had been built specially for Mahlke.

The naval battle in the Gulf of Danzig lasted from the first of September to the second of October. The score, after the capitu-

lation on Hela Peninsula, was as follows: The Polish units *Gryf,*
Wicher, Baltyk, as well as the three mine sweepers of the *Czaika*
class, the *Mewa,* the *Jaskolka,* and the *Czapla,* had been destroyed
by fire and sunk in their ports; the German destroyer *Leberecht*
had been damaged by artillery fire, the mine sweeper *M 85* ran
into a Polish antisubmarine mine north of Heisternest and lost a
third of its crew.

Only the remaining, slightly damaged vessels of the *Czaika* class
were captured. The *Zuraw* and the *Czaika* were soon commissioned under the names of *Oxthöft* and *Westerplatte;* as the third,
the *Rybitwa,* was being towed from Hela to Neufahrwasser, it began to leak, settle, and wait for Joachim Mahlke; for it was he who
in the following summer raised brass plaques on which the name
Rybitwa had been engraved. Later, it was said that a Polish officer and a bosun's mate, obliged to man the rudder under German
guard, had flooded the barge in accordance with the well-known
Scapa Flow recipe.

For some reason or other it sank to one side of the channel,
not far from the Neufahrwasser harbor buoy and, though it lay
conveniently on one of the many sandbanks, was not salvaged,
but spent the rest of the war right there, with only its bridge, the
remains of its rail, its battered ventilators, and the forward gun
mount (the gun itself had been removed) emerging from the water — a strange sight at first, but soon a familiar one. It provided
you, Joachim Mahlke, with a goal in life; just as the battleship
Gneisenau, which was sunk in February '45 just outside of Gdynia harbor, became a goal for Polish schoolboys; though I can only
wonder whether, among the Polish boys who dove and looted the
Gneisenau, there was any who took to the water with the same
fanaticism as Mahlke.

Chapter 3

He was not a thing of beauty. He could have had his Adam's apple
repaired. Possibly that piece of cartilage was the whole trouble.

But it went with the rest of him. Besides, you can't prove everything by proportions. And as for his soul, it was never introduced

to me. I never heard what he thought. In the end, all I really had to go by was his neck and its numerous counterweights. It is true that he took enormous bundles of margarine sandwiches to school and to the beach with him and would devour quantities of them just before going into the water. But this can only be taken as one more reminder of his mouse, for the mouse chewed insatiably.

There were also his devotions at the altar of the Virgin. He took no particular interest in the Crucified One. It struck me that though the bobbing on his neck did not cease when he joined his fingertips in prayer, he swallowed in slow motion on these occasions and contrived, by arranging his hands in an exaggeratedly stylized pose, to distract attention from that elevator above his shirt collar and his pendants on strings, shoelaces, and chains — which never stopped running.

Apart from the Virgin he didn't have much truck with girls. Maybe if he had had a sister? My girl cousins weren't much use to him either. His relations with Tulla Pokriefke don't count, they were an anomaly and would not have been bad as a circus act — remember, he was planning to become a clown — for Tulla, a spindly little thing with legs like toothpicks, might just as well have been a boy. In any case, this scrawny girl child, who swam along with us when she felt like it during our second summer on the barge, was never the least embarrassed when we decided to give our swimming trunks a rest and sprawled naked on the rusty bridge, with very little idea what to do with ourselves.

You can draw a good likeness of Tulla's face with the most familiar punctuation marks. The way she glided through the water, she might have had webs between her toes. Always, even on the barge, despite seaweed, gulls, and the sour smell of the rust, she stank of carpenter's glue, because her father worked with glue in her uncle's carpenter's shop. She was all skin, bones, and curiosity. Calmly, her chin in the cup of her hand, Tulla would look on when Winter or Esch, unable to contain himself, produced his modest offering. Hunching over so that the bones of her spine stuck out, she would gaze at Winter, who was always slow in getting there, and mutter: "Man, that's taking a long time!"

But when, finally, the stuff came and splashed on the rust, she would begin to fidget and squirm, she would throw herself down on her belly, make little rat's eyes and look and look, trying to discover heaven-knows-what, turn over, sit up, rise to her knees and her feet, stand slightly knock-kneed over the mess. and begin to stir it with a supple big toe, until it foamed rust-red: "Boy! That's the berries! Now you do it, Atze."

Tulla never wearied of this little game — yes, game, the whole thing was all perfectly innocent. "Aw, you do it," she would plead in that whining voice of hers. "Who hasn't done it yet? It's your turn."

She always found some good-natured fool who would get to work even if he wasn't at all in the mood, just to give her something to goggle at. The only one who wouldn't give until Tulla found the right words of encouragement — and that is why I am narrating these heroic deeds — was the great swimmer and diver Joachim Mahlke. While all the rest of us were engaging in this time-honored, nay Biblical, pursuit, either one at a time or — as the manual puts it — with others, Mahlke kept his trunks on and gazed fixedly in the direction of Hela. We felt certain that at home, in his room between snowy owl and Sistine Madonna, he indulged in the same sport.

He had just come up, shivering as usual, and he had nothing to show. Schilling had just been working for Tulla. A coaster was entering the harbor under its own power. "Do it again," Tulla begged, for Schilling was the most prolific of all. Not a single ship in the roadstead. "Not after swimming. I'll do it again tomorrow," Schilling consoled her. Tulla turned on her heel and stood with outspread toes facing Mahlke, who as usual was shivering in the shadow of the pilothouse and hadn't sat down yet. A high-seas tug with a forward gun was putting out to sea.

"Won't you? Aw, do it just once. Or can't you? Don't you want to? Or aren't you allowed to?"

Mahlke stepped half out of the shadow and slapped Tulla's compressed little face left right with his palm and the back of his hand. His mouse went wild. So did the screwdriver. Tulla, of course, didn't shed one single tear, but gave a bleating laugh with her mouth closed; shaking with laughter, she arched her india-rubber frame effortlessly into a bridge, and peered through her spindly legs at Mahlke until he — he was back in the shade again and the tug was veering off to northwestward said: "OK. Just so you'll shut your yap."

Tulla came out of her contortion and squatted down normally with her legs folded under her, as Mahlke stripped his trunks down to his knees. The children at the Punch-and-Judy show gaped in amazement: a few deft movements emanating from his right wrist, and his pecker loomed so large that the tip emerged from the shadow of the pilothouse and the sun fell on it. Only when we had all formed a semicircle did Mahlke's jumping Jim return to the shadow.

"Won't you let me just for a second?" Tulla's mouth hung open. Mahlke nodded and dropped his right hand, though without un-curving his fingers. Tulla's hands, scratched and bruised as they always were, approached the monster, which expanded under her questioning fingertips; the veins stood out and the glans protruded.

"Measure it!" cried Jürgen Kupka. Tulla spread the fingers of her left hand. One full span and another most. Somebody and then somebody else whispered: "At least twelve inches!" That was an exaggeration of course. Schilling, who otherwise had the longest, had to take his out, make it stand up, and hold it beside Mahlke's: Mahlke's was first of all a size thicker, second a matchbox longer, and third looked much more grownup, dangerous, and worthy to be worshiped.

He had shown us again, and then a second time he showed us by producing not one but two mighty streams in quick succession. With his knees not quite together, Mahlke stood by the twisted rail beside the pilothouse, staring out in the direction of the harbor buoy, a little to the rear of the low-lying smoke of the vanishing high-seas tug; a torpedo boat of the *Gull* class was just emerging from the harbor, but he didn't let it distract him. Thus he stood, showing his profile, from the toes extending just over the edge to the watershed in the middle of his hair: strangely enough, the length of his sexual part made up for the otherwise shocking pro-tuberance of his Adam's apple, lending his body an odd, but in its way perfect, harmony.

No sooner had Mahlke finished squirting the first load over the rail than he started in all over again. Winter timed him with his waterproof wrist watch; Mahlke's performance continued for ap-proximately as many seconds as it took the torpedo boat to pass from the tip of the breakwater to the buoy; then, while the torpedo boat was rounding the buoy, he unloaded the same amount again;

the foaming bubbles lurched in the smooth, only occasionally rippling swell, and we laughed for joy as the gulls swooped down, screaming for more.

Joachim Mahlke was never obliged to repeat or better this performance, for none of us ever touched his record, certainly not when exhausted from swimming and diving; sportsmen in everything we did, we respected the rules.

For a while Tulla Pokriefke, for whom his prowess must have had the most direct appeal, courted him in her way; she would always be sitting by the pilothouse, staring at Mahlke's swimming trunks. A few times she pleaded with him, but he always refused, though good-naturedly.

"Do you have to confess these things?"

Mahlke nodded, and played with his dangling screwdriver to divert her gaze.

"Will you take me down sometime? By myself I'm scared. I bet there's still a stiff down there."

For educational purposes, no doubt, Mahlke took Tulla down into the fo'c'sle. He kept her under much too long. When they came up, she had turned a grayish yellow and sagged in his arms. We had to stand her light, curveless body on its head.

After that Tulla Pokriefke didn't join us very often and, though she was more regular than other girls of her age, she got increasingly on our nerves with her drivel about the dead sailor in the barge. She was always going on about him. "The one that brings him up," she promised, "can you-know-what."

It is perfectly possible that without admitting it to ourselves we all searched, Mahlke in the engine room, the rest of us in the fo'c'sle, for a half-decomposed Polish sailor; not because we really wanted to lay this unfinished little number, but just so.

Yet even Mahlke found nothing except for a few half-rotted pieces of clothing, from which fishes darted until the gulls saw that something was stirring and began to say grace.

No, he didn't set much store by Tulla, though they say there was something between them later. He didn't go for girls, not even for Schilling's sister. And all my cousins from Berlin got out of him was a fishy stare. If he had any tender feelings at all, it was for boys; by which I don't mean to suggest that Mahlke was queer;

in those years spent between the beach and the sunken barge, we none of us knew exactly whether we were male or female. Though later there may have been rumors and tangible evidence to the contrary, the fact is that the only woman Mahlke cared about was the Catholic Virgin Mary. It was for her sake alone that he dragged everything that can be worn and displayed on the human neck to St. Mary's Chapel. Whatever he did, from diving to his subsequent military accomplishments, was done for her or else — yes, I know, I'm contradicting myself again — to distract attention from his Adam's apple. And perhaps, in addition to Virgin and mouse, there was yet a third motive: Our school, that musty edifice that defied ventilation, and particularly the auditorium, meant a great deal to Joachim Mahlke; it was the school that drove you, later on, to your supreme effort.

And now it is time to say something about Mahlke's face. A few of us have survived the war; we live in small small towns and large small towns, we've gained weight and lost hair, and we more or less earn our living. I saw Schilling in Duisburg and Jürgen Kupka in Braunschweig shortly before he emigrated to Canada. Both of them started right in about the Adam's apple. "Man, wasn't that something he had on his neck! And remember that time with the cat. Wasn't it you that sicked the cat on him..." and I had to interrupt: "That's not what I'm after; it's his face I'm interested in."

We agreed as a starter that he had gray or gray-blue eyes, bright but not shining, anyway that they were not brown. The face thin and rather elongated, muscular around the cheekbones. The nose not strikingly large, but fleshy, quickly reddening in cold weather. His over-hanging occiput has already been mentioned. We had difficulty in coming to an agreement about Mahlke's upper lip. Jürgen Kupka was of my opinion that it curled up and never wholly covered his two upper incisors, which in turn were not vertical but stuck out like tusks — except of course when he was diving. But then we began to have our doubts; we remembered that the little Pokriefke girl also had a curled-up lip and always visible incisors. In the end we weren't sure whether we hadn't mixed up Mahlke and Tulla, though just in connection with the upper lip. Maybe it was only she whose lip was that way, for hers was, that much is certain. In Duisburg Schilling — we met in the station restaurant, because his wife had some objection to unannounced visitors — reminded me of the caricature that had created an uproar in our class for several days. In '41 I think it was, a big, tall character turned up in our class, who had been evacuated from Latvia with his family. In spite of his cracked voice, he was a fluent talker; an aristocrat, always fashionably dressed, knew Greek, lectured like a book, his father was a baron, wore a fur cap in the winter, what *was* his name? — well, anyway, his first name was Karel. And he could draw, very quickly, with or without models: sleighs surrounded by wolves, drunken Cossacks, Jews suggesting *Der Stürmer*, naked girls riding on lions, in general lots of naked girls with long porcelainlike legs, but never smutty, Bolsheviks devouring babies, Hitler disguised as Charlemagne, racing cars driven by ladies with long flowing scarves; and he was especially clever at drawing caricatures of his teachers or fellow students with pen, brush, or crayon on every available scrap of paper or with chalk on the blackboard; well, he didn't do Mahlke on paper, but with rasping chalk on the blackboard.

He drew him full face. At that time Mahlke already had his ridiculous part in the middle, fixated with sugar water. He represented the face as a triangle with one corner at the chin. The mouth was puckered and peevish. No trace of any visible incisors that might have been mistaken for tusks. The eyes, piercing points under sorrowfully uplifted eyebrows. The neck sinuous, half in profile, with a monstrous Adam's apple. And behind the head and sorrowful features a halo: a perfect likeness of Mahlke the Redeemer. The effect was immediate.

We snorted and whinnied on our benches and only recovered our senses when someone hauled off at the handsome Karel So-and-So, first with his bare fist, then, just before we managed to separate them, with a steel screwdriver.

It was I who sponged your Redeemer's countenance off the blackboard.

Chapter 4

With and without irony: maybe you wouldn't have become a clown but some sort of creator of fashions; for it was Mahlke who during the winter after the second summer on the barge created the pompoms: two little woolen spheres the size of ping-pong balls, in solid or mixed colors, attached to a plaited woolen cord that was worn under the collar like a necktie and tied into a bow so that the two pompoms hung at an angle, more or less like a bow tie. I have checked and am able to state authoritatively that beginning in the third winter of the war, the pompoms came to be worn almost all over Germany, but mostly in northern and eastern Germany, particularly by high-school students. It was Mahlke who introduced them to our school. He might have invented them. And maybe he actually did. He had several pair made according to his specifications by his Aunt Susi, mostly out of the frayed yarn unraveled from his dead father's much-darned socks. Then he wore the first pair to school and they were very very conspicuous on his neck.

Ten days later they were in the dry-goods stores, at first in cardboard boxes bashfully tucked away by the cash register, but soon attractively displayed in the showcases. An important factor in their success was that they could be had without coupons. From Langfuhr they spread triumphantly through eastern and northern Germany; they were worn — I have witnesses to bear me out — even in Leipzig, in Pirna, and months later, after Mahlke had discarded his own, a few isolated pairs made their appearance as far west as the Rhineland and the Palatinate. I remember the exact day when Mahlke removed his invention from his neck and will speak of it in due time.

We wore the pompoms for several months, toward the end as a protest, after Dr. Klohse, our principal, had branded this article of apparel as effeminate and unworthy of a German young man, and forbidden us to wear pompoms inside the school building or even in the recreation yard. Klohse's order was read in all the classrooms, but there were many who complied only during actual classes. The pompoms remind me of Papa Brunies, a pensioned teacher who had been recalled to his post during the war; he was delighted with the merry little things; once or twice, after

Mahlke had given them up, he even tied a pair of them around his own stand-up collar, and thus attired declaimed Eichendorff: "Weathered gables, lofty windows..." or maybe it was something else, but in any case it was Eichendorff, his favorite poet. Oswald Brunies had a sweet tooth and later, ostensibly because he had eaten some vitamin tablets that were supposed to be distributed among the students, but probably for political reasons — Brunies was a Freemason — he was arrested at school. Some of the students were questioned. I hope I didn't testify against him. His adoptive daughter, a doll-like creature who took ballet lessons, wore mourning in public; they took him to Stutthof, and there he stayed — a dismal, complicated story, which deserves to be written, but somewhere else, not by me, and certainly not in connection with Mahlke.

Let's get back to the pompoms. Of course Mahlke had invented them to make things easier for his Adam's apple. For a time they quieted the unruly jumping jack, but when the pompoms came into style all over the place, even in Sixth, they ceased to attract attention on their inventor's neck. I can still see Mahlke during the winter of '42 — which must have been hard for him because diving was out and the pompoms had lost their efficacy — always in monumental solitude, striding in his high, black laced shoes, down Osterzeile and up Bärenweg to St. Mary's Chapel, over crunching cinder-strewn snow. Hatless. Ears red, brittle, and prominent. Hair stiff with sugar water and frost, parted in the middle from crown to forehead. Brows knitted in anguish. Horror-stricken, watery-blue eyes that see more than is there. Turned-up coat collar. The coat had also come down to him from his late father. A gray woolen scarf, crossed under his tapering to scrawny chin, was held in place, as could be seen from a distance, by a safety pin. Every twenty paces his right hand rises from his coat pocket to feel whether his scarf is still in place, properly protecting his neck — I have seen clowns, Grock in the circus, Charlie Chaplin in the movies, working with the same gigantic safety pin. Mahlke is practicing: men, women, soldiers on furlough, children, singly and in groups, grow toward him over the snow. Their breath, Mahlke's too, puffs up white from their mouths and vanishes over their shoulders. And the eyes of all who approach him are focused, Mahlke is probably thinking, on that comical, very comical, excruciatingly comical safety pin.

In the same dry, hard winter I arranged an expedition over the frozen sea to the ice-bound mine sweeper with my two girl cousins, who had come from Berlin for Christmas vacation, and Schilling to make things come out even. The girls were pretty, sleek, tousled blonde, and spoiled from living in Berlin. We thought we would show off some and impress them with our barge. The girls were awfully ladylike in the streetcar and even on the beach, but out there we were hoping to do something really wild with them, we didn't know what.

Mahlke ruined our afternoon. In opening up the harbor channel, the icebreakers had pushed great boulders of ice toward the barge; jammed together, they piled up into a fissured wall, which sang as the wind blew over it and hid part of the barge from view. We caught sight of Mahlke only when we had mounted the ice barrier, which was about as tall as we were, and had pulled the girls up after us. The bridge, the pilothouse, the ventilators aft of the bridge, and whatever else had remained above water formed a single chunk of glazed, bluish-white candy, licked ineffectually by a congealed sun. No gulls. They were farther out, over the garbage of some ice-bound freighters in the roadstead.

Of course Mahlke had turned up his coat collar and tied his scarf, with the safety pin out in front, under his chin. No hat, but round, black ear muffs, such as those worn by garbage men and the drivers of brewery trucks, covered his otherwise protruding ears, joined by a strip of metal at right angles to the part in his hair.

He was so hard at work on the sheet of ice over the bow that he didn't notice us; he even seemed to be keeping warm. He was trying with a small ax to cut through the ice at a point which he presumed to be directly over the open forward hatch. With quick short strokes he was making a circular groove, about the size of a manhole cover. Schilling and I jumped from the wall, caught the girls, and introduced them to him. No gloves to take off; he merely shifted the ax to his left hand. Each of us in turn received a prickly-hot right hand, and a moment later he was chopping again. Both girls had their mouths slightly open. Little teeth grew cold. Frosty breath beat against their scarves and frosty-eyed they stared at his ice-cutting operations. Schilling and I were through. But though furious with him, we began to tell about his summertime accomplishments as a diver: "Metal plates, absolutely, and a fire extinguisher, and tin cans, he opened them right up and guess what was in them — human flesh! And when he brought up the phonograph something came crawling out of it, and one time he.... "

The girls didn't quite follow, they asked stupid questions, and addressed Mahlke as Mister. He kept right on hacking. He shook his head and ear muffs as we shouted his diving prowess over the ice, but never forgot to feel for his muffler and safety pin with his free hand. When we could think of nothing more to say and were just standing there shivering, he would stop for a moment every twenty strokes or so, though without ever standing up quite straight, and fill the pause with simple, modest explanations. Embarrassed, but at the same time self-assured, he dwelt on his lesser exploits and passed over the more daring feats, speaking more of his work than of adventures in the moist interior of the sunken mine sweeper. In the meantime he drove his groove deeper and deeper into the ice. I wouldn't say that my cousins were exactly fascinated by Mahlke; no, he wasn't witty enough for that and his choice of words was too commonplace. Besides, such little ladies would never have gone all out for anybody wearing black ear muffs like a granddaddy. Nevertheless, we were through. He turned us into shivering little boys with running noses, standing there definitely on the edge of things; and even on the way back the girls treated us with condescension.

Mahlke stayed on; he wanted to finish cutting his hole, to prove to himself that he had correctly figured the spot over the hatch. He didn't ask us to wait till he had finished, but he did delay our departure for a good five minutes when we were already on top of the wall, by dispensing a series of words in an undertone, not at us, more in the direction of the ice-bound freighters in the roadstead.

Still chopping, he asked us to help him. Or was it an order, politely spoken? In any case he wanted us to make water in the wedge-shaped groove, so as to melt or at least soften the ice with warm urine. Before Schilling or I could say: "No dice," or "We just did," my little cousins piped up joyfully: "Oh yes, we'd love to. But you must turn your backs, and you too, Mr. Mahlke."

After Mahlke had explained where they should squat — the whole stream, he said, has to fall in the same place or it won't do any good — he climbed up on the wall and turned toward the beach. While amid whispering and tittering the sprinkler duet went on behind us, we concentrated on the swarms of black ants near Brösen and on the icy pier. The seventeen poplars on the Beach Promenade were coated with sugar. The golden globe at the tip of the Soldiers' Monument, an obelisk towering over Brösen Park, blinked at us excitedly. Sunday all over.

When the girls' ski pants had been pulled up again and we stood around the groove with the tips of our shoes, the circle was still steaming, especially in the two places where Mahlke had cut crosses with his ax. The water stood pale yellow in the ditch and seeped away with a crackling sound. The edges of the groove were tinged a golden green. The ice sang plaintively. A pungent smell persisted because there were no other smells to counteract it, growing stronger as Mahlke chopped some more at the groove and scraped away about as much slush as a common bucket might have held. Especially in the two marked spots, he succeeded in drilling shafts, in gaining depth.

The soft ice was piled up to one side and began at once to crust over in the cold. Then he marked two new places. When the girls had turned away, we unbuttoned and helped Mahlke by thawing an inch or two more of the ice and boring two fresh holes. But they were still not deep enough. He himself did not pass water, and we didn't ask him to; on the contrary we were afraid the girls might try to encourage him.

As soon as we had finished and before my cousins could say a word, Mahlke sent us away. We looked back from the wall; he had pushed up muffler and safety pin over his chin and nose; his neck was still covered but now his pompoms, white sprinkled red, were taking the air between muffler and coat collar. He was hacking again at his groove, which was whispering something or other about the girls and us — a bowed form barely discernible through floating veils of sun-stirred laundry steam.

On the way back to Brösen, the conversation was all about him. Alternately or both at once, my cousins asked questions. We didn't always have the answer. But when the younger one wanted to know why Mahlke wore his muffler so high up and the other one started in on the muffler too, Schilling seized on the opportunity and described Mahlke's Adam's apple, giving it all the qualities of a goiter. He made exaggerated swallowing motions, imitated Mahlke chewing, took off his ski cap, gave his hair a kind of part in the middle with his fingers, and finally succeeded in making the girls laugh at Mahlke; they even said he was an odd-ball and not quite right in the head.

But despite this little triumph at your expense — I put in my two cents' worth too, mimicking your relations with the Virgin Mary — we made no headway with my cousins beyond the usual necking in the movies. And a week later they returned to Berlin.

Here I am bound to report that the following day I rode out to Brösen bright and early; I ran across the ice through a dense coastal fog, almost missing the barge, and found the hole over the fo'c'sle completed. During the night a fresh crust of ice had formed; with considerable difficulty, I broke through it with the heel of my shoe and an iron-tipped cane belonging to my father, which I had brought along for that very purpose. Then I poked the cane around through the cracked ice in the gray-black hole. It disappeared almost to the handle, water splashed my glove; and then the tip struck the deck, no, not the deck, it jutted into empty space. It was only when I moved the cane sideways along the edge of the hole that it met resistance. And I passed iron over iron: the hole was directly over the open forward hatch. Exactly like one plate under another in a pile of plates, the hatch was right under the hole in the ice — well, no, that's an exaggeration, not *exactly,* there's no such thing: either the hatch was a little bigger or the hole was a little bigger; but the fit was pretty good, and my pride in Joachim Mahlke was as sweet as chocolate creams. I'd have liked to give you my wrist watch.

I stayed there a good ten minutes; I sat on the circular mound of ice — it must have been all of eighteen inches high. The lower third was marked with a pale-yellow ring of urine from the day before. It had been our privilege to help him. But even without our help Mahlke would have finished his hole. Was it possible that he could manage without an audience? Were there shows he put on only for himself? For not even the gulls would have admired your hole in the ice over the forward hatch, if I hadn't gone out there to admire you.

He always had an audience. When I say that always, even while cutting his circular groove over the ice-bound barge, he had the Virgin Mary behind or before him, that she looked with enthusiasm upon his little ax, the Church shouldn't really object; but even if the Church refuses to put up with the idea of a Virgin Mary forever engaged in admiring Mahlke's exploits, the fact remains that she always watched him attentively: I know. For I was an altar boy, first under Father Wiehnke at the Church of the Sacred Heart, then under Gusewski at St. Mary's Chapel. I kept on assisting him at Mass long after I had lost my faith in the magic of the altar, a process which approximately coincided with my growing up. The comings and goings amused me. I took pains too. I didn't shuffle like most altar boys. The truth is, I was never sure, and to this day I am not sure, whether there might not after all be something behind or in front of the altar or in the tabernacle.... At any rate Father Gusewski was always glad to have me as one of his two altar boys, because I never swapped cigarette pictures between offering and consecration, never rang the bells too loud or too long, or made a business of selling the sacramental wine. For altar boys are holy terrors: not only do they spread out the usual juvenile trinkets on the altar steps; not only do they lay bets, payable in coins or worn-out ball bearings — Oh no. Even during the gradual prayers they discuss the technical details of the world's warships, sunk or afloat, and substitute snatches of such lore for the words of the Mass, or smuggle them in between Latin and Latin: *"Introibo ad altare Dei* — Say, when was the cruiser *Eritrea* launched? — Thirty-six. Special features? — *Ad Deum, qui laetificat juventutem meam.* — Only Italian cruiser in East African waters. Displacement? — *Deus fortitudo mea* — Twenty-one hundred and seventy-two tons. Speed? — *Et introibo ad altare Dei* — Search me. Armament? — *Sicut erat in principio* — Six hundred-and-fifty-millimeter guns, four seventy-fives.... Wrong! — *et nunc et semper* — No, it's right. Names of the German artillery training ships? — *et in saecula saeculorum, Amen.* — *Brummer* and *Bremse.*"

Later on I stopped serving regularly at St. Mary's and came only when Gusewski sent for me because his boys were busy with Sunday hikes or collecting funds for Winter Aid.

I'm telling you all this only to explain my presence at the main altar, for from there I was able to observe Mahlke as he knelt at the altar of the Virgin. My, how he could pray! That calflike look. His eyes would grow steadily glassier. His mouth peevish, perpetually moving without punctuation. Fishes tossed up on the beach gasp for air with the same regularity. I shall try to give you an idea of how relentlessly Mahlke could pray. Father Gusewski was distributing communion. When he came to Mahlke, who always, seen from the altar, knelt at the outer left, this particular kneeler was one who had forgotten all caution, allowing his muffler and gigantic safety pin to shift for themselves, whose eyes had congealed, whose head and parted hair were tilted backward, who allowed his tongue to hang out, and who, in this attitude, left an agitated mouse so exposed and defenseless that I might have caught it in my hand. But perhaps Joachim Mahlke realized that his cynosure was convulsed and exposed. Perhaps he intentionally accentuated its frenzy with exaggerated swallowing, in order to attract the glass eyes of the Virgin standing to one side of him; for I cannot and will not believe that you ever did anything whatsoever without an audience.

Chapter 5

I never saw him with pompoms at St. Mary's Chapel. Although the style was just beginning to take hold, he wore them less and less. Sometimes when three of us were standing in the recreation yard, always under the same chestnut tree, all talking at once over our woolen doodads, Mahlke removed his pompoms from his neck; then, after the second bell had rung, he would tie them on again, irresolutely, for lack of a better counterweight.

When for the first time a graduate of our school returned from the front, a special bell signal called us to the auditorium though classes were still in progress. On the return journey he had stopped briefly at the Führer's Headquarters, and now he had the coveted lozenge on his neck. He stood, not behind but beside the old-brown pulpit, at the end of the hall, against a background of three tall windows, a row of potted leafy plants, and the faculty gathered in a semicircle. Lozenge on neck, red rosebud mouth, he projected his voice into the space over our heads and made little explanatory gestures. Mahlke was sitting in the row ahead of me and Schilling. I saw his ears turn a flaming transparent red; he leaned back stiffly, and I saw him, left right, fiddling with something on his neck, tugging, gagging, and at length tossing something under his bench: something woolen, pompoms, a green and red mixture I think they were. The young fellow, a lieutenant in the Air Force, started off hesitantly and rather too softly, with an appealing awkwardness; he even blushed once or twice, though there was nothing in what he was saying to warrant it: " ... well, boys, don't get the idea that life in the Air Force is like a rabbit hunt, all action and never a dull moment. Sometimes nothing happens for whole weeks. But when they sent us to the Channel, I says to myself, if things don't start popping now, they never will. And I was right. On the very first mission a formation with a fighter escort came straight at us, and believe me, it was some merry-go-round. In and out of the clouds, winding and circling the whole time. I try to gain altitude, down below me there's three Spitfires circling, trying to hide in the clouds. I says to myself, it's just too bad if I can't ... I dive, I've got him in my sights, bam, he's trailing smoke. Just time to turn over on my left wing tip when there's a second Spitfire coming toward me in my sights, I go straight for his nose, it's him or me; well, as you can see, it's him that went into the drink, and I says to myself, as long as you've got two, why not try the third and so on, as long as your gas holds out. So I see seven of them down below me, they've broken formation and they're trying to get away. I pick out one of them, I've got a good sun well in back of me. He gets his, I repeat the number, turns out OK, I pull back the stick as far as she'll go, and there's the third in my line of fire: he goes into a spin, I must have got him, instinctively I trail him, lose him, clouds, got him again, give another burst, he drops into the pond, but so do I pretty near; I honestly can't tell you how I got my crate upstairs again. Anyway, when I come home flapping my wings — as you probably know, you must have seen it in the newsreels, we come in flapping our wings if we've bagged anything — I can't get the landing gear down. Jammed. So I had to make my first crash landing. Later in the officers' club they tell me I've been marked up for a certain six, it's news to me; as you can imagine, I'd been too excited to count. I was mighty happy, but about four o'clock we've got to go up again. Well, to make a long story short, it was pretty much the same as in the old days when we played handball in our good old recreation yard — 'cause the stadium hadn't built yet. Maybe Mr. Mallenbrandt remembers: either didn't shoot a single goal or I'd shoot nine in a row; that's how it was that day: six that morning and three more in the afternoon. That was my ninth to seventeenth; but it wasn't until a good six months later, when I had my full forty, that I was commended by our CO, and by the time I was decorated at the Führer's Headquarters I had forty-four under my belt; 'cause we guys up at the Channel just about lived in our crates. The ground crews got relieved, not us. There were some that couldn't take it. Well, now I'll tell you something funny for relief. In every airfield there's a squadron dog. One day it was beautiful weather and we decided to take Alex, our dog. . . . "

Such, approximately, were the words of the gloriously decorated lieutenant. In between two air battles, as an interlude, he told the story of Alex, the squadron dog, who had been compelled to learn parachute jumping. There was also the little anecdote about the corporal who was always too slow in getting up when the alert was sounded and was obliged to fly several missions in his pajamas.

The lieutenant laughed with his audience; even the graduating class laughed, and some of the teachers indulged in a chuckle. He had graduated from our school in '33 and was shot down over the Ruhr in '43. His hair was dark brown, unparted, combed rigorously back; he wasn't very big, looked rather like a dapper little waiter in a night club. While speaking he kept one hand in his pocket, but took it out whenever he needed two hands to illustrate an air battle with. His use of his outspread palms was subtle and masterful; with a twist of his shoulders, he could make you see his plane banking as it circled in quest of victims, and he had no need of long, explanatory sentences. His chopped phrases were more like cues for his pantomime. At the height of his act he roared out engine noises or stuttered when an engine was in trouble. It was safe to assume that he had practiced his number at his airfield officers' club, especially as the term "officers' club" kept cropping up in his narrative: "We were sitting peacefully in the officers' club...I was just heading for the officers' club 'cause I wanted to.... In our officers' club there's a... " But even aside from his mime's hands and his realistic sound effects, he knew how to appeal to his audience; he managed, for instance, to get in a few cracks at some of our teachers, who still had the same nicknames as in his day. But he was always pleasant, full of harmless mischief. And no boaster. He never claimed credit for the difficult things he had done, but put everything down to his luck: "I've always been lucky, even in school, when I think of some of my report cards.... " And in the middle of a schoolboy's joke he suddenly remembered three of his former classmates who, as he said, shall not have died in vain. He concluded his talk not with the names of the three dead comrades, but with this naive, heartfelt admission: "Boys, let me tell you this: every last one of us who's out there fighting likes to think back on his school days and, believe me, we often do."

We clapped, roared, and stamped at great length. Only when my hands were hot and burning did I observe that Mahlke was holding back and contributing no applause.

Up front Dr. Klohse shook both his former student's hands demonstratively as long as the applause went on. Then, after gripping the frail figure for a moment by the shoulders, he turned abruptly away, and took up his stance behind the pulpit, while the lieutenant quickly sat down.

The principal's speech went on and on. Boredom spread from the lush green plants to the oil painting on the rear wall of the auditorium, a portrait of Baron von Conradi, the founder of our school. Even the lieutenant, a slender figure between Brunies and Mallenbrandt, kept looking at his fingernails. In this lofty hall Klohse's cool peppermint breath, which suffused all his mathematics classes, substituting for the odor of pure science, wasn't much of a help. From up front his words barely carried to the middle of the auditorium: "Thosewhocomeafterus — Andinthishour — whenthetravelerreturns — butthistimethehomeland — andletusnever — pureofheart — asIsaidbefore — pureofheart — andifanyonedisagreeslet — andinthishour — keepclean — toconcludewiththewordsofSchiller — ifyourlifeyoudonotstake — thelaurelneverwillyoutake — Andnowbacktowork!"

Dismissed, we formed two clusters at the narrow exits. I pushed in behind Mahlke. He was sweating and his sugar-water hair stood up in sticky blades around his ravaged part. Never, not even in gym, had I seen Mahlke perspire. The stench of three hundred schoolboys stuck like corks in the exits. Beads of sweat stood out on Mahlke's flushed anxiety cords, those two bundles of sinew running from the seventh vertebra of his neck to the base of his jutting occiput. In the colonnade outside the folding doors, amid the hubbub of the little Sixths, who had resumed their perpetual game of tag, I caught up with him. I questioned him head on: "Well, what do you say?"

Mahlke stared straight ahead. I tried not to look at his neck. Between two columns stood a plaster bust of Lessing: but Mahlke's neck won out. Calmly and mournfully, as though speaking of his aunt's chronic ailments, his voice said: "Now they need a bag of forty if they want the medal. At the beginning and after they were through in France and in the north, it only took twenty — if it keeps on like this...."

I guess the lieutenant's talk didn't agree with you. Or you wouldn't have resorted to such cheap compensations. In those days luminous buttons and round, oval, or open-work plaques were on display in the windows of stationery and dry-goods stores. They glowed milky-green in the darkness, some disclosing the contours of a fish, others of a flying gull. These little plaques were purchased mostly by elderly gentlemen and fragile ladies, who wore them on their coat collars for fear of collisions in the blacked-out streets; there were also canes with luminous stripes.

You were not afraid of the blackout, and yet you fastened five or six plaques, a luminous school of fish, a flock of gliding gulls, several bouquets of phosphorescent flowers, first on the lapels of your coat, then on your muffler; you had your aunt sew half a dozen luminous buttons from top to bottom of your coat; you turned yourself into a clown. In the winter twilight, through slanting snowflakes or well-nigh uniform darkness, I saw you, I still see you and always will, striding toward me down Bärenweg, enumerable from top to bottom and back, with one two three four five six coat buttons glowing moldy-green: a pathetic sort of ghost, capable at most of scaring children and grandmothers — trying to distract attention from an affliction which no one could have seen in the pitch-darkness. But you said to yourself, no doubt: No blackness can engulf this overdeveloped fruit; everyone sees, suspects, feels it, wants to grab hold of it, for it juts out ready to be grabbed; if only this winter were over, so I could dive again and be under water.

Chapter 6

But when the summer came with strawberries, special communiqués, and bathing weather, Mahlke didn't want to swim. On the first of June we swam out to the barge for the first time. We weren't really in the mood. We were annoyed at the Thirds who swam with us and ahead of us, who sat on the bridge in swarms, dived, and brought up the last hinge that could be unscrewed. "Let me come with you, I can swim now," Mahlke had once pleaded. And now it was Schilling, Winter, and myself who pestered him: "Aw, come along. It's no fun without you. We can sun ourselves on the barge. Maybe you'll find something interesting down below."

Reluctantly, after waving us away several times, Mahlke stepped into the tepid soup between the beach and the first sandbank. He swam without his screwdriver, stayed between us, two arms' lengths behind Hotten Sonntag, and for the first time I saw him swim calmly, without excitement or splashing. On the bridge he sat huddled in the shadow of the pilothouse and no one could persuade him to dive. He didn't even turn his neck when the Thirds vanished into the fo'c'sle and came up with trinkets. Yet Mahlke could have taught them a thing or two. Some of them even asked him for pointers — but he scarcely answered. The whole time he looked out through puckered eyes over the open sea in the direction of the harbor mouth buoy, but neither inbound freighters, nor outbound cutters, nor a formation of torpedo boats could divert him. Maybe the submarines got a slight rise out of him. Sometimes, far out at sea, the periscope of a submerged U-boat could be seen cutting a distinct stripe of foam. The 750-ton vessels, built in series at the Schichau Dockyards, were given trial runs in the Gulf or behind Hela; surfacing in the deep channel, they put in to-

ward the harbor and dispelled our boredom. Looked good as they
rose to the surface, periscope first. The moment the conning tower
emerged, it spat out one or two figures. In dull-white streams the
water receded from the gun, ran off the bow and then the stern.
Men scrambled out of the hatches, we shouted and waved — I'm
not sure whether they answered us, though I still see the motion of
waving in every detail and can still feel it in my shoulders. Whether
or not they waved back, the surfacing of a submarine strikes the
heart, still does — but Mahlke never waved.

. . . and once — it was the end of June, summer vacation hadn't
started yet and the lieutenant commander hadn't yet delivered his
lecture in our school auditorium — Mahlke left his place in the
shade because a Third had gone down into the fo'c'sle of the mine
sweeper and hadn't come up. Mahlke went down the hatch and
brought the kid up. He had wedged himself in amidships, but he
hadn't got as far as the engine room. Mahlke found him under the
deck between pipes and bundles of cable. For two hours Schilling
and Hotten Sonntag took turns working on the kid according to
Mahlke's directions. Gradually, the color came back into his face,
but when we swam ashore we had to tow him.

The next day Mahlke was diving again with his usual enthusiasm, but without a screwdriver. He swam across at his usual speed,
leaving us all behind; he had already been under once when we
climbed up on the bridge.

The preceding winter's ice and February storms had carried
away the last bit of rail, both gun mounts, and the top of the pilothouse. Only the encrusted gull droppings had come through in
good shape and, if anything, had multiplied. Mahlke brought up
nothing and didn't answer the questions we kept thinking up. But
late in the afternoon, after he had been down ten or twelve times
and we were starting to limber up for the swim back, he went
down and didn't come up. We were all of us out of our minds.

When I speak of a five-minute intermission, it doesn't mean a
thing; but after five minutes as long as years, which we occupied
with swallowing until our tongues lay thick and dry in dry hollows, we dove down into the barge one by one: in the fo'c'sle
there was nothing but a few baby herring. Behind Hotten Sonntag I ventured through the bulkhead for the first time, and looked
superficially about the former officers' mess. Then I had to come

up, shot out of the hatch just before I would have burst, went down again, shoved my way twice more through the bulkhead, and didn't give up until a good half hour later. Seven or eight of us lay flat on the bridge, panting. The gulls circled closer and closer; must have noticed something.

Luckily, there were no Thirds on the barge. We were all silent or all talking at once. The gulls flew off to one side and came back again. We cooked up stories for the lifeguard, for Mahlke's mother and aunt, and for Klohse, because there was sure to be an investigation at school. Because I was Mahlke's neighbor, they saddled me with the visit to his mother on Osterzeile. Schilling was to tell our story to the lifeguard and in school.

"If they don't find him, we'll have to swim out here with a wreath and have a ceremony."

"We'll chip in. We'll each contribute at least fifty pfennigs."

"We can throw him overboard from here, or maybe just lower him into the fo'c'sle."

"We'll have to sing something," said Kupka. But the hollow tinkling laughter that followed this suggestion did not originate with any of us: it came from inside the bridge. We all gaped at some unknown point, waiting for the laughter to start up again, but when it did, it was a perfectly normal kind of laughter, had lost its hollowness, and came from the fo'c'sle. The waters parting at his watershed, Mahlke pushed out of the hatch, breathing scarcely harder than usual, and rubbed the fresh sunburn on his neck and shoulders. His bleating was more good-natured than scornful. "Well," he said, "have you got that funeral oration ready?"

Before we swam ashore, Mahlke went down again. Winter was having an attack of the weeping jitters and we were trying to pacify him. Fifteen minutes later Winter was still bawling, and Mahlke was back on the bridge, wearing a set of radio operator's earphones which from the outside at least looked undamaged, almost new; amidships Mahlke had found the way into a room that was situated inside the command bridge, above the surface of the water; the former radio shack. The place was bone-dry, he said, though somewhat clammy. After considerable stalling he admitted that he had discovered the entrance while disentangling the young Third from the pipes and cables. "I've camouflaged it. Nobody'll ever find it. But it was plenty of work. It's my private property now, in case you have any doubts. Cozy little joint. Good place to hide if things get hot. Lots of apparatus, transmitter and so on. Might try to put it in working order one of these days."

But that was beyond Mahlke's abilities and I doubt if he ever tried. Or if he did tinker some without letting on, I'm sure his efforts were unsuccessful. He was very handy and knew all there was to know about making ship models, but he was hardly a radio technician. Besides, if Mahlke had ever got the transmitter working and started broadcasting witty sayings, the Navy or the harbor police would have picked us up.

In actual fact, he removed all the apparatus from the cabin and gave it to Kupka, Esch, and the Thirds; all he kept for himself was the earphones. He wore them a whole week, and it was only when he began systematically to refurnish the radio shack that he threw them overboard.

The first thing he moved in was books — I don't remember exactly what they were. My guess is that they included *Tsushirna, The Story of a Naval Battle,* a volume or two of Dwinger, and some religious stuff. He wrapped them first in old woolen blankets, then in oilcloth, and calked the seams with pitch or tar or wax. The bundle was carried out to the barge on a driftwood raft which he, with occasional help from us, towed behind him as he swam. He claimed that the books and blankets had reached their destination almost dry. The next shipment consisted of candles, an alcohol burner, fuel, an aluminum pot, tea, oat flakes, and dehydrated vegetables. Often he was gone for as much as an hour; we would begin to pound frantically, but he never answered. Of course we admired him. But Mahlke ignored our admiration and grew more and more monosyllabic; in the end he wouldn't even let us help him with his moving. However, it was in our presence that he rolled up the color print of the Sistine Madonna, known to me from his room on Osterzeile, and stuffed it inside a hollow curtain rod, packing the open ends with modeling clay. Madonna and curtain rod were towed to the barge and maneuvered into the cabin. At last I knew why he was knocking himself out, for whom he was furnishing the former radio shack.

My guess is that the print was damaged in diving, or perhaps that the moisture in the airless cabin (it had no portholes or communication with the ventilators, which were all flooded in the first place) did not agree with it, for a few days later Mahlke was wearing something on his neck again, appended to a black shoelace: not a screwdriver, but the bronze medallion with the so-called Black Madonna of Czestochowa in low relief. Our eyebrows shot up knowingly; ah-ha, we thought, there's the Madonna routine again. Before we had time to settle ourselves on the bridge, Mahlke disappeared down the forward hatch. He was back again in no more than fifteen minutes, without shoelace and medallion, and he seemed pleased as he resumed his place behind the pilothouse.

He was whistling. That was the first time I heard Mahlke whistle. Of course he wasn't whistling for the first time, but it was the first time I noticed his whistling, which is tantamount to saying that he was really pursing his lips for the first time. I alone — being the only other Catholic on the barge — knew what the whistling was about: he whistled one hymn to the Virgin after another. Leaning on a vestige of the rail, he began with aggressive good humor to beat time on the rickety side of the bridge with his dangling feet; then over the muffled din, he reeled off the whole Pentecost sequence *"Veni, Sancte Spiritus"* and after that — I had been expecting it — the sequence for the Friday before Palm Sunday. All ten stanzas of the *Stabat Mater dolorosa,* including *Paradisi Gloria* and *Amen,* were rattled off without a hitch. I myself, who had once been Father Gusewski's most devoted altar boy but whose attendance had become very irregular of late, could barely have recollected the first lines.

Mahlke, however, served Latin to the gulls with the utmost ease, and the others, Schilling, Kupka, Esch, Hotten Sonntag, and whoever else was there, listened eagerly with a "Boyohboy" and "Ittakesyourbreathaway." They even asked Mahlke to repeat the *Stabat Mater,* though nothing could have been more remote from their interests than Latin or liturgical texts.

Still, I don't think you were planning to turn the radio shack into a chapel for the Virgin. Most of the rubbish that found its way there had nothing to do with her. Though I never inspected your hideout — we simply couldn't make it — I see it as a miniature edition of your attic room on Osterzeile. Only the geraniums and cactuses, which your aunt, often against your will, lodged on the window sill and the four-story cactus racks, had no counterpart in the former radio shack; otherwise your moving was a perfect job.

After the books and cooking utensils, Mahlke's ship models, the dispatch boat *Cricket* and the torpedo boat of the *Wolf* class, scale 1:1250, were moved below decks. Ink, several pens, a ruler, a school compass, his butterfly collection, and the stuffed snowy owl were also obliged to take the dive. I presume that Mahlke's furnishings gradually began to look pretty sick in this room where water vapor could do nothing but condense. Especially the butterflies in their glassed-over cigarboxes, accustomed as they were to dry attic air, must have suffered from the dampness.

But what we admired most about this game of moving man, which went on for days, was precisely its absurdity and deliberate destructiveness. And the zeal with which Joachim Mahlke gradually returned to the former Polish mine sweeper so many of the objects which he had painstakingly removed two summers before — good old Pilsudski, the plates with the instructions for operating this or that machine, and so on — enabled us, despite the irritating Thirds, to spend an entertaining, I might even say exciting, summer on that barge for which the war had lasted only four weeks.

To give you an example of our pleasures: Mahlke offered us music. You will remember that in the summer of 1940, after he had swum out to the barge with us perhaps six or seven times, he had slowly and painstakingly salvaged a phonograph from the fo'c'sle or the officers' mess, that he had taken it home, repaired it, and put on a new turntable covered with felt. This same phonograph, along with ten or a dozen records, was one of the last items to find their way back again. The moving took two days, during which time he couldn't resist the temptation to wear the crank around his neck, suspended from his trusty shoelace.

Phonograph and records must have come through the trip through the flooded fo'c'sle and the bulkhead in good shape, for that same afternoon he surprised us with music, a hollow tinkling whose source seemed to shift eerily about but was always somewhere inside the barge. I shouldn't be surprised if it shook loose the rivets and sheathing. Though the sun was far down in the sky, we were still getting some of it on the bridge, but even so that sound gave us gooseflesh. Of course we would shout: "Stop it. No.

Go on! Play another!" I remember a well-known *Ave Maria*, as long-lasting as a wad of chewing gum, which smoothed the choppy sea; he just couldn't manage without the Virgin.

There were also arias, overtures, and suchlike — have I told you that Mahlke was gone on serious music? From the inside out Mahlke regaled us with something passionate from *Tosca,* something enchanted from Humperdinck, and part of a symphony beginning with dadada daaah, known to us from popular concerts.

Schilling and Kupka shouted for something hot, but that he didn't have. It was Zarah who produced the most startling effects. Her underwater voice laid us out flat on the rust and bumpy gull droppings. I don't remember what she sang in that first record. It was always the same Zarah. In one, though, she sang something from an opera with which we had been familiarized by a movie called *Homeland.* "AlasIhavelosther," she moaned. "Thewindsangmeasong," she sighed. "Onedayamiraclewillhappen," she prophesied. She could sound organ tones and conjure the elements, or she could dispense moments of languor and tenderness. Winter hardly bothered to stifle his sobs and in general our eyelashes were kept pretty busy.

And over it all the gulls. They were always getting frantic over nothing, but when Zarah revolved on the turntable down below, they went completely out of their heads. Their glass-cutting screams, emanating no doubt from the souls of departed tenors, rose high over the much-imitated and yet inimitable, dungeon-deep plaint of this tear-jerking movie star gifted with a voice, who in the war years earned an immense popularity on every front including the home front.

Mahlke treated us several times to this concert until the records were so worn that nothing emerged but a tortured gurgling and scratching. To this day no music has given me greater pleasure, though I seldom miss a concert at Robert Schumann Hall and whenever I am in funds purchase long-playing records ranging from Monteverdi to Bartók. Silent and insatiable, we huddled over the phonograph, which we called the Ventriloquist. We had run out of praises. Of course we admired Mahlke; but in the eerie din our admiration shifted into its opposite, and we thought him so repulsive we couldn't look at him. Then as a low-flying freighter hove into view, we felt moderately sorry for him. We were also afraid of Mahlke; he bullied us. And I was ashamed to be seen on the street with him. And I was proud when Hotten Sonntag's sister or the little Pokriefke girl met the two of us together outside the Art Cinema or on Heeresanger. You were our theme song. We would lay bets: "What's he going to do now? I bet you he's got a sore throat again. I'm taking all bets: Someday he's going to hang himself, or he'll get to be something real big, or invent something terrific."

And Schilling said to Hotten Sonntag: "Tell me the honest truth; if your sister went out with Mahlke, to the movies and all, tell me the honest truth; what would you do?"

Chapter 7

The appearance of the lieutenant commander and much-decorated U-boat captain in the auditorium of our school put an end to the concerts from within the former Polish mine sweeper *Rybitwa*. Even if he had not turned up, the records and the phonograph couldn't have held out for more than another three or four days. But he did turn up, and without having to pay a visit to our barge he turned off the underwater music and gave all our conversations about Mahlke a new, though not fundamentally new, turn.

The lieutenant commander must have graduated in about '34. It was said that before volunteering for the Navy he had studied some at the university: theology and German literature. I can't help it, I am obliged to call his eyes fiery. His hair was thick and kinky, maybe wiry would be the word, and there was something of the old Roman about his head. No submariner's beard, but aggressive eyebrows that suggested an overhanging roof. His forehead was that of a philosopher-saint, hence no horizontal wrinkles, but two vertical lines, beginning at the bridge of the nose and rising in search of God. The light played on the uppermost point of the bold vault. Nose small and sharp. The mouth he opened for us was a delicately curved orator's mouth. The auditorium was over-crowded with people and morning sun. We were forced to huddle in the window niches. Whose idea had it been to invite the two

upper classes of the Gudrun School? The girls occupied the front
rows of benches; they should have worn brassieres, but didn't.

When the proctor called us to the lecture, Mahlke hadn't wanted
to attend. Flairing some possible gain in prestige for myself, I took
him by the sleeve. Beside me, in the window niche — behind us the
windowpanes and the motionless chestnut trees in the recreation
yard — Mahlke began to tremble before the lieutenant commander had even opened his mouth. Mahlke's hands clutched Mahlke's
knees, but the trembling continued. The teachers, including two
lady teachers from the Gudrun School, occupied a semicircle of
oak chairs with high backs and leather cushions, which the proctor had set up with remarkable precision. Dr. Moeller clapped his
hands, and little by little the audience quieted down for Dr. Klohse,
our principal. Behind the twin braids and pony tails of the upper-
class girls sat Fourths with pocketknives; braids were quickly
shifted from back to front. Only the pony tails remained within
reach of the Fourths and their knives. This time there was an introduction. Klohse spoke of all those who are out there fighting
for us, on land, on the sea, and in the air, spoke at length and
with little inflection of himself and the students at Langemarck,
and on the Isle of Ösel fell Walter Flex. Quotation: Maturebut-
pure — the manly virtues. Then some Fichte or Arndt. Quotation:
Onyoualoneandwhatyoudo. Recollection of an excellent paper on
Fichte or Arndt that the lieutenant commander had written in Second: "One of us, from our midst, a product of our school and its
spirit, and in this spirit let us..."

Need I say how zealously notes were passed back and forth between us in the window niches and the girls from Upper Second.
Of course the Fourths mixed in a few obscenities of their own.
I wrote a note saying Godknowswhat either to Vera Plötz or to
Hildchen Matull, but got no answer from either. Mahlke's hands
were still clutching Mahlke's knees. The trembling died down.
The lieutenant commander on the platform sat slightly crushed
between old Dr. Brunies, who as usual was calmly sucking hard
candy, and Dr. Stachnitz, our Latin teacher. As the introduction
droned to an end, as our notes passed back and forth, as the
Fourths with pocketknives, as the eyes of the Führer's photograph
met those of the oil-painted Baron von Conradi, as the morning sun slipped out of the auditorium, the lieutenant commander

moistened his delicately curved orator's mouth and stared morosely at the audience, making a heroic effort to exclude the girl students from his field of vision. Cap perched with dignity on his parallel knees. Under the cap his gloves. Dress uniform. The hardware on his neck plainly discernible against an inconceivably white shirt. Sudden movement of his head, half followed by his decoration, toward the lateral windows: Mahlke trembled, feeling no doubt that he had been recognized, but he hadn't. Through the window in whose niche we huddled the U-boat captain gazed at dusty, motionless chestnut trees; what, I thought then or think now, what can he be thinking, what can Mahlke be thinking, or Klohse while speaking, or Brunies while sucking, or Vera Plötz while your note, or Hildchen Matull, what can he he he be thinking, Mahlke or the fellow with the orator's mouth? For it would have been illuminating to know what a U-boat captain thinks while obliged to listen, while his gaze roams free without crosswires and dancing horizon, until Joachim Mahlke feels singled out; but actually he was staring over schoolboys' heads, through double windowpanes, at the dry greenness of the poker-faced trees in the recreation yard, giving his orator's mouth one last moistening with his bright-red tongue, for Klohse was trying, with words on peppermint breath, to send a last sentence out past the middle of the auditorium: "And today it beseems us in the homeland to give our full attention to what you sons of our nation have to report from the front, from every front."

The orator's mouth had deceived us. The lieutenant commander started out with a very colorless survey such as one might have found in any naval manual: the function of the submarine. German submarines in the First World War: Weddigen and the *U 9*, submarine plays decisive role in Dardanelles campaign, sinking a total of thirteen million gross register tons. Our first 250-ton subs, electric when submerged, diesel on the surface, the name of Prien was dropped, Prien and the *U 47*, and Lieutenant Commander Prien sent the *Royal Oak* to the bottom — hell, we knew all that — as well as the *Repulse*, and Schuhart sank the *Courageous*, and so on and so on. And then all the old saws: "The crew is a body of men who have sworn to stand together in life and death, for far from home, terrible nervous strain, you can imagine, living in a sardine can in the middle of the Atlantic or the Arctic, cramped humid hot, men obliged to sleep on spare torpedoes, nothing stirring for days on end, empty horizon, then suddenly a convoy, heavily guarded, everything has to go like clockwork, not an unnecessary syllable; when we bagged our first tanker, the *Arndale,* 17,200 tons, with two fish amidships, believe it or not, I thought of you, my dear Dr. Stachnitz, and began to recite out loud, without turning off the intercom, *qui quae quod, cuius cuius cuius* ... until our exec called back: Good work, skipper, you may take the rest of the day off. But a submarine mission isn't all shooting and tube one fire and tube two fire; for days on end it's the same monotonous sea, the rolling and pounding of the boat, and overhead the sky, a sky to make your head reel, I tell you, and sunsets ... "

Although the lieutenant commander with the hardware on his neck had sunk 250,000 gross register tons, a light cruiser of the *Despatch* class and a heavy destroyer of the *Tribal* class, the details of his exploits took up much less space in his talk than verbose descriptions of nature. No metaphor was too daring. For instance: " ... swaying like a train of priceless, dazzlingly white lace, the foaming wake follows the boat which, swathed like a bride in festive veils of spray, strides onward to the marriage of death."

The tittering wasn't limited to the pigtail contingent; but in the ensuing metaphor the bride was obliterated: "A submarine is like a whale with a hump, but what of its bow wave? It is like the twirling, many times twirled mustache of a hussar."

The lieutenant commander also had a way of intoning dry technical terms as if they had been dark words of legend. Probably his lecture was addressed more to Papa Brunies, his former German teacher, known as a lover of Eichendorff, than to us. Klohse had mentioned the eloquence of his school themes, and perhaps he wished to show that his tongue had lost none of its cunning. Such words as "bilge pump" and "helmsman" were uttered in a mysterious whisper. He must have thought he was offering us a revelation when he said "master compass" or "repeater compass." Good Lord, we had known all this stuff for years. He saw himself as the kindly grandmother telling fairy tales. The voice in which he spoke of a dog-watch or a watertight door or even something as commonplace as a "choppy cross sea!" It was like listening to dear old Andersen or the Brothers Grimm telling a spooky tale about "sonar impulses."

When he started brushing in sunsets, it got really embarrassing: "And before the Atlantic night descends on us like a flock of ravens transformed by enchantment into a black shroud, the sky takes on colors we never see at home. An orange flares up, fleshy and unnatural, then airy and weightless, bejeweled at the edges as in the paintings of old masters; and in between, feathery clouds; and oh what a strange light over the rolling full-blooded sea!"

Standing there with his sugar candy on his neck, he sounded the color organ, rising to a roar, descending to a whisper, from watery blue to cold-glazed lemon yellow to brownish purple. Poppies blazed in the sky, and in their midst clouds, first silver, then suffused with red: "So must it be," these were his actual words, "when birds and angels bleed to death." And suddenly from out of this sky, so daringly described, from out of bucolic little clouds, he conjured up a seaplane of the *Sunderland* type. It came buzzing toward his U-boat but accomplished nothing. Then with the same orator's mouth but without metaphors, he opened the second part of his lecture. Chopped, dry, matter-of-fact: "I'm sitting in the periscope seat. Just scored a hit. Probably a refrigerator ship. Sinks stern first. We take the boat down at one one zero. Destroyer comes in on one seven zero. We come left ten degrees. New course: one two zero, steady on one two zero. Propeller sounds fade, increase, come in at one eight zero, ash cans: six...seven...eight... eleven: lights go out; pitch-darkness, then the emergency lighting comes on, and one after another the stations report all clear. Destroyer has stopped. Last bearing one six zero, we come left ten degrees. New course four five...."

Unfortunately, this really exciting fillet was followed by more prose poems: "The Atlantic winter" or "Phosphorescence in the Mediterranean," and a genre painting: "Christmas on a submarine," with the inevitable broom transformed into a Christmas tree. In conclusion he rose to mythical heights: the homecoming after a successful mission, Ulysses, and at long last: "The first sea gulls tell us that the port is near."

I don't know whether Dr. Klohse ended the session with the familiar words "And now back to work," or whether we sang "Welovethestorms." I seem, rather, to recall muffled but respectful applause, disorganized movements of getting up, begun by girls and pigtails. When I turned around toward Mahlke, he was gone;

I saw his hair with the part in the middle bob up several times by the right-hand exit, but one of my legs had fallen asleep during the lecture and for a few moments I was unable to jump from the window niche to the waxed floor.

It wasn't until I reached the dressing room by the gymnasium that I ran into Mahlke; but I could think of nothing to start a conversation with. While we were still changing, rumors were heard and soon confirmed. We were being honored: the lieutenant commander had asked Mallenbrandt, his former gym teacher, for leave to participate in the good old gym class, though he was out of shape. In the course of the two hours which as usual on Saturday closed the school day, he showed us what he could do. In the second hour, we were joined by the Firsters.

Squat, well built, with a luxuriant growth of black hair on his chest. From Mallenbrandt he had borrowed the traditional red gym pants, the white shin with the red stripe at chest level, and the black C embedded in the stripe. A cluster of students formed around him while he was dressing. Lots of questions: "...may I look at it close up? How long does it take? And what if? But a friend of my brother's in the mosquito boats says...." He answered patiently. Sometimes he laughed for no reason but contagiously. The dressing room whinnied; and the only reason why Mahlke caught my attention just then was that he didn't join in the laughter; he was busy folding and hanging up his clothes.

The trill of Mallenbrandt's whistle called us to the gymnasium, where we gathered around the horizontal bar. The lieutenant commander, discreetly seconded by Mallenbrandt, directed the class. Which meant that we were not kept very busy, because he was determined to perform for us, among other things, the giant swing ending in a split. Aside from Hotten Sonntag only Mahlke could compete, but so execrable were his swing and split — his knees were bent and he was all tensed up — that none of us could bear to watch him. When the lieutenant commander began to lead us in a series of free and carefully graduated ground exercises, Mahlke's Adam's apple was still dancing about like a stuck pig. In the vault over seven men, he landed askew on the mat and apparently turned his ankle. After that he sat on a ladder off to one side and must have slipped away when the Firsters joined us at the beginning of the second hour. However, he was back again for the basketball game against the First; he even made three or four baskets, but we lost just the same.

Our Neo-Gothic gymnasium preserved its air of solemnity just as St. Mary's Chapel in Neuschottland, regardless of all the painted plaster and ecclesiastical trappings Father Gusewski could assemble in the bright gymnastic light of its broad window fronts, never lost the feel of the modern gymnasium it had formerly been. While there clarity prevailed over all mysteries, trained our muscles in a mysterious twilight: our gymnasium had ogival windows, their panes broken up by rosettes and flamboyant tracery. In the glaring light of St. Mary's Chapel, offering, transubstantiation, and communion were disenchanted motions that might have been performed in a factory; instead of wafers, one might just as well have handed out hammers, saws, or window frames, or for that matter gymnastic apparatus, bats and relay sticks, as in former days. While in the mystical light of our gymnasium the simple act of choosing the two basketball teams, whose ten minutes of play was to wind up the session, seemed solemnly moving like an ordination or confirmation ceremony. And when the chosen ones stepped aside into the dim background, it was with the humility of those performing a sacred rite. Especially on bright mornings, when a few rays of sun found their way through the foliage in the yard and the ogival windows, the oblique beams, falling on the moving figures of athletes performing on the trapeze or rings, produced strange, romantic effects. If I concentrate, I can still see the squat little lieutenant commander in altar-boy-red gym pants, executing airy, fluid movements on the flying trapeze, I can see his flawlessly pointed feet — he performed barefoot — diving into a golden sunbeam, and I can see his hands — for all at once he was hanging by his knees — reach out for a shaft of agitated golden dust. Yes, our gymnasium was marvelously old-fashioned; why, even the dressing room obtained its light through ogival windows; that was why we called it the Sacristy.

Mallenbrandt blew his whistle; after the basketball game both classes had to line up and sing "Tothemountainswegointheearly-dewfallera"; then we were dismissed. In the dressing room there was again a huddle around the lieutenant commander. Only the Firsters hung back a little. After carefully washing his hands and armpits over the one and only washbasin — there were no

showers — the lieutenant commander put on his underwear and
stripped off his borrowed gym togs so deftly that we didn't see
a thing. Meanwhile he was subjected to more questions, which
he answered with good-natured, not too condescending laughter.
Then, between two questions, his good humor left him. His hands
groped uncertainly. Covertly at first, then openly, he was looking
for something. He even looked under the bench. "Just a minute,
boys, I'll be back on deck in a second," and in navy-blue shorts,
white shirt, socks but no shoes, he picked his way through students, benches, and zoo smell: Pavilion for Small Carnivores. His
collar stood open and raised, ready to receive his tie and the ribbon
bearing the decoration whose name I dare not utter. On the door
of Mallenbrandt's office hung the weekly gymnasium schedule.
The lieutenant commander knocked and went right in.

Who didn't think of Mahlke as I did? I'm not sure I thought of
him right away, I should have, but the one thing I am sure of is
that I didn't sing out: "Hey, where's Mahlke?" Nor did Schilling
nor Hotten Sonntag, nor Winter Kupka Esch. Nobody sang out;
instead we all ganged up on sickly little Buschmann, a poor devil
who had come into the world with a grin that he couldn't wipe off
his face even after it had been slapped a dozen times.

The half-dressed lieutenant commander came back with Mallenbrandt in a terry-cloth bathrobe. "Whowasit?" Mallenbrandt
roared. "Lethimstepforward!" And we sacrificed Buschmann to his
wrath. I too shouted Buschmann; I even succeeded in telling myself
as though I really believed it: Yes, it must have been Buschmann,
who else could it be?

But while Mallenbrandt, the lieutenant commander, and the
upper-class monitor were flinging questions at Buschmann all together, I began to have pins and needles, superficially at first,
on the back of my neck. The sensation grew stronger when
Buschmann got his first slap, when he was slapped because even
under questioning he couldn't get the grin off his face. While my
eyes and ears waited for a clear confession from Buschmann, the
certainty crawled upward from the back of my neck: Say, I wonder
if it wasn't a certain So-and-So!

My confidence seeped away; no, the grinning Buschmann was
not going to Confess; even Mallenbrandt must have suspected as
much or he would not have been so liberal with his slaps. He had

stopped talking about the missing object and only roared between one slap and the next: "Wipe that grin off your face. Stop it, I say. I'll teach you to grin."

I may say, in passing, that Mallenbrandt did not achieve his aim. I don't know whether Buschmann is still in existence; but if there should be a dentist, veterinary, or physician by the name of Buschmann — Heini Buschmann was planning to study medicine — it is certainly a grinning Dr. Buschmann; for that kind of thing is not so easily got rid of, it is long-lived, survives wars and currency reforms, and even then, in the presence of a lieutenant commander with an empty collar, waiting for an investigation to produce results, it proved superior to the blows of Mr. Mallenbrandt.

Discreetly, though all eyes were on Buschmann, I looked for Mahlke, but there was no need to search; I could tell by a feeling in my neck where he was inwardly singing his hymns to the Virgin. Fully dressed, not far away but removed from the crowd, he was buttoning the top button of a shirt which to judge by the cut and stripes must have been still another hand-me-down from his father. He was having trouble getting his distinguishing mark in under the button.

Apart from his struggles with his shirt button and the accompanying efforts of his jaw muscles, he gave an impression of calm. When he realized that the button wouldn't close over his Adam's apple, he reached into the breast pocket of his coat, which was still hanging up, and produced a rumpled necktie. No one in our class wore a tie. In the upper classes there were a few fops who affected ridiculous bow ties. Two hours before, while the lieutenant was still regaling the auditorium about the beauties of nature, he had worn his shirt collar open; but already the tie was in his breast pocket, awaiting the great occasion.

This was Mahlke's maiden voyage as a necktie wearer. There was only one mirror in the dressing room and even so it was covered with spots. Standing before it, but only for the sake of form, for he didn't step close enough to see anything much, he tied on his rag — it had bright polka dots and was in very bad taste, I am convinced today — turned down his collar, and gave the enormous knot one last tug. Then he spoke up, not in a very loud voice but with sufficient emphasis that his words could be distinguished from the sounds of the investigation that was still in progress and the slaps which Mallenbrandt, over the lieutenant commander's objections, was still tirelessly meting out. "I'm willing to bet," Mahlke said, "that Buschmann didn't do it. But has anybody searched his clothing?"

Though he had spoken to the mirror, Mahlke found ready listeners. His necktie, his new act, was noticed only later, and then not very much. Mallenbrandt personally searched Buschmann's clothes and soon found reason to strike another blow at the grin: in both coat pockets he found several opened packages of condoms, with which Buschmann carried on a retail trade in the upper classes; his father was a druggist. Otherwise Mallenbrandt found nothing, and the lieutenant commander cheerfully gave up, knotted his officer's tie, turned his collar down, and, tapping at the spot which had previously been so eminently decorated, suggested to Mallenbrandt that there was no need to take the incident too seriously: "It's easily replaced. It's not the end of the world. Just a silly boyish prank."

But Mallenbrandt had the doors of the gymnasium and dressing room locked and with the help of two Firsters searched our pockets as well as every corner of the room that might have been used as a hiding place. At first the lieutenant commander was amused and even helped, but after a while he grew impatient and did something that no one had ever dared to do in our dressing room: he began to chain smoke, stamping out the butts on the linoleum floor. His mood soured visibly after Mallenbrandt had silently pushed up a spittoon that for years had been gathering dust beside the washbowl and had already been searched as a possible hiding place.

The lieutenant commander blushed like a schoolboy, tore the cigarette he had just begun from his delicately curved orator's mouth, and stopped smoking. At first he just stood there with his arms folded; then he began to look nervously at the time, demonstrating his impatience by the sharp left hook with which he shook his wrist watch out of his sleeve.

He took his leave by the door with gloved fingers, giving it to be understood that he could not approve of the way this investigation was being handled, that he would put the whole irritating business into the hands of the principal, for he had no intention of letting his leave be spoiled by a bunch of ill-behaved brats.

Mallenbrandt tossed the key to one of the Firsters, who created an embarrassing pause by his clumsiness in unlocking the dressing-room door.

Chapter 8

The investigation dragged on, ruining our Saturday afternoon and bringing no results. I remember few details and those are hardly worth talking about, for I had to keep an eye on Mahlke and his necktie, whose knot he periodically tried to push up higher; but for Mahlke's purposes a hook would have been needed. No, you were beyond help.

But what of the lieutenant commander? The question seems hardly worth asking, but it can be answered in few words. He was not present at the afternoon investigation, and it may well have been true, as unconfirmed rumors had it, that he spent the afternoon with his fiancée, looking through the city's three or four medal shops. Somebody in our class claimed to have seen him on Sunday at the Four Seasons Café, sitting with his fiancée and her parents, and allegedly nothing was missing between his collarbones: the visitors to the café may have noticed, with a certain awe, who was sitting there in their midst, trying his well-mannered best to cut the recalcitrant cake of the third war year with a fork.

I didn't go to the café that Sunday. I had promised Father Gusewski to serve as his altar boy at early Mass. Shortly after seven Mahlke came in with his bright necktie and was unable, despite the aid of the usual five little old women, to dispel the emptiness of the former gymnasium. He received communion as usual on the outer left. The previous evening, immediately after the investigation at school, he must have come to St. Mary's Chapel and confessed; or perhaps, for one reason or another, you whispered into Father Wiehnke's ear at the Church of the Sacred Heart.

Gusewski kept me, inquired after my brother, who was fighting in Russia, or maybe he had stopped fighting, for there had been no news of him for several weeks. Once again I had ironed and starched all the altar covers and the alb, and it is perfectly possible that he gave me a roll or two of raspberry drops; what I know for sure is that Mahlke was gone when I left the sacristy. He must have been one car ahead of me. On Max-Halbe-Platz I boarded the trailer of a No. 9 car. Schilling jumped on at Magdeburger Strasse after the car had gathered considerable speed. We spoke of something entirely different. Maybe I offered him some of Father Gusewski's raspberry drops. Between Saspe Manor and Saspe Cemetery, we overtook Hotten Sonntag. He was riding a lady's bicycle and carrying the little Pokriefke girl astraddle on the baggage rack. The spindly little thing's thighs were still as smooth as frogs' legs, but she was no longer flat all over. The wind showed that her hair had grown longer.

We had to wait at the Saspe siding for the car coming from the opposite direction, and Hotten Sonntag and Tulla passed us. At the Brösen stop the two of them were waiting. The bicycle was leaning against a wastepaper basket provided by the beach administration. They were playing brother and sister, standing there with their little fingers linked. Tulla's dress was blue blue washing blue, and in every way too short too tight too blue. Hotten Sonntag was carrying the bundle of bathrobes etc. We managed to exchange a few silent glances, and to catch each other's meaning. At length words fell from the supercharged silence: "Of course it was Mahlke, who else could it have been? What a guy!"

Tulla wanted details, squirmed up to us, and wheedled with a pointed forefinger. But neither of us called the object by name. She got no more out of us than a terse "WhoelsebutMahlke" and an "It'sasclearasday." But Schilling, no, it was I, dreamed up a new title. Into the gap between Hotten Sonntag's head and Tulla's head I inserted the words: "The Great Mahlke. The Great Mahlke did it, only the Great Mahlke can do such things."

And the title stuck. All previous attempts to fasten nicknames on Mahlke had been short-lived. I remember "Soup Chicken"; and when he stood aloof, we had called him "Swallower" or "The Swallower." But the first title to prove viable was my spontaneous cry: "The Great Mahlke!" And in these papers I shall speak now and then of "The Great Mahlke."

At the cashier's window we got rid of Tulla. She disappeared into the ladies' cabins, stretching her dress with her shoulder blades. Before the verandalike structure in front of the men's bathhouse lay the sea, pale and shaded by fair-weather clouds, blowing across the sky in dispersed order. Water: 65. Without having to search, the three of us caught sight, behind the second sandbank, of somebody swimming frantically on his back, splashing and foaming as he headed for the superstructure of the mine sweeper. We agreed that only one of us should swim after him. Schilling and I suggested Hotten Sonntag, but he preferred to lie with Tulla Pokriefke behind the sun screen on the family beach and sprinkle sand on frogs' legs. Schilling claimed to have eaten too much breakfast: "Eggs and all. My grandma from Krampitz has chickens and some Sundays she brings in two or three dozen eggs."

I could think of no excuse. I rarely observed the rule about fasting before communion and I had eaten breakfast very early. Besides, it was neither Schilling nor Hotten Sonntag who had said "The Great Mahlke," but I. So I swam after him, in no particular hurry.

Tulla Pokriefke wanted to swim along with me, and we almost came to blows on the pier between the ladies' beach and the family beach. All arms and legs, she was sitting on the railing. Summer after summer she had been wearing that same mouse-gray, grossly darned child's bathing suit; what little bosom she had was crushed, elastic cut into her thighs, and between her legs the threadbare wool molded itself in an intimate dimple. Curling her nose and spreading her toes, she screamed at me. When in return for some present or other — Hotten Sonntag was whispering in her ear — she agreed to withdraw, three or four little Thirds, good swimmers, whom I had often seen on the barge, came climbing over the railing; they must have caught some of our conversation, for they wanted to swim to the barge though they didn't admit it. "Oh no," they protested, "we're going somewhere else. Out to the breakwater. Or just to take a look." Hotten Sonntag attended to them: "Anybody that swims after him gets his balls polished."

After a shallow dive from the pier I started off, changing my stroke frequently and taking my time. As I swam and as I write, I tried and I try to think of Tulla Pokriefke, for I didn't and still don't want to think of Mahlke. That's why I swam backstroke, and that's why I write that I swam backstroke. That was the only way I could see Tulla Pokriefke sitting on the railing, a bag of bones in mouse-gray wool; and as I thought of her, she became smaller, crazier, more painful; for Tulla was a thorn in our flesh — but when I had the second sandbank behind me, she was gone, thorn and dimple had passed the vanishing point, I was no longer swimming away from Tulla, but swimming toward Mahlke, and it is toward you that I write: I swam breaststroke and I didn't hurry.

I may as well tell you between two strokes — the water will hold me up — that this was the last Sunday before summer vacation. What was going on at the time? They had occupied the Crimea, and Rommel was advancing again in North Africa. Since Easter we had been in Upper Second. Esch and Hotten Sonntag had volunteered, both for the Air Force, but later on, just like me who kept hesitating whether to go into the Navy or not, they were sent to the Panzer Grenadiers, a kind of high-class infantry. Mahlke didn't volunteer; as usual, he was the exception. "You must be nuts," he said. However, he was a year older, and there was every likelihood that he would be taken before we were; but a writer mustn't get ahead of himself.

I swam the last couple of hundred yards all in breaststroke, but still more slowly in order to save my breath. The Great Mahlke was sitting as usual in the shadow of the pilothouse. Only his knees were getting some sun. He must have been under once. The gargling remnants of an overture wavered in the fitful breeze and came out to meet me with the ripples. That was his way: dove down into his den, cranked up the phonograph, put on a record, came up with dripping watershed, sat down in the shade, and listened to his music while above him the screams of the gulls substantiated the doctrine of transmigration.

No, not yet. Once again, before it is too late, let me turn over on my back and contemplate the great clouds shaped like potato sacks, which rose from Putziger Wiek and passed over our barge in endless procession, providing changes of light and a cloud-long coolness. Never since — except at the exhibition of our local children's painting which Father Alban organized two years ago at our settlement house with my help, have I seen such beautiful, potato-sack-shaped clouds. And so once again, before the battered rust of the barge comes within reach, I ask: Why me? Why not Hotten Sonntag or Schilling? I might have sent the Thirds, or Tulla with

Hotten Sonntag. Or the whole lot of them including Tulla, for the Thirds, especially one of them who seems to have been related to her, were always chasing after the little bag of bones. But no, bidding Schilling to make sure that no one followed me, I swam alone. And took my time.

I, Pilenz — what has my first name got to do with it? — formerly an altar boy dreaming of every imaginable future, now secretary at the Parish Settlement House, just can't let magic alone; I read Bloy, the Gnostics, Böll, Friedrich Heer, and often with profound emotion the *Confessions* of good old St. Augustine. Over tea brewed much too black, I spend whole nights discussing the blood of Christ, the Trinity, and the sacrament of penance with the Franciscan Father Alban, who is an open-minded man though more or less a believer. I tell him about Mahlke and Mahlke's Virgin, Mahlke's neck and Mahlke's aunt, Mahlke's sugar water, the part in the middle of his hair, his phonograph, snowy owl, screwdriver, woolen pompoms, luminous buttons, about cat and mouse and *mea culpa*. I tell him how the Great Mahlke sat on the barge and I, taking my time, swam out to him alternating between breaststroke and backstroke; for I alone could be termed his friend, if it was possible to be friends with Mahlke. Anyway I made every effort. But why speak of effort? To me it was perfectly natural to trot along beside him and his changing attributes. If Mahlke had said: "Do this and that," I would have done this and that and then some. But Mahlke said nothing. I ran after him, I went out of my way to pick him up on Osterzeile for the privilege of going to school by his side. And he merely put up with my presence without a word or a sign. When he introduced the pompom vogue, I was the first to take it up and wear pompoms on my neck. For a while, though only at home, I even wore a screwdriver on a shoelace. And if I continued to gratify Gusewski with my services as an altar boy, it was only in order to gaze at Mahlke's neck during holy communion. When in 1942, after Easter vacation — aircraft carriers were battling in the Coral Sea — the Great Mahlke shaved for the first time, I too began to scrape my chin, though no sign of a beard was discernible. And if after the submarine captain's speech Mahlke had said to me: "Pilenz, go swipe that business on the ribbon," I would have taken medal and ribbon off the hook and kept it for you.

But Mahlke attended to his own affairs. And now he was sitting in the shadow of the pilothouse, listening to the tortured remains of his underwater music: *Cavalleria Rusticana* — gulls overhead — the sea now smooth now ruffled now stirred by short-winded waves — two fat ships in the roadstead — scurrying cloud shadows — over toward Putzig a formation of speedboats: six bow waves, a few trawlers in between — I can already hear the gurgling of the barge, I swim slowly, breaststroke, look away, look beyond, in between the vestiges of the ventilators I can't remember exactly how many — and before my hands grip the rust, I see you, as I've been seeing you for a good fifteen years: You! I swim, I grip the rust, I see You: the Great Mahlke sits impassive in the shadow, the phonograph record in the cellar catches, in love with a certain passage which it repeats till its breath fails; the gulls fly off; and there you are with the ribbon and *it* on your neck.

It was very funny-looking, because he had nothing else on. He sat huddled, naked and bony in the shade with his eternal sunburn. Only the knees glared. His long, semirelaxed pecker and his testicles lay flat on the rust. His hands clutching his knees. His hair plastered in strands over his ears but still parted in the middle. And that face, that Redeemer's countenance! And below it, motionless, his one and only article of clothing, the large, the enormous medal a hand's breadth below his collarbone.

For the first time the Adam's apple, which, as I still believe — though he had auxiliary motors — was Mahlke's motor and brake, had found its exact counterweight. Quietly it slumbered beneath his skin. For a time it had no need to move, for the harmonious cross that soothed it had a long history; it had been designed in the year 1813, when iron was worth its weight in gold, by good old Schinkel, who knew how to capture the eye with classical forms: slight changes in 1871, slight changes in 1914–18, and now again slight changes. But it bore no resemblance to the *Pour le Mérite,* a development of the Maltese Cross, although now for the first time Schinkel's brain child moved from chest to neck, proclaiming symmetry as a Credo.

"Hey, Pilenz! What do you think of my trinket? Not bad, eh?"

"Terrific! Let me touch it."

"You'll admit I earned it."

"I knew right away that you'd pulled the job."

"Job nothing. It was conferred on me only yesterday for sinking five ships on the Murmansk run plus a cruiser of the *Southampton* class...."

Both of us determined to make a show of lightheartedness; we grew very silly, bawled out every single verse of "We're sailing against England," made up new verses, in which neither tankers nor troop transports were torpedoed amidships, but certain girls and teachers from the Gudrun School; forming megaphones of our hands, we blared out special communiqués, announcing our sinkings in terms both high-flown and obscene, and drummed on the deck with our fists and heels. The barge groaned and rattled, dry gull droppings were shaken loose, gulls returned, speedboats passed in the distance, beautiful white clouds drifted over us, light as trails of smoke, comings and goings, happiness, shimmering light, not a fish leaped out of the water, friendly weather; the jumping jack started up again, not because of any crisis in the throat, but because he was alive all over and for the first time a little giddy, gone the Redeemer's countenance. Wild with glee, he removed the article from his neck and held the ends of the ribbon over his hip bones with a mincing little gesture. While with his legs, shoulders, and twisted head he performed a fairly comical imitation of a girl, but no particular girl, the great iron cookie dangled in front of his private parts concealed no more than a third of his pecker.

In between — your circus number was beginning to get on my nerves — I asked him if he meant to keep the thing; it might be best, I suggested, to store it in his basement under the bridge, along with the snowy owl, phonograph, and Pilsudski.

The Great Mahlke had other plans and carried them out. For if Mahlke had stowed the object below decks; or better still, if I had never been friends with Mahlke; or still better, both at once: the object safe in the radio shack and I only vaguely interested in Mahlke, out of curiosity or because he was a classmate — then I should not have to write now and I should not have to say to Father Alban: "Was it my fault if Mahlke later..." As it is, I can't help writing, for you can't keep such things to yourself. Of course it is pleasant to pirouette on white paper — but what help are white clouds, soft breezes, speedboats coming in on schedule, and a flock of gulls doing the work of a Greek chorus; what good can any magical effects of syntax do me; even if I drop capitals and punctuation, I shall still have to say that Mahlke did not stow his bauble in the former radio shack of the former Polish mine sweeper *Rybitwa,* that he did not hang it between Marshal Pilsudski and the Black Madonna, over the moribund phonograph and the decomposing snowy owl, that he went down under with his trinket on his neck, but stayed barely half an hour, while I counted sea gulls, preening himself — I can swear to that — with his prize piece for the Virgin's benefit. I shall have to say that he brought it up again through the fo'c'sle hatch and was wearing it as he slipped on his trunks and swam back to the bathhouse with me at a good steady pace, that holding his treasure in his clenched fist, he smuggled it past Schilling, Hotten Sonntag, Tulla Pokriefke, and the Thirds, into his cabin in the gentlemen's section.

I was in no mood for talking and gave Tulla and her entourage only half an idea of what was up before vanishing into my cabin. I dressed quickly and caught Mahlke at the No. 9 car stop. Throughout the ride I tried to persuade him, if it had to be, to return the medal personally to the lieutenant commander, whose address it would have been easy to find out.

I don't think he was listening. We stood on the rear platform, wedged in among the late Sunday morning crowd. From one stop to the next he opened his hand between his shirt and mine, and we both looked down at the severe dark metal with the rumpled, still wet ribbon. When we reached Saspe Manor, Mahlke held the medal over the knot of his tie, and tried to use the platform window as a mirror. As long as the car stood motionless, waiting for the car in the opposite direction to pass, I looked out over one of his ears, over the tumbledown Saspe Cemetery toward the airfield. I was in luck: a large trimotored Ju 52 was circling cautiously to a landing. That helped me.

Yet it was doubtful whether the Sunday crowd in the car had eyes to spare for the Great Mahlke's exhibition. Amid benches and bundles of beach equipment, they were kept busy struggling with small children worn out from bathing. The whining and blubbering of children, rising, falling, rising, squelched, and ebbing off into sleep, echoed from the front to the rear platform and back — not to mention smells that would have turned the sweetest milk sour.

At the terminus on Brunshöferweg we got out and Mahlke said over his shoulder that he was planning to disturb the noonday repose of Dr. Waldemar Klohse, our principal, that he was going in alone and there was no point in my waiting for him.

Klohse — as we all knew — lived on Baumbachallee. I accompanied the Great Mahlke through the tiled underpass, then I let him go his way; he did not hurry, I would even say that he zigzagged slightly. He held the ends of the ribbon between thumb and forefinger of his left hand; the medal twirled, serving as a propeller on his course to Baumbachallee.

An infernal idea! And why did he have to carry it out! If you had only thrown the damn thing up into the linden trees: in that residential quarter full of shade-dispensing foliage there were plenty of magpies that would have carried it off to their secret store, and tucked it away with the silver teaspoon, the ring and the brooch and the kit and boodle.

Mahlke was absent on Monday. The room was full of rumors. Dr. Brunies conducted his German class, incorrigibly sucking the Cebion tablets he should have distributed to his pupils. Eichendorff lay open before him. Sweet and sticky, his old man's mumble came to us from the desk: a few pages from the *Scamp,* then poems: *The Mill Wheel, The Little Ring, The Troubadour* — Two hearty journeymen went forth — If there's a fawn you love the best — The song that slumbers in all things — Mild blows the breeze and blue. Not a word about Mahlke.

It was not until Tuesday that Klohse came in with a gray portfolio, and took his stance beside Dr. Erdmann, who rubbed his hands in embarrassment. Over our heads resounded Klohse's cool breath: a disgraceful thing had happened, and in these fateful times when we must all pull together. The student in question — Klohse did not mention the name — had already been removed from the establishment. It had been decided, however, that other authorities, the district bureau for example, would not be notified. In the interests of the school the students were urged to observe a manly silence, which alone could minimize the effects of such scandalous behavior. Such was the desire of a distinguished alumnus, the lieutenant commander and U-boat captain, bearer of the and so on....

And so Mahlke was expelled, but—during the war scarcely anyone was thrown out of secondary school for good—transferred to
the Horst Wessel School, where his story was kept very quiet.

Chapter 9

The Horst Wessel School, which before the war had been called
the Crown Prince Wilhelm School, was characterized by the same
dusty smell as our Conradinum. The building, built in 1912, I
think, seemed friendlier than our brick edifice, but only on the
outside. It was situated on the southern edge of the suburb, at the
foot of Jeschkental Forest; consequently Mahlke's way to school
and my way to school did not intersect at any point when school
resumed in the autumn.

But there was no sign of him during the summer vacation
either—a summer without Mahlke!—the story was that he had
signed up for a premilitary training camp offering courses in radio operation. He displayed his sunburn neither in Brösen nor
at Glettkau Beach. Since there was no point in looking for him
at St. Mary's Chapel, Father Gusewski was deprived of one of
his most reliable altar boys. Altar Boy Pilenz said to himself: No
Mahlke, no Mass.

The rest of us lounged about the barge from time to time,
but without enthusiasm. Hotten Sonntag tried in vain to find
the way into the radio shack. Even the Thirds had heard rumors of an amazing and amazingly furnished hideaway inside the
bridge. A character with eyes very close together, whom the in-
fants submissively addressed as Störtebeker, dove indefatigably.
Tulla Pokriefke's cousin, a rather sickly little fellow, came out to
the barge once or twice, but never dove. Either in my thoughts or
in reality I tried to strike up a conversation with him about Tulla;
I was interested in her. But she had ensnared her cousin as she had
me—what with, I wonder? With her threadbare wool, with her in-
eradicable smell of carpenter's glue? "It's none of your God-damn
business!" That's what the cousin said to me—or might have.

Tulla didn't swim out to the barge; she stayed on the beach, but
she had given up Hotten Sonntag. I took her to the movies twice,

but even so I had no luck; she'd go to the movies with anybody. It was said that she had fallen for Störtebeker, but if so her love was unrequited, for Störtebeker had fallen for our barge and was looking for the entrance to Mahlke's hideout. As the vacation drew to an end there was a good deal of whispering to the effect that his diving had been successful. But there was never any proof: he produced neither a waterlogged phonograph record nor a decaying owl feather. Still, the rumors persisted; and when, two and a half years later, the so-called Dusters, a somewhat mysterious gang supposedly led by Störtebeker, were arrested, our barge and the hiding place under the bridge appear to have been mentioned. But by then I was in the Army; all I heard was a line or two in letters — for until the end, or rather as long as the mails were running, Father Gusewski wrote me letters ranging from pastoral to friendly. In one of the last, written in January '45 — as the Russian armies were approaching Elbing — there was something about a scandalous assault of the Dusters on the Church of the Sacred Heart, where Father Wiehnke officiated. In this letter Störtebeker was referred to by his real name; and it also seems to me that I read something about a three-year-old child whom the gang had cherished as a kind of mascot. I am pretty certain, though sometimes I have my doubts, that in his last or next to last letter — I lost the whole packet and my diary as well near Cottbus — there was some mention of the barge which had its big day before the onset of the summer vacation of '42, but whose glory paled in the course of the summer; for to this day that summer has a flat taste in my mouth — what was summer without Mahlke?

Not that we were really unhappy about his absence. I myself was glad to be rid of him, so I didn't have to chase after him the whole time; but why, I wonder, did I report to Father Gusewski as soon as school began again, offering my services at the altar? The reverend father's eyes crinkled with delight behind his rimless glasses and grew smooth and solemn behind the self-same glasses only when — we were sitting in the sacristy and I was brushing his cassock — I asked, as though in passing, about Joachim Mahlke. Calmly, raising one hand to his glasses, he declared: "Yes, yes, he is still one of the most faithful members of my congregation; never misses a Sunday Mass. You know, I presume, that he was away for four weeks, at a so-called premilitary training camp; but

I shouldn't like to think that you're coming back to us only on Mahlke's account. Speak up, Pilenz!"

Exactly two weeks earlier, we had received news that my brother Klaus, a sergeant in the Army, had fallen in the Kuban. I spoke of his death as my reason for wishing to resume my duties as an altar boy. Father Gusewski seemed to believe me; at any rate he tried to believe in me and in my renewed piety.

I don't recollect the particulars of Winter's or Hotten Sonntag's face. But Father Gusewski had thick wavy hair, black with the barest sprinkling of gray, which could be counted on to sprinkle his cassock with dandruff. Meticulously tonsured, the crown of his head had a bluish glint. He gave off an aroma compounded of hair tonic and Palmolive soap. Sometimes he smoked Turkish cigarettes in an ornately carved amber holder. He enjoyed a reputation for progressiveness and played ping-pong in the sacristy with the altar boys and those preparing for their first communion. He liked the ecclesiastical linen, the humeral and the alb, to be immoderately starched, a chore attended to by a certain Mrs. Tolkmit or, when the old lady was ailing, by a handy altar boy, often myself. He himself appended sachets of lavender to every maniple, every stole, to all the Mass vestments, whether they lay in chests or hung in closets. Once when I was about thirteen, he ran his small, hairless hand down my back under my shirt from my neck to the waist of my gym shorts, but stopped there because my shorts had no elastic band and I tied them in front with tapes. I didn't give the incident much thought, for Father Gusewski had won my sympathy with his friendly, often boyish ways. I can still remember his ironic benevolence; so not another word about the occasional wanderings of his hand; all perfectly harmless, it was really my Catholic soul he was looking for. All in all, he was a priest like hundreds of others; he maintained a well-selected library for a working-class congregation that read little; his zeal was not excessive, his belief had its limits — in regard to the Assumption, for instance — and he always spoke, whether over the corporal about the blood of Christ or in the sacristy about ping-pong, in the same tone of unctuous serenity. It did strike me as silly when early in 1940 he put in a petition to have his name changed — less than a year later he called himself, and had others call him, Father Gusewing. But the fashion for Germanizing polish-sounding names ending in *ki* or *ke* or *a*—like Formella—was taken up by lots of people in whose days: Lewandowski became Lengnisch; Mr. Olczewski, our butcher, had himself metamorphosed into a Mr. Ohlwein; Jürgen Kupka's parents wanted to take the East Prussian name of Kupkat, but their petition, heaven knows why, was rejected. Perhaps in emulation of one Saul who became Paul, a certain Gusewski wished to become Gusewing—but in these papers Father Gusewski will continue to be Gusewski; for you, Joachim Mahlke, did not change your name.

When for the first time after summer vacation I served early Mass at the altar, I saw him again and anew. Immediately after the prayers at the foot of the altar — Father Gusewski stood on the Epistle side and was busy with the Introit — I sighted him in the second pew, before the altar of Our Lady. But it was only between the reading of the Epistle and the gradual, and more freely during the Gospel reading, that I found time to examine his appearance. His hair was still parted in the middle and still held in place with the usual sugar water; but he wore it a good inch longer. Stiff and candied, it fell over his two ears like the two sides of a steep-pointed roof: he would have made a satisfactory Jesus the way he held up his joined hands on a level with his forehead without propping his elbows; beneath them I perceived a bare, unguarded neck that concealed none of its secrets; for he was wearing his shirt collar open and folded over his jacket collar in the manner hallowed by Schiller: no tie, no pompoms, no pendants, no screwdriver, nor any other item from his copious arsenal. The only heraldic beast in an otherwise vacant field was the restless mouse which he harbored under his skin in place of a larynx, which had once attracted a cat and had tempted me to put the cat on his neck. The area between Adam's apple and chin was still marked with a few crusty razor cuts. At the Sanctus I almost came in too late with the bell.

At the communion rail Mahlke's attitude was less affected. His joined hands dropped down below his collarbone and his mouth smelled as though a pot of cabbage were simmering on a small flame within him. Once he had his wafer, another daring innovation captured my attention: in former days Mahlke, like every other communicant, had returned directly from the communion rail to his place in the second row of pews; now he prolonged and interrupted this silent itinerary, first striding slowly and stiffly to the middle of the altar of Our Lady, then falling on both knees, not on the linoleum floor but on a shaggy carpet which began shortly before the altar steps. Then he raised his joined hands until they were level with his eyes, with the part in his hair, and higher still he held them out in supplication and yearning to the over-life-size plaster figure which stood childless, a virgin among virgins, on a silver-plated crescent moon, draped from shoulders to ankles in a Prussian-blue starry mantle, her long-fingered hands folded over her flat bosom, gazing with slightly protuberant glass eyes at the ceiling of the former gymnasium. When Mahlke arose knee after knee and reassembled his hands in front of his Schiller collar, the carpet had imprinted a coarse, bright-red pattern on his kneecaps.

Father Gusewski had also observed certain aspects of Mahlke's new style. Not that I asked questions. Quite of his own accord, as though wishing to throw off or to share a burden, he began immediately after Mass to speak of Mahlke's excessive zeal, of his dangerous attachment to outward forms. Yes, Father Gusewski was worried; it had seemed to him for some time that regardless of what inner affliction brought Mahlke to the altar, his cult of the Virgin bordered on pagan idolatry.

He was waiting for me at the door of the sacristy. I was so frightened I almost ran back in again, but at once he took my arm, laughed in a free and easy way that was completely new, and talked and talked. He who had formerly been so monosyllabic spoke about the weather — Indian summer, threads of gold in the air. And then abruptly, but in the same conversational tone and without even lowering his voice: "I've volunteered. I can't understand it. You know how I feel about all that stuff: militarism, playing soldier, the current overemphasis on martial virtues. Guess what branch of service. Don't make me laugh. The Air Force is all washed up. Paratroopers? Wrong again! Why wouldn't you think of the submarines? Well, at last! That's the only branch that still has a chance. Though of course I'll feel like an ass in one of those things and I'd rather do something useful or funny. You remember I wanted to be a clown. Lord, what ideas a kid will get!

"I still think it's a pretty good idea. Otherwise things aren't so bad. Hell, school is school. What fool ideas I used to have. Do you remember? Just couldn't get used to this bump. I thought it was some kind of disease. But it's perfectly normal. I've known

people, or at least I've seen some, with still bigger ones; they don't
get upset. The whole thing started that day with the cat. You
remember. We were lying in Heinrich Ehlers Field. A Schlagball
tournament was going on. I was sleeping or daydreaming, and that
gray beast, or was it black, saw my neck and jumped, or one of
you, Schilling I think, it's the kind of thing he would do, took the
cat... Well, that's ancient history. No, I haven't been back to the
barge. Störtebeker? Never heard of him. Let him, let him. I don't
own the barge, do I? Come and see us soon."

It was not until the third Sunday of Advent — all that autumn
Mahlke had made me a model altar boy — that I accepted his invitation. Until Advent I had been obliged to serve all by myself.
Father Gusewski had been unable to find a second altar boy. Actually I had wanted to visit Mahlke on the first Sunday of Advent
and bring him a candle, but the shipment came too late and it was
not until the second Sunday that Mahlke was able to place the
consecrated candle on the altar of Our Lady. "Can you scare up
some?" he had asked me. "Gusewski won't give me any." I said
that I'd do what I could, and actually succeeded in procuring one
of those long candles, pale as potato shoots, that are so rare in
wartime; for my brother's death entitled my family to a candle. I
went on foot to the rationing office and they gave me a coupon after I had submitted the death certificate. Then I took the streetcar
to the religious-articles shop in Oliva, but they were out of candles. I had to go back again and then a second time, and so it was
only on the second Sunday of Advent that I was able to give you
your candle and see you kneel with it at the altar of Our Lady,
as I had long dreamed of seeing you. Gusewski and I wore violet
for Advent. But your neck sprouted from a white Schiller collar
which was not obscured by the reversed and remodeled overcoat
you had inherited from an engine driver killed in an accident, for
you no longer — another innovation! — wore a muffler fastened
with a large safety pin.
    And Mahlke knelt stiffly and at length on the coarse carpet on
the second Sunday of Advent and again on the third, the day I
decided to take him at his word and drop in on him in the afternoon. His glassy unquivering gaze — or if it quivered, it was when
I was busy at the altar — was aimed over the candle at the belly of

the Mother of God. His hands formed a steep roof over his forehead and its thoughts, but he did not touch his forehead with his
crossed thumbs.

And I thought: Today I'll go. I'll go and take a look at him. I'll
study him. Yes, so I will. There must be something behind all that.
Besides, he had invited me.

Osterzeile was a short street: and yet the one-family houses with
their empty trellises against house fronts scrubbed till they were
sore, the uniform trees along the sidewalks — the lindens had lost
their poles within the last year but still required props — discour-
aged and wearied me, although our Westerzeile was identical, or
perhaps it was because our Westerzeile had the same smell and cel-
ebrated the seasons with the same Lilliputian garden plots. Even
today when, as rarely happens, I leave the settlement house to visit
friends or acquaintances in Stockum or Lohhausen, between the
airfield and the North Cemetery, and have to pass through streets
of housing development which repeat themselves just as weari-
somely and dishearteningly from house number to house number,
from linden to linden, I am still on the way to visit Mahlke's
mother and Mahlke's aunt and you, the Great Mahlke; the bell
is fastened to a garden gate that I might have stepped over without
effort, just by stretching my legs a little. Steps through the wintry
but snowless front garden with its top-heavy rosebushes wrapped
for the winter. The flowerless flower beds are decorated with Baltic
sea shells broken and intact. The ceramic tree frog the size of a
rabbit is seated on a slab of rough marble embedded in crusty garden soil that has crumbled over it in places. And in the flower bed
on the other side of the narrow path which, while I think of it,
guides me from the garden gate to the three brick steps before the
ocher-stained, round-arched door, stands, just across from the tree
frog, an almost vertical pole some five feet high, topped with a
birdhouse in the Alpine manner. The sparrows go on eating as I
negotiate the seven or eight paces between flower bed and flower
bed. It might be supposed that the development smells fresh, clean,
sandy, and seasonal — but Osterzeile, Westerzeile, Bärenweg, no,
the whole of Langfuhr, West Prussia, or Germany for that matter,
smelled in those war years of onions, onions stewing in margarine;
I won't try to determine what else was stewing, but one thing that

could always be identified was freshly chopped onions, although onions were scarce and hard to come by, although jokes about the onion shortage, in connection with Field Marshal Göring, who had said something or other about short onions on the radio, were going the rounds in Langfuhr, in West Prussia, and all over Germany. Perhaps if I rubbed my typewriter superficially with onion juice, it might communicate an intimation of the onion smell which in those years contaminated all Germany, West Prussia and Langfuhr, Osterzeile as well as Westerzeile, preventing the smell of corpses from taking over completely.

I took the three brick steps at one stride, and my curved hand was preparing to grasp the door handle when the door was opened from within — by Mahlke in Schiller collar and felt slippers. He must have refurbished the part in his hair a short while before. Neither light nor dark, in rigid, freshly combed strands, it slanted backward in both directions from the part. Still impeccably neat; but when I left an hour later, it had begun to quiver as he spoke and droop over his large, flamboyant ears.

We sat in the rear of the house, in the living room, which received its light from the jutting glass veranda. There was cake made from some war recipe, potato cake; the predominant taste was rose water, which was supposed to awaken memories of marchpane. Afterward preserved plums, which had a normal taste and had ripened during the fall in Mahlke's garden — the tree, leafless and with whitewashed trunk, could be seen in the left-hand pane of the veranda. My chair was assigned to me: I was at the narrow end of the table, looking out, while Mahlke, opposite me at the other end, had the veranda behind him. To the left of me, illumined from the side so that gray hair curled silvery, Mahlke's aunt; to the right, her right side illumined, but less glittering because combed more tightly, Mahlke's mother. Although the room was overheated, it was a cold wintry light that outlined the fuzzy edges of her ears and a few trembling wisps of loose hair. The wide Schiller collar gleamed whiter than white at the top, blending into gray lower down: Mahlke's neck lay flat in the shadow.

The two women were rawboned, born and raised in the country. They were at a loss what to do with their hands and spoke profusely, never at the same time, but always in the direction of

Joachim Mahlke even when they were addressing me and asking about my mother's health. They both spoke to me through him, who acted as our interpreter: "So now your brother Klaus is dead. I knew him only by sight, but what a handsome boy!"

Mahlke was a mild but firm chairman. When the questions became too personal — while my father was sending APO letters from Greece, my mother was indulging in intimate relations, mostly with noncoms — well, Mahlke warded off questions in that direction: "Never mind about that, Auntie. Who can afford to judge in times like this when everything is topsy-turvy? Besides, it's really no business of yours, Mamma. If Papa were still alive, he wouldn't like it, he wouldn't let you speak like that."

Both women obeyed him or else they obeyed the departed engine driver whom he quietly conjured up whenever his aunt or mother began to gossip. When they spoke of the situation at the front — confusing the battlefields of Russia with those of North Africa, saying El Alamein when they meant the Sea of Azov — Mahlke managed quietly, without irritation, to guide the conversation into the right geographical channels: "No, Auntie, that naval battle was at Guadalcanal, not in Karelia."

Nevertheless, his aunt had given the cue and we lost ourselves in conjectures about the Japanese and American aircraft carriers that might have been sunk off Guadalcanal. Mahlke believed that the carriers *Hornet* and *Wasp*, the keels of which had been laid only in 1939, as well as the *Ranger*, had been completed in time to take part in the battle, for either the *Saratoga* or the *Lexington*, perhaps both, had meanwhile been sunk. We were still more in the dark about the two big Japanese carriers, the *Akagi* and the *Kaga*, which was decidedly too slow to be effective. Mahlke expressed daring opinions: only aircraft carriers, he said, would figure in the naval battles of the future, there was no longer any point in building battleships, it was the small, fast craft and the carriers that counted. He went into details. When he rattled off the names of the Italian *esploratori*, both women gaped in amazement and Mahlke's aunt clapped her bony hands resoundingly; there was something girlish about her enthusiasm, and in the silence that followed her clapping, she fiddled with her hair in embarrassment.

Not a word fell about the Horst Wessel School. I almost seem to remember that, as I was getting up to go, Mahlke laughingly mentioned his old nonsense about his neck, as he put it, and even went so far — his mother and aunt joined in the laughter — as to tell the story about the cat: this time it was Jürgen Kupka who put the cat on his throat; if only I knew who made up the story, he or I, or who is writing this in the first place!

In any case — this much is certain — his mother found some wrapping paper and packed up two little pieces of potato cake for me as I was taking my leave. In the hall, beside the staircase leading to the upper story and his attic, Mahlke pointed out a photograph hanging beside the brush bag. The whole width of the photograph was taken up with a rather modern-looking locomotive with tender, belonging to the Polish railways — the letters PKP could be clearly distinguished in two places. In front of the engine stood two men, tiny but imposing, with folded arms. The Great Mahlke said: "My father and Labuda the fireman, shortly before they were killed in an accident near Dirschau in '34. But my father managed to prevent the whole train from being wrecked; they awarded him a medal posthumously."

Chapter 10

Early in the new year I thought I would take violin lessons — my brother had left a violin — but we were enrolled as Air Force auxiliaries and today it is probably too late although Father Alban keeps telling me that I ought to. And it was he who encouraged me to write about Cat and Mouse: "Just sit yourself down, my dear Pilenz, and start writing. Yes, yes, there was too much Kafka in your first poetic efforts and short stories, but even so, you've got a style of your own: if you won't take up the fiddle, you can get it off your chest by writing — the good Lord knew what He was doing when He gave you talent."

So we were enrolled in the Brösen-Glettkau shore battery, or training battery if you will, behind the gravel-strewn beach promenade, amid dunes and blowing beach grass, in buildings that smelled of tar, socks, and the beach grass used to stuff our mattresses. There might be lots of things to say about the daily life of an Air Force auxiliary, a schoolboy in uniform, subjected in the morning to gray-haired teachers and the traditional methods of education and in the afternoon obliged to memorize gunnery instructions and the secrets of ballistics; but this is not the place to tell my story, or the story of Hotten Sonntag's simple-minded vigor, or to recount the utterly commonplace adventures of Schilling — here I am speaking only of you; and Joachim Mahlke never became an Air Force auxiliary.

Just in passing and without trying to tell a coherent story beginning with cat and mouse, some students from the Horst Wessel School, who were also being trained in the Brösen-Glettkau shore battery, contributed a certain amount of new material: "Just after Christmas they drafted him into the Reich Labor Service. Oh yes, he graduated, they gave him the special wartime diploma. Hell, examinations were never any problem for him, he was quite a bit older than the rest of us. They say his battalion is out on Tuchler Heath. Cutting peat maybe. They say things are happening up there. Partisans and so on."

In February I went to see Esch at the Air Force hospital in Oliva. He was lying there with a fractured collarbone and wanted cigarettes. I gave him some and he treated me to some sticky liqueur. I didn't stay long. On the way to the streetcar bound for Glettkau I made a detour through the Castle Park. I wanted to see whether the good old whispering grotto was still there. It was: some convalescent alpine troops were trying it out with the nurses, whispering at the porous stone from both sides, tittering, whispering, tittering. I had no one to whisper with and went off, with some plan or other in mind, down a birdless, perhaps brambly path which led straight from the castle pond and whispering grotto to the Zoppot highway. It was rather like a tunnel because of the bare branches that joined overhead and it kept growing frighteningly narrower. I passed two nurses leading a hobbling, laughing, hobbling lieutenant, then two grandmothers and a little boy who might have been three years old, didn't want to be connected with the grandmothers, and was carrying but not beating a child's drum. Then out of the February-gray tunnel of brambles, something else approached and grew larger: Mahlke.

We were both ill at ease. There was something eerie, almost awesome, about a meeting on such a path without forks or byways, cut off even from the sky: it was fate or the rococo fantasy of a French landscape architect that had brought us together — and to this day I avoid inextricable castle parks designed in the manner of good old Le Nôtre.

Of course a conversation started up, but I couldn't help staring transfixed at his head covering; for the Labor Service cap, even when worn by others than Mahlke, was unequaled for ugliness: a crown of disproportionate height sagged forward over the visor; the whole was saturated with the color of dried excrement; the crown was creased in the middle in the manner of a civilian hat, but the bulges were closer together, so close as to produce the plastic furrow which explains why the Labor Service head covering was commonly referred to as "an ass with a handle." On Mahlke's head this hat made a particularly painful impression, for it seemed to accentuate the very same part in the middle that the Labor Service had forced him to give up. We were both of us on edge as we stood facing one another between and beneath the brambles. And then the little boy came back without the grandmothers, pounding his tin drum, circumnavigated us in a semicircle with magical overtones, and at last vanished down the tapering path with his noise.

We exchanged a hasty good-by after Mahlke had tersely and morosely answered my questions about fighting with partisans on Tuchler Heath, about the food in the Labor Service, and as to whether any Labor Service Maidens were stationed near them. I also wanted to know what he was doing in Oliva and whether he had been to see Father Gusewski. I learned that the food was tolerable, but that he had seen no sign of any Labor Service Maidens. He thought the rumors about fighting partisans to be exaggerated but not entirely unfounded. His commander had sent him to Oliva for some parts: official business, justifying a two days' absence. "I spoke to Gusewski this morning, right after early Mass." Then a disparaging wave of the hand: "Hell can freeze over, he'll always be the same!" and the distance between us increased, because we were taking steps.

No, I didn't look after him. Unbelievable, you think? But if I say "Mahlke didn't turn around in my direction," you won't doubt me. Several times I had to look behind me because there was no one, not even the little boy with his noise box, coming toward me to help.

Then as I figure it, I didn't see you for a whole year; but not to see you was not, and still is not, to forget you and your fearful symmetry. Besides, there were reminders: if I saw a cat, whether gray or black or pepper-and-salt, the mouse ran into my field of vision forthwith; but still I hesitated, undecided whether the mouse should be protected or the cat goaded into catching it.

Until summer we lived at the shore battery, played endless games of handball, and on visiting Sundays rollicked to the best of our ability in the beach thistles, always with the same girls or their sisters; I alone accomplished nothing at all. Hesitation was my trouble; I haven't got over it yet, and this weakness of mine still inspires me with the same ironical reflections. What else occupied our days? Distributions of peppermint drops, lectures about venereal diseases; in the morning *Hermann and Dorothea,* in the afternoon the 98-K rifle, mail, four-fruit jam, singing contests. In our hours off duty we sometimes swam out to our barge, where we regularly found swarms of the little Thirds who were coming up after us and who irritated us no end, and as we swam back we couldn't for the life of us understand what for three summers had so attached us to that mass of rust encrusted with gull droppings. Later we were transferred to the 88-millimeter battery in Pelonken and then to the Zigankenberg battery. There were three or four alerts and our battery helped to shoot down a four-motor bomber. For weeks several orderly rooms submitted rival claims to the accidental hit — and through it all, peppermint drops, *Hermann and Dorothea,* and lots of saluting.

Because they had volunteered for the Army, Hotten Sonntag and Esch were sent to the Labor Service even sooner than I. Hesitating as usual, unable to make up my mind which branch of service I favored, I had missed the deadline for volunteering. In February 1944, with a good half of our class, I took and passed the final examinations — which differed little from the usual peacetime variety — and promptly received notice to report for Labor Service. Discharged from the Air Force Auxiliaries, I had a good two weeks ahead of me and was determined to do something con-

clusive in addition to winning my diploma. Whom did I light on
but Tulla Pokriefke, who was sixteen or over and very accessible,
but I had no luck and didn't get anywhere with Hotten Sonntag's
sister either. In this situation and state of mind—I was comforted
to some extent by letters from one of my cousins; the whole family
had been evacuated to Silesia after an air raid had left their house
a total loss—I made a farewell visit to Father Gusewski, promised
to help at the altar during the furloughs I hoped I would get, and
was given a new Missal and a handy metal crucifix, specially man-
ufactured for Catholic recruits. Then at the corner of Bärenweg
and Osterzeile on my way home, I ran into Mahlke's aunt, who
wore thick glasses when she went out and was not to be avoided.

Before we had even exchanged greetings, she began to talk, at
a good clip in spite of her rural drawl. When people came by, she
gripped my shoulder and pulled until one of my ears approached
her mouth. Hot, moist sentences. She began with irrelevant chit-
chat. The shopping situation: "You can't even get what you've got
coupons for." I learned that onions were not to be found, but that
brown sugar and barley grits were obtainable at Matzerath's and
that Ohlwein, the butcher, was expecting some canned pork. Finally, with no cue from me, she came to the point: "The boy is
better now, though he don't exactly say so in his letters. But he's
never been one to complain, he's just like his father, who was my
brother-in-law. And now they've put him in the tanks. He'll be
safer than in the infantry and dry when it rains."

Then whispers crept into my ear and I learned of Mahlke's new
eccentricities, of the infantile pictures he drew under the signature
of his letters.

"The funny part of it is that he never drew when he was little,
except for the water colors he had to make in school. But here's
his last letter in my pocketbook. Dear, how rumpled it is! Oh,
Mr. Pilenz, there's so many people want to see how the boy is
doing."

And Mahlke's aunt showed me Mahlke's letter. "Go ahead and
read it." But I didn't read. Paper between gloveless fingers. A dry,
sharp wind came circling down from Max-Halbe-Platz and nothing could stop it. Battered my heart with the heel of its boot and
tried to kick the door in. Seven brothers spoke within me, but none
of them followed the writing. There was snow in the wind but

I could still see the letter paper distinctly, though it was grayish brown, poor quality. Today I may say that I understood immediately, but I just stared, wishing neither to look nor to understand; for even before the paper crackled close to my eyes, I had realized that Mahlke was starting up again: squiggly line drawings under neat Sütterlin script. In a row which he had taken great pains to make straight, but which was nevertheless crooked because the paper was unlined, eight, twelve, thirteen, fourteen unequally flattened circles and on every kidney a wartlike knob, and from each wart a bar the length of a thumbnail, projecting beyond the lopsided boiler toward the left edge of the paper. And on each of these tanks — for clumsy as the drawings were, I recognized the Russian T-34 — there was a mark, mostly between turret and boiler, a cross indicating a hit. And in addition — evidently the artist didn't expect the viewers of his work to be very bright — all fourteen of the T-34s — yes, I'm pretty sure there were fourteen of them — were canceled very emphatically with large crosses in blue pencil.

Quite pleased with myself, I explained to Mahlke's aunt that the drawings obviously represented tanks that Joachim had knocked out. But Mahlke's aunt didn't show the least surprise, plenty of people had already told her that, but what she couldn't understand was why there were sometimes more, sometimes fewer of them, once only eight and, in the letter before last, twenty-seven.

"Maybe it's because the mails are so irregular. But now, Mr. Pilenz, you must read what our Joachim writes. He mentions you too, in connection with candles, but we've already got some." I barely skimmed through the letter: Mahlke was thoughtful, inquiring about all his aunt's and mother's major and minor ailments — the letter was addressed to both of them — varicose veins, pains in the back, and so on. He asked for news of the garden: "Did the plum tree bear well this year? How are my cactuses doing?" Only a few words about his duties, which he called fatiguing and responsible: "Of course we have our losses. But the Blessed Virgin will protect me as in the past." Would his mother and aunt kindly give Father Gusewski one or if possible two candles for the altar of Our Lady? And then: "Maybe Pilenz can get you some; they have coupons." He furthermore asked them to offer prayers to St. Judas Thaddaeus — a nephew twice-removed of the Virgin Mary, Mahlke knew his Holy Family — and also have a Mass said for his late lamented father, who "left us without receiving the sacraments." At the end of the letter, more trifles and some pale landscape painting: "You can't imagine how run-down everything is here, how wretched the people are and all the many children. No electricity or running water. Sometimes I begin to wonder what it's all for, but I suppose it has to be. And someday if you feel like it and the weather is good, take the car out to Brösen — but dress warmly — and look out to the left of the harbor mouth, but not so far out, to see whether the super-structure of a sunken ship is still there. There used to be an old wreck there. You can see it with the naked eye, and Auntie has her glasses — it would interest me to know if it's still..."

I said to Mahlke's aunt: "You can spare yourself the ride. The barge is still in the same place. And give Joachim my best when you write. He can set his mind at rest, nothing changes around here, and nobody's likely to walk off with the barge."

And even if the Schichau Dockyards had walked off with it, that is, raised it, scrapped or refitted it, would it have done you any good? Would you have stopped scribbling Russian tanks with childish precision on your letters and crossing them off with blue pencil? And who could have scrapped the Virgin? And who could have bewitched our good old school and turned it into birdseed? And the cat and the mouse? Are there stories that can cease to be?

Chapter 11

With Mahlke's scribbled testimonials before my eyes, I had to live through three more days at home. My mother was devoting her attentions to a construction foreman from the Organisation Todt — or maybe she was still cooking the saltless-diet dishes that found the way to Lieutenant Stiewe's heart — one of these gentlemen at any rate had made himself at home in our apartment and, apparently unaware of the symbolism of the thing, was wearing the slippers my father had broken in. In an atmosphere of cozy comfort that might have been cut out of a woman's magazine, my mother bustled from one room to the next in mourning; black was becoming to her, she wore it to go out and she wore it to stay in. On the sideboard she had erected a kind of altar for my fallen brother: first in a black frame and under glass a passport photo enlarged past recognition, showing him as a sergeant but without the visor cap; second, similarly framed and covered with glass, the death notices from the *Vorposten* and the *Neueste Nachrichten;* third, she had tied up a packet of his letters in a black silk ribbon; to which, fourth, she had appended the Iron Crosses, first and second class, and the Crimean Medal, and placed the bundle to the left of the photographs; while fifth and on the right, my brother's violin and bow, resting on some music paper with notes on it — my brother had tried his hand at composing violin sonatas — formed a counterweight to the letters.

If today I occasionally miss my elder brother Klaus, whom I scarcely knew, what I felt at the time was mostly jealousy on account of that altar; I visualized my own enlarged photo thus framed in black, felt slighted, and often chewed my fingernails when I was alone in our living room with my brother's altar, which refused to be ignored.

One fine morning as the lieutenant lay on the couch preoccupied with his stomach and my mother in the kitchen cooked saltless gruel, I would certainly have smashed that altar — photo, death notices, and perhaps the fiddle as well; my fist would have lost its temper without consulting me. But before that could happen, my departure date came, depriving me of a scene that would still be stageworthy: so well had death in the Kuban, my mother by the sideboard, and I, the great procrastinator, prepared the script. Instead, I marched off with my imitation-leather suitcase, and took the train to Konitz via Berent. For three months between Osche and Reetz, I had occasion to familiarize myself with Tuchler Heath. Everywhere wind and sand. Spring days to gladden the hearts of insect lovers. Rolling, round juniper berries. Wherever you turned, bushes and things to take aim at: the idea was to hit the two cardboard soldiers behind the fourth bush on the left. Over the birches and butterflies beautiful clouds with no place to go. In the bogs, circular, shiny-dark ponds where you could fish with hand grenades for perch and moss-covered carp. Nature wherever you looked. And movies in Tuchel.

Nevertheless and in spite of birches, clouds, and perch, I can give only a rough sketch, as in a sandbox, of this Labor Service battalion with its compound of shacks nestling in a copse, its flagpole, garbage pits, and off to one side of the school shack, its latrine. My only justification for telling you even this much is that a year before me, before Winter, Jürgen Kupka, and Bansemer, the Great Mahlke had worn denims and clodhoppers in the same compound, and literally left his name behind him: in the latrine, a roofless wooden box plunked down amid the broom and the overhead murmuring of the scrub pines. Here the two syllables — no first name — were carved, or rather chipped, into a pine board across from the throne, and below the name, in flawless Latin, but in an unfounded, runic sort of script, the beginning of his favorite sequence: *Stabat Mater dolorosa* . . . The Franciscan monk Jacopone da Todi would have been ever so pleased, but all it meant to me was that even in the Labor Service I couldn't get rid of Mahlke. For while I relieved myself, while the maggot-ridden dross of my age group accumulated behind me and under me, you gave me and my eyes no peace: loudly and in breathless repetition, a painstakingly incised text called attention to Mahlke, whatever I might decide to whistle in opposition.

And yet I am sure that Mahlke had had no intention of joking. Mahlke couldn't joke. He sometimes tried. But everything he did, touched, or said became solemn, significant, monumental; so also his runic inscription in the pine wood of a Reich Labor Service latrine named Tuchel-North, between Osche and Reetz. Digestive aphorisms, lines from lewd songs, crude or stylized anatomy — nothing helped. Mahlke's text drowned out all the more or less wittily formulated obscenities which, carved or scribbled from top to bottom of the latrine wall, gave tongues to wooden boards.

What with the accuracy of the quotation and the awesome secrecy of the place, I might almost have got religion in the course of time. And then this gloomy conscience of mine wouldn't be driving me to do underpaid social work in a settlement house, I wouldn't spend my time trying to discover early Communism in Nazareth or late Christianity in Ukrainian kolkhozes. I should at last be delivered from these all-night discussions with Father Alban, from trying to determine, in the course of endless investigations, to what extent blasphemy can take the place of prayer. I should be able to believe, to believe something, no matter what, perhaps even to believe in the resurrection of the flesh. But one day after I had been chopping kindling in the battalion kitchen, I took the ax and hacked Mahlke's favorite sequence out of the board and eradicated your name.

It was the old story of the spot that found no takers, kind of grisly-moral and transcendent; for the empty patch of wood with its fresh fibers spoke more eloquently than the chipped inscription. Besides, your message must have spread with the shaving, for in the barracks, between kitchen, guardroom, and dressing room, stories as tall as a house began to go around, especially on Sundays when boredom took to counting flies. The stories were always the same, varying only in minor detail. About a Labor Service man named Mahlke, who had served a good year before in Tuchel-North battalion and must have done some mighty sensational things. Two truck drivers, the cook, and the room orderly had been there the whole time, every shipment had passed them by. Without significantly contradicting one another, they spoke roughly as follows: "This is how he looked the first day. Hair down to here. Well, they sent him to the barber. Don't make me laugh. He needed more than a barber: ears like an egg beater and a neck, a neck, what a neck! He also had...and once when...and for instance when he...but the most amazing thing about him was when I sent the whole pack of new recruits to Tuchel to be deloused because as room orderly I...When they were all under the shower, I says to myself, my eyes are playing tricks on me, so I look again, and I says to myself, mustn't get envious now, but that dick of his, take it from me, a monster, when he got excited it would stand up to or maybe more, anyway he made good use of it with the commander's wife, a strapping piece of in her forties, because the damn-fool commander — he's been transferred to France, a nut — sent him over to his house, the second from the left in Officers' Row, to build a rabbit hutch. At first Mahlke, that was his name, refused, no he didn't fly off the handle, he just quietly quoted chapter and verse from the Service regulations. That didn't do him a bit of good. The chief personally chewed his ass out till he could hardly and for the next two days he was shoveling shit in the latrine. I hosed him off from a respectful distance, because the boys wouldn't let him into the washroom. Finally he gave in and went toddling over with tools and boards. All that fuss over rabbits! He must have really screwed that old lady! Every day for more than a week she sent for him to work in the garden; every morning Mahlke toddled off and was back again for roll call. But that rabbit hutch wasn't making any headway at all, so finally it dawned on the chief. I don't know if he caught them bare ass, maybe on the kitchen table or maybe between the sheets like mamma and papa, anyway, he must have been struck speechless when he saw Mahlke's, anyway he never said one word about it here in the barracks: it's not hard to see why. And he sent Mahlke off on official trips whenever he could to Oliva and Oxhöft for spare parts, just to get that stud and his nuts out of the battalion. Because the chief's old lady must have had mighty hot pants to judge by the size of his you know. We still get rumors from the orderly room: they correspond. Seems there was more to it than sex. You never know the whole story. And the very same Mahlke — I was there — smoked out a partisan ammunition dump single-handed near Gross-Bislaw. It's a wild story. A plain ordinary pond like there's so many around here. We were out there partly for work, partly for field training. We'd been lying beside this pond for half an hour, and Mahlke keeps looking and looking, and finally he says: Wait a minute, there's something fishy down there. The platoon leader, can't remember his name, grinned, so did we, but he said to go ahead. Before you could say boo, Mahlke has his clothes off and dives into the muck. And what do you know: the fourth time under, but not two feet below the surface, he finds the entrance to an ultra-modern ammunition dump with a hydraulic loading system. All we had to do was carry the stuff away, four truckloads, and the chief had to commend him in front of the whole battalion. In spite of the business with his old lady, they say he even put him in for a medal. He was in the Army when it came, but they sent it on. He was going into the tanks if they took him."

I restrained myself at first. The same with Winter, Jürgen Kupka, and Bansemer; we all clammed up when the conversation came around to Mahlke. When we chanced to pass Officers' Row — on hikes or on our way to the supply room — we would exchange furtive smiles of connivance, for the second house on the left still had no rabbit hutch. Or a meaningful glance would pass between us because a cat lurked motionless in the gently waving grass. We became a kind of secret clan, though I wasn't very fond of Winter and Kupka, and still less of Bansemer.

Four weeks before the end of our stint, the rumors began to creep in. Partisans had been active in the region; we were on twenty-four-hour alert, never out of our clothes, though we never caught anybody and we ourselves suffered no losses. The same room orderly who had issued Mahlke his uniform and taken him to be deloused brought the news from the office: "In the first place there's a letter from Mahlke to the former commander's wife. It's being forwarded to France. In the second place, there's a letter from way up, full of questions about Mahlke. They're still working on it. I always knew that Mahlke had it in him. But he certainly hasn't let any grass grow under his feet. In the old days you had to be an officer if you wanted something nice to wrap around your neck, no matter how badly it ached. Nowadays every enlisted man gets his chance. He must be just about the youngest. Lord, when I think of him with those ears..."

At that point words began to roll out of my mouth. Then Winter spoke up. And Jürgen Kupka and Bansemer had their own two cents' worth to put in.

"Oh, Mahlke. We've known him for years."

"We had him in school."

"He had a weakness for neckwear when he was only fourteen."

"Christ, yes. Remember when he swiped that lieutenant commander's thingamajig off the hook in gym class. Here's how it..."

"Naw, you gotta begin with the phonograph."

"What about the canned goods? I suppose that was nothing. Right in the beginning he always wore a screwdriver..."

"Wait a minute! If you want to begin at the beginning, you'll have to go back to the Schlagball match in Heinrich Ehlers Field. Here's how it was: We're lying on the ground and Mahlke's asleep. So a gray cat comes creeping across the field, heading straight for Mahlke. And when the cat sees that neck bobbing up and down, she says to herself, my word, that's a mouse. And she jumps..."

"That's the bunk. Pilenz picked up the cat and put it...You going to tell me different?"

Two days later we had official confirmation. It was announced at morning roll call: A former Labor Service man from Tuchel-North battalion, serving first as a simple machine-gunner, then as a sergeant and tank commander, always in the thick of battle, strategically important position, so and so many Russian tanks, and furthermore, etcetera etcetera.

Our replacements were expected and we were beginning to turn in our rags when I received a clipping that my mother had cut out of the *Vorposten*. There it was printed in black and white: A son of our city, always in the thick of battle, first as a simple machine-gunner, later as a tank commander, and so on and so on.

Chapter 12

Marl, sand, glittering bogs, bushes, slanting groups of pines, ponds, hand grenades, carp, clouds over birches, partisans behind the broom, juniper juniper (good old Löns, the naturalist, had come from around there), the movie house in Tuchel — all were left behind. I took nothing with me but my cardboard suitcase and a little bunch of tired heather. Even during the trip I began irrationally but stubbornly to look for Mahlke, while throwing the heather between the tracks after Karthaus, in every suburban station and finally in Central Station, outside the ticket windows, in the crowds of soldiers who had poured out of the furlough trains, in the doorway of the control office, and in the streetcar to Langfuhr. I felt ridiculous in my outgrown civilian-schoolboy clothes and convinced that everyone could read my mind. I didn't go home — what had I to hope for at home? — but got out near our school, at the Sports Palace car stop.

I left my suitcase with the caretaker, but asked him no questions. Sure of what to expect, I raced up the big granite stairway, taking three or more steps at a time. Not that I expected to catch him in the auditorium — both doors stood open, but inside there were only cleaning women, upending the benches and scrubbing them — for whom? I turned off to the left: squat granite pillars good for cooling feverish foreheads. The marble memorial tablet for the dead of both wars: still quite a lot of room to spare. Lessing in his niche. Classes were in session, for the corridors were empty, except for one spindle-legged Fourth carrying a rolled map through the all-pervading octagonal stench. 3a — 3b — art room — 5a — glass case for stuffed mammals — what was in it now? A cat, of course. But where was the delirious mouse? Past the conference room. And there at the end of the corridor, with the bright front window at his back, between the secretariat and the principal's office, stood the Great Mahlke, mouseless — for from his neck hung that very special article, the abracadabra, the magnet, the exact opposite of an onion, the galvanized four-leaf clover, good old Schinkel's brain child, the trinket, the all-day sucker, the thingamajig, the Iwillnotutterit.

And the mouse? It was asleep, hibernating in June. Slumbering beneath a heavy blanket, for Mahlke had put on weight. Not that anyone, fate or an author, had erased or obliterated it, as Racine obliterated the rat from his escutcheon, tolerating only the swan. Mahlke's heraldic animal was still the mouse, which acted up in its dreams when Mahlke swallowed; for from time to time the Great Mahlke, notwithstanding his glorious decoration, had to swallow.

How he looked? I have said that he had filled out in action, not too much, about two thicknesses of blotting paper. You were half leaning, half sitting on the white enameled window sill. You were wearing the banditlike combination of black and field-gray, common to all those who served in the Tank Corps: gray bloused pants concealed the shafts of black, highly polished combat boots. The black, tight-fitting tanker's jacket bunched up under the arms, making them stand out like handles, but it was becoming even so and made you look frail in spite of the few pounds you had gained. No decorations on the jacket. And yet you had both Crosses and some other thing, but no wound insignia: the Virgin had made you invulnerable. It was perfectly understandable that there should be nothing on the chest to distract attention from the new eye-catcher. Around your waist a worn and negligently polished pistol belt, and below it only a hand's breadth of goods, for the tanker's jacket was very short, which is why it was sometimes called a monkey jacket. Sagging from the weight of the pistol, which hung down nearly to your ass, the belt relieved the stiffness of your attitude and gave you a lopsided, jaunty look. But your gray field cap sat straight and severe without the then as now customary tilt; a rectilinear crease down the middle recalled your old love of symmetry and the part that divided your hair in your schoolboy and diving days, when you planned, or so you said, to become a clown. Nevertheless, the Redeemer's hairdo was gone. Even before curing your chronic throat trouble with a piece of metal, they must have given you the ludicrous brush cut which was then characteristic of recruits and today gives some of our pipe-smoking intellectuals their air of functional asceticism. But the countenance was still that of a redeemer: the eagle on your inflexibly vertical cap spread its wings over your brow like the dove of the Holy Ghost. Thin skin, sensitive to the light. Blackheads on fleshy nose. Lowered eyelids traversed by fine red veins. And when I stood breathless between you and the stuffed cat, your eyes scarcely widened.

A little joke: "Greetings, Sergeant Mahlke!"

My joke fell flat. "I'm waiting for Klohse. He's giving a math class somewhere."

"He'll be mighty pleased."

"I want to speak to him about the lecture."

"Have you been in the auditorium?"

"My lecture's ready, every word of it."

"Have you seen the cleaning women? They're scrubbing down the benches."

"I'll look in later with Klohse. We'll have to discuss the seating arrangement on the platform."

"He'll be mighty pleased."

"I'm going to suggest that they limit the audience to students from the lower Third up."

"Does Klohse know you're waiting?"

"Miss Hersching from the secretariat has gone in to tell him."

"Well, he'll be mighty pleased."

"My lecture will be short but full of action."

"I should think so. Good Lord, man, how did you swing it so quick?"

"Have a little patience, my dear Pilenz: all the circumstances will be discussed in my lecture."

"My, won't Klohse be pleased!"

"I'm going to ask him not to introduce me."

"Mallenbrandt maybe?"

"The proctor can announce the lecture. That's enough."

"Well, he'll be mighty..."

The bell signal leaped from floor to floor, announcing that classes were at an end. Only then did Mahlke open both eyes wide. Short, sparse lashes. His bearing was meant to be free and easy, but he was tensed to leap. Disturbed by something behind my back, I turned half toward the glass case: the cat wasn't gray, more on the black side. It crept unerringly toward us, disclosing a white bib. Stuffed cats are able to creep more convincingly than live ones. "The Domestic Cat," said a calligraphed cardboard sign. The bell stopped, an aggressive stillness set in; the mouse woke up and the cat took on more and more meaning. Consequently I cracked a little joke and another little joke in the direction of the window; I said something about his mother and his aunt; I talked, in order to give him courage, about his father, his father's locomotive, his father's death near Dirschau, and his father's posthumous award for bravery: "How happy your father would be if he were still alive!"

But before I had finished conjuring up Mahlke's father and persuading the mouse that there was no need to fear the cat, Dr. Waldemar Klohse, our principal, stepped between us with his high, smooth voice. Klohse uttered no congratulations, he didn't address Mahlke as Sergeant or Bearer of the Thingamajig, nor did he say, Mr. Mahlke, I am sincerely pleased. After evincing a pointed interest in my experience in the Labor Service and in the natural beauties of Tuchler Heath — "you will remember that Löns grew up there" — he sent a trim column of words marching over Mahlke's field cap: "So you see, Mahlke, you've made it after all. Have you been to the Horst Wessel School? My esteemed colleague, Dr. Wendt, will certainly be glad to see you. I feel sure that you will wish to deliver a little lecture for the benefit of your former schoolmates, to reinforce their confidence in our armed forces. Would you please step into my office for a moment?"

And the Great Mahlke, his arms raised like handles, followed Dr. Klohse into the principal's office and in the doorway whisked his cap off his stubblehead. Oh, that bumpy dome! A schoolboy in uniform on his way to a solemn conference, the outcome of which I did not wait for, although I was curious to know what the already wide-awake and enterprising mouse would say, after the interview, to that cat which though stuffed had never ceased to creep.

Nasty little triumph! Once again I enjoyed my moment of superiority. Just wait and see! He can't won't can't give in. I'll help him. I'll speak to Klohse. I'll find words to touch his heart. Too bad they've taken Papa Brunies to Stutthof. He'd come out with his good old Eichendorff in his pocket and extend a helping hand.

But no one could help Mahlke. Perhaps if I had spoken to Klohse. But I did speak to him; for half an hour I let him blow peppermint breath in my face. I was crushed, and my answer was very feeble: "By all reasonable standards, sir, you are probably right. But couldn't you in view of, I mean, in this particular case? On the one hand, I understand you perfectly. Yes, it can't be denied, a school has to have discipline. What's done can't be undone, but on the other hand, and because he was so young when he lost his father..."

And I spoke to Father Gusewski, and to Tulla, whom I asked to speak to Störtebeker and his gang. I went to see my former group leader in the Young Folk. He had a wooden leg from Crete and was sitting behind a desk in the section headquarters on Winterplatz. He was delighted with my proposal and cursed all schoolmasters: "Sure thing, we'll do it. Bring him over. I dimly remember him. Wasn't there some sort of trouble? Forget it. I'll drum up the biggest crowd I can. Even the League of German Girls and the Women's Association. I can get a hall across from the postal administration, seats three hundred and fifty..."

Father Gusewski wanted to gather his old ladies and a dozen Catholic workers in the sacristy, for the public meeting halls were not available to him.

"Perhaps, to bring his talk into line with the concerns of the Church," Father Gusewski suggested, "your friend could say something about St. George to begin with and conclude with a word or two about the power of prayer in times of great distress." He was eagerly looking forward to the lecture.

The young delinquents associated with Störtebeker and Tulla Pokriefke thought they had a cellar that would fill the bill. A youngster by the name of Rennwand, whom I knew slightly —

he served as an altar boy in the Church of the Sacred Heart —
spoke of the place in the most mysterious terms: Mahlke would
need a safe-conduct and would have to surrender his pistol. "Of
course we'll have to blindfold him on the way. And he'll have to
sign a pledge not to tell a living soul, but that's a mere formality.
Of course we'll pay well, either in cash or in Army watches. We
don't do anything for nothing and we don't expect him to."

But Mahlke accepted none of these possibilities, and he was not
interested in pay. I tried to prod him: "What do you want anyway?
Nothing's good enough for you. Why don't you go out to Tuchel-
North? There's a new batch of recruits. The room orderly and the
cook remember you. I'm sure they'd be pleased as Punch to have
you make a speech."

Mahlke listened calmly to all my suggestions, smiling in places,
nodded assent, asked practical questions about organizing the
meeting in question, and once the obstacles were disposed of,
tersely and morosely rejected every single proposition, even an invitation from the regional party headquarters, for from the start
he had but one aim in mind: the auditorium of our school. He
wanted to stand in the dust-swarming light that trickled through
Neo-Gothic ogival windows. He wanted to address the stench of
three hundred schoolboys, farting high and farting low. He wanted
the whetted scalps of his former teachers around him and behind him. He wanted to face the oil painting at the end of the
auditorium, showing Baron von Conradi, founder of the school,
caseous and immortal beneath heavy varnish. He wanted to enter the auditorium through one of the old-brown folding doors
and after a brief, perhaps pointed speech, to leave through the
other; but Klohse, in knickers with small checks, stood barring
both doors at once: "As a soldier, Mahlke, you ought to realize.
No, the cleaning women were scrubbing the benches for no particular reason, not for you, not for your lecture. Your plan may have
been excellently conceived, but it cannot be executed. Remember
this, Mahlke: There are many mortals who love expensive carpets
but are condemned to die on plain floorboards. You must learn
renunciation, Mahlke."

Klohse compromised just a little. He called a meeting of the
faculties of both schools, which decided that "Disciplinary con-
siderations make it imperative..."

And the Board of Education confirmed Klohse's report to the effect that a former student, whose past history, even though he, but particularly in view of the troubled and momentous times, though without wishing to exaggerate the importance of an offense which, it must be admitted, was none too recent, nevertheless and because the case is unique of its kind, the faculty of both schools has agreed that...

And Klohse wrote a purely personal letter. And Mahlke read that Klohse was not free to act as his heart desired. Unfortunately, the times and circumstances were such that an experienced schoolmaster, conscious of his professional responsibilities, could not follow the simple, paternal dictates of his heart; in the interests of the school, he must request manly co-operation in conformity to the old Conradinian spirit; he would gladly attend the lecture which Mahlke, soon, he hoped, and without bitterness, would deliver at the Horst Wessel School; unless he preferred, like a true hero, to choose the better part of speech and remain silent.

But the Great Mahlke had started down a path resembling that tunnel-like, overgrown, thorny, and birdless path in Oliva Castle Park, which had no forks or byways but was nonetheless a labyrinth. In the daytime he slept, played backgammon with his aunt, or sat listless and inactive, apparently waiting for his furlough to be over. But at night he crept with me — I behind him, never ahead of him, seldom by his side — through the Langfuhr night. Our wanderings were not aimless: we concentrated on Baumbachallee, a quiet, genteel, conscientiously blacked-out lane, where nightingales sang and Dr. Klohse lived. I weary behind his uniformed back: "Don't be an ass. You can see it's impossible. And what difference does it make? The few days' furlough you've got left. Good Lord, man, don't be an ass...."

But the Great Mahlke wasn't interested in my tedious appeals to reason. He had a different melody in his protuberant ears. Until two in the morning we besieged Baumbachallee and its two nightingales. Twice he was not alone, and we had to let him pass. But when after four nights of vigilance, at about eleven o'clock, Dr. Klohse turned in from Schwarzer Weg alone, tall and thin in knickers but without hat or coat, for the air was balmy, and came striding up Baumbachallee, the Great Mahlke's left hand shot out and seized Klohse's shirt collar with its civilian tie. He pushed the schoolman against the forged-iron fence, behind which bloomed roses whose fragrance — because it was so dark — was overpowering, louder even than the voices of the nightingales. And taking the advice Klohse had given him in his letter, Mahlke chose the better part of speech, heroic silence; without a word he struck the school principal's smooth-shaven face left right with the back and palm of his hand. Both men stiff and formal. Only the sound of the slaps alive and eloquent; for Klohse too kept his small mouth closed, not wishing to mix peppermint breath with the scent of the roses.

That happened on a Thursday and took less than a minute. We left Klohse standing by the iron fence. That is to say, Mahlke about-faced and strode in his combat boots across the gravel-strewn sidewalk beneath the red maple tree, which was not red at night but formed a black screen between us and the sky. I tried to give Klohse something resembling an apology, for Mahlke — and for myself. The slapped man waved me away; no longer looked slapped but stood stiff as a ramrod, his dark silhouette, sustained by roses and the voices of rare birds, embodying the school, its founder, the Conradinian spirit, the Conradinum; for that was the name of our school.

After that we raced through lifeless suburban streets, and from that moment on neither of us had a word to spare for Klohse. Mahlke talked and talked, with exaggerated coolness, of problems that seemed to trouble him at that age — and myself, too, to some extent. Such as: Is there a life after death? Or: Do you believe in transmigration? "I've been reading quite a bit of Kierkegaard lately," he informed me. And "you must be sure to read Dostoevski. Later, when you're in Russia. It will help you to understand all sorts of things, the mentality and so on."

Several times we stood on bridges across the Striessbach, a rivulet full of horse leeches. It was pleasant to lean over the railing and wait for rats. Each bridge made the conversation shift from schoolboy banalities — erudition, for instance, about the armor plate, firepower, and speed of the world's battleships — to religion and the so-called last questions. On the little Neuschottland bridge we gazed for a long while at the star-studded June sky and then — each for himself — into the stream. Mahlke in an undertone, while below us the shallow outlet of Aktien pond, carrying away the yeasty vapors of Aktien Brewery, broke over shoals of tin cans: "Of course I don't believe in God. He's just a swindle to stultify the people. The only thing I believe in is the Virgin Mary. That's why I'm never going to get married."

There was a sentence succinct and insane enough to be spoken on a bridge. It has stayed with me. Whenever a brook or canal is spanned by a small bridge, whenever there is a gurgling down below and water breaking against the rubbish which disorderly people the world over throw from bridges into rivulets and canals, Mahlke stands beside me in combat boots and tanker's monkey jacket, leaning over the rail so that the big thingamajig on his neck hangs down vertical, a solemn clown triumphing over cat and mouse with his irrefutable faith: "Of course not in God. A swindle to stultify the people. There's only Mary. I'll never get married."

And he uttered a good many more words which fell into the Striessbach. Possibly we circled Max-Halbe-Platz ten times, raced twelve times up and down Heeresanger. Stood undecided at the terminus of Line No. 5. Looked on, not without hunger, as the streetcar conductors and marcelled conductorettes, sitting in the blued-out trailer, bit into sandwiches and drank out of thermos bottles.

...and then came a car — or should have — in which the conductorette under the cocked cap was Tulla Pokriefke, who had been drafted as a wartime helper several weeks before. We'd have spoken to her and I would certainly have made a date with her if she had been working on Line No. 5. But as it was, we saw her little profile behind the dark-blue glass and we were not sure.

I said: "You ought to give it a try with her."

Mahlke, tormented: "I just told you that I'm never going to get married."

I: "It would cheer you up."

He: "And who's going to cheer me up afterward?"

I tried to joke: "The Virgin Mary of course."

He had misgivings: "What if she's offended?"

I offered my help. "If you want me to, I'll be Gusewski's altar boy tomorrow morning."

I was amazed at the alacrity with which he said: "It's a deal!" And he went off toward the trailer which still held out the promise of Tulla Pokriefke's profile in a conductor's cap. Before he got in, I called out: "Say, how much more furlough have you got left?"

And from the door of the trailer the Great Mahlke said: "My train left four and a half hours ago. If nothing has gone wrong, it must be pulling into Modlin."

Chapter 13

"Misereatur vestri omnipotens Deus, et, dimissis peccatis vestris,... " The words issued light as a soap bubble from Father Gusewski's pursed lips, glittered in all the colors of the rainbow, swayed hesitantly, broke loose from the hidden reed, and rose at last, mirroring windows, the altar, the Virgin, mirroring you me everything — and burst painlessly, struck by the bubbles of the absolution: *"Indulgentiam, absolutionem et remissionem peccatorum vestrorum...."* and the moment these new bubbles of spirit were pricked in their turn by the Amen of the seven or eight faithful, Gusewski elevated the host and began with full-rounded lips to blow the big bubble, the bubble of bubbles. For a moment it trembled terror-stricken in the draft; then with the bright-red tip of tongue, he sent it aloft; and it rose and rose until at length it fell and passed away, close to the second pew facing the altar of Our Lady: *"Ecce Agnus Dei...."*

Of those taking communion, Mahlke was first to kneel. He knelt before the "LordIamnotworthythatthoushouldstenterundermyroof" had been repeated three times. Even before I steered Gusewski down the altar steps to the communicants' rail, he leaned his head back, so that his face, peaked after a sleepless night, lay parallel to the whitewashed concrete ceiling, and parted his lips with his tongue. A moment's wait, while over his head the priest makes a small quick sign of the Cross with the wafer intended for this communicant. Sweat oozed from Mahlke's pores and formed glistening beads which quickly broke, punctured by the stubble of his beard. His eyes stood out as though boiled. Possibly the blackness of his tanker's jacket enhanced the pallor of his face. Despite the wooliness of his tongue, he did not swallow. In humble self-effacement the iron object that had rewarded his childish scribbling and crossing-out of so and so many Russian tanks crossed itself and lay motionless over his top collar button. It was only when Father Gusewski laid the host on Mahlke's tongue and Mahlke partook of the light pastry, that you swallowed; and then the thingamajig joined in.

Let us all three celebrate the sacrament, once more and forever: You kneel, I stand behind dry skin. Sweat distends your pores. The reverend father deposits the host on your coated tongue. All three of us have just ended on the same syllable, whereupon a mechanism pulls your tongue back in. Lips stick together. Propagation of sobs, the big thingamajig trembles, and I know that the Great Mahlke will leave St. Mary's Chapel fortified, his sweat will dry; if immediately afterward drops of moisture glistened on his face, they were raindrops. It was drizzling.

In the dry sacristy Gusewski said: "He must be waiting outside. Maybe we should call him in, but..."

I said: "Don't worry, Father. I'll take care of him."

Gusewski, his hands busy with the sachets of lavender in the closet: "You don't think he'll do anything rash?"

For once I made no move to help him out of his vestments: "You'd better keep out of it, Father." But to Mahlke, when he stood before me wet in his uniform, I said: "You damn fool, what are you hanging around here for? Get down to the assembly point on Hochstriess. Tell them some story about missing your train. I refuse to have anything to do with it."

With those words I should have left him, but I stayed and got wet. Rain is a binder. I tried to reason with him: "They won't bite your head off if you're quick about it. Tell them something was wrong with your mother or your aunt."

Mahlke nodded when I made a point, let his lower jaw sag from time to time, and laughed for no reason. Then suddenly he bubbled over: "It was wonderful last night with the Pokriefke kid. I wouldn't have thought it. She's not the way she puts on. All right, I'll tell you the honest truth: it's because of her that I don't want to go back. Seems to me that I've done my bit — wouldn't you say so? I'm going to put in a petition. They can ship me out to Gross-Boschpol as an instructor. Let other people be brave. It's not that I'm scared, I've just had enough. Can you understand that?"

I refused to fall for his nonsense; I pinned him down. "Oho, so it's all on account of the Pokriefke kid. Hell, that wasn't her. She works on the No. 2 Line to Oliva, not on the No. 5. Everybody knows that. You're scared shitless, that's all. I can see how you feel."

He was determined that there should be something between them. "You can take my word for it about Tulla. The fact is she took me home with her, lives on Elsenstrasse. Her mother doesn't mind. But you're right, I've had my bellyful. Maybe I'm scared too. I was scared before Mass. It's better now."

"I thought you didn't believe in God and all that stuff."

"That's got nothing to do with it."

"OK, forget it. And now what?"

"Maybe Störtebeker and the boys could... You know them pretty well, don't you?"

"No dice. I'm having no further dealings with those characters. It's not healthy. You should have asked the Pokriefke kid in case you really..."

"Wise up. I can't show my face on Osterzeile. If they're not there already, it won't be long — say, could I hide in your cellar, just for a few days?"

That too struck me as unhealthy. "You've got other places to hide. What about your relatives in the country? Or in Tulla's uncle's woodshed.... Or on the barge."

For a while the word hung in mid-air. "In this filthy weather?" Mahlke said. But the thing was already decided; and though I refused stubbornly and prolixly to go with him, though I too spoke of the filthy weather, it gradually became apparent that I would have to go: rain is a binder.

We spent a good hour tramping from Neuschottland to Schellmühl and back, and then down the endless Posadowskiweg. We took shelter in the lee of at least two advertising pillars, bearing always the same posters warning the public against those sinister and unpatriotic figures Coalthief and Spendthrift, and then we resumed our tramp. From the main entrance of the Women's Hospital we saw the familiar backdrop: behind the railroad embankment, the gable roof and spire of the sturdy old Conradinum; but he wasn't looking or he saw something else. Then we stood for half an hour in the shelter of the Reichskolonie car stop, under the echoing tin roof with three or four grade-school boys. At first they spent the time roughhousing and pushing each other off the bench. Mahlke had his back turned to them, but it didn't help.

Two of them came up with open copybooks and said something in broad dialect. "Aren't you supposed to be in school?" I asked.

"Not until nine. In case we decide to go."

"Well, hand them over, but make it fast."

Mahlke wrote his name and rank in the upper left-hand corner of the last page of both copybooks. They were not satisfied, they wanted the exact number of tanks he had knocked out — and Mahlke gave in; as though filling out a money order blank, he wrote the number first in figures, then in letters. Then he had to write his piece in two more copybooks. I was about to take back my fountain pen when one of the kids asked: "Where'd you knock 'em off, in Bjälgerott [Byelgorod] or Schietemier [Zhitomir]?"

Mahlke ought just to have nodded and they would have subsided. But he whispered in a hoarse voice: "No, most of them around Kovel, Brody, and Brzezany. And in April when we knocked out the First Armored Corps at Buczacz."

The youngsters wanted it all in writing and again I had to unscrew the fountain pen. They called two more of their contemporaries in out of the rain. It was always the same back that held still for the others to write on. He wanted to stretch, he would have liked to hold out his own copybook; they wouldn't let him: there's always one fall guy. Mahlke had to write Kovel and Brody-Brzezany, Cherkassy and Buczacz. His hand shook more and more, and again the sweat oozed from his pores. Questions spurted from their grubby faces: "Was ya in Kriewäurock [Krivoi Rog] too?" Every mouth open. In every mouth teeth missing. Paternal grandfather's eyes. Ears from the mother's side. And each one had nostrils: "And where dya think they'll send ya next?"

"He ain't allowed to tell. What's the use of asking?"

"I bet he's gonna be in the invasion."

"They're keepin 'im for after the war."

"Ask him if he's been at the Führer's HQ?"

"How about it, Uncle?"

"Can't you see he's a sergeant?"

"You gotta picture?"

" 'Cause we collect 'em."

"How much more furlough time ya got?"

"Yeah, whenner ya leavin?"

"Ya still be here tomorrow?"

"Yeah, when's yer time up?"

Mahlke fought his way out, stumbling over satchels. My fountain pen stayed in the shelter. Marathon through crosshatching. Side by side through puddles: rain is a binder. It was only after we passed the stadium that the boys fell back. But still they shouted after us; they had no intention of going to school. To this day they want to return my fountain pen.

When we reached the kitchen gardens outside Neuschottland, we stopped to catch our breath. I had a rage inside me and my rage was getting kittens. I thrust an accusing forefinger at the accursed thingamajig and Mahlke quickly removed it from his neck. Like the screwdriver years before, it was attached to a shoelace. Mahlke wanted to give it to me, but I shook my head. "Hell, no, but thanks for nothing."

But he didn't toss the scrap metal into the wet bushes; he had a back pocket.

How am I going to get out of here? The gooseberries behind the makeshift fences were unripe: Mahlke began to pick with both hands. My pretext cast about for words. He gobbled and spat out skins. "Wait for me here, I'll be back in half an hour. You've got to have something to eat or you won't last long on the barge."

If Mahlke had said "Be sure you come back," I would have lit out for good. He scarcely nodded as I left; with all ten fingers he was reaching through the fence laths at the bushes; his mouth full of berries, he compelled loyalty: rain is a binder.

Mahlke's aunt opened the door. Good that his mother wasn't home. I could have taken some edibles from our house, but I thought: What's he got his family for? Besides, I was curious about his aunt. I was disappointed. She stood there in her kitchen apron and asked no questions. Through open doors came the smell of something that makes teeth squeak: rhubarb was being cooked at the Mahlkes'.

"We're giving a little party for Joachim. We've got plenty of stuff to drink, but in case we get hungry..."

Without a word she went to the kitchen and came back with two two-pound cans of pork. She also had a can opener, but it wasn't the same one that Mahlke had brought up from the barge when he found the canned frogs' legs in the galley. While she was out wondering what to give me — the Mahlkes always had their cupboards full, relatives in the country — I stood restless in the hallway, gazing at the photograph of Mahlke's father and Fireman Labuda. The locomotive had no steam up.

The aunt came back with a shopping net and some newspaper to wrap the cans and can opener in. "Before you eat the pork," she said, "you'll have to warm it up some. If you don't, it'll be too heavy; it'll sit on your stomach."

If asked before leaving whether anyone had been around asking for Joachim, the answer was no. But I didn't ask, I just turned around in the doorway and said: "Joachim sends you his love," though Mahlke hadn't sent anything at all, not even to his mother.

He wasn't curious either when I reappeared between the gardens in the same rain, hung the net on a fence lath, and stood rubbing my strangled fingers. He was still gobbling unripe gooseberries, compelling me, like his aunt, to worry about his physical well-being: "You're going to upset your stomach. Let's get going." But even then he stripped three handfuls from the dripping bushes and filled his pants pockets. As we looped around Neuschottland and the housing development between Wolfsweg and Bärenweg, he was still spitting out hard gooseberry skins. As we stood on the rear platform of the streetcar trailer and the rainy airfield passed by to the left of us, he was still pouring them in.

He was getting on my nerves with his gooseberries. Besides, the rain was letting up. The gray turned milky; made me feel like getting out and leaving him alone with his gooseberries. But I only said: "They've already come asking about you. Two plainclothesmen."

"Really?" He spat out the skins on the platform floor. "What about my mother? Does she know?"

"Your mother wasn't there. Only your aunt."

"Must have been shopping."

"I doubt it."

"Then she was over at the Schielkes' helping with the ironing."

"I'm sorry to say she wasn't there either."

"Like some gooseberries?"

"She's been taken down to the military district. I wasn't going to tell you."

We were almost in Brösen before Mahlke ran out of gooseberries. But as we crossed the beach, in which the rain had cut its pattern, he was still searching his sopping pockets for more. And when the Great Mahlke heard the sea slapping against the beach and his eyes saw the Baltic, the barge as a far-off backdrop, and the shadows of a few ships in the roadstead, he said: "I can't swim." Though I had already taken off my shoes and pants. The horizon drew a line through both his pupils.

"Is this a time to make jokes?"

"No kidding. I've got a bellyache. Damn gooseberries."

At this I swore and looked through my pockets and swore some more and found a mark and a little change. I ran to Brösen and rented a boat for two hours from old man Kreft. It wasn't as easy as it looks on paper, though Kreft didn't ask very many questions and helped me to launch the boat. When I pulled up on the beach, Mahlke lay writhing in the sand, uniform and all. I had to kick him to make him get up. He shivered, sweated, dug both fists into the pit of his stomach; but even today I can't make myself believe in that bellyache in spite of unripe gooseberries on an empty stomach.

"Why don't you go behind the dunes? Go ahead. On the double!" He walked hunched over, making curved tracks, and disappeared behind the beach grass. Maybe I could have seen his cap, but though nothing was moving in or out, I kept my eyes on the breakwater. When he came back, he was still bunched over but he helped me to shove off. I sat him down in the stern, stowed the net with the cans in it on his knees, and put the wrapped can opener in his hands. When the water darkened behind the second sandbank I said: "Now *you* can take a few strokes."

The Great Mahlke didn't even shake his head; he sat doubled up, clutching the wrapped can opener and looking through me; for we were sitting face to face.

Although I have never again to this day set foot in a rowboat, we are still sitting face to face: and his fingers are fidgeting. His neck is bare, but his cap straight. Sand trickling from the folds in his uniform. No rain, but forehead dripping. Every muscle tense. Eyes popping out of his head. With whom has he exchanged noses? Both knees wobbling. No cat offshore. But the mouse scurrying.

Yet it wasn't cold. Only when the clouds parted and the sun burst through the seams did spots of gooseflesh pass over the scarcely breathing surface of the water and assail our boat. "Take a few strokes, it'll warm you up." The answer was a chattering of teeth from the stern. And from intermittent groans chopped words were born into the world: " . . . fat lot of good. Might have guessed. Fuss for a lot of nonsense. Too bad. It would have been a good lecture. Would have started in with explanations, the sights, armor-piercing shells, Maybach engines, and so on. When I was a loader, I had to come up all the time to tighten up bolts, even under fire. But I wasn't going to talk about myself the whole time. My father and Labuda, the fireman. A few words about the accident near Dirschau. How my father by his courage and self-sacrifice. The way I always thought of my father as I sat there at the sights. Hadn't even received the sacraments when he. Thanks for the candles that time. O thou, most pure. Mother inviolate. Through whose intercession partake. Most amiable. Full of grace. It's the honest truth. My first battle north of Kursk proved it. And in the tangle outside Orel when they counterattacked. And in August by the Vorskla the way the Mother of God. They all laughed and put the division chaplain on my tail. Sure, but then we stabilized the front. Unfortunately, I was transferred to Center Sector, or they wouldn't have broken through so quick at Kharkov. She appeared to me again near Korosten when the 59th Corps. She never had the child, it was always the picture she was holding. Yes, Dr. Klohse, it's hanging in our hall beside the brush bag. And she didn't hold it over her breast, no, lower down. I had the locomotive in my sights, plain as day. Just had to hold steady between my father and Labuda. Four hundred. Direct hit. See that, Pilenz? I always aim between turret and boiler. Gives them a good airing. No, Dr. Klohse, she didn't speak. But to tell you the honest truth, she doesn't have to speak to me. Proofs? She held the picture, I tell you. Or in mathematics. Suppose you're teaching math. You assume that parallel lines meet at infinity. You'll admit that adds up to something like transcendence. That's how it was that time in the second line east of Kazan. It was the third day of Christmas. She came in from the left and headed for a clump of woods at convoy speed, twenty miles an hour. Just had to keep her in my sights. Hey, Pilenz, two strokes on the left, we're missing the barge."

At first Mahlke's outline of his lecture was little more than a chattering of teeth, but then he had them under control. Through it all he kept an eye on our course. The rhythm at which he spoke made me row so fast that the sweat poured from my forehead, while his pores dried and called it a day. Not for a single stroke was I sure whether or not he saw anything more over the expanding bridge than the customary gulls.

Before we hove alongside, he sat relaxed in the stern playing negligently with the can opener, which he had taken out of its paper. He no longer complained of bellyache. He stood before me on the barge, and when I had tied up, his hands busied themselves on his neck: the big thingamajig from his rear pocket was in place again. Rubbed his hands, the sun broke through, stretched his legs: Mahlke paced the deck as though taking possession, hummed a snatch of litany, waved up at the gulls, and played the cheery uncle who turns up for a visit after years of adventurous absence, bringing himself as a present. O happy reunion! "Hello, boys and girls, you haven't changed a bit!"

I found it hard to join in the game: "Get a move on. Old man Kreft only gave me the boat for an hour and a half. At first he said only an hour."

Mahlke calmed down: "OK, never detain a busy man. Say, do you see that bucket, the one next to the tanker, she's lying pretty low. I'll bet she's a Swede. Just for your information, we're going to row out there as soon as it gets dark. I want you back here at nine o'clock. I've a right to ask that much of you — or haven't I?"

The visibility was poor and of course it was impossible to make out the nationality of the freighter in the roadstead. Mahlke began to undress elaborately, meanwhile spouting a lot of incoherent nonsense. A few words about Tulla Pokriefke: "A hot number, take it from me." Gossip about Father Gusewski: "They say he sold goods on the black market. Altar cloths too. Or rather the coupons for the stuff." A couple of funny stories about his aunt: "But you've got to give her credit for one thing, she always got along with my father, even when they were both kids in the country." More about the locomotive: "Say, you might drop back at our house and get the picture, with or without the frame. No, better let it go. Just weigh me down."

He stood there in red gym pants, a vestige of our school tradition. He had carefully folded his uniform into the regulation bundle and stowed it away in his old-accustomed place behind the

pilothouse. His boots looked like bedtime. "You got everything?"
I asked. "Don't forget the opener." He shifted the medal from left
to right and chattered schoolboy nonsense as if he hadn't a care in
the world: "Tonnage of the Argentine battleship *Moreno?* Speed in
knots? How much armor plate at the waterline? Year built? When
remodeled? How many hundred-and-fifty-millimeter guns on the
Vittorio Veneto?"

I answered sluggishly, but I was pleased to find that I still had
the dope. "Are you going to take both cans at once?"

"I'll see."

"Don't forget the can opener. There it is."

"You're looking out for me like a mother."

"Well, if I were you, I'd start going downstairs."

"Right you are. The place must be in a pretty sad state."

"You're not supposed to spend the winter there."

"The main thing is I hope the lighter works. There's plenty of
alcohol."

"I wouldn't throw that thing away. Maybe you can sell it as a
souvenir someplace. You never can tell."

Mahlke tossed the object from hand to hand. He slipped off
the bridge and started looking step by step for the hatch, holding out his hands like a tightrope walker, though one arm was
weighed down by the net with the two cans in it. His knees made
bow waves. The sun broke through again for a moment and his
backbone and the sinews in his neck cast a shadow to leftward.

"Must be half past ten. Maybe later."

"It's not as cold as I expected."

"It's always that way after the rain."

"My guess is water sixty-five, air sixty-eight."

There was a dredger in the channel, not far from the harbor-
mouth buoy. Signs of activity on board, but the sounds were pure
imagination, the wind was in the wrong direction. Mahlke's mouse
was imaginary too, for even after his groping feet had found the
rim of the hatch, he showed me only his back.

Over and over the same custom-made question dins into my
ears: Did he say anything else before he went down? The only
thing I am halfway sure of is that angular glance up at the bridge,
over his left shoulder. He crouched down a moment to moisten
himself, darkening the flag-red gym pants, and with his right

hand improved his grip on the net with the tin cans — but what about the all-day sucker? It wasn't hanging from his neck. Had he thrown it away without my noticing? Where is the fish that will bring it to me? Did he say something more over his shoulder? Up at the gulls? Or toward the beach or the ships in the roadstead? Did he curse all rodents? I don't think I heard you say: "Well, see you tonight." Headfirst and weighed down with two cans of pork, he dove: the rounded back and the rear end followed the neck. A white foot kicked into the void. The water over the hatch resumed its usual rippling play.

Then I took my foot off the can opener. The can opener and I remained behind. If only I had got right into the boat, cast off and away: "Hell, he'll manage without it." But I stayed, counting the seconds. I let the dredger with its rising and falling chain buckets count for me, and frantically followed its count: thirty-two, thirty-three rusty seconds. Thirty-six, thirty-seven mud-heaving seconds. For forty-one, forty-two badly oiled seconds, forty-seven, forty-eight, forty-nine seconds, the dredger with its rising, falling, dipping buckets did what it could: deepened the Neufahrwasser harbor channel and helped me measure the time: Mahlke, with his cans of pork but no can opener, with or without the black candy whose sweetness had bitterness for a twin, must by then have moved into the erstwhile radio shack of the Polish mine sweeper *Rybitwa*.

Though we had not arranged for any signals, you might have knocked. Once again and again once again, I let the dredger count thirty seconds for me. By all calculable odds, or whatever the expression is, he must have... The gulls, cutting out patterns between barge and sky, were getting on my nerves. But when for no apparent reason the gulls suddenly veered away, the absence of gulls got on my nerves. I began, first with my heels, then with Mahlke's boots, to belabor the deck of the bridge: flakes of rust went flying, crumbs of gull dropping danced at every blow. Can opener in hammering fist, Pilenz shouted: "Come up! You've forgotten the can opener, the can opener...." Wild, then rhythmic shouting and hammering. Then a pause. Unfortunately, I didn't know Morse code. Two-three two-three, I hammered. Shouted myself hoarse: "Can o-pen-er! Can o-pen-er"

Ever since that Friday I've known what silence is. Silence sets in when gulls veer away. Nothing can make more silence than a dredger at work when the wind carries away its iron noises. But it was Joachim Mahlke who made the greatest silence of all by not responding to my noise.

So then I rowed back. But before rowing back, I threw the can opener in the direction of the dredger, but didn't hit it.

So then I threw away the can opener and rowed back, returned old man Kreft's boat, had to pay an extra thirty pfennigs, and said: "Maybe I'll be back again this evening. Maybe I'll want the boat again."

So then I threw away, rowed back, returned, paid extra, said I'd be, sat down in the streetcar and rode, as they say, home.

So then I didn't go straight home after all, but rang the doorbell on Osterzeile, I asked no questions, just got them to give me the locomotive and frame, for hadn't I said to Mahlke and to old man Kreft too for that matter: "Maybe I'll be back again this evening...."

So my mother had just finished making lunch when I came home with the photograph. One of the heads of the labor police at the railroad car factory was eating with us. There was no fish, and beside my plate there was a letter for me from the military district.

So then I read and read my draft notice. My mother began to cry, which embarrassed the company. "I won't be leaving until Sunday night," I said, and then, paying no attention to our visitor: "Do you know what's become of Papa's binoculars?"

So then, with binoculars and photograph, I rode out to Brösen on Saturday morning, and not that same evening as agreed — the fog would have spoiled the visibility, and it was raining again. I picked out the highest spot on the wooded dunes, in front of the Soldiers' Monument. I stood on the top step of the platform — above me towered the obelisk crowned with its golden ball, sheenless in the rain — and for half if not three quarters of an hour I held the binoculars to my eyes. It was only when everything turned to a blur that I lowered the glasses and looked into the dog-rose bushes.

So nothing was moving on the barge. Two empty combat boots were clearly distinguishable. Gulls still hovered over the rust, then gulls settled like powder on deck and shoes. In the roadstead the same ships as the day before. But no Swede among them, no neutral ship of any kind. The dredger had scarcely moved. The weather seemed to be on the mend. Once again I rode, as they say, home. My mother helped me to pack my cardboard suitcase.

So then I packed: I had removed the photograph from the frame and, since you hadn't claimed it, packed it at the bottom. On top of your father, on top of Fireman Labuda and your father's locomotive that had no steam up, I piled my underwear, the usual rubbish, and the diary which was lost near Cottbus along with the photograph and my letters.

Who will supply me with a good ending? For what began with cat and mouse torments me today in the form of crested terns on ponds bordered with rushes. Though I avoid nature, educational films show me these clever aquatic birds. Or the newsreels make me watch attempts to raise sunken freight barges in the Rhine or underwater operations in Hamburg harbor: it seems they are blasting the fortifications near the Howald Shipyard and salvaging aerial mines. Men go down with flashing, slightly battered helmets, men rise to the surface. Arms are held out toward them, the helmet is unscrewed, removed: but never does the Great Mahlke light a cigarette on the flickering screen; it's always somebody else who lights up.

When a circus comes to town, it can count on me as a customer. I know them all, or just about; I've spoken with any number of clowns in private, out behind the trailers; but usually they have no sense of humor, and if they've ever heard of a colleague named Mahlke, they won't admit it.

I may as well add that in October 1959 I went to Regensburg to a meeting of those survivors of the war who, like you, had made Knights's Cross. They wouldn't admit me to the hall. Inside, a Bundeswehr band was playing, or resting between pieces. During one such intermission, I had the lieutenant in charge of the order squad page you from the music platform: "Sergeant Mahlke is wanted at the entrance." But you didn't show up. You didn't surface.

Translated by Ralph Manheim

Part Two

THE MEETING
AT TELGTE

Note

The historical background to the events and personalities dealt with in this novel may be unfamiliar to English and American readers. Leonard Forster has provided an afterword and notes on the dramatis personae (pp. 224–32) identifying the historical, literary, and commercial streams that had their confluence at Telgte.

See also volume 7 in The German Library, *Seventeenth Century German Prose,* edited by Lynne Tatlock. —*Ed.*

Chapter 1

The thing that hath been tomorrow is that which shall be yesterday. Our stories of today need not have taken place in the present. This one began more than three hundred years ago. So did many other stories. Every story set in Germany goes back that far. If I am writing down what happened in Telgte, it is because a friend, who gathered his fellow writers around him in the forty-seventh year of our century, is soon to celebrate his seventieth birthday; and yet he is older, much older than that — and we, his present-day friends, have all grown hoary white with him since those olden times.

Up from Jutland and down from Regensburg came Lauremberg and Greflinger on foot; others came on horseback or in covered wagons. While some were sailing down rivers, old Weckherlin took ship from London to Bremen. From far and near they came, from all directions. A merchant, to whom due dates mean profit and loss, might well have been amazed at the punctual zeal displayed by those men of mere verbal action, especially at a time when the towns and countryside were still, or once again, ravaged, overgrown with nettles and thistles, depopulated by plague, and when all the roads were unsafe.

So much so that Moscherosch and Schneuber, who had come from Strassburg, reached their appointed destination stripped of everything they owned (except their portfolios, useless to highwaymen), Moscherosch laughing and richer by a satire, Schneuber lamenting and already dreading the horrors of the return journey. (His arse was sore from blows with the flat of the sword.)

Only because Czepko, Logau, Hofmannswaldau, and other Silesians, provided with a safe-conduct issued by Wrangel, had attached themselves to various Swedish battalions, whose foraging raids took them as far as Westphalia, were they able to reach Osnabrück undiminished; but they suffered as if in their own flesh from the daily atrocities of the foraging parties, who showed no concern for any poor devil's religion. No remonstrances would hold Wrangel's horsemen in check. The student Scheffler (a discovery of Czepko's) was almost done in while trying to shield a peasant woman who, like her husband before her, was to be impaled before the eyes of her children.

Johann Rist came via Hamburg from nearby Wedel on the Elbe. A coach had brought Mülbe, the Strassburg publisher, from Lüneburg. The route taken by Simon Dach, whose invitations had provoked all this effort, from the Kneiphof section of Königsberg, was indeed the longest, but also the safest, for he had traveled in the retinue of Frederick William, Elector of Brandenburg. The previous year Frederick William had become engaged to Louise of Orange, and Dach had been privileged to recite his panegyric verses in Amsterdam. It was then that the many letters of invitation, complete with designation of the meeting place, were written, and that, with the elector's help, provision was made for their delivery. (The elector's ubiquitous political agents were often required to double as couriers.) This was how Gryphius received his invitation, though he had been traveling for the past year with the Stettin merchant Wilhelm Schlegel, first in Italy, then in France, and Dach's letter was delivered to him on his return journey (in Speyer, to be exact). He set out at once and brought Schlegel with him.

Augustus Buchner, magister of letters, arrived punctually from Wittenberg. After declining several times, Paul Gerhardt nevertheless arrived on time. Philipp Zesen, whose letter caught up with him in Hamburg, traveled from Amsterdam with his publisher. No one wanted to miss the meeting. Nothing, no school, state, or court function, could keep them away. Those who lacked funds for the journey went looking for patrons. Those who, like Greflinger, had found no patron were carried to their destination by obstinacy. And those whose obstinacy might have deterred them from starting in time were infected with travel fever by the news that others were already on their way. Even such men as Zesen and Rist, who counted each other as enemies, were intent on meeting. Logau's curiosity about the meeting proved even stronger than his scorn for the assembled poets. Their local surroundings were too constricting. No business transaction, however intricate, no love affair, however diverting, could resist the force that drew them together. Moreover, the peace negotiations brought increasing unrest. No one wanted to be by himself.

But eagerly as the gentlemen had responded to Dach's invitation in their hunger for literary exchange, they soon lost heart when they failed to find quarters in Oesede, the village near Osnabrück where the meeting was to be held. Though reservations had been made in plenty of time, the Black Horse, where the conferees were to have lodged, had been commandeered by the staff of Swedish War Councilor Erskein, who had recently put the demands of Wrangel's armies for indemnification before the peace conference, so adding appreciably to the cost of the peace. What rooms were not occupied by regimental secretaries and colonels in Count Königsmark's army were piled high with documents. The great hall, where they planned to meet, to carry on the discussions for which they had so fervently longed and to read their manuscripts to one another, had been turned into a storeroom. Everywhere horsemen and musketeers were lounging about. Couriers came and went. Erskein made himself inaccessible. A provost, to whom Dach presented a document showing that he had rented the Black Horse, was seized with a fit of circumfluously infectious laughter when Dach requested that his down payment be reimbursed by the Swedes. Brusquely rebuffed, Dach came back. Strong, stupid men. Their armored emptiness. Their grinning dullness. None of the Swedish officers had ever heard of the illustrious visitors. Grudgingly, they let them rest a while in the taproom. The landlord advised them to move on to the Oldenburg region, where everything, even lodging, was available.

Already the Silesians were thinking of going on to Hamburg, Gerhardt of returning to Berlin, Moscherosch and Schneuber of proceeding to Holstein with Rist; already Weckherlin had decided to take the next ship to London; already most of the travelers, not without recriminations against Dach, were threatening to let the meeting go hang, and already Dach — ordinarily the soul of equanimity — was beginning to have doubts about his plan; already they were standing in the street with their luggage, uncertain which way to turn, when — well before nightfall — the Nuremberg contingent arrived: Harsdörffer with his publisher Endter and young Birken; they were accompanied by a red-bearded fellow who called himself Christoffel Gelnhausen and whose gangling youthfulness — he seemed to be in his middle twenties — was contradicted by his pockmarked face. In his green doublet and plumed hat he looked like something out of a storybook. Someone said that he had been begotten by Count Mansfeld's soldiery on their way through — but Gelnhausen turned out to be more real than he looked. He was in command of a detachment of imperial horsemen and musketeers, who were camped at the edge of town because the territory of the towns where the peace conference was being held had been declared neutral ground, barred to the military action of both parties.

When Dach had described the poets' sorry situation to the Nurembergers, and Gelnhausen had offered his services in a long-winded speech well larded with tropes, Harsdörffer took Dach aside. True, he said, the fellow prates like an itinerant astrologer — he had introduced himself to the assemblage as Jupiter's favorite, whom, as they could see, Venus had punished in France — but he had wit, and was better read than his clowning might lead one to suspect. Moreover, he was serving as a secretary at the headquarters of the Schauenburg regiment, then stationed in Offenburg. In Cologne, where the Nurembergers had arrived by ship from Würzburg, Gelnhausen had helped them out of difficulties incurred when Endter had attempted to sell a stack of books without a license. Fortunately Gelnhausen had been able to talk them clear of clerical suspicion, which scented "heretical machinations." His lies, said Harsdörffer, are as inspired as any romances; his eloquence reduces the very Jesuits to silence; not just the church fathers, but all the gods and their planets are at his fingertips; he is familiar with the seamy side of life, and wherever he goes, in Cologne, in Recklinghausen, in Soest, he knows his way about. Quite possibly, Harsdörffer concluded, he might help them.

Gerhardt warned them against dealing with a man of the imperial party. Hofmannswaldau stood dumbfounded, hadn't the fellow just quoted a passage from Opitz's translation of the *Arcadia*? Moscherosch and Rist thought they should listen at least to the regimental secretary's proposals, especially after Schneuber of Strassburg had asked him about certain particulars of life in the bustling garrison town of Offenburg and received bathhouse gossip in reply.

In the end, Gelnhausen was given leave to explain himself to the assembled and now desperately unquartered gentlemen. His words seemed as trustworthy as the sheen of the double row of buttons on his green doublet. Being a cousin of Mercury and therefore as restlessly active as that god, he was, so he averred, bound for Münster in any case — at the bidding of his master, an acolyte of Mars, in other words a colonel — carrying a secret message to Count Trauttmannsdorff, who, in his capacity as head of the emperor's negotiating team, had been crammed full of wisdom by the peevish Saturn — in order that peace might dawn at last. The trip came to less than thirty miles. Under an almost full moon. And through flat country. And if their lordships decided to avoid priest-ridden Münster, they would pass through Telgte, a snug little town which, though impoverished, had remained unscarred, since the townspeople had managed to beat off the Hessians and had not wearied of feeding the Königsmark regimental treasury. And since, as they must know, Telgte had long been a place of pilgrimage, there he would find quarters for their lordships, those pilgrims of the Muses. For he learned early on to find lodging for all manner of gods.

When old Weckherlin asked what they, as Protestants, had done to deserve so much Catholic favor (after all, Gelnhausen was bearing swift tidings to the Catholic party), the regimental secretary replied that he cared little for religion, as long as no one interfered with his own. And that his message for Trauttmannsdorff was not so secret as all that, since everyone knew that the Saxon regiments in Marshal Turenne's camp had mutinied against their foreign overlords and dispersed. Such news ran on ahead, so there was no point in hurrying. He therefore preferred to oblige a dozen homeless poets, all the more so since he himself — by Apollo! — wielded the pen, though for the present only in Colonel Schauenburg's regimental chancellery.

At that Dach accepted his offer. Whereupon Gelnhausen stopped talking tortuous foolishness and issued orders to his horsemen and musketeers.

Chapter 2

Since the start of the peace negotiations, which by then had been in progress for almost three years, the road from Osnabrück via Telgte to Münster had been much traveled in both directions, from the Protestant to the Catholic camp and contrariwise, by couriers in carriages and on horseback, bearing an archive-glutting mass of petitions, memoranda, scheming missives, invitations to festivities, and agents' reports on the latest military movements, which had been going on undeterred by the peace negotiations. The military lineup of the contending parties was not determined by religious allegiance: Catholic France, with papal approval, had fought against Spain, the Habsburgs, and Bavaria; the Protestant Saxons sometimes had one and sometimes the other foot in the imperial camp; a few years earlier, the Lutheran Swedes had attacked the Lutheran Danes. In deep secret Bavaria was bargaining for possession of the Palatinate. Other factors were armies that had mutinied or changed sides, internal conflicts in the Netherlands, the eternal lamentations of the Silesian Estates, the impotence of the imperial cities, the changing but not diminishing land hunger of the allies, in consequence of which, when the conference agreed the year before that Alsace should be ceded to France and Pomerania to Sweden, the delegates from Strassburg and the Baltic towns ran themselves and their horses ragged (in vain) on the road between Osnabrück and Münster. Which was not to be surprised at, for the state of the roads to and from the conference towns was equaled only by the state of the negotiations and of Germany itself.

In any event, though Gelnhausen borrowed, or, rather, requisitioned, four wagons in next to no time, they took longer than expected to convey the homeless gentlemen — more than twenty in number — from the foothills of Teutoburg Forest through the Tecklenburg plain to Telgte. (The sacristan's offer to provide temporary quarters in an empty convent near Oesede, where the Swedes had lodged, was declined, for the devastated building was lacking in the slightest comfort; only Logau and Czepko, who distrusted Gelnhausen, spoke in favor of accepting.)

The colors of the summer evening were fading behind them when Simon Dach paid the bridge toll for his party. And immediately after the bridge across the outer Ems, but before the inner arm of the river, which bounds the city on the Ems Gate side, Gelnhausen, in his own characteristic way, billeted the company at the Bridge Tavern, a thatch-roofed, tall-gabled stone structure planted in the middle of the otherwise unoccupied water meadows and at first sight showing little war damage. Taking aside the landlady, with whom he was evidently acquainted, he exchanged whispers with her and then introduced her to Dach, Rist, and Harsdörffer as Libuschka, a friend of long years' standing. An aging woman under a layer of face paint, she was wrapped in a horse blanket and wore soldier's breeches, but spoke with refinement and claimed descent from the Bohemian nobility. From the very start, she said, her father had fought for the Protestant cause with Bethlen Gabor. Cognizant of the honor being shown her house, she promised to provide the company with lodging, perhaps not at once, but very shortly.

Thereupon Gelnhausen and his imperial troops created such a hubbub outside the stables, in front of the tavern, in the front hall, on the stairs, and outside all the rooms that the chained dogs came close to choking. They didn't stop until all the guests and their coachmen had been jolted out of their sleep. No sooner had the gentlemen — they were Hanseatic merchants come from Lemgo, on their way to Bremen — gathered in front of the Bridge Tavern than Gelnhausen commanded them to leave the house forthwith. And he backed up his order by informing them that all who loved their lives should keep their distance, since several of the listless, wasted figures in and around the wagons had been stricken with the plague and were candidates for the charnel house. He and his detachment, he explained, were escorting a group of unfortunates whom it was necessary to remove, lest their presence incommode the peace negotiations, for which reason he, body physician to Signor Chigi, the papal nuncio, had not only imperial, but Swedish orders as well, to convey the diseased persons to quarantine. He therefore bade the merchants leave immediately and without argument, barring which he would be obliged to burn their vehicles and wares on the riverbank. The plague — as everyone knew and as he, a physician endowed with all the wisdom of Saturn, could assure them — was no respecter of wealth, but on the contrary delighted in ravishing treasures and took special pleasure in searing gentlemen in Brabant cloth with its torrid breath.

When the merchants asked for a written statement justifying their eviction, Gelnhausen drew his sword, called it his goose quill, asked to whom his first missive should be addressed, and added that in the name of the emperor and his adversaries he must urgently — by Mars and his ferocious dogs! — request the departing guests of the Bridge Tavern to observe the strictest silence concerning the reason for their sudden departure.

After this address, the inn was quickly evacuated. Carriages had never been harnessed more briskly. If anyone hesitated, the musketeers sprang to his help. Before Dach and several of the poets could protest loudly enough the immorality of Gelnhausen's trick, the house had been taken over. With misgivings, to be sure, but reassured by Moscherosch and Greflinger, who took the proceedings as a farce deserving to be laughed at, the poets repaired to the evacuated rooms and still-warm beds.

Since in addition to the merchant Schlegel, several printers from Strassburg, Amsterdam, Hamburg, and Breslau had, in their capacity as publishers, accepted Dach's invitation, the landlady Libuschka was easily compensated for her loss, especially because the evicted Hanseatics had left several bolts of cloth and a few pieces of silverware behind them, not to mention four kegs of Rhenish brown beer.

Gelnhausen's soldiers made themselves at home in the stables that were built onto one side of the house. From the entrance hall, between the taproom and the kitchen (to which the great hall was attached), the poets climbed two flights of stairs to the top floor of the Bridge Tavern. Already they were easier in their minds. Only the choice of rooms permitted of some friction. Zesen quarreled with Lauremberg after having had words with Rist. The medical student Scheffler was in tears. Since there were not enough rooms, Dach bedded him, Birken, and Greflinger in the attic straw.

At that point it became known that old Weckherlin's pulse was failing. Schneuber, who shared a room with Moscherosch, demanded ointment for his wounds. Gerhardt and Magister Buchner both wanted rooms to themselves. Hofmannswaldau doubled up with Gryphius, Czepko with Logau. Harsdörffer kept close to Endter, his publisher. Rist was drawn to Zesen and Zesen to Rist. In all this the landlady and her maids lent the new guests a helping hand. Libuschka was familiar with some of the gentlemen's names. She was able to recite several stanzas of Gerhardt's hymns. She gratified Harsdörffer with elegant quotations from his *Garden of the Pegnitz Pastoral.* And, later, sitting in the taproom with Moscherosch and Lauremberg — who had no desire for bed but preferred to stay up until morning over brown beer, bread, and cheese — she was able, in succinct sentences, to sum up several of the dream visions from Moscherosch's *Philander.* She might have been made to order for a meeting of poets, so well read was landlady Libuschka — or Courage, as she was called by Gelnhausen, who joined them after a while and was toasted for his prowess as a billeting officer.

Simon Dach also stayed awake. He lay in his room and once again mentally enumerated those he had summoned in letters, persuaded en route, forgotten intentionally or unintentionally, included in his list on someone's recommendation, or rejected, as well as those who had not yet arrived, among them his friend Albert, for whom the second bed in his room stood ready.

Sleep-banishing, sleepy-making worries: Maybe Schottel would come after all. (But the man from Wolfenbüttel stayed away, because Buchner had been invited.) The Nuremberg party made excuses for Klaj's absence on grounds of illness. Heaven help us if Rompler should come after all. Could Prince Ludwig reasonably be expected? (But the head of the Fruit-bearing Society remained in Köthen, offended: the prince detested Dach, who did not belong to the Order of the Palm Tree and made no bones about being a commoner.)

How fortunate that they had left word at the Black Horse in Oesede, saying where they would meet, in a different town but for the same reasons, namely, to rescue their cruelly maltreated language and to be near the peace negotiations. There they would sit until everything, the distress of the fatherland as well as the splendor and misery of poetry, had been discussed.

Opitz and Fleming would be missed. Would it be possible to keep theorizing to a minimum? Would anyone else turn up uninvited? Pondering these questions and physically longing for his wife, Regina, Dach slipped into sleep.

Chapter 3

Or perhaps before retiring he wrote a letter to his Regina, née Pohl, who everywhere — in the Kneiphof quarter of Königsberg, by the students at the academy, among Dach's friends Albert, Blum, and Roberthin, and even by the elector — was referred to as Dach's Pohlin.* His letter started on a note of despair, then veered to amusement at the peripeties of the hunt for lodgings, and ended by commending the proceedings of the meeting to God's wisdom and mercy. Without delving into the deeper meaning of events, it merely recorded: how brutally the Swedes had expelled them from Oesede; how Gelnhausen, commonly referred to as Christoffel or Stoffel, had requisitioned four harnessed covered wagons from the carriage pool of the Protestant Estates; how at night, under a waxing moon, spared by the storms that were rumbling in the distance, they had followed the pitch torches of the imperial horsemen down the rutted Münster road as far as Telgte; how while still on the road Moscherosch, Greflinger, and Lauremberg had started swilling brandy, bellowing street songs, and teasing the always dignified Gerhardt; how Czepko and old Weckherlin had boldly leapt to the defense of the sensitive Gerhardt, with the result that, at least in three of the four wagons, hymns had been sung the rest of the way, and Gerhardt's recently published "Now hushed are woods and waters, At rest toil's sons and daughters, The world aslumber lies" had infected even the topers; and how nearly the whole company, including Gryphius (who had been sitting beside Dach and had grown fat all over), had fallen asleep while singing, so that no one had had time to reflect on Gelnhausen's outrageous trick of talking their company sick with plague so eloquently that the effluvia might have been smelled, until the end of the journey, when it was too late; and how despite or because of the damnable yet amusing (and he himself chose to be amused) immorality of the thing, they had all finally gone to bed, some laughing at the terrified haste of the fleeing moneybags and still drinking to the cruel joke, others quietly praying God for forgiveness, but all too tired to permit of any quarrels among the Silesians, Nuremberg-

---

*Pohlin, which is the feminine form of Pohl, sounds the same as *Polin,* Polish woman. — *Trans.*

ers, and Strassburgers, which might have imperiled the meeting. Only between Rist and Zesen had there been flashes, as expected. On the other hand, since Schottel was not coming, Buchner promised to observe moderation. The Silesians, Dach's letter went on, had brought a frightened student with them; Hofmannswaldau wasn't acting at all like a scion of the nobility; all except Rist, who could not refrain from preaching, and Gerhardt, who was a stranger to literary life, were friendly to one another; even that whoremaster Greflinger was accommodating and had sworn by the infidelity of his Flora to behave with reasonable propriety; at the most, treachery might be expected of Schneuber, whom he, Dach, mistrusted. But if need be, he would know how to hold the company in check. Apart from the boozers in the taproom and himself, who was thinking of his Regina, only the double imperial guard that Gelnhausen had drawn up outside the Bridge Tavern for their protection were still awake. The landlady, though undoubtedly a trollop, was nevertheless an extraordinary woman, speaking fluent Italian with Gryphius, even standing up to Magister Buchner in Latin, and as thoroughly at home in the world of letters as a fox in a goose pen. Thus everything was turning out amazingly well, as though pursuant to a higher plan. The one thing that made him uneasy was the popish surroundings. Rumor had it that secret meetings of Anabaptists were being held in Telgte. The ghost of Knipperdolling still haunted the place. A spooky sort of town, but clearly suitable for a congress.

What more Simon Dach wrote to his Regina I shall leave to the two of them. Only his last, sleep-bringing thoughts are still within my reach: they circled around pros and cons, lagged behind and ran ahead of events, made various persons enter and exit, repeated themselves. I shall put them in order.

Dach had no doubts about the utility of the meeting that had been so long in preparation. As long as the war was going on, meetings had been more longed for than planned. Opitz, for instance, contemplating such a gathering only a short while before his death, had written from his haven in Danzig: "A meeting of all possible poets should be held in Breslau or in Prussia, to unite our confraternity in these days of the fatherland's division...."

But no one, not even Opitz, would have been so acceptable to the dispersed writers as Dach, whose wide-ranging mind and generously dispensed warmth made for a gathering of sufficient scope to encompass a lone vagrant like Greflinger, an aristocratic aesthete like Hofmannswaldau, and the unliterary Gerhardt, but who nevertheless imposed restrictions, for no invitations were sent to the poetasters who toadied to princely patrons and were interested only in turning out encomiums and precommissioned elegies. Dach had gone so far as to ask his own prince, who could recite several of Dach's poems by heart and had contributed to the general travel fund, to remain benevolently absent.

Though certain members of the company (among them Buchner and Hofmannswaldau) had advised Dach to wait for the conclusion of the peace treaty or to hold the meeting at a distance from the war that was still raging — possibly in Polish Lissa or in unscarred Switzerland; though Zesen and the German-minded Association, which he had founded in Hamburg in the early forties, wished, in competition with Dach and in collaboration with Rompler's Upright Society of the Pine Tree, to organize a countermeeting — Dach's persistence and political firmness had proved decisive. As a young man (under Opitz's influence), he had corresponded with Grotius, Bernegger, and the Heidelberg group around Lingelsheim, and consequently, though not active in diplomacy, as Opitz and Weckherlin still were at the time, he had regarded himself as an irenicist, a man of peace, ever since. In spite of Zesen, who backed down, and in opposition to the intrigues of the Strassburg magister Rompler, who was not invited, Simon Dach won out: it was arranged that in the forty-seventh year of the century (after twenty-nine years of war, the peace negotiations had not yet been concluded), a meeting should be held somewhere between Münster and Osnabrück, for the purpose of giving new force to the last remaining bond between all Germans, namely, the German language they held in common, and — if only from the sidelines — uttering a political word or two.

After all, they were not nobodies. Everything had been laid waste, words alone kept their luster. And where princes had disgraced themselves, poets had earned respect. They, not the powerful, were assured of immortality.

In any event Simon Dach was convinced that the meeting, if not he himself, was important. For — on a small scale and far from shot and shell, as they said in Königsberg — he had gathered poets and friends of the arts around him. Not only on Magister-gasse, where thanks to a Kneiphof ordinance he enjoyed lifelong residence privileges, but also in the garden of Heinrich Albert the cathedral organist, on Lomse Island in the river Pregel, friends had met to read one another poems, most of which had been commissioned or written to celebrate one occasion or another: the usual poems and songs in honor of some marriage, which Albert would set to music. In jest the friends called themselves the Cucumber Lodge Society, knowing that side by side with other associations, such as the Fruit-bearing Order of the Palm Tree or the Strassburg Upright Society of the Pine Tree, or even with the Pegnitz Shepherds of Nuremberg, they were merely one branch of far-flung German poesy.

Early that afternoon, when the gentlemen had slept their fill, or slept off their drink, and had gathered in the great hall, Dach, knowing how eager they were to hear the whole tree murmur and feeling that a pun on his name was in order, made the following introductory remarks, proceeding after his fashion to speak now gaily, now gravely: "Let us, dear friends, foregather in my name — for it is I who invited you — as under one roof,* to the end that each of us may contribute according to his powers and through the resulting harmony establish a German-minded Pegnitz, Fruit-bearing, Upright Cucumber Lodge and Pine Tree Associations, and that in the forty-seventh year of this woeful century, our hitherto drowned-out voice be heard above all the long-winded talk of peace and despite the continuing clamor of battle; for what we have to say is not foreign-contaminated chatter, but part and parcel of our language: Where, O Germany, shall I leave you? For well nigh thirty years, by murder and rapine, Thou hast destroyed thyself, the guilt is thine...."

Chapter 4

Dach took these lines from his recently completed but not yet published poem lamenting the destruction of the cucumber bower on

---

Dach = roof. — *Trans.*

Lomse Island, which had been the meeting place of the Königsberg poets and had been sacrificed to the construction of a highway. Albert the cathedral organist had composed a three-part song in its memory.

Since Dach's lines aroused attention, Hofmannswaldau, Rist, Czepko, and others urged the author to recite the whole lament, which he did only later, on the third day, for he did not wish to open the meeting with his own production. Nor did he allow any further introductory speeches. (Zesen intended to say something fundamental about his German-minded Association and its division into guilds. Rist would have counterattacked, for he was already gestating the Order of Elbe Swans, which he was subsequently to found.)

Instead, Simon Dach, hoping to bring the company to look on Gerhardt as somewhat less of a stranger, asked him to say a prayer for the success of the meeting. Gerhardt stood up to do so, with Old Lutheran gravity and not without threatening with damnation the false prophets present; he must have had in mind the Silesian mystics or the Calvinists, if any.

Curtailing the silence that followed the prayer, Dach summoned his "most honored friends" to give a thought to those poets whose place would have been there among them had death not ravished them. All rose to their feet as he solemnly listed "those who too soon departed from us," naming first Opitz, then Fleming, then the political mentor of his generation, the irenicist Lingelsheim, then Zincgref; and finally he startled the assembly — Gryphius's countenance was clouded with displeasure — by evoking the memory of the Jesuit Spee von Langenfeld.

True, many of those present were acquainted with (and had indeed been influenced by) the much imitated Jesuit theater, and in his student days Gryphius had seen fit to translate several of the Jesuit Jakob Balde's Latin odes into German; true, Gelnhausen, whom no one outside of Harsdörffer (and Greflinger) regarded as a member of the assembly, had represented himself as a Catholic without giving anyone umbrage — but the posthumous honoring of Spee struck several of the Protestant gentlemen as going too far, even though they had accepted Dach's recommendation of tolerance. It would have provoked a loud protest or a wave of silent disgruntlement if Hofmannswaldau had not come to the help of

Dach, who was trying, with a stern frown, to quell the general agitation by first quoting the "Penitential Hymn of a Contrite Heart" from Spee's anthology, *The Nightingale's Rival,* which had not yet been published, but copies of which were in circulation — "At nightfall when the darkness Clothes us black in shadow" — and then, as fluently as though he had carried the Latin original engraved in his mind, paraphrasing several passages from the *Cautio Criminalis,* Spee's indictment of the Inquisition and of torture. He then proceeded to laud the Jesuit's courage and (looking Gryphius straight in the eye) reminded his audience of how in blackest Würzburg Spee had seen some two hundred pitiful women subjected to torture; how when, maddened by pain, they had confessed, he had comforted them on their way to the stake; and finally of how, after committing his cruel experience to writing, he had published his eyewitness report as an indictment. And Hofmannswaldau concluded with the challenge: "Who among you can boast such courage?"

No answer was possible. Old Weckherlin was in tears. As though to add meaning, the student Scheffler said that Spee, like Opitz, had been carried off by the plague. Dach only made a note of the name and then handed Logau a printed text, wishing him — since all the dead were to be remembered — to read one of the sonnets that Fleming, who had died soon after Opitz, had written (while traveling in Nogaian Tartary) in his honor. And Logau also read his own elegy on the "Bober Swan,"* as Opitz was occasionally called: "In Latin there are many poets, Virgil is the greatest one. Likewise, among German singers, Opitz stands alone."

After honoring Lingelsheim, the friend of peace, Dach, in memory of Zincgref, read two selections from his book of precepts — light anecdotes that would relieve the tension — and, when he had finished, read one more on request.

Thus strained solemnity eased into amicable exchanges. Especially the older men knew stories about the departed. Weckherlin spoke of the young Opitz's doings in Heidelberg, in the days of the late lamented Lingelsheim. Buchner knew exactly what Fleming would have written if his Baltic Elsabe had not been unfaith-

---

*Opitz was ennobled as Opitz von Boberfeld. The Bober is a river on which his native town is situated. — *Trans.*

ful to him. The question was raised: why had Spee's poems thus far found no publisher? Then there was talk of student years in Leiden: Gryphius and Hofmannswaldau, Zesen and young Scheffler had been fed wild visionary ideas there. Someone (I?) asked why, in honoring the dead, Dach had neglected to mention the "Görlitz shoemaker," since after all the followers of Böhme were here represented.

In the meantime the landlady and her maids had served a rather modest collation in the taproom. Dumplings floated in a soup fat with sausage broth. Flatbread was broken. Brown beer was on hand. You broke off a chunk, you dipped, you slobbered, you dipped again. Laughter went round and round. (What was the right way to pronounce this town on the Ems? Telgte or Telchte, or should one go so far as to say Tächte like the native maids?) Dach passed alongside the table, saying a few words to each man, and reconciling those who like Buchner and young Birken were becoming embroiled in argument ahead of time.

A discussion of the language was scheduled for after the meal. What had wrecked it, and what might make it well again? What rules should be laid down, and what rules would hamper the poetic flow? How might the so-called natural language, which Buchner disparaged as a "purely mystical concept," be nurtured with better fare and so develop into a national language? What should pass as High German and what place should be allotted to the dialects? For learned and polyglot as they all were — Gryphius and Hofmannswaldau were eloquent in seven tongues — they all mouthed and whispered, babbled and bellowed, declaimed and postured, in some sort of regional German.

Though he had been living and teaching mathematics in Danish Zeeland ever since Wallenstein's invasion of Pomerania, Lauremberg expressed himself in his native Rostock brogue, and Rist the Holstein preacher answered him in Low German. After thirty years of residence in London, the diplomat Weckherlin still spoke an unvarnished Swabian. And into the predominantly Silesian conversation, Moscherosch mixed his Alemannic, Harsdörffer his peppery Franconian, Buchner and Gerhardt their Saxon, Greflinger his Lower Bavarian gargle, and Dach a Prussian kneaded and shaped between Memel and Pregel. Gelnhausen told his wretched bawdy tales and decanted clownish wisdom in three different dialects, for in the course of the war Stoffel had acquired the Westphalian and Alemannic stammer on top of his native Hessian.

Though they spoke a confusing variety of languages, they made themselves clearly understood, and their German was free and unfettered. But that did not detract from their prowess in linguistic theory. No line of poetry but was subjected to some rule.

Chapter 5

When Simon Dach gave the signal, the company moved with astonishing discipline from the taproom to the great hall; to him the poets subordinated their often childish willfulness. They accepted his authority. Rist and Zesen forsook (for a while) their deep-rooted contentiousness. Greflinger had always longed for such a father. It genuinely amused the aristocrat Hofmannswaldau to sacrifice his habits to the commoner Dach. The princes of learning — Harsdörffer with residence in Nuremberg, Buchner of Wittenberg — would gladly (under the warming influence of wine) have chosen Dach as their regent. And because for some years Weckherlin, who had grown bilious at court, had no longer been serving the King of England but had become a secretary of state under Parliament, he inclined to the will of the majority; along with the rest he acceded to Dach's sign, meanwhile uttering an ironic comment on the democratic puritanism of his elective home, where a certain Cromwell had turned poets into fire-eaters.

Only the student Scheffler had absented himself. While the company were still on their soup, he had wandered off through the Ems Gate and into town. There he went looking for the goal of the annual pilgrimage to Telgte, a woodcarved Pietà: Mary sitting stiffly, holding the death-stiffened body of her son.

When all had gathered in a semicircle around Dach, on benches and chairs and, these being insufficient, on milking stools and beer kegs under the beamed ceiling, the summer came in to them for a while through the open windows, mingling its buzzing of flies with their expectant silence or whispered exchanges. Schneuber was trying to convince Zesen of something. Weckherlin was explaining to Greflinger how secret agents went about coding their reports, a skill he had acquired in the service of various masters. The land-lady's two donkeys could be heard outside, and from farther away the tavern dogs.

Next to Dach, who had allowed himself an armchair, a stool stood in wait for the speaker of the moment. Symbolic emblems, such as were customary at regional gatherings — the palm of the Fruit-bearing Society, for instance — had not been set up and did not adorn the background. Perhaps in the interest of simplicity. Or possibly because no significant emblem had occurred to them. Maybe one would turn up later on.

Without making an introductory speech, but merely calling the assembly to order by clearing his throat, Dach called on the first speaker, Augustus Buchner, the elderly and in every muscle austere Saxon magister of letters, a man so incapable of expressing himself without lecturing that even his silence suggested a lecture. He could be so ponderously silent that his mute periods might have been cited as figures of speech.

From his *Short Guide to German Poetry,* a work widely distributed in manuscript copies, Buchner read the tenth chapter, entitled "On the Measure of Verses and Their Varieties." His remarks, which he regarded as supplementary to Opitz's theoretical writings, dealt with the proper use of "dactylic words," reproved old Ambrosius Lobwasser of blessed memory for "mixing incorrect *pedes* into his alexandrines," and gave examples of a form of dactylic ode, the last four lines of which were trochaic in the bucolic manner.

Buchner's contribution was sprinkled with bows to Opitz — who, however, had to be contradicted here and there — and with gibes at the absent Schottel, that "preceptor of princes," for his servility and his addiction to secret societies. Though Abraham von Franckenberg was not named, the word "Rosicrucian" was mentioned. Occasionally the speaker switched to scholarly Latin. Even when talking extemporaneously, he could quote just about anything. (In the Fruit-bearing Society, to which he belonged, he was known as The Enjoyed One.)

When Dach threw the floor open to disputation, no one wished at first to question Buchner's authority, though most of the gentlemen were versed in theory, skilled in their craft, metrically surefooted, attuned to argumentative cross fire, eloquent beyond measure, and inclined to contradict even when words of approval were on the tips of their tongues. Merely because Rist, taking the tone of the preacher that he was, termed all criticism of Opitz "depraved and reprehensible," Zesen, who had studied under Buchner, replied that those were the words of a man, namely, the Elbe Swan master of Opitzism, whose entire work was a dull-witted parroting of Opitz.

After Harsdörffer's learned defense of the Nuremberg pastorals, which had, he believed, been attacked by Buchner, and Weckherlin's observation that in spite of Opitz's interdiction, he had made correct use of dactylic words long before Buchner, Gryphius distilled a drop of bitterness: such poetic schools, he declared, could at best promote soulless prolixity; to which Buchner agreed, adding that for that reason he, unlike certain other teachers of literature, would refrain from publishing his lectures.

Next Dach called on Sigmund Birken, whose hair hung down to his shoulders in curls that were constantly taking on new life. His round face disclosed childlike eyes and moist, pouting lips. One wondered why so much beauty should have need of theory.

After Birken had read the twelfth chapter from the manuscript of his *German Rhetoric and Poetic Art,* consisting of rules for actors, prescribing that an author should put appropriate speech into the mouths of his characters — "thus children should speak childishly, old people wisely, women chastely and gently, heroes bravely and heroically, peasants crudely" — Greflinger and Lauremberg jumped on him. Nothing but boredom, they declared, could come of that! Typical of the Pegnitz school! Wishy-washy! And Moscherosch scoffed: In what century was this young fop living?

Harsdörffer tried rather halfheartedly to help his protégé. Such dramatic rules, he said, were demonstrable in the ancients. Gerhardt praised Birken's rule that horrors should not be shown directly but, at most, narrated. Gryphius, though said to be working on tragedies, was nevertheless silent. And Buchner's silence thundered menacingly.

At that point Gelnhausen asked for the floor. No longer swaggering in a green doublet with gold buttons, but (like Greflinger) wearing the baggy breeches of a soldier, he sat on one of the window seats and fidgeted impatiently until Dach gave him leave to speak. He wished only, said Stoffel, to observe that to his higgledy-piggledy knowledge old people often talked childishly, children wisely, women crudely, and peasants chastely, whereas even on the point of death the heroes he had known spoke profanely. Only the Devil had spoken gently to him, usually at crossroads. Whereupon the regimental secretary gave an extemporaneous sampling of the speech of the persons cited, concluding with the Prince of Hell.

Even Gryphius laughed. And Dach closed the disputation on a conciliatory note by throwing out the question: was it advisable, since life confronted us daily with bloody deeds and obscenity, to show them on the stage as well? He himself, he held, was inclined to agree with young Birken's rule, provided it were not applied too rigidly.

Then he called on Hans Michael Moscherosch, whose satires from the first part of his *Visions of Philander of Sittewald,* though published and widely known, were nevertheless received with pleasure, especially the mocking ditty:

> Most every tailor, sad to say,
> Dabbles in languages today,
> Latin and French — why not Bulgarian? —
> When in his cups, the dumb vulgarian...

This fell in with the general outrage at the mutilation of the German language, in whose impressionable soil the French, Spanish, and Swedish campaigns had left their hoof and wheel marks.

When landlady Libuschka called in from the doorway to ask whether the *signores* would care for a *boccolino* of *rouge,* the company answered in all the foreign languages then current in Germany. Each of those present, even Gerhardt, proved a master of mumbo-jumbo parody. And Moscherosch, on the one hand a sturdy fellow apt to be the first to laugh at his own jokes, but on the other hand a man inclined to profundity and belonging to the Order of the Palm Tree, in which he bore the epithet of The Dreamer, gave further samples of his satirical prowess. He scoffed at forced rhymes and pastoral circumlocutions. Without naming names he struck blows at the Pegnitz school. Several times he called himself a "good German," even though his name was of Moorish origin, as he pointed out for the benefit of anyone who might be toying with the thought of a rhyme for "stew." (It so happened that the bottom-of-the-barrel wine that the landlady had her maids serve was of Spanish origin.)

Then, from the just-printed first part of his *Poetic Funnel*, Harsdörffer read instructions as to the best way of handling his crash course for future poets — "After all, the six hours need not be successive and on the same day" — and then won general applause by taking out a manuscript and reading a brief encomium on the German language, which "more than any foreign tongue could imitate the sound and note of every creature, for it ... whirs like the swallow, croaks like the raven, chirps like the sparrow, lisps and whispers with the flowing brook...."

Obviously, we could never have come to any agreement as to whether to write *"teutsch"* or *"deutsch,"* but any praise of the German language in either spelling gave us a lift. Each of us thought up some new nature-imitating onomatopoeia to demonstrate the German art of word making. Soon (to Buchner's irritation) we were discussing Schottel's catalogue of linguistic inventions and praising his "snowy-milk-white" and other finds. When it came to improving the language and Germanizing foreign words, we found ourselves in agreement. Even Zesen's suggestion of replacing "convent" with *"Jungfernzwinger"* ("virgins' dungeon") met with approval.

It took Lauremberg's long poem, "On Old-Fashioned Poetry and Rhymes," which struck vigorous Low German blows at the new-fashioned High German, to divide the company again, though Lauremberg was a hard man to argue with. He knew his adversaries' arguments in advance — "Our language is accepted By every chancellery; Wherever German speech is written, High German it must be" — and praised his unspoiled Nether German as against the stilted, affected, now euphuistic, now bombastic chancellery, or High, German: "So stiff and glumpish one can scarce determine, Whether it's French or honest German."

Yet not only the modernists Zesen and Birken, but Buchner and Logau as well, rejected all dialects as vehicles of poetry. High German alone, they held, should be developed into an instrument of ever-increasing refinement, which would succeed — where sword and pike had failed — in sweeping the fatherland clean of foreign domination. Rist submitted that in that case it would be necessary to do away with all such old-fashioned claptrap as sacrilegious invocations of the Muses and references to those abominable heathen gods. Gryphius declared that, in opposition to Opitz, he had long held that dialects were needed to give force to the "main" language, but that since his studies in Leiden he had, not without regret, become stricter in his usage.

It was again Gelnhausen who, from the window seat, informed the company that whether, on the banks of the Rhine, people said *"Kappes,"* or between the Ems and the Weser said *"Kumst,"* cabbage was meant in either case. The linguistic controversy, he said, made no sense to him, but Lauremberg's poem had demonstrated to the satisfaction of every ear that Low German speech could lend winning sound to stilted discourse. Therefore, in his opinion, they should subsist side by side and mixed, and people so intent on cleanliness that the broom was never out of reach would end up sweeping life away.

Rist and Zesen wanted (both in alliance and opposition to each other) to raise objections, but Dach supported Stoffel.

He, too, he submitted, let his native Prussian flow like buttermilk into some of his lighter songs, and he had collected songs sung by the common people, hoping, with the help of Albert the organist, to make them suitable for singing by the general public. He then began to sing some of his verses in an undertone— "Annie of Tharaw, my true love of old, She is my life and my goods and my gold" —and after a while he was not singing alone, but in chorus with Lauremberg, Greflinger, Rist, and even with Gryphius's mighty voice, until at last Annie of Samland put an end to the linguistic controversy: "The threads of our two lives are woven in one."

Thereupon Simon Dach suspended the congress for that day. Dinner, he announced, was served in the taproom; if anyone found it too modest, he should bear in mind that a Croatian foraging party had only recently requisitioned the landlady's provisions, driven off her calves, slaughtered her hogs, and consumed or, to put it bluntly, gobbled up her last goose. Nevertheless, there would be plenty to eat.... And hadn't the afternoon given them pleasure with its argument and counterargument?

When they left the great hall, the medical student was back among them. His eyes were as wide as if he had beheld a miracle, but all that had happened was that the priest of the church had shown him the Telgte Pietà, which was hidden in a barn. To Czepko, who was standing beside him, Scheffler said that the Mother of God had told him that just as God was in him, she was in every maiden's womb.

Chapter 6

What the landlady bade her maids dish up was not so very meager: steaming millet porridge in deep wooden bowls, with rendered lard and bits of bacon poured over it. On the side, boiled sausages and coarse bread. In addition, her garden, which lay behind the house, protected by the wilderness that fenced it round (which the Croatian foragers must have overlooked), had yielded onions, carrots, and black radishes, all of which were served raw and tasted good with the brown beer.

The company praised the simple fare. Even those ordinarily spoiled and pampered declared fulsomely that their palates had not enjoyed such blessings in a long, long time. Weckherlin excoriated English cooking. Hofmannswaldau called the rustic offering a meal for the gods. Alternately in Latin and German, Harsdörffer and Birken spoke of comparable meals recorded in classical pastorals. And in the word flux of the Wedel pastor, Rist, whom Dach had appointed to say grace, the Emsland millet porridge was transformed into manna from heaven.

Only Gelnhausen first muttered to himself, then loudly reproved the landlady: What did Courage think she was doing! He could never expect his horsemen and musketeers, meanly lodged in her stable, to eat such swill more than once! If they remained loyal to the emperor, it was in the expectation of daily roast chicken, breast of beef, and jowl of pork, for, as everyone knew, their pay was inadequate. If the food served them wasn't crispy-succulent enough, they'd be serving the Swedes tomorrow. For just as a musket demanded dry powder, so a musketeer had to be kept in a good humor. And if Mars withdrew his protection, the swan-throated Apollo would find himself at the mercy of every reckless snickersnee. Meaning that without a military guard the poets' disputation couldn't last a day. He felt in duty bound to inform the gentlemen, as forbearingly as possible, not only—as Courage was well aware—that all Westphalia, especially the Tecklenburg area, was rich in forests and thickets, but also that the river Ems was crawling with highwaymen from end to end.

He then withdrew with Libuschka, who apparently recognized that Gelnhausen's horsemen and musketeers required additional sustenance. Left alone for a while, the literary men, some frightened and others indignant at Gelnhausen's impudence, relieved their feelings in disputation. Never fear. They would manage to forget the danger facing their meeting through skillful recourse to the dactylic words for which they were always searching; the world could come to an end, and in the midst of the rumbling and roaring these gentlemen would quarrel over the correct or incorrect use of metric feet. In the last analysis — and Gryphius, with the verbal splendor of his sonnets, was not alone in having said so — all was vanity.

And so the company were soon back at the table, chewing and spooning in literary converse. At one end — facing Dach — Buchner, gesticulating as he spoke, expressed his suspicion of the absent Schottel, whom he accused of a coup against the Fruit-bearing Society. Whereupon Harsdörffer and his publisher, Endter, who had made secret arrangements with Schottel, parodied the magister's manner of speaking. On all sides the absent were thoroughly vilipended, quarrels crisscrossed, mockery was overdone, conferees belabored one another with stones transmuted into words. One group, straddling their bench, kept captious count of Lauremberg's Low German *"pedes"*: in another corner Zesen and Birken reviled the late Opitz, whose rules were termed relentless fences and whose images were disparaged as colorless. Both modernists accused Rist, Czepko, and (in covert whispers) Simon Dach of perpetual "Opitzizing." On the other hand, Rist, who was sitting with Weckherlin and Lauremberg, waxed indignant over the immorality of the Pegnitz Shepherds: why, in Nuremberg, they were even admitting women to the sessions of the Order of Flowers. A good thing Dach hadn't invited any ladies, considering how fashionable their rhymed soul-mush had become.

Still others were standing around the seated Gryphius, who, though only thirty, was already well upholstered on all sides, bloated no doubt by grief and disgust with the world. His coat

stretched tight in many places. His double chin, already beto-
kening a third. He spoke with the voice of a prophet and could
thunder even when he lacked lightning. In a small circle, he invoked humanity, and as he spoke the question — What is man? —
found answer in ever-renewed images, each of which expunged
the last: delusion on all sides. Gryphius dealt annihilation. Everything he did disgusted him. For all his impetuous need to write, he
was perpetually, in a torrent of words, abjuring literature. At the
same time, his disgust with everything written, let alone printed,
went hand in hand with his eagerness to see everything he had
recently poured forth — certain tragedies, for example, and various projected comedies or satires — published without delay. That
is why, hardly a moment after pondering grandiloquent scenes,
he was able without transition to bid farewell to "letters and all
such trumpery," for no sooner do they come into being than decay sets in. Now that peace was in the offing, he declared, he
preferred to make himself useful. The Glogau Estates had long
been urging him to become their syndic. Though he had formerly
abominated Opitz's only too adroit diplomacy, today he deemed
activity conducive to the commonweal all the more indispensable.
At a time when law and morality, even more than the devastated
countryside, were everywhere in ruins, the prime imperative was
to put order into chaos, for order alone could provide a blindly
errant people with something to hold on to. Flowery pastorals and
euphonious verses would accomplish nothing.

Such talk of abjuring the written word provoked Logau, who
was standing to one side, to emit maxims all ready for the printer.
If the shoemaker were to turn baker, he observed, the upshot
would be leathery bread. And Weckherlin said that his almost
thirty years of toil in the government service meant less to him than
a single one of his odes, which he intended, the new ones along
with those that were feeble with age, to send to the printer's soon.

And undeterred by Gryphius, who continued in ever-new images
to proclaim the death of literature and the order-fostering rule of
reason, the publishers, who had hitherto maintained a certain reserve, now went weaseling around the room in quest of promising
manuscripts. Weckherlin's new book had already been placed in
Amsterdam. Moscherosch lent ear to the advances of Naumann,
the Hamburg bookseller. After as good as closing a deal with Rist,

whose works had hitherto appeared in Lüneburg, for a volumi-
nous manuscript celebrating the forthcoming peace, the publisher
Endter vied with Mülbe of Strassburg and Elzevihr of Holland in
trying to persuade the resourceful Hofmannswaldau to procure
for them — that is, for one of the three — the manuscript of the
deceased Jesuit Spee's *The Nightingale's Rival,* for, they said, provided it had merit, they would be willing to publish the work
of a Papist. Hofmannswaldau held out hope to all three and allegedly — so Schneuber vituperated later on — accepted advances
from all three. Nevertheless, *The Nightingale's Rival* by Friedrich
von Spee was not published until 1649, and then by Friessem in
Catholic Cologne.

So the evening waxed. A few of the gentlemen were moved to
take the air in the landlady's garden but were soon driven back
by the veils of gnats blown in from the Ems. Dach was amazed at
the stubborn industry of Libuschka, who, warring with nettles and
thistles, had managed to grow vegetables in the wilderness. With
just such courage his friend Albert had induced his little garden to
grow around the cucumber bower. Nothing remained of it. Soon
there would be nothing left to praise but the thistle, that latter-day
flower and symbol of adverse times.

Then they stood for a while in the courtyard or stretched their
legs in the direction of the outer Ems, where stood an abandoned fulling mill. From there they were able to see that their
meeting was being held on an island (Emshagen by name) separated from the town, between the two arms of the river. They
spoke knowingly of the damaged, towerless town wall and admired Moscherosch's tobacco pipe. They chatted with the maids,
one of whom (like the late Fleming's beloved) was named Elsabe,
and, while the tavern dogs cavorted around them, apostrophized
the tethered mules in Latin. They made biting or comical remarks
against or about one another and argued a while as to whether,
according to Schottel's instructive color scale, Libuschka's hair
should be termed "pitch" or "coal" black, or whether it was per-
missible to characterize the early dusk as "donkey-fallow." They
laughed at Greflinger, who, standing with legs wide-planted like
a Swedish ensign, was telling the musketeers about his campaigns
under Baner and Torstenson. Several groups were about to stroll
down the Hauptstrasse in the direction of the Ems Gate — for

the town of Telgte was still unknown to them — when one of the imperial horsemen of Stoffel's guard rode into the courtyard and handed a message to Gelnhausen, who was standing in the stable doorway with the landlady and the sergeant of musketeers. It was soon known to all that Trauttmannsdorff, the emperor's chief negotiator, had suddenly — on the sixteenth day of July — left Münster in manifestly high spirits and set out for Vienna, to the discomfiture of the conference and all its participants.

In a trice the conversation turned political and moved to the taproom, where a fresh keg of brown beer was opened. Only the youngsters — Birken, Greflinger, and, hesitantly, the student Scheffler — stayed in the courtyard with Zesen and approached the maids. Each made a grab or (in Scheffler's case) was grabbed; Zesen alone was left empty-handed, and, his feelings hurt by Greflinger's mockery, went down to the river. He wanted to be alone with himself.

But no sooner had I caught sight of him standing above the outer Ems, which had dug deep into its sandy bed, than two corpses, tied together, were washed against the bank. Though bloated, they could be recognized as a man and a woman. After brief hesitation — an eternity for Zesen — the pair broke loose from the tangled reeds, spun around playfully in the current, escaped from the eddy, and glided downstream to the mill weir where evening was blending into night, leaving nothing behind except potential metaphors, which Zesen began at once to pad with resounding neologisms. He was so hard pressed by language that he had no time to be horrified.

Chapter 7

In the taproom conjectures were exchanged over beer. His smile — since Trauttmannsdorff passed for a gloomy man — could only be interpreted as a sign of Papist triumph, Habsburg advantage, new loss for the Protestant camp, and further postponement of the peace — such were the opinions with which the gentlemen added to one another's fears. Especially the Silesians saw themselves forsaken. Czepko had a foreboding that they would all be abandoned to the Jesuits.

They edged away from Gelnhausen, who made light of the imperial legate's sudden departure. What, he asked, was there to be surprised at, when you stopped to think that ever since Wrangel had replaced the gout-ridden Torstenson, he had done nothing but carry on private warfare to fill his pockets, preferring an invasion of Bavaria in quest of spoils to a march on Vienna through gaunt Bohemia. Nor were the French doing very well by the Protestant cause, now that — according to a street song current in Paris — Anne of Austria was darning Mazarin's socks while the cardinal was anointing her royal courage.*

Exactly, cried Libuschka; she had known the score ever since she had lost her maidenhead. Seven times she had been married, mostly to imperial, but also to Hessian cavalry captains, and once almost to a Dane. And each time, whether a priest or a Lutheran minister had blessed the union, she had been used and reviled as a "courage." That's the military for you, as bad on one side as on the other. And Stoffel here — whom everybody, first in Hanau, later in Soest, and then again at the spa where they had gone to cure the love pox — had addressed as Simpel — Run, Simpel! Come here, Simpel! Hurry up, Simpel! — had no more in his codpiece than her dear departed captains.

---

*How did "courage" get to mean the female sex organ and by extension a peddler of the same? And how, for that matter, did Libuschka come to be known as Courage? Thereby hangs a tale. As a young girl Libuschka, to protect her virginity from the imperial troops who had occupied the Bohemian town of Bragoditz, where she lived, dressed as a boy, took the name of Janko, and went to work as a groom for a German cavalryman, who soon passed her on to a captain. Libuschka-Janko served the captain well, acquired the ways of a fighting man, and even took part in foraging expeditions. One day she got into a fight with another groom, who had insulted the Bohemian nation. When her antagonist tried to grab her "by the utensil which she had not," her fear of being unmasked redoubled her strength and she gave him a sound thrashing. The story came to the captain's ears. To continue in Libuschka's words: "When he asked me why I had beaten the fellow so villainously, I replied: 'Because he grabbed at my courage, where no man's hand had ever ventured before.' You see, I wanted to express myself allusively and not with Swabian crudeness. ... And since my virginity was on its last legs in any case, for that groom would surely have betrayed me, I bared my snow-white bosom and showed the captain my hard, alluring breasts." Grimmelshausen, *Lebensbeschreibung der Erzbetrügerin und Landstörzerin Courasche. — Trans.*

"You shut your trap, Courage, or I'll shut it for you!" Geln-hausen shouted. Didn't she know that an account had been open since their course of medical treatment in Swabia?

She'd open an account for him, all right, she replied; she'd make him pay for all the brats born in his wake in one garrison town after another.

What, he cried, was this nonsense about brats? When she, Courage, had never brought any brats into the world, but sat bar-ren on a donkey that ate nothing but thistles. She herself was a thistle that needed to be hacked out wherever it grew. Roots and all!

Whereupon landlady Libuschka, as though Gelnhausen had ac-tually taken a knife to her, jumped on the table among the beer mugs, stamped till the beer mugs danced, suddenly picked up her skirts, dropped her breeches, turned her arse in Stoffel's direction, and gave him a well-aimed answer.

"Hey, Gryf!" cried Moscherosch. "What do you think of that? What splendid dialogues and curtain scenes the writers of German tragedies could cull from her!"

Everyone laughed. Even from Gryphius, who a moment before had been deep in gloom, laughter erupted. Weckherlin wanted to hear "Courage's thunder" again. And after Logau had delivered himself of a maxim to the effect that a fart had deeper meaning than the sound might suggest, the company soon recovered from the dismay caused by Trauttmannsdorff's sudden departure. (Only Paul Gerhardt sought out his room in horror. For he had an inti-mation of the turn that the landlady's nether wind would give the gentlemen's conversation.)

Over their brown beer they treated one another to crude and double-meaningful anecdotes. Moscherosch had several unprinted calendars full of them in readiness. With turns of phrase that ob-scured more than they revealed, Hofmannswaldau related how shamelessly Opitz had carried on with several daughters of Bres-lau burghers, yet avoided paying alimony. Old Weckherlin drained the sink of London's iniquity, taking special pleasure in exhibit-ing the nakedness of the Puritan hypocrites, the new ruling class. From Schneuber the company learned the intimate secrets of aris-tocratic ladies who, in frequenting the Society of the Pine Tree, had not only couched their thoughts in rhyme but had also couched themselves with Rompler and his friends. Naturally Lauremberg contributed. Everyone opened his tap. Even Gryphius, inclining to pressure, served up a few tidbits brought back from his trip to Italy, for the most part anecdotes about whoring monks, which Harsdörffer tried to outdo and Hofmannswaldau embroidered into stories about triangles and squares: this exercise gave them occasion to display their learning, for, in introducing or winding up a tale about bumptious trollops or randy monks, they would indicate their French or Italian sources.

When the amazed Simon Dach remarked that he evidently lived in the wrong place, since he could report no such happenings from Königsberg-Kneiphof, where the goings-on were sometimes crude but never so outrageous, his contribution was found particularly amusing. And if, prodded by Harsdörffer and others, landlady Libuschka and Gelnhausen (temporarily reconciled) had not told a few stories, he from his life as a soldier — the Battle of Witt-stock — she from her days as a sutler at the camp outside Mantua, and then a few bawdy tales from their time together at the spa, the evening would have gone on merrily with storytelling and keg tapping. But when the two of them lined up the gruesome particulars of what had happened in Magdeburg when Tilly and his butchers fell on the city, the listeners were numbed; brazenly Libuschka told them how much she had gained in the looting. She boasted of baskets full of gold chains she had cut off the necks of slaughtered women. In the end Gelnhausen poked her to make her stop. Magdeburg's suffering admitted of no reaction but silence.

Speaking into the stillness, Dach said it was late, time for sleep. Stoffel's and especially Libuschka's unvarnished report, which had thoughtlessly been asked of them, showed, said Dach, where laughter had to stop and how dearly we pay for too much laughter, with the result that they all, with their laughter in their throats, were driven to gulping. And this had happened because horror had become a commonplace even to persons of sensibility. May the Lord forgive them and favor them in His mercy.

Dach sent the company to bed like children, without even the nightcap that Lauremberg and Moscherosch tried to insist on. He wanted to hear no more laughter, however subdued. Enough wit had been squandered. Luckily, he said, the pious Gerhardt had gone early to his room. Rist — ordinarily a vigorous preacher —

ought really to have put a stop to the verbal whoring. No, he wasn't angry with anyone, he, too, had joined in the laughter. For the present there was nothing more to be said. But tomorrow, when manuscripts would again be read for the benefit of all, he hoped, as anyone who knew him would testify, to be of good cheer with the rest of them.

When all was still in the house — except for the landlady, who was putting her kitchen in order and most likely had Gelnhausen with her — Simon Dach passed once again through the corridors and looked in at the attic, where the youngsters were bedded on straw. There they lay, and the maids were with them. Birken lay held in arms like a child. How deeply they had exhausted themselves. Only Greflinger started up and wanted to explain. But Dach motioned him with his fingers to stay quiet and under his blanket. Let them enjoy themselves. If anyone had sinned, it was not here in the straw, but in the taproom. (And I had joined in the laughter, I had let stories occur to me, I had started the trouble, and — once it was started — I had willingly sat in the seat of the scornful.) After casting a last look, Dach was glad to see that the bashful Scheffler had ended up with one of the maids.

When at last he started back to his room — possibly to write a letter — he heard horses, wagon wheels, the dogs, and then voices in the courtyard. That must be my Albert, Dach hoped.

Chapter 8

He did not come alone. The Königsberg cathedral organist, who had made a name for himself well beyond the borders of Prussia as a composer and a publisher and was known in particular for the successive volumes of his "arias," was accompanied by his cousin Heinrich Schütz, *Kapellmeister* at the court of Saxony, who was on his way to Hamburg and then to Glückstadt, where he hoped to find a long-coveted invitation to the Danish court. There was nothing more to keep him in Saxony. In his early sixties like Weckherlin, but more robust than the Swabian, who had worn himself out in government service, Schütz was a man of austere authority and stern grandeur, whom no one (except Albert, and he only in part) could fathom. His presence — far from overbearing, he seemed troubled by fear of being in the way — raised the tone of the poets' gathering but at the same time reduced the measure of its importance. A man whom no group could endure had come to their meeting.

I won't claim to be wiser than I was then — but everyone knew that, little as Schütz questioned his God and devoted as he had proved to be his prince in spite of repeated Danish offers, his only true allegiance was to his own aspirations. Never, even in his incidental compositions, had he achieved the mediocrity required by Protestants for their daily use. He had provided neither his elector nor Christian of Denmark with anything more than the strictest minimum of courtly music. Though still as active as in the prime of life, he rejected the usual busyness. When the publishers of his works insisted on additions conducive to use in the churches, such as the notation of the thorough bass, Schütz, in his prefaces, deplored these adjuncts and warned against their use, since in his opinion the basso continuo should never be anything but a rarely used expedient.

Since he attached more importance than did any other composer to the written word, and since his music was designed to serve and interpret the word, to enhance it, underline its gestures, and give it greater depth, breadth, and elevation, Schütz was strict with words and confined himself for the most part either to the traditional Latin liturgy or to the text of Luther's Bible. In his main work, his religious music, he had thus far eschewed the productions of contemporary poets, with the exception of Becker's *Psalter* and a few of the poems written by Opitz in his youth; urgently as he had appealed to us for texts, the German poets had nothing to offer him. Consequently, when Simon Dach heard his guest's name, his first feeling, before he could experience pleasure, was one of alarm.

They stood for a while in the courtyard, exchanging *politesses.* Over and over again Schütz apologized for arriving uninvited. As though to justify himself, he observed that he had been acquainted for years with some of the gentlemen (Buchner, Rist, Lauremberg). Dach, for his part, tried to put into words the honor that was being shown them. Gelnhausen's imperial guard stood in the background, holding torches. The musketeers thought they were witnessing the arrival of a prince, though Schütz's travel costume was that of a burgher and his luggage could be carried in two hands. (The other guest, they believed, must be the prince's gentleman-in-waiting.)

The travelers had come by way of Oesede, where they had found the instructions to proceed to Telgte. Since Schütz was traveling with a safe-conduct signed by the Elector of Saxony, there had been no difficulty in securing fresh horses. As though to identify himself, he showed the document with an almost childlike pride, meanwhile talking of one thing and another: an uneventful trip, with nothing untoward to report; the flat countryside had been well lighted by the full moon; the fields were fallow, overgrown with weeds; he was more tired than hungry; he would gladly sleep on the stove bench if no bed was available; he knew all about inns, for his father had been the landlord of the Schützenhof in Weissenfels on the Saale, which was often full beyond capacity.

With difficulty Dach and Albert persuaded the *Kapellmeister* to move into Dach's room. When the landlady appeared (with Gelnhausen in the background) and heard the guest's name, she hastened to greet him in a burst of Italian as Maestro Sagittario.*
All were even more surprised (and Schütz a little shaken) when Gelnhausen, after serviceably stationing himself beside the newcomer's luggage, began in a pleasing tenor to sing the first motet of the *Cantiones sacrae,* a supradenominational work which had accordingly circulated in Catholic as well as Protestant regions: *"O bone, O dulcis, O benigne Jesu...."*

And Stoffel explained that while serving as a baggage boy in Breisach when the town was being besieged by the Weimar troops, he had sung in the choir, because singing made hunger more bearable. Then he picked up the luggage and drew Schütz and all the others after him. The landlady came last, taking a jug of apple cider and some black bread to the newcomer's room at his request.

Later Libuschka made up a makeshift bed in the taproom for Dach and Albert, who had declined to take over her alcove beside the kitchen. She addressed her flow of talk chiefly to Albert: how hard it was in such times for an unattached woman to preserve her honor; how beautiful she had been in former days, and

---

Sagittario is Italian and *Schütze* is German for "archer." — *Trans.*

what sufferings had made her wiser.... In the end Stoffel dragged her out of the room. A very special cement knitted him and Courage together.

No sooner had the two of them gone than the guests were again disturbed. Zesen's horrified face appeared in the open window on one side of the taproom. He had come from the river, he spluttered; it was full of corpses; first he had seen just two of them; they had been tied together, and that reminded him of his Markhold and Rosemunde; then more and more had come drifting down; the moon had lighted their floating flesh; he could find no words for so much death; the house was beset by evil omens; there would never be peace; because the language had not been kept pure; because mutilated words had swelled up like drifting corpses. He would write what he had seen. Just that. Immediately. He would find tones that had never before been heard.

Dach closed the window. Finally, after listening to Zesen first with horror, then with amusement, the two friends were alone. Time and again they embraced each other, now and then slapping each other's back and grumbling rough-hewn terms of endearment that could never have been fitted into dactylic meter. Though only a short while ago Dach, to punish the company for their smutty stories, had sent them to their rooms without a nightcap, he now filled mugs with brown beer for himself and Albert. Several times they touched mug to mug.

When the two friends lay in the dark, the organist told Dach what a hard time he had had persuading Schütz to come. His distrust of writers and their far too many words had increased in the last few years. When Rist had provided him with nothing and Lauremberg's libretti had served him poorly at the Danish court, he had taken up one of Schottel's operas, but Schottel's stilted verbiage still disgusted him. So it was not love for his kinsman that had moved Albert's world-famous cousin to detour via Telgte, but the hope that Gryphius might read some dramatic work that would supply him with the text for an opera. And Albert reiterated the hope that one manuscript or another might find grace in the eyes of his exacting cousin.

Simon Dach worried as he lay in the darkness; would his motley and quarrelsome literary circus — the wild Greflinger, the testy Gerhardt, so ready, as he had just shown, to take umbrage, the disturbed Zesen — would they behave with adequate decorum in the presence of so distinguished a visitor?

In the midst of his worries sleep overcame him. Only the beams of the Bridge Tavern remained awake. Or did something else happen during the night?

Chapter 9

In the room that he shared with his counterpart, Rist, Zesen continued for quite some time to line up sonorous words until he fell asleep over a line in which swollen, ballooning corpses were likened to Rosemunde's flesh and his own.

In the meantime a courier from Osnabrück rode across the Ems and past the Bridge Tavern on his way to Münster, and another rode in the opposite direction; both were carrying news that would be stale by the time it reached its destination. The tavern dogs barked.

Then, after looking down on the river for a long time, the full moon stood over the tavern and its guests. No one evaded its influence. From it emanated change.

That must be why the three couples in the attic straw bedded themselves in different and contrary wise; for when they awoke in the gray of dawn, Greflinger, who at the start of his night in the straw had lain with the dainty and delicate maid, now found himself with the bony one, whose name was Marthe. And the plump maid, Elsabe by name, who had lain at first with the retiring Scheffler, found herself lying with Birken, whereas the dainty and delicate maid, Marie, who had fallen at first to Greflinger's lot, now lay asleep as though bound by chains to Scheffler. When they woke one another up and (moved by the moon) saw themselves wrongly paired, they didn't wish to lie as they were, but they no longer knew exactly with whom they had originally tumbled into the straw. After another change, it is true, each man and his maid thought they were lying right, but the full moon, which had long changed its place, was still exerting its influence. As though called by the unfaithful Flora, who had given his songs their sheen but had for years been the wedded wife of another, Greflinger, who had black hair covering the whole length of his back, crawled to the plump Elsabe; the dainty and delicate Marie flung herself on the pouting, angelic lips of Birken, who always, whether with the bony, the plump, or the dainty and delicate maid, thought he was lying with a nymph; and the tall, rawboned Marthe forced Scheffler between her limbs, in order, as previously the plump maid and the dainty and delicate maid had done, to fulfill the promise that the wooden Telgte Madonna had given him the day before. And time and time again the frail young student poured out his soul with his sperm.

So it came about that for the third time all six began to thresh the attic straw, after which each was acquainted with each; no wonder that the bedfellows failed to hear what else happened that early morning.

But I know. Five horsemen led their saddled mounts out the stable and into the courtyard. Gelnhausen was there. No door squeaked, no iron struck stone. The horses trod slowly and silently. Their hoofs had been wrapped in rags. And with sure hands — no leather slapped, the shafts were well oiled on their pins — two musketeers harnessed one of the covered wagons that the imperial troops had requisitioned in Oesede. A third brought muskets for himself and the other two and thrust them under the canvas. No need for words. Everything went off as though rehearsed. Not a murmur out of the tavern dogs.

Only the landlady of the Bridge Tavern whispered something to Gelnhausen, instructions no doubt, for Stoffel, already mounted, punctuated her words with nods of the head. As though playing a part, Libuschka (formerly known as Courage) stood wrapped in a horse blanket beside the sometime huntsman of Soest, who still (or once again) looked dashing in a green doublet with gold buttons and a plumed hat.

Only Paul Gerhardt woke up when the team tugged at the covered wagon and the emperor's horsemen rode out of the courtyard. He was just in time to see Gelnhausen turn in his saddle, draw his sword, and with his free hand wave laughingly at the landlady, who made no sign in answer, but was still standing stiffly in the courtyard, wrapped in her blanket, when the wagon and riders were curtained off by the alders before being swallowed up by the Ems Gate.

Then the birds started in. Or perhaps it was only then that Gerhardt heard how many birds had been ushering in the Telgte morning. Larks, finches, blackbirds, titmice, starlings. In the elderberry bushes behind the stable, in the copper beech in the middle of the courtyard, in the four lime trees that had been planted on the weather side of the tavern, from the birch and alder woods invaded by the scrub from the outer bank of the Ems, also in the nests the sparrows had built themselves in the weather-beaten thatched roof that was failing apart around the rear gable. From all directions the morning began with birds. (There were no cocks left in the town.)

When landlady Libuschka broke loose from her freeze and slowly, shaking her head and muttering plaintively, shuffled out of the courtyard, she, who the day before had raucously set the tone and had still impressed the gentlemen as a valid target, became an old woman; abandoned to herself, wrapped in her horse blanket.

For which reason Paul Gerhardt, who now started on his morning prayers, included poor Courage in his plea: he prayed that the Lord and merciful Father might not in His wrath punish the wretched woman too severely for her sins; that He might look with forbearance upon her future trespasses, for the war had made this poor woman what she was and corrupted many another pious soul besides her. Then he prayed, as he had every morning for years, that peace might come soon, bringing safety to all true believers, and to the heretics, who denied the true God, either ultimate insight or merited punishment. Among the heretics the pious man numbered not only, as any orthodox Lutheran traditionally would have, the Catholics of the clerical party, but also the Huguenots, Zwinglians, Calvinists, and all mystical fantasts; for which reason the piety of the Silesian repelled him.

Gerhardt was truly pious only in his conception of God — and in his hymns, which carried farther than he in his bigotry would have liked. For years, ever since he had been tutoring children in Berlin and hoping vainly for a parsonage, simple words had come to him, few in number yet sufficient to provide Lutheran congregations with ever-new songs in rhymed stanzas, so that everywhere, in homes and in what churches the war had left standing (even in Catholic regions), people sang with the pious Gerhardt — in the old-fashioned manner and to the unassuming melodies of Crüger and later of Ebeling; his "Morning Song," for example — "Awake, my heart, and sing" — the last stanzas of which, "To the Creator of all things, the giver of all gifts, the guardian and protector...," had been written on the way to Telgte; all nine stanzas would shortly be set to music by Johann Crüger.

Even if Gerhardt had been able to, nothing and no one could have induced him to write anything else — odes, elegant sonnets, or satires, let alone lewd pastorals. He was not a literary man, and the folk song had given him more than he had learned from Opitz (and his executor Buchner). His hymns had nature in them and did not speak figuratively. Consequently, he had at first declined to attend the poets' meeting. It was solely as a favor to Dach, whose practical piety just barely fitted into Gerhardt's concept of religion, that he had agreed to come. But exactly as he had foreseen, he had immediately taken umbrage at everything and everyone: at Hofmannswaldau with his perpetual witty talk; at Gryphius with his self-satisfied, all-encompassing disgust of the world which he had not yet milked dry; at the muddled aestheticist prattle of the supposedly gifted Zesen; at the way Lauremberg kept serving up the same old satire; at Czepko's pansophic ambiguities; at Logau's blasphemous tongue; at Rist's bluster, and the busy comings and goings of the publishers. All that, the glib talk and perpetual know-it-allness of the literati, so repelled him that he stood by no one but himself (his obstinately independent mind), belonged to no literary group, and no sooner arrived than longed to go home; but the pious man stayed on.

And when Paul Gerhardt, after pleading for the salvation of the shameless landlady and the damnation of all enemies of the true faith, continued his morning prayer, he entreated the Lord at length to enlighten his Calvinist prince, who was summoning Huguenots and other heretics to the March of Brandenburg as settlers, for which reason Gerhardt could not love him. Then he included the poets in his prayer.

He begged the Almighty God and Father to endow the most learned but abysmally erring gentlemen — the worldly-wise Weckherlin and the shady (because of his dubious origins) Moscherosch, the wicked Greflinger and even the clownish Stoffel, though a Catholic — with right words. His fingers interlocked, he prayed with fervor that the congress might in all things praise the glory of God, the supreme judge.

As a postscript to his morning prayer, he begged that he might at long last be granted a parsonage, if possible in Brandenburg; but it was not until four years later that Paul Gerhardt became rural dean of Mittenwalde, where he was at last enabled to marry the already aging love of his tutorial days, his pupil Anna Berthold, and wrote hymn after hymn, all with many stanzas.

Then Simon Dach rang the bell in the taproom. All those who were still asleep woke up. The young men found themselves maidless in the attic straw. Marthe, Elsabe, and Marie were already at work in the kitchen. They cut stale bread into the morning soup, of which Heinrich Schütz also partook after seating himself, a stranger though known to all, at the long table, between Gerhardt and Albert.

Chapter 10

How radiantly that summer's day began. Light poured through every window, lending a touch of warmth to a house kept cool by the dampness of the walls. And the hour was also brightened by the joy of the conferees at the presence of their distinguished guest.

Immediately after the morning soup, still in the taproom (this time Czepko had said grace), Simon Dach stood up and addressed the company. Before they went back to their manuscripts, he said, it was fitting that a cordial welcome be given to the illustrious guest, but this, he felt, must be done by someone more proficient than himself, a mere music lover. His Albert — as he called the cathedral organist — was more at home with motets and madrigals, whereas he, Dach, for want of knowledge, could offer no more than wondering admiration. At the most he was able to appreciate ditties with thorough-bass accompaniments. Then he sat down, relieved.

After an elaborate exordium, Heinrich Albert sketched in the honored guest's career: How under the patronage first of the Landgrave of Kassel, then of the Elector of Saxony, young Schütz, though destined by his parents for the study of the law, had stud-

ied composition in Venice under the world-famous Gabrieli, whom
he could have succeeded as organist in charge of both organs at
St. Mark's basilica, but it had meant more to him to return to his
own country. Not until much later, when war had begun to exact its murderous toll from Germany, had he gone back to Italy to
continue his studies under the illustrious Monteverdi, after which,
fully the great man's equal, he had returned with the most modern music, having so mastered his craft that he was now able to
give voice to the joys and sorrows of men, their anguished silence and their anger, their weary waking and tormented sleep,
their yearning for death and their fear of God, and not last to the
praise of His goodness. All this, for the most part, according to
the uniquely true words of Scripture. And in innumerable works:
in religious concerti, in musical exequies, in his *Story of the Resurrection,* or — as recently as two years ago — in his setting of *The
Seven Words on the Cross.* All these had been at once severe and
tender, simple and artful. For which reason most of his works had
proved too difficult for the common cantor or the scantily trained
choral singer. He himself, Albert owned, had often despaired of
Schütz's intricate polyphony, and had done so again only recently
when, in preparation for the festival of the Reformation, he had attempted the Ninety-eighth Psalm — "Sing unto the Lord" — with
his Kneiphof choir and had acknowledged failure in the face of its
antiphony. However, he did not wish on so joyful an occasion to
offend the master with the everlasting lament of the church organist, especially as the *Kapellmeister* knew from hard experience how
difficult it was in times so long unsettled by war to keep competent
singers and violinists. Even proud Dresden was wanting in instru-
mentalists. Receiving no proper pay, the foreign virtuosi sought
the security and regularity that came from princely favor. He was
barely able to feed his few boy choristers. Ah, if only God in His
mercy would grant peace at long last, for then performers might
once more be as skillful as the exacting master demanded.

Then, quite casually, Albert stated Schütz's request for leave to
listen in at the manuscript reading, in the hope of being inspired
at last to compose madrigals, as Monteverdi had done, to words
in his own language, or of hearing some dramatic work on which
to base an opera, just as twenty years past the late Opitz's *Dafne*
had been amenable to his music; in which connection he felt that

he still owed the here-present Magister Buchner a debt of thanks for his help as an intermediary.

All waited somewhat uneasily for the guest's answer, for all the time that Albert had been eulogizing the master, deploring his difficult mode of composition, and finally stating his wishes, nothing had happened in Schütz's face. The creases in his high, careworn forehead had not so much as deepened, let alone relaxed. His eyes were still focused every bit as attentively upon something sad, situated well outside the room. His mouth — under his mustache and above his beard, both of which were carefully cut in the manner of the long-dead Gustavus Adolphus — drooped at the corners. His grayish-brown hair, which he wore combed back. His immobility, scarcely stirred by his breathing.

When at last he spoke, his statement of thanks was brief. He had merely, he said, carried further what Johann Gabriel had taught him. The touch of childishness with which this always dignified man showed everyone at the table the ring that he wore on his left hand seemed strange, perhaps even a trifle absurd. Giovanni Gabrieli, he informed the company, had given him that ring just before his death. In a single sentence he disposed of the difficult polyphony Albert had mentioned: music, he said, required that sort of artistry, if it was to keep faith with the pure word of God. Then came a first judgment, spoken softly but audible the whole length of the table. Those who wished to make things easier for themselves and remain outside the domain of art could, he recommended, confine themselves to strophic songs with thorough-bass accompaniment. But now, he concluded, he was eager to hear something of which he himself was incapable — skillfully written words.

Schütz, who had spoken seated, stood up, so giving the signal, without Dach's having to speak again, for a general move into the spacious hall. All left the table; only Gerhardt hesitated, because he took Schütz's disparaging remarks about strophic songs as aimed solely at himself. Weckherlin had to plead with him and finally drag him into the other room.

Dach had other difficulties with Gryphius, who did not wish to read, and certainly not immediately, from the tragedy he had recently completed in Strassburg, on his way back from France. Very well, he would comply if need be, but not at that particular moment and not merely because Schütz — with all due respect to his greatness — so desired. Besides, he was no writer of operas, he lacked the passion for courtly pomp. Let Dach call on others first, perhaps on the youngsters. Apparently the night had not agreed with them. They were yawning in three parts and sagging at the knees. Even Greflinger was as silent as the tomb. Perhaps some of their own verse, sleepy as it might make others, would wake its authors.

All this made sense to Dach. But when Rist and Moscherosch asked leave to open the session with a manifesto that the two of them, assisted by Hofmannswaldau and Harsdörffer, had sat up drafting until late into the night and reworked in the morning — an appeal for peace to be addressed by the poets of Germany to their princes — the Königsberg magister feared for the cohesion of his literary family. "Later, friends!" he cried. "Later! First let us feed Master Schütz with our ink-stained labors. Politics is the gout-racked spouse of peace. She won't run away from us."

By then we were sitting in our usual places in the great hall. From outside we could hear, farther away than the day before, the mules tethered in the Emshagen wilderness. Someone (Logau?) asked where Stoffel was. Gerhardt kept silent. Not until Harsdörffer repeated the question did the landlady provide information: The regimental secretary had been called to Münster on pressing business. At the crack of dawn.

Libuschka had recovered her spirits. Light of foot, she was everywhere at once, now with curled hair. She had not spared the face paint. Her maids carried a comfortable easy chair with wide armrests into the semicircle. In the light from the window to one side of him, Heinrich Schütz sat as though upraised, presenting his careworn brow to the assembly.

Chapter 11

It was still early morning when the second day of reading began. An ornament had now been placed beside the still-empty reader's stool: a tall thistle, dug from the landlady's garden and planted in an earthenware pot. Thus isolated and taken as a thing apart, the thistle was beautiful.

Without allusion to this "symbol of war-ravaged times," Dach proceeded to the order of the day. He had no sooner settled, with an air of old, established routine, in his chair facing the semicircle, than he called on the youngsters — Birken Scheffler Greflinger — to read successively from the stool at his side (now placed next to the thistle).

Sigmund Birken, a wartime child of Bohemian extraction, had fled to Nuremberg; welcomed by Harsdörffer, Klaj, and their group of Pegnitz Shepherds, he had met with idyllic support and encouragement in patrician homes and, as borne out by his reading of the previous day, had early given evidence of theoretical zeal. Under the name of Floridan in the Pegnitz Shepherds and known to Zesen's German-minded Association as The Sweet-smelling One, he had been applauded for his hymns, his prose and verse idylls, and his allegorical plays. Because of the enthusiastic reception given some years later to his Nuremberg production of a pageant entitled *The Departure of War and the Entrance of Peace into Germany* before a military audience, he was shortly thereafter ennobled by the emperor and received into the Order of the Palm Tree under the name of The Well-grown. Everywhere, at home and on his travels, he kept a succinct diary, for which reason his belongings, when he lodged in the attic straw of the Bridge Tavern, included a "Journal" ornamented with a flower-tendril design.

Birken the sound painter, for whom everything became sound and form and who, in keeping with the most modern sensibility, gave nothing its name but transposed everything into images, read a few painstakingly wrought, here bulging, there narrowing, figure poems in cross and heart shape, which were beautiful in appearance but called forth no applause from the company, because the form did not come out in the reading. More enthusiasm was aroused by a poem that, in playful words, made Peace and Justice exchange kisses: "...the sweetest kisses are sweeter than sweet...."

What Harsdörffer and Zesen (the one learnedly, the other with high-flown interpretations) praised as epoch-making innovation gave Buchner occasion for long-winded misgivings, permitted Moscherosch to parody the poet's whole manner but most particularly the rhyme "sweating-fretting" in the heart-shaped poem, and almost made Rist jump out of his clerical skin. A good thing, he cried, that poor Opitz had been spared this "Zesenized Birkenry."

The "gracefully tumbling" words had appealed to old Weckherlin. Logau, as usual, expressed himself tersely. Where meaning was absent, he said, why shouldn't singsong and dingdong exchange compliments?

Next Johann Scheffler, who was soon to become a physician and later on, as a priest (under the name of Angelus Silesius), was to promote the Jesuit Counter-Reformation, sat beside the thistle. At first hesitating and muddling his words, then more composed, fortified no doubt by Czepko's "Chin up, student!," he read an early version of his hymn "Thee will I love, my strength, my tower," which came later on to be sung by all denominations. Then he recited a few epigrams that ten years later were to make their way in their definitive form under the title *Der cherubinische Wandersmann* (*The Cherubinic Wanderer*) but for the present puzzled the assembly, because no one, with the possible exception of Czepko and Logau, could make anything of lines such as "I know God cannot live an instant without me," not to mention "When God lay hid in womb of maiden chaste, The circle then was by the point embraced."

Gerhardt jumped up as though stung by a wasp: Another Silesian will-o'-the-wisp! That accursed shoemaker* still speaking out of the mouths of his pupils. Hocus-pocus and mystical rubbish! And he warned the gathering against the false glitter of God-abusing paradox.

As a pastor of the Wedel congregation, Rist felt called upon to agree, in a voice as though from the pulpit with everything Gerhardt had said. But he refrained from putting it more plainly, since he suspected Papist poison hidden in the rubbish.

To the surprise of all, the Lutheran Gryphius put in a word for Scheffler. Alien as it was to him, he declared, the charm of this miraculously self-contained order was balm to his soul.

The next to read was Georg Greflinger, the object of Dach's paternal favor and solicitude, a tall, broad-shouldered young fellow whom the war had driven as a child from a sheep pasture to Re-

---

*The Silesian mystic Jakob Böhme (1575–1624). —*Trans.*

gensburg, later forcing him into the Swedish service and making him so restless that he was constantly traveling between Vienna and Paris, Frankfurt, Nuremberg, and the Baltic towns, everywhere entangling himself in one love affair after another. Only recently his longest engagement had been cast aside by the daughter of a Danzig artisan, who had thus become the faithless Flora of his poems. Not until the following year was he to marry in Hamburg, settle down, and embark on a profitable business career, for concurrently with devoting four thousand alexandrines to the history of the Thirty Years' War, he opened a news agency and, beginning in the late fifties, published a weekly newspaper, the *Nordische Mercur.* Wholly concerned with earthly matters, Greflinger recited two bawdy ditties, the one wittily praising infidelity — "When Flora was jealous" — the other rollicking — "Hylas doesn't want a wife" — and both well suited to being read out loud. While the young man, parodying himself and his military bearing, was still declaiming his jests, the assembly was seized with merriment. The lines "No one girl is enough for me, Whoring, whoring, whoring is my life" were followed by modest laughter. The restraint was all for the benefit of Schütz. Though Dach and Albert were both amused, they did not contradict Gerhardt when, in the ensuing discussion period, he took exception to the praise meted out by Moscherosch and Weckherlin. Such doggerel, he said, was only fit for the gutter. Were they trying to bring down God's wrath on the heads of the assembly?

Heinrich Schütz sat silent.

Then came a disturbance, for the landlady's three maids, who (with Dach's permission) had been listening at the back of the hall, started giggling over Greflinger's bawdy songs, couldn't stop, tried desperately to hold it in, sputtered, tittered, whimpered internally, screamed as though frantic, and all so infectiously that the gathering was carried away by Marthe Elsabe Marie. Harsdörffer laughed so hard that he swallowed the wrong way and his publisher had to slap him on the back. Even from the impassive Schütz the three-part offering wrung a smile. Emanating from Lauremberg, the news was spread about by Schneuber that the giggling Marie had wet both her legs. More laughter. (I saw Scheffler blush.) Only the pious Gerhardt found his judgment confirmed. "What did I tell you? Fit only for the gutter! The stinking gutter!"

Then, after sending the maids into the kitchen with a glance backed up by a gesture, Simon Dach called on Andreas Gryphius to read from his tragedy *Leo Armenius*. (And under his breath he asked Schütz to forgive the assemblage for their childish foolery.)

The moment Gryphius took his seat, the company fell silent. At first he stared at the roof beams. Then in a powerful voice Gryf — as Hofmannswaldau, the systematically antagonistic friend of his youth, called him — launched into his introductory remarks: "At a time when our fatherland lies buried beneath its ashes, transformed into a theater of vanity, I have been at pains, in the present tragedy, to set before us the transience of human affairs...." He then announced that his *Leo Armenius* was to be dedicated to his gracious patron the merchant Wilhelm Schlegel, there present, because he had written the play while traveling with Schlegel and could not have done so without his encouragement. Next he briefly outlined the plot, named Constantinople as the scene of General Michael Balbus's conspiracy against the Emperor Leo Armenius, and assured the assembled semicircle that it took more than the rabid overturning of the old order to create a new one.

Only then did Gryphius, giving weight to every word but evidently going on for several manuscript pages too many — quite a few members of the audience, and not only the youngsters but Weckherlin and Lauremberg as well, fell asleep — read the expository passage beginning with Balbus's conspiratorial harangue: "The blood that you have risked for throne and crown" interspersed with the cries of the conspirators, "His deeds upon his head! The day is dawning," and ending with Crambe's oath: "Your sword. We vow To turn the prince's awesome power to lightest dust...."

He continued with the arrest scene, larded with exclamations such as "Heaven help us! What is this!" — which the bound general concludes with the scornful words, "Stood I in flaming brimstone, yet would I proclaim: This is the meed of virtue, this the hero's thanks...."

As an intermezzo Gryphius read the courtiers' strictly constructed three-part statement of the benefits and dangers of the human tongue, the first member or thesis being "Man's very life depends upon his tongue," followed by the antithesis, "Man's death depends on the tongue of every man," while the choral edifice is completed by the third member: "Thy life, O man, and death depend upon thy tongue...."

After the much too verbosely dragged-out trial scene — "Take him to prison; keep an eye on door and locks" — and the Emperor Leo's impassioned monologue passing sentence on the conspirator — "On all the round of earth no drama is so great As when who plays with fire to ashes is reduced" — Gryphius proceeded at long last to the final scene, if not of the play, then at least of his reading.

The dialogue between the Emperor Leo and the Empress Theodosia made a fit ending, for thanks to the empress's eloquent plea that Balbus should not go to the stake until after the holy feast of the Nativity — "Justice has taken its course, let it be mercy's turn" — she succeeds in softening the emperor's grim resolve — "Heaven will bless the head that punishes grim vice" — just a little. "Oh, do not execute stern judgment on the feast day. To God and me, I know, you'll not deny such favor."

Gryphius, who had plenty of breath in reserve and whose mighty voice still filled the hall, would gladly have carried on with the Chorus of Courtiers — "O everlasting vanity, thou mover of all things" — but Dach (with a hand on the reader's shoulder) bade him let well enough alone. The listeners, he said, had heard enough to form an ample picture. He, at all events, felt as though buried beneath an avalanche of words.

Again the assembly sat silent. The light that had piled up outside seeped in through the open windows. Czepko, seated to one side, was watching a butterfly. So much summer after such somber scenes.

Old Weckherlin, who had been awakened from his slumbers by the lively argument and counterargument of the last scene, was first to ask for the floor. Only a misunderstanding could have made him so bold. He praised the author and the end of his play. How gratifying that order should have been maintained and that attempted crime should have met with royal mercy. He hoped that in like manner God would come to the help of poor England, where Cromwell was conducting himself like Balbus in the play. One could not help worrying day and night about the king's safety.

The order-loving secretary of state was rudely corrected by Magister Buchner. The lines they had heard, said Buchner, must make the coming catastrophe clear to all; Gryphius's tragedy was great, and unique in Germany, because it did not in the traditional manner assign guilt one-sidedly, but on every side deplored man's frailty and weakness, his vain attempts to do good, since present tyranny was always superseded by new tyranny. Buchner had special praise for the three-part tongue metaphor spoken by the Chorus of Courtiers and called attention to its learned emblematization of the long-tongued purple snail, already mentioned by Aristotle. Then, however, the magister, as though acquitting himself of a duty, expressed mild misgivings about some of the rhymes.

Harsdörffer, speaking as a patriot, criticized the foreign subject matter of the play. It was incumbent, he declared, upon an author with such command of the language as Gryphius had to lend his word-compelling powers to German tragedy, and to it alone.

The scene of action was of no account, said Logau, only the making mattered. And that he must condemn. Such was the welter of words that they drowned in a purple broth, or stabbed one another to death, though the author's intent was manifestly to indict the royal purple and condemn the eternal warfare of the princes. Gryphius's reason advocated order, but his logorrhea wallowed in insurrection.

Partly to state his opinion, but still more in defense of his friend, Hofmannswaldau observed: Yes, Gryf was like that, in love with chaos; his words were in such conflict with one another that they were always turning gray misery to splendor and golden sunlight into darkest gloom; by the power of his words, he laid bare his weakness. But, then, if like Logau he were poorer in language, he could easily make three plays out of one scene.

True enough, Logau replied, he lacked Gryphius's palette, he didn't write with a brush.

Nor with a pen, Hofmannswaldau retorted. More with a stylus.

The contest of wits might have continued and entertained the company for some time, if not for Heinrich Schütz, who suddenly stood up and spoke over the heads of the poets. Yes, he said, he had heard it all. Beginning with the poems, then the speech divided into scenes and apportioned according to roles. First, he would like to praise the clear and beautifully denuded verses of the young medical student, whose name had unfortunately escaped him. If, as he had just heard, the student's name was indeed Johann Scheffler, he would make a note of it. On first hearing, he thought he would be able to compose an eight-part a cappella antiphonal setting for the distich about the rose, or else perhaps for the epigram on essence and accident, which he read: "Become essential, man! When the world fails at last, Accident falls away But Essence, that stands fast." Such words had breath. And if it did not seem presumptuous, he would say that insight such as this was otherwise to be found only in the Holy Scriptures.

But now to the others. Unfortunately, young Birken's verses had passed him by; he would have to read them over; only another reading would show whether there was as much sense as sound in them. Further, he would not deny that, if nothing else, Master Greflinger's ribald songs, the like of which were known to him from his cousin Albert's collection of arias and at which, in view of all the sacrilege rampant throughout the fatherland, he could not take moral umbrage, had a quality conducive to the composition of madrigals. Few German poets, as he knew to his misfortune, mastered that art. How he envied Monteverdi, for whom Guarini had written the loveliest pieces, as had Marino. In the hope of being favored with such texts, he wished to encourage the young man to cultivate the German madrigal, as the late lamented Opitz had attempted to do. Such free-flowing verse, bound by no regular stanza form, could be merry, plaintive, argumentative, even playfully, wildly nonsensical, provided it had breath and left room for the music.

He regretted to say that he found no such room in the dramatic scenes he had heard. Highly as he esteemed the harsh earnestness of Master Gryphius's sonnets, staunchly as he seconded the author's castigation of the vanity of this world, and for all the enduring beauty he perceived in what had just been read, he, as a composer, could find no room among the many, all too many words. No room for a tranquil gesture to unfold. In such a crush no cry of grief could ring out or find an echo. True, everything was said as compactly as could be, but one sharp contour canceled out the next, and the outcome was an overcrowded void. For all the stormy onslaught of words, no movement resulted. To set such a drama to music, one would have to unleash a war of flies. Alas, alas! How fortunate Monteverdi had been to have Maestro Rinuccini at hand with tractable libretti. God bless any poet capable of providing him, Schütz, with a text as beautiful as Arianna's lament. Or something on the order of Tancredi's battle with Clorinda, set so ravishingly to music after the words of Tasso.

But that would be asking too much. He must content himself with less. When the fatherland was laid low, poetry could hardly be expected to flower.

These words were followed not so much by silence as by consternation. Gryphius sat as though thunderstruck. And I, too, felt the blow, as did many others. Gerhardt in particular was galled that only the will-o'-the-wispish Scheffler and the bawdy Greflinger should have been applauded. Already he was on his feet, prepared to attack. He was not at a loss for an answer. He knew what sort of music the word needed. He would show this friend of the Italians, this lover of all that was foreign, this Signor Henrico Sagittario. He would tell him in plain German. He wouldn't mince words....

But Gerhardt was not given leave just yet. Neither Rist nor Zesen, both of whom were perishing to answer, obtained permission. (Nor did I, full as I was of ready words.) Taking a sign from the landlady at the door as an excuse, Simon Dach adjourned the session. Before quarreling, he suggested, they should spoon up their noonday soup in peace.

While the gentlemen were rising from their chairs, Harsdörffer inquired whether Gelnhausen was back, for, so he said, he missed Stoffel.

Chapter 12

Tasty and fatless. The bacon rind had already done service the day before. A soup that sated but briefly, yet hoped to be long remembered. Barley grits seasoned with chervil. Accompanied by short rations of black bread. Not enough to fill the youngsters' bellies. Greflinger grumbled. Hofmannswaldau, who only the day before had been moved by the meager fare to praise the simple life, observed that simplicity could be overdone. Then he pushed his half-filled bowl over to young Birken. Spoon in soup, Gryphius stirred up thoughts that expanded Silesian hunger into cosmic hunger. Logau joked tersely and testily about the contemporary art of stretching soup. Czepko kept silence over his spoon. Others (Moscherosch, Weckherlin) had stayed away or (like Buchner) had gone to their rooms with their steaming bowls. (Later on, Schneuber circulated the rumor that he had seen one of the maids — Elsabe — following the magister with some extra food wrapped in a cloth.)

As for Schütz, he remained at the table plying his spoon while his cousin Albert entertained him with stories of better days. In the mid-thirties both men had enjoyed King Christian's favor at the court of Copenhagen. Sagittario was heard laughing.

When Harsdörffer, who had been chosen to say grace on this occasion, remarked that few words were needed, since the chervil soup must surely be taken as penance enough, Simon Dach reminded him that a war was still in progress, but, on the other hand, he and the merchant Schlegel and a few of the publishers were going to explore Telgte and would no doubt come back with something they could get their teeth into for supper.

Not even the rats, cried Lauremberg, were finding anything in Telgte. The town was gutted and boarded up, only a sprinkling of inhabitants were left. The gates were barely guarded, and the streets were deserted, except for stray dogs. He and Schneuber had gone there that morning, prepared to pay ready money for a couple of chickens. There was nothing left to cackle in Telgte.

Strange that the pious Gerhardt should have got so worked up. They should have made more careful preparations. Dach, who had done the inviting, should have made sure such strict necessities as bacon and beans were available; after all, he enjoyed his prince's favor. Couldn't a little something have been diverted from his Calvinist larder? He, Gerhardt, asked for no more than the basic needs of every Christian. And moreover, if a guest such as the Saxon court *Kapellmeister* deigned to visit with mere writers of strophic songs, he was entitled to expect better fare.

To this Dach replied: Yes, he deserved to be chided. But he would tolerate no aspersions on his prince's religion. Were the Brandenburg Edicts of Tolerance unknown to Gerhardt?

To them, said Gerhardt, he would not bow. (And much later, as deacon of the Church of St. Nicholas in Berlin, he was to demonstrate his sectarian zeal to the point of being relieved of his office.)

How fortunate that there was still plenty of Rhenish brown beer. Rist made conciliatory gestures. As a Wittenberg authority, Buchner called his former students to order. And when the landlady gave the company hope that Gelnhausen would bring something substantial back with him from Münster, the poets dropped the soup controversy and sank their teeth into phrases and sentences: easily satisfied word-ruminants, finding, if need be, satiety in self-quotation.

Though Schütz's criticism did not prevent Gryphius, however deeply distressed only a moment before, from brushing in the somber scenes of several new tragedies for the benefit of a quickly gathered group of listeners, Schütz's praise had made the Breslau student's manuscripts interesting to several publishers, and young Scheffler did not see how he could decline their offers. Endter of Nuremberg held out the lure of a position as medical officer in that town, and Elzevihr suggested the possibility of a return to Leiden for further study, for he could tell by listening to the student where he — like the young Gryphius in his time — had broadened his mind.

But Scheffler stood firm. He would have to ask counsel elsewhere. (And that no doubt is why I later saw him hurrying once again through the Ems Gate to Telgte, there to kneel, surrounded by the usual old women, before the wooden Pietà....)

Logau and Harsdörffer, at the other end of the long table, asked what had driven Gelnhausen to Münster so early in the morning, and landlady Libuschka spoke from behind her hand as though revealing a secret. Stoffel, she said, had been summoned to the imperial chancellery. Rebellion was not confined to the Weimar troops, and there had also been a mutiny among the Bavarians, who had made their separate peace with the Swedes. General Werth of the cavalry had gone over to the emperor and was trying to breathe new life into the war. His men were a merry crew — she knew them well. She had taken two officers from his regiments as husbands and bed companions, though not for very long. Libuschka then explained why she had given Wallenstein's regiments a wide berth and lost herself in anecdotes about harum-scarum campaigns, in the course of which it became known that three years before she had invaded Holstein with Gallas's troops and taken her cut at the pillage of Wedel — how fortunate that Rist was emoting somewhere else. Then she spoke of earlier times, how in her middle twenties, still in the bloom of her youth, in breeches and on horseback, she had served under Tilly and — at the Battle of Lutter — taken a Danish captain prisoner. He would surely, being a nobleman, have made her a countess if the changing fortunes of war had not....

It goes without saying that Libuschka had an audience. She knew more than many of the poets about the ups and downs of the contending powers. The course of the war, she said, was decided not by diplomacy, but by the problem of finding winter quarters.

Her stories made them forget Stoffel's mission. As long as she was talking, spreading herself with leaps of time over three decades, even old Weckherlin was eager to hear the Battle of Wimpfen, the Protestant disaster of his youth, described as seen from both banks of the Neckar, and the miracle that favored the Spaniards — the apparition of a white-clad Virgin Mary — accounted for. According to the landlady, a cloud created by exploding ammunition had blown over the battlefield and admitted of Catholic interpretations.

Only when Moscherosch and Rist took turns in reading the appeal of the poets to the princes, which they had drafted in collaboration with Harsdörffer and Hofmannswaldau, but which Dach had not wished them to read that morning, did the company lose interest in the landlady and become inflamed by the fatherland's distress. That, after all, was the reason for their meeting. To make themselves heard. They could at least muster words, if not regiments.

Because Rist was the first to read, the appeal began with a word of fear: "Germany, the most glorious empire in the world, is now bled white, devastated and despoiled. That is the truth. For nigh on thirty years God has visited cruel Mars, accursed war, that most frightful punishment and plague, upon unrepentant Germany for the monstrous wickedness of its innumerable sins. That is the truth! Today the hard-pressed fatherland, lying at its last gasp, yearns to be blessed once more with noblest peace. Wherefore at Telgte, which according to an old interpretation means 'young oak tree,' the poets here assembled have resolved to communicate their

views to the German and foreign princes and establish them as
the truth...."

Then Moscherosch listed the heads of the parties. First the emperor, then the electors were named in the old order (without
Bavaria, but including the Palatinate), with all the respect that
Hofmannswaldau's elegant pen had been able to formulate. Then
the foreign crowns were invoked, and immediately thereafter, the
whole lot of them, of whatever denomination, German, French,
and Swedish, were castigated, for the German rulers had opened
up the fatherland to foreign hordes, while the foreigners had chosen Germany as their battlefield, so that it now lay dismembered
and unrecognizable, all loyalty lost with the old order and all
beauty destroyed. The poets alone, so said the appeal, still knew
what deserved the name of German. With many "ardent sighs and
tears" they had knitted the German language as the last bond; they
were the other, the true Germany.

After that (again by Rist and Moscherosch) various demands
were lined up, including reinforcement of the Estates, retention by
the empire of Pomerania and Alsace, reinstatement of the Palatinate as an independent electorate, restoration of the elective kingdom of Bohemia, and — it goes without saying — religious freedom for all denominations, including the Calvinists. (The Strassburg contingent had made this a condition of their adherence.)

Though at first this manifesto — which was read loudly and emphatically, paragraph by paragraph — aroused enthusiasm, voices
were soon heard wishing its arrogance lessened, its demands
curtailed, and its practical implications clarified. As was to be
expected, Gerhardt took exception to the special mention of the
Calvinists. Buchner (now returned from his room) criticized (with
a glance at Schütz) the over-sharp condemnation of Saxony. Such
"scribbling," said Weckherlin, would neither move Maximilian to
take a single step against the Spaniards, nor spur the landgravine
of Hesse against the Swedes. As for the Palatinate, it was gone forever. Logau then declared, tongue in cheek, that once the French
cardinal received their epistle, he would abandon all spoils and
evacuate Alsace and Breisach forthwith, while one could fancy Oxenstierna, in response to so touchingly German an appeal, losing
all interest in Pomerania, including the island of Rügen.

At that Greflinger was fired to indignation. Why was the old slyboots so down on the Swedes? If the heroic Gustavus Adolphus hadn't shipped across the Baltic, even Hamburg would have become Papist. And if Saxony and Brandenburg hadn't time and again hung back like cowards, they might, in league with the Swedes, have advanced to the Danube and beyond. And if Wrangel's cavalry hadn't visited Bavaria the year before, his own hometown of Regensburg would have been closed to him forever.

The Swedes and no one else, cried Lauremberg, had thrown Wallenstein out of Mecklenburg. Hear! cried the Silesians; who, if not the Swedes, would defend them against Rome? For all the hardship of the occupation, there was reason to be grateful. All attacks on the Swedish crown would have to be deleted. Intimidated, young Scheffler sat silent. When Schneuber argued that in that case the French must also be spared, because France had crucially weakened Spain, Zesen said what Rist had been wanting to say: then their document would not be a protest, but only a statement of the usual helplessness. No need to trumpet that. That's not what they had met for. So why were they sitting there?

Heinrich Schütz, who had attended the debate as though absent, answered the question: For the sake of the written words, which poets alone had the power to write in accordance with the dictates of art. And also to wrest from helplessness — he knew it well — a faint "and yet."

With that we could agree. Quickly, as though to take advantage of the brief moment of peace, Simon Dach said that he liked the text, even if it could not be used; that Master Schütz, ordinarily so severe, had only said mildly what everyone knew — that poets were without power, except to write true if useless words. Let them, he recommended, sleep on the appeal; overnight, perhaps, they would arrive at a more propitious version. Then he called the assembly into the great hall for a new disputation. For there, he announced, Gerhardt would at last reply to the world-famous guest.

Chapter 13

The chervil soup with barley grits may have appeased previously envenomed spirits, or perhaps the appeal to the princes had drained the poets; they sat listlessly in the semicircle as Gerhardt, in a tone of moderation, delivered his speech against the Dresden *Kapellmeister.*

Heinrich Schütz's opinion that German poetry was lacking in breath and clogged with verbiage, that the crush of words left no room for music to unfold with gentle or agitated gestures — this bad mark, with the explanatory gloss that the war had no doubt caused the garden of poetry to wither, remained in force, for, when called on by Dach, Gerhardt spoke in generalities. The guest, he said, looked at everything from the vantage point of his high art; in taking so lofty a view, he lost sight of the simple word, which should serve God before it bowed to art. Wherefore true faith demanded songs that would stand as a barrier to all temptation. Such songs were made for plain people, the congregation should be able to sing them without difficulty. They should, to be precise, have many stanzas, so that from stanza to stanza the singing Christian might soar above his weakness, fortify his faith, and find consolation in evil times. Schütz, said Gerhardt, had scorned to provide poor sinners with the kind of hymns they needed. Even Becker's *Psalter,* as he had heard said in many places, was too convoluted for the church congregations. He, Gerhardt, therefore preferred to lean on his friend Johann Cröger, who as a cantor knew how to work with strophic songs. For Cröger, art was not a lonely tower. He did not cherish the brilliant orchestras of the princes, but set store by the cares of the common man. Along with other, not necessarily world-famous, composers, he was quite content to serve the daily needs of the Christian congregations and compose music for such strophic hymns as the too-soon-departed Fleming's "I leave to his good pleasure," or the revered Johann Rist's "O Ewigkeit, du Donnerwort" ("Eternity, thou word of fear"), or our amiable Simon Dach's "Oh, how blessed are ye saints together," or the recently abused but truly eloquent Gryphius's "The glory of this earth must turn to dust and ashes," or the stanzas that he, Gerhardt, had written in utter devotion to the Lord: "Awake, my heart, and sing," or the more recent "O world behold thy life, upon the Cross doth hang," or "Now all give thanks and praise," or what he had written right here in his room at Telgte: "Thank God, it hath resounded, the blessed voice of joy and peace, Murders reign is bounded, and spear and sword at last may cease...."

Like a good Saxon, Gerhardt recited every one of the six stanzas, the fourth of which — "and strew fresh seed upon the once so verdant fields, now turned to thicket or parched and barren heath" — found simple words for the state of the fatherland. The assembly was grateful to him. Rist humbly thanked him. Once again young Scheffler was in tears. Gryphius stood up, went over to Gerhardt, and grandly threw his arms around him. After that the general mood was one of thoughtfulness. Schütz sat as though under a bell jar. Albert a prey to inner distress. Dach blew his nose loudly, several times.

Then, speaking into the once more erupting silence, Logau said he wished only to observe that pious hymns, such as those diligently penned for the churches by many here present, were no fit subject for literary discussion. A very different matter, in his opinion, was the high art of Master Schütz, which could not concern itself with the common strophic hymn, because its towering eminence placed it beyond the daily needs of the common man, and yet, though over the heads of the congregations, it redounded solely to the praise of God. Furthermore, said Logau, what Master Schütz had said about the breathless language of the German poets warranted careful consideration. He, in any event, thanked the composer for his lesson.

Czepko and Hofmannswaldau voiced their agreement, Rist and again Gerhardt wished to express a contrary opinion, Gryphius threatened violent eruption, and Buchner, after overlong silence, was pregnant with a long speech. A dispute might well have arisen, especially since Dach seemed irresolute, as though considering himself defenseless before the threatened upsurge of eloquence; but then, unexpectedly (and without being asked), Schütz spoke again.

Seated, he spoke softly, apologizing for having been the occasion of so much misunderstanding. Only his excessive desire for dispassionate yet moving texts had been to blame. He therefore felt obliged to explain once again what sort of language could serve as a handmaiden to music.

Only then did he stand up and, illustrating his thought with the example of his Passion music *The Seven Words on the Cross,* explained what he as a musician demanded of a text — what sustained measures it must admit of, what heightening leave room for. How the gesture implicit in the word must expand in song. To what ecstatic heights words of deep sorrow might rise. Finally, with his still mellifluous old man's voice, he sang the passage about Mary and the apostle: "Woman, woman, behold thy son...John, John, behold thy mother...." Then he sat down again and, seated, once more startling the assembly, proclaimed, first in Latin — *"Ut sol inter planetas..."* — and then in German, the motto of Henrico Sagittario: "As the sun amidst the planets, so let music shine amidst the liberal arts."

Still pleased (or horrified) at the moving song, Dach had not noticed, or had pretended not to notice, this new display of arrogance. In any event, he called for more readings without transition: first Zesen, then Harsdörffer and Logau, and last, Johann Rist. Those called were successively willing. Only Rist warned his listeners that he would be obliged to read from a bungled first draft. Each reading was followed by pertinent discussion, which stuck close to the text and no longer, except for the usual excursions into morality, lost itself in theoretical mazes. Sometimes one, sometimes another left the room, either to pass water, or to run into Telgte, or to throw dice with the remaining musketeers in the sunshine outside the stable. (When Weckherlin brought in a complaint next day that money had been stolen from his room, Greflinger was suspected at first, because Schneuber had seen him playing dice.)

Philipp Zesen — The Well-phrasing One, as he was named the following year as a new and soon-to-be-ennobled member of the Fruit-bearing Society — that restless, high-strung, truly youthful man, forever anticipating his innovations with explanatory verbiage, and at all times consumed by several internal fires that stole one another's air, spoke at first chaotically, neglecting to name the subject — corpses drifting in the Ems — of the "terrifying image" that would have to be incorporated into his script if love was to find its appropriate conclusion. Then he collected himself on the stool beside the thistle and read from a pastoral novel already published in Holland, in which a young German by the name of Markhold courts the Venetian Rosemunde in vain, because he, a

Lutheran, cannot marry a Catholic unless he promises to have any prospective daughters brought up within the church.

This conflict, which had considerable actuality and still more future, held the company's interest, though the book was known to most of those present, and Zesen's newfangled spelling had already provoked several hostile pamphlets (and first of all a polemic by Rist).

Though Harsdörffer and Birken defended the innovator and intrepid word-builder and Hofmannswaldau praised the gallant flow of the narrative, nevertheless the Adriatic Rosemunde's swoons, her frequent "unwellness" — "Her half-open eyes, her bloodless lips, her silenced tongue, her pallid cheeks, her livid, motionless hands" — provoked disturbing laughter from Rist and others (Lauremberg and Moscherosch) during the reading, and joyous parodies during the discussion period.

Zesen looked as though he were being whipped. He scarcely heard Logau cry out: "You can't deny his courage!" When Buchner finally attempted to check his former student's emotional overflow with cool, authoritative, Opitz-involving discourse, Zesen took refuge in a violent nosebleed. How much of it the gaunt man had. It spurted over his round white collar. It dripped into his still-open book. Dach broke off the discussion. Someone (Czepko or the publisher Elzevihr) helped Zesen to the back of the room and made him lie down on the cool floor, where the bleeding soon stopped.

By then Harsdörffer was sitting beside the thistle: The Playful One, as he was known in the Fruit-bearing Society. An always relaxed, self-assured gentleman with a feeling for novelty, who saw himself more as a learned mentor to talented young men and — exclusively in the interest of Nuremberg — as a patrician statesman, then as an inspired poet. Thus, to the general satisfaction, he read some of his riddles, and the company found entertainment in trying to solve them. By turns a featherbed, a man's shadow, an icicle, the malignant and succulent crab,* and, finally, a dead child in the womb were artfully concealed within a quatrain. Harsdörffer's jocose delivery somewhat diminished the effect.

After much praise, in which Gryphius joined, Birken inquired cautiously, as though asking his mentor for advice, whether it was

---

*German *Krebs* = both "cancer" and "crab." — *Trans.*

seemly to couch a child that had died in the womb in so light-footed a verse form.

After qualifying Birken's question as nonsense, citing and then confuting criticisms from Rist and Gerhardt which had not even been uttered, Buchner, magister of letters, declared that a riddle had just as much right to be cheerful as to be pregnant with a tragic solution; of course, he added, this laconic construct could claim to be nothing more than a minor art form, but it was quite appropriate to the Pegnitz Shepherds.

By then the country nobleman who, though impoverished, had nevertheless found security as administrator of the Duke of Brieg's properties had taken his place on the stool and, by spitting two of his three hand-sized sheets of paper on its thorns, given the plant a collateral, ironic meaning. The Belittler was his title in the Fruit-bearing Society. And Logau spoke with his trusted succinctness. Sarcastically and too irreverently for some of the listeners' taste, he said more in two lines than a long dissertation could have unsaid. About the religions, for instance: "Lutheran, Papist, Calvinist — these faiths exist all three. But who can tell us just what is Christianity?" Or in view of the coming peace: "When peace is made amid such devastation, Hangmen and jurisconsults will dominate the nation."

After two poems of some length, one being the monologue of a wartime dog, Logau concluded with a couplet dealing with feminine fashion, which he wished expressly to dedicate to land-lady Libuschka's maids: "Womenfolk are so confiding, Wear their dresses cut so low, That the rolling hills give tiding Of the sultry warmth below."

After Hofmannswaldau and Weckherlin, even Gryphius showed approval. As did Buchner by his silence. Someone thought he had detected a smile on Schütz's face. Rist publicly contemplated trying the couplet about the religions on his Wedel congregation when next he addressed them from the pulpit. When — the others had a good idea why — the pious Gerhardt raised his hand, Dach overlooked it and answered the overlooked would-be questioner by saying that if anyone were to take umbrage at Logau's outspokenness, he would shut him up that night with the three maids, for he knew of certain gentlemen who had descended from the hills to the lowlands in their company.

While the poets cast mocking glances at one another, while Greflinger whistled a tune, while Birken smiled with moist lips, Schneuber waxed offensive under his breath, and Lauremberg inquired what had become of young Scheffler. Buchner said: Oh, well, haste was in order. With time so short, only brief subsidiary action was possible.

Meanwhile, amid laughter, the "Elbe Swan" had occupied the stool between Dach and the thistle. Such was the name sometimes given to Johann Rist, by way of allusion to Opitz, the "Bober Swan," by the friends with whom Rist, as a member of the Fruit-bearing Society, in which he was known as The Valiant One, corresponded. Everything about Rist was imposing, his resounding parsonical word flow, his chamberlainlike entrances, his homespun marshland humor, his gigantic frame always clad in the best broadcloth, his beard, his firm, substantial nose, and even, what with his crafty way of narrowing his left eye, his watery gaze. He had an opinion about everything. Nothing escaped him uncontradicted. Though he wasted his strength in feuds (not only with Zesen), he was nevertheless an industrious writer. Irresolutely at first, he now began to rummage through his papers; then finally he gave himself a jolt and was ready.

Rist informed his audience that, by way of anticipating the peace treaty that was still being negotiated amid the din of battle, he had begun to write a dramatic work to be entitled *Germany Jubilant over the Peace*. In it, a female figure would appear as Truth. "For Truth must proclaim or announce to you certain things that will be dear to the hearts of many, but to many may possibly bring no little sorrow. Therefore, ye Germans, give ear!"

He read a few scenes of the first interlude, in which a war-weary junker, talking with two peasants, deplores their moral depravity. The peasants, he explains, have been bled by the soldiery, and from the soldiery, they have learned the art of bleeding others. Just like the soldiers, they steal, loot, extort, drink, and whore. Consequently, they dread the coming of peace, which may well mean the end of their dissolute life. When in response the peasants Drewes Kikintlag and Beneke Dudeldey praise their merry life as highwaymen and drunkards in pithy Low German — "What's the war to us? Let 'em fight, let 'em bleed, as long as there's plenty to drink at our hostler Peter Langwamme's house" — the nobleman waxes indignant in stilted chancellery German: "May God have mercy, what is this I hear? Would you wretches rather suffer the brutal pressures of war than live in concord, peace, and tranquillity under your lawful authorities?" But the peasants prefer the chaotic wartime conditions to the extortionate taxes they can look forward to once peace breaks out. They fear the old order and its return, disguised as a new order. The war levies imposed by one army or another are not nearly so hard to bear as the future burden of taxation.

Rist read the short scene in which, as though reversing their roles, the officer praises peace while the peasants want to prolong the war, with the skill of an actor holding first one, then another mask over his face. Too bad that only a few could follow the Holstein dialect. After his reading, the author had to translate the pithiest bits for Moscherosch, Harsdörffer, Weckherlin, and the Silesians, and, losing their flavor in the process, they became as flat as the junker's speeches. Consequently, the discussion revolved not so much around the scene from Rist's peace play, as around the general decline of morality.

Everyone knew of dreadful examples: How when Breisach was besieged, homeless children were butchered and eaten. How in places where order had been put to flight, the mob set themselves up as masters. How the most flea-bitten yokels swaggered about in city finery. And everyone knew of highwaymen in Franconia, in Brandenburg, behind every bush. For the tenth time, Schneuber complained of how he had been robbed on his way from Strassburg with Moscherosch. There was talk of evildoers, some already hanged and others still running around loose. Harsh words were devoted to the Swedes and their ruthless foraging expeditions. But while numerous Silesian voices were still chronicling and multiplying gruesome details (the Swedish drink, charred feet), the regimental secretary suddenly (I had been hearing noise — the barking of the tavern mongrels — outside for some time) burst into the room.

Still in his green doublet, still with a feather in his hat, he leapt into the midst of the gentlemen, saluted in the imperial manner, and proclaimed the end of the barley-soup era: no more short rations, for five geese, three suckling pigs, and a fat sheep had come his way. In his passage he had been showered with sausages. If the gentlemen didn't believe him, he declared, they could see all that for themselves. Already his men could be seen turning spits in the courtyard. There would be a feast to which the assembled poets need only contribute Lucullean double rhymes, Epicurean iambi, Bacchanalian epigrams, Dionysian dactyls, and words of Platonic wisdom. For even if it was too soon to celebrate the peace, they could at least celebrate the fast gasps of the war. He therefore entreated them to go right out into the courtyard and marvel at the skill with which Stoffel, known from Bohemia to Breisgau, from the Spessart Mountains to the plains of Westphalia as Simplicius, had foraged for German poetry.

They did not go out at once. Dach insisted on order. It was still up to him, he said, whether or not to adjourn the session, and until such time he would countenance further argument and rebuttal. After all, they wouldn't want the Elbe Swan to have sung in vain.

And so for a short period of give and take we prolonged the discussion of Rist's scene and of the moral depravity that had swept the country. Gryphius suggested that if the scene were played before the dull, unthinking public, they would applaud the peasants rather than the junker. Moscherosch praised Rist for having the courage to dramatize the grievous state of the country. But — Czepko asked himself and others — were the peasants not right in fearing the return of the old order? Yes, cried Lauremberg, but what order could one wish for if not the good, old one?

For fear of giving the argument further fuel with an inquiry into the question of a new and possibly just order, and because the aroma of roast meat was already rising from the courtyard, Simon Dach signaled the increasingly restless gathering that the afternoon session was adjourned. Several poets — and not only the youngsters — hurried out into the open. Others took their time. The last to leave the great hall were Dach, Gerhardt, and Schütz, the last two engaged in quiet conversation, as though reconciled. Only the thistle, in its place beside the empty stool, remained behind. Outside, the goings-on were dithyrambic.

Chapter 14

The five geese were already lined up on one spit and the thrée suckling pigs on the second, while the sheep stuffed with sausages was turning on the third. The long table from the taproom had been moved up to the bushes bordering the outer arm of the Ems, so that it remained untouched by the smoke from the fires that were flaring in the middle of the courtyard. Landlady Libuschka and her maids rushed back and forth between house and courtyard, setting the table. Closer inspection revealed that the tablecloths had formerly done service on an altar. The plates, cups, mugs, and bowls seemed to belong in one of the many Westphalian moated castles. Apart from two-pronged serving forks, there was no other cutlery.

Blowing across the courtyard in the direction of the stable, the smoke veiled the alders that fringed the inner arm of the Ems and bordered the town, the gables of the Herrenstrasse, and off to one side the parish church. Gelnhausen's musketeers attended the roasting spits. Since they caught the fat dripping from the geese, pigs, and sheep in earthenware bowls, they were able to baste the roasts continually with goose, pork, and mutton fat. From the juniper bushes that covered the Emshagen as far as the fulling mill, the stableboy brought dry fagots, which from time to time made the fires smoke more abundantly. The town of Telgte lay flat-painted behind the animated picture into which the tavern dogs kept moving, sometimes singly, sometimes gathered into a pack. (Later they fought over the bones.)

Meanwhile Gelnhausen's horsemen were busy driving stakes into the ground, on which to stretch patterned canvas — that might have been taken from the tent of a Hessian colonel — over the laid table like a canopy. Garlands were plaited of fresh foliage, and wild roses from the landlady's garden woven into them. Soon garlands were affixed to the stakes of the canopy. The fringes around its edges were twisted into tassels, on which hung bells that later, when a breeze came up, contributed to the festive mood.

Although it was still day and the dusk was taking its time in failing, Gelnhausen brought five heavy silver candlesticks of ecclesiastical origin, still fitted with almost unused candies, from the covered wagon that had been harnessed that morning and had brought the geese and pigs and sheep, altar cloths and canopy.

Stoffel then placed the three-armed silver pieces on the table. After several attempts to position them informally, he adopted a military stance as though lining up a company. Off to one side in groups, the poets saw all that; and I kept the record.

When under Gelnhausen's supervision a figure the size of a small boy, cast in bronze and representing Apollo, was brought from the inexhaustible covered wagon, when finally this work of art was placed in the middle of the table (after the candlesticks had once again been moved), Simon Dach felt obliged to do something more than stand dumbfounded, admiring the display with mounting trepidation. Taking aside first the landlady, then Gelnhausen, he asked where and by what right these treasures had been seized, how paid for, or with whose permission borrowed. So much miscellaneous richness — meat linen metal — did not, he said, fall from the trees.

Yes, said Gelnhausen, all that was true, and he also had to admit that the geese, pigs, and sheep came from Catholic houses, but the whole transaction could only be regarded as honorable, for on the occasion of his necessarily secret visit to Münster — and there were incidentals that he was still unable to divulge — several of the delegates to the peace conference had spoken with enthusiasm of the meeting of German poets, which had been bruited about by then. Monsignor Chigi, the papal nuncio, had commissioned him to ask Harsdörffer to write a personal dedication into his, Chigi's, copy of the *Conversation Plays for Women*, a first edition dated 1641, which he carried with him at all times. Venetian Ambassador Contarini sent greetings to Maestro Sagittario, who was still remembered at St. Mark's, and took the liberty of informing him once again that Master Schütz's return to Venice would at any time call forth not one but many ovations. The Marquis de Sable had immediately sent a courier to Cardinal Mazarin with the news of the poets' gathering, and would have his palace put in order if the company would do him the honor. Only the Swedish ambassador, newly arrived from Osnabrück, had made eyes like a calf in a thunderstorm on hearing the world-famous names, which were Greek to him, even though the great Oxenstierna was his father. But Count Johann von Nassau, who had been representing the emperor at the conference since Trauttmannsdorff's departure, had been all the more cordial and had hastened to bid Isaak Volmar, a high official at the imperial chancellery, to provide for the well-being of the poets who had traveled so far, and make certain they did not lack for sustenance, refreshment, or loving gifts. And here, sure enough, was a gold ring for Herr Dach, here finely wrought silver cups, and here, and here.... Whereupon Volmar, equipped with written instructions concerning the forthcoming banquet, had turned Gelnhausen's knowledge of the country to account. He, Gelnhausen, had hurried hither and thither. For indeed he knew Westphalia like the back of his hand. As the once famous huntsman of Soest, he had familiarized himself with every nook and cranny in the triangle formed by Dorsten, Lippstadt, and Coesfeld. Münster itself had been unable to offer much; everything went to the embassies. But the surrounding countryside still had resources. In short: as an imperial agent acting on instructions from Count von Nassau, he had had little difficulty in carrying out the order, for one thing because the region was more Catholic than the Pope ever meant it to be. There was plenty of everything. Only game would be wanting. Would Herr Dach care to see the list? Every single item checked off — wine, cheese, and so on. Was Master Dach displeased?

At first Dach had listened to the report (rounded out with anecdotes about the doings in Münster and adorned with here uncited subordinate clauses invoking members of the ancient pantheon as witnesses) by himself, then accompanied by Logau, Harsdörffer, Rist, and Hofmannswaldau, and finally surrounded by us all. He had listened at first with distrust, then with increasing wonderment, and at the end feeling somewhat flattered. He toyed with the gold ring, which embarrassed him. The silver cups passed from hand to hand. Though Logau (from old habit) might make a barbed remark or two, though there might seem to be a bit of exaggeration in the report, the company were not loath to accept greetings and commendations from persons so highly placed. And when Gelnhausen produced from his courier's bag a copy of the *Conversation Plays for Women* — true enough, a first edition, dated 1641! — the *ex libris* of which identified the owner as Fabio Chigi, the papal nuncio (later Pope Alexander VII), held out the book, and smilingly asked Harsdörffer to write in a dedication at his convenience, everyone was convinced that there could be nothing dishonorable about the forthcoming banquet; even Logau was mute.

Residual doubts — could they as good Lutherans accept these popish gifts? — were dispelled by Dach, who reminded Gryphius, and finally Rist and Gerhardt as well, of the revered Opitz's willingness to serve the Catholic cause, of how as an irenicist in the tradition of the learned Grotius and as a student of the late Lingelsheim, the Bober Swan had at all times advocated freedom of religion and opposed all exclusivity. Ah, if only the peace proved such that Lutherans would dine at one table with Catholics and Catholics with Lutherans and Calvinists. As for himself, in any event, even a Catholic suckling pig made his mouth water.

And then the landlady called out that the meat was ready to carve.

Chapter 15

At last! cried Greflinger, shaking his black curls, which tumbled over his shoulders. Rist and Lauremberg felt certain of having deserved this roast meat. But Czepko and Logau had misgivings: what if the Devil had kindled the three cooking fires? Birken was determined to do justice to what he had so long gone without. And he promised the silent Scheffler, whose eyes were on the maids, that he would. With wolfish hunger Moscherosch thrust himself between Harsdörffer and his publisher. When Gryphius boasted of his spacious stomach, Hofmannswaldau reminded him of the transience of the palate's joys. Schneuber's arse was still so sore that even in the presence of such gastronomic delights he found it hard to sit down. Old Weckherlin thought he had better wrap a goose breast in his handkerchief as a provision for hungry times ahead, and he advised Gerhardt to do the same. Looking past Zesen, who was staring spellbound at the cooking fires, Gerhardt threatened to impose moderation on the company when he said grace. But Dach, who had his Albert beside him, said that on this occasion young Birken would pray aloud for all. Albert cast a searching look around him and asked a question of the merchant Schlegel, who passed it on to the publisher Mülbe by way of Elzevihr, but by the time the question had reached Buchner, it had answered itself: Schütz was absent from the table.

How do I know all this? I was sitting in their midst, I was there. It was no secret to me that landlady Libuschka had sent one of her maids to town to recruit wenches for the night. Who was I? Neither Logau nor Gelnhausen. Still others might have been invited— Neumark, for instance, but he stayed in Königsberg; or Tscherning, whose absence was especially deplored by Buchner. Whoever I may have been, I knew that the wine in the casks was sacramental. My ear picked up what the imperial musketeers called out to one another while carving the geese, the pigs, and the sheep. I had seen Schütz — as soon as he had entered the courtyard, caught sight of the preparations, and listened for a moment to Gelnhausen — go back into the house and climb the stairs to his room. I even knew what no one else did, that while the banquet of the German poets was getting under way at the Bridge Tavern in Telgte, the Bavarian delegates in Münster were pledging Alsace to France and obtaining the Palatinate (plus a promise of the electoral dignity) in return. Wretched horse trading! I could have cried, but I laughed, because I was privileged to be there, to be present while under the Hessian canopy, in the gathering dusk, the candles in the Catholic candlestick were lighted and we clasped our hands. For now Birken, who was sitting next to Scheffler, stood up, half concealed from me by the child-size Apollo but equally beautiful, to pronounce an out-and-out Protestant grace: "May Lord Jesus set us free, In the world the world to flee...." Then, standing in his place halfway down the table, the outer Ems behind him and before him the town, darkened against the sky — Dach spoke again to them all, though the carved meat was already steaming in the seignorial porcelain. Possibly because Birken's grace had been too somber and unworldly— "Let us, while we are living, mortify our flesh" — Dach, whose Christianity was of a more practical nature, wished to provide earthly encouragement. If even the spirit did not live by the spirit alone, it was fitting, he said, that a proper morsel should fall to the lot of poor poets, those forever hungry onlookers. Consequently, he would not trouble Gelnhausen — to whom thanks — with further questions about the whence, but let well enough alone. And in the hope that God's blessing rested on everything that the table bore so superabundantly, he bade his friends do well by their far from spoiled palates. And might the present banquet provide an ample foretaste of the peace to come!

They fell to. With both hands. With elbows devoutly propped. With Silesian, Franconian, Elbian, Brandenburgian, Alemannic hunger. Similarly the horsemen, the musketeers, the tavern mongrels, the stableboy, the maids, and the town wenches. They attacked the geese, the pigs, and the sheep. Half of what the sheep had had inside it, the blood sausages and liver sausages, had been put on the table, while half had stayed with the cooks. Into the juice, which dripped from rounded beards, pointed beards, and twirled mustaches and stood fatty in the dishes, they dipped freshly baked white bread. How crisply the skin of the suckling pigs crackled. The juniper fagots had lent their savor to the meat, especially to the mutton.

Only the landlady and Gelnhausen kept moving restlessly back and forth. They continued to serve up the food — millet steamed in milk with raisins, bowls full of crystallized ginger, sweet pickles, plum butter, great jugs of red wine, dry goat cheese, and lastly the sheep's head, which had been prepared in the kitchen. Into the mouth Libuschka had wedged a large beet; she had encased the neck in a gentlemanly white collar, and with a crown of marsh marigolds transformed the head into a crowned sheep's head. As Courage carried it in, her queenly bearing gave further dignity to the head she was dishing up.

That admitted of jokes. The sheep's head demanded comparisons. Homage was paid to it in iambi and trochees, in trisyllabic feet, Buchnerian dactyls, and alexandrines, with metathesis, alliteration, internal rhymes, and nimble improvisations. Assuming the role of a betrayed sheep, Greflinger bewailed the loss of his faithless Flora; the others resorted to political allusions.

"Nor eagle proud nor lion, Adorns the German blazon, But the good submissive sheep" was Logau's contribution. Moscherosch made the emblematic beast of the Germans "converse in courtly Spanish wise." Gryphius, who was shoveling the food in as though determined to engulf the world, desisted from the forepaw of a piglet for the time it took to rhyme: "The sheep that bleats for peace forever Will get it from the butcher's cleaver."

Augustus Buchner, magister of letters, put up with hasty rhymes, pretended not to hear Zesen's "Three four seven eight eleven, All good sheep will go to heaven," and only remarked on how lucky it was that the stern Schütz had been spared such tidbits....In response to which the startled Dach desisted from the goose leg he had coated with plum butter, looked around at the likewise startled company, and asked his Albert to go quickly and see to their guest.

The cathedral organist found the old man in his room, lying coatless on his bed. Raising himself a little, Schütz said it was kind of them to notice his absence, but he would like to rest another little while. He had many new impressions to think over. The realization, for example, that cutting wit, such as Logau's, was not conducive to music. Yes indeed. He was ready to believe that a merry mood prevailed down there in the courtyard. The merriment rose up to his room polyphonically, making a mockery of thoughts such as this: if, as he believed, reason was prejudicial to music, if, in other words, the writing of music was at cross-purposes with the rational writing of words, how, then, was it possible that Logau should nevertheless, with cool, unclouded mind, achieve beauty? Cousin Albert might well be inclined to smile at such hairsplitting and call him a lawyer manqué. Ah, yes, if only he had persevered in his study of the law, before music had taken up all his attention. But his period of apprenticeship in Marburg had sharpened his wits, which still came in handy. Given a little time, he could see through the finest fabric of lies. Some little thread was always missing. Now take that ruffian Stoffel, who, to be sure, spun more amusingly than some of the visiting poets: the world of lies he concocted had a logic of its own. What? Was Cousin Albert still taken in? In that case he would not disturb his sweet simplicity. Yes, yes, he would be down after a while for a glass of something. Sooner or later. No need to worry. His cousin should just go and make merry.

Only when Albert was halfway through the door did Schütz speak briefly of his accumulated worries. He called his circumstances in Dresden wretched. On the one hand, he regarded his return to Weissenfels as desirable; on the other, he was in a hurry to go to Hamburg and beyond to Glückstadt. There he hoped to find a message from the Danish court, an invitation to Copenhagen: operas, ballets, sprightly madrigals....Lauremberg had given him hope. The crown prince was devoted to the arts. In any case he was carrying with him a printed score of the second part of the *Sinphoniae sacrae,* dedicated to the prince. Then Schütz lay down again but did not close his eyes.

In the courtyard the news that the Dresden *Kapellmeister* would come down for a while later on was received with relief. Partly because it was not vexation that was keeping the world-famous man away, and partly because the stern guest would still be absent for a time from the poets' merry-to-tumultuous board. We welcomed the prospect of being among ourselves for a while longer.

Greflinger and Schneuber had motioned the landlady's three maids over to the table as well as — with Gelnhausen's encouragement — a few of the wenches from Telgte. Elsabe was sitting on Moscherosch's lap. Someone, presumably old Weckherlin, had foisted two excessively low-cut women on the pious Gerhardt. The dainty and delicate Marie leaned on the student Scheffler with the familiarity of old acquaintance, and the young man was soon heaped with mockery. In which pursuit Lauremberg and Schneuber distinguished themselves. Was Marie substituting for the Blessed Virgin? Was he intending to become a Catholic by mating with her? And suchlike offensive remarks, until Greflinger gave them a piece of his Bavarian mind and showed his fists.

Elsewhere Rist, whose preacher's hand had been exploring one of the town wenches' topography, was insulted by Logau. The Belittler had only wanted to tell The Valiant One that his busy treasure hunting seemed to leave him no free hand for the wine jug. Whereupon Rist, gesticulating with both hands, had waxed loudly bellicose. Logau's wit, he declared, was corrosive because it lacked wholesome humor, and because it lacked wholesome humor it was no better than irony, and because it was ironical it was not German, and because it was not German, it was intrinsically "un-German and anti-German."

This gave rise to a new disputation, during which the maids and wenches were as good as forgotten. The argument over the essence of irony and of humor kept the company too busy to do anything but reach thirstily for the wine jugs. Soon Logau stood alone, for Zesen now joined Rist in denigrating, and in the most literal sense "damning," his belittling view of things, people, and conditions as alien, un-German, Gallic, and, in a word, ironic; for once in agreement, Rist and Zesen termed the usually two-line epigrams of the always insidious Logau mere works of the Devil. Why? Because irony is the work of the Devil. Why of the Devil? Because it's French and therefore diabolical.

Hofmannswaldau tried to put an end to this all too German quarrel, but his humor hardly served the purpose. Old Weckherlin, freshly returned from England, was amused by the old-country uproar. Fortified with wine but no longer a master of words, Gryphius contributed fiendish laughter. When Moscherosch ventured a word in Logau's favor, remarks were dropped about his name, which couldn't be Moorish and was certainly — by God! — not German in origin. Lauremberg shouted the evil word from ambush. A fist struck the table. Wine sloshed over. Greflinger scented a brawl. Dach had risen to stem this outburst of violence with his thus far respected "That's enough, children!" when out of the darkness Heinrich Schütz came striding across the courtyard and sobered the company.

Although the guest begged the poets not to let him disrupt their conversation, the humor-irony controversy evaporated forthwith. No one had meant any harm. The maids and wenches withdrew to the still-flaming cooking fires. Buchner relinquished the chair intended for Schütz. Dach gave vent to his joy that the guest had finally come — better late than never. Landlady Libuschka wanted to slice him some hot leg of mutton. Gelnhausen poured wine. But Schütz neither ate nor drank. In silence he surveyed the table and then looked out at the fires in the courtyard, around which the musketeers and horsemen had begun their own festivities. One of the musketeers was a passable bagpiper. Two, then three couples were seen dancing before and behind the fire in varying illumination.

After contemplating the bronze Apollo for some time and the silver candlesticks only briefly, Schütz turned to Gelnhausen, who was still standing beside him with a wine jug. And flung the question straight in Stoffel's face: how had one of the horsemen and that musketeer — the one dancing there! — come by their head wounds? He demanded a straight answer and no evasions.

Whereupon all those at the table learned that a bullet had grazed the horseman and a dragoon's saber had wounded the musketeer — only slightly, praise God.

When Schütz questioned further, it was learned that an engagement had occurred between Gelnhausen's imperial troops and a

Swedish detachment stationed in Vechta. But they had put the foraging Swedes to flight.

And taken spoils in the process? Schütz persisted.

It then came to light that the Swedes had just slaughtered the geese, pigs, and sheep on the farm of a peasant whom, admittedly, Gelnhausen had been planning to visit. The good man, whom sad to say the Swedes had spitted to his barn door, was an old acquaintance from the days when he, Gelnhausen, had been known throughout the region as the huntsman of Soest. Ah, he and his green doublet with the gold buttons had...

Schütz wasn't standing for any digressions. It finally came out that the church silver, the child-size Apollo, the Hessian tent canvas, the castle porcelain, and the altar cloths, not to mention the plum butter, crystallized ginger, sweet pickles, cheese, and white bread, had been found in a covered wagon captured from the Swedes.

As though to keep his report as realistic as possible, Gelnhausen explained how it had been necessary to transfer the cargo, because in trying to get away, the Swedish vehicle had sunk axle-deep into a bog.

Who had given him the order for this robbery?

That, said Gelnhausen, seemed to be roughly the gist of Count von Nassau's instructions as passed on to him by the imperial chancellery. It was not robbery, however, but a military engagement that had resulted in the transfer of the foragers' loot. Exactly as ordered.

What was the precise wording of this imperial order?

The count had sent cordial and courteous greetings and bidden him, Gelnhausen, see to the material needs of the assembled poets.

Did this solicitude necessarily imply loot — that is, as an assortment of roast meat, sausages, two casks of wine, finely wrought bronze, and other luxuries?

In view of yesterday's experience with the fare at the Bridge Tavern, the count's instructions to provide for their material needs could not have been carried out more nutritively. And as for the modest festive setting, had Plato not written...?

As though to leave no area of shadow, Schütz then asked Stoffel whether, apart from the peasant, other persons had been injured in the disgraceful robbery. And Gelnhausen replied casually that it had all happened so quickly, but as far as he could remember, the rough manners of the Swedes had not agreed with the hired man and the maidservant. And as she lay dying, the peasant woman had worried about her little boy, whom he, Gelnhausen, praise God, had seen running into the nearby woods, so escaping the butchery.

Stoffel went on to say that he knew a story that had had a similar sad beginning in the Spessart Mountains. For that was just what had happened to him as a boy. "Paw and Maw" had perished miserably. But he was still alive. God grant that as much good fortune could come the way of the little Westphalian boy.

The festive board was a picture of desolation. Piles of bones big and little. Puddles of wine. The formerly crowned, now half-eaten sheep's head. The disgust. The burned-down candies. The savagely barking mongrels. The belts on the canopy tinkled in mockery. The general gloom was deepened by the merriment of the horsemen and musketeers; around the fires, with the women, they sang, laughed, and bellowed undismayed. It took a shout from the landlady to silence the bagpiper. Off to one side, Birken vomited. The poets stood in groups. Scheffler was not alone in weeping: Czepko and the merchant Schlegel did likewise. Gerhardt was heard praying under his breath. Still under the influence of wine, Gryphius staggered around the table. Logau assured Buchner that he had suspected skulduggery from the start. (With some difficulty I restrained Zesen from going to the Ems to see corpses drifting.) And Simon Dach stood there like a broken man, breathing heavily. His Albert opened his shirt. Only Schütz kept his composure.

He was still in his armchair by the table. And from his seat he advised the poets to go on with their meeting and dispense with useless lamentations. In the eyes of God, he said, their complicity in the horror was slight. Their undertaking, however, which would benefit the language and help their unfortunate fatherland, remained great and must be carried on. He hoped he had not interfered with it.

Then he stood up and said good-bye — especially to Dach, warmly to Albert, to the others with a gesture. Before setting out, he informed the company that he was leaving early because of his hurry to get to Hamburg and beyond, not because of the shameful incident.

Brief orders were given — Dach sent Greflinger for Schütz's luggage. Then the *Kapellmeister* took Gelnhausen aside, and they walked a few steps together. To judge by his tone, the old man spoke kindly, words of comfort. Once he laughed, then both laughed. When Stoffel went down on his knees before him, Schütz pulled him up. It seems, as Harsdörffer later reported, that he told the regimental secretary never again to put his murderous fictions into practice, but to write them down bravely, for life had given him lessons enough.

Along with the covered wagon, two imperial horsemen escorted Schütz as far as Osnabrück. By torchlight the gentlemen stood in the courtyard. Then Simon Dach summoned the gathering to the taproom, where the long table was again standing as though nothing had happened.

Chapter 16

"O empty dream, whereon we mortals build..." Everything went sour. Horror clouded the mirrors. The meanings of words were reversed. Hope languished beside the silted well. Built on desert sand, no wall stood firm. In all the world nothing endured but mockery. The world's false glitter. The green branch foredoomed to wither. The whited sepulcher. The painted corpse. The plaything of false fortune... "What is the life of man, with all its shifts and changes, But a fantasy of time!"

Since the beginning of the war, but more disastrously since young Gryphius's first sonnets, published in Lissa, everything had struck them as hopeless. For all the lusts that swelled their sentence structure, for all the daintiness with which they clipped nature, transforming it into a pastoral rich in grottoes and mazes, for all their facility in devising sonorous words and sound patterns that obliterated more meaning than they communicated, always in the last stanza the earth became a vale of tears. Even the lesser poets found no difficulty in celebrating death as liberation. Avid for honor and fame, they rivaled one another in framing the vanity of human endeavor in sumptuous images. The younger poets were especially quick to dispose of life in their verses. But the older ones as well were so used to taking leave of this earth and its frippery that the valeoftearsishness and deathwhereisthystingishness of their industriously (and for modest reward) penned commissions could easily be regarded as fashionable and nothing more; for which reason Logau, who kept a cool head and sided with reason, often poked fun at his colleagues' rhymed yearning for death. And several moderate proponents of the "All is vanity" thesis joined him now and then in looking behind the somber backs of one another's cards and discovering their bright-colored faces.

Accordingly, not only Logau and Weckherlin, but also the shrewd and experienced Hofmannswaldau and Harsdörffer regarded as pure superstition the current belief that the end of the world would soon corroborate the poetic croakings that had been at such pains to bring it about. But the others — and with them the satirists and even the worldly-wise Dach — saw the Day of Judgment within reach, not always, to be sure, but whenever the political horizon, as often happened, darkened, or the commonplace problems of life tangled themselves into a knot — when, after Gelnhausen's confession, for example, the poets' banquet could only be regarded as an orgy of gluttony and their merrymaking was turned to lamentation.

Only Gryphius, the master of gloom, emanated good cheer. This sort of mood was his stock in trade. Serenely he stood firm amid chaos. To his mind, all human order was built on delusion and futility.

Consequently, he laughed. Why all the fuss? Had they ever known a feast that did not automatically drown itself in horror?

For the present, however, the assembled poets could not stop staring into the jaws of hell. That was the pious Gerhardt's hour. Rist, too, was hard at work. Out of Zesen's mouth Satan triumphed in sound patterns. Young Birken's pouting lips drooped pathetically. The more inward-looking Scheffler and Czepko were seen to seek salvation in prayer. All the publishers, especially Mülbe, whose usual occupation was forging plans, foresaw the end of their trade. And Albert recalled lines by his friend Dach:

> See how all life on earth doth pass,
> Now that death's snout obscene

Is with us drinking from our glass
And wiping all our dishes clean.

It was only when the poets seated around the table had savored
their misery long enough that they began to accuse themselves and
one another. Harsdörffer in particular was accused of foisting a
highwayman on their company. Just because the fellow was always
ready with a quip, said Buchner angrily, the Pegnitz Shepherds
had deemed him worthy of a recommendation. Zesen chided Dach
for having let the crude vagabond speak at their confidential sessions. Moscherosch, on the other hand, pointed out that they were
indebted to the swine for their lodgings. And Hofmannswaldau
scoffed that this first, by no means negligible, deception had
only made most of them laugh. Once again Gryphius triumphed
(though modestly): What did they expect? Everyone wallowed in
sin. Everyone was burdened with guilt. Gathered together as they
all were in their sinfulness, regardless of station, death alone could
make the crooked straight before God.

To Dach's mind this verdict of universal guilt amounted to a universal acquittal. He would have none of it. The present problem,
he said, was not to deplore man's innate depravity or to seek out
individual culprits, but to assign responsibility. And that he must
charge first of all to himself. He, more than anyone else, must
acknowledge the guilt. It would never occur to him to turn their
disgrace, which was primarily his disgrace, into an amusing story
to tell in Königsberg. But as to what they should do now, he, too,
was at a loss. Schütz — a pity he'd gone — was right. The meeting
must be carried to its conclusion. They couldn't just run away.

When Harsdörffer took all responsibility on himself and offered
to leave, no one would hear of it. Buchner said his accusations had
been uttered in the heat of anger. If Harsdörffer went, he would
go, too.

Might they not, merchant Schlegel suggested, consider holding a
court of honor of the kind customary in the Hanseatic towns, and
judge Gelnhausen's crime in his presence? Since he, Schlegel, was
not of the same station as the poets, he would be willing to serve
as judge.

Cries of Yes! A trial! The fellow, cried Zesen, must not be allowed to attend further readings and molest them with his insolent

interruptions. Rist protested that the final framing of the poets' appeal for peace, scheduled for the next day, must not take place in the presence of a common tramp, and Buchner added that, much as the scoundrel might have picked up here and there, he was utterly uneducated.

All seemed to favor the court of honor. When Logau asked whether the verdict, which could not be in doubt, should be pronounced now or later, and who was prepared to seek out Stoffel among his musketeers and summon him into court, no one volunteered. When Lauremberg cried out that since Greflinger felt happiest in the baggy breeches of a soldier, he was the man to do it, it became evident that Greflinger was absent.

Schneuber's instant suspicion: He's in league with Gelnhausen. But when Zesen went further in his imputations — suggesting that "they" must be planning further "injury to the German poets" — Dach made it clear that he had never had an ear for calumny. He himself would go. It was his duty, and his alone, to summon Gelnhausen.

This Albert and Gerhardt would not countenance. It would be dangerous, said Weckherlin, to provoke the drunken imperials at such an hour. And after the usual argument, Moscherosch's suggestion of calling the landlady was also rejected. In response to Rist's shout that they should convict the fellow *in absentia*, Hofmannswaldau retorted that that sort of trial was not to his liking, and if that was what they wanted, they could convict him, too.

Once again general perplexity. All sat silent around the long table. Only Gryphius chose to be amused at the renewed upsurge of lamentation. The only remedy for life, said he, was death.

At length Dach put an end to the procedural controversy. Early next morning, he announced, before the start of the final readings, he would confront the regimental secretary. Then he bade us all, in God's name, to retire for the night.

Chapter 17

Greflinger — to relieve the suspense — had gone fishing. From the weir of the fulling mill he had cast a net into the outer Ems and set out lines; but the two other youngsters found deep, blessed, scarcely dream-ruffled sleep. The repeated exertions of the night before, when, stirred by the full moon, they and Greflinger had lain with the maids, had made them heavy-headed enough to fall straight from the general gloom into the attic straw. Scheffler was breathing regularly before Birken; whereas the three maids found no rest when the last cooking fire had burned down but, along with the town wenches, fell to those musketeers not on guard duty. The night life in the stable could be heard across the court-yard and through the front windows of the tavern. Perhaps to counter the din with sounds of equal volume, the publishers and authors kept themselves awake with literary arguments in several of the rooms.

Paul Gerhardt found sleep by praying, long in vain but then successfully, for deliverance from the far-echoing lusts of the flesh. Dach and Albert — they, too, experienced in dealing with sinful noise — guided their fatigue to its goal. In their room, where nothing of Schütz remained, they read the Bible to each other — the Book of Job, needless to say....

But restlessness remained. A searching for everything and nothing. Perhaps it was still the influence of the full moon that brought movement into the house and kept us restless. Hardly less fat, it hung over the Emshagen. I'd have liked to bark at it, to howl with the tavern dogs. But with the poets I carried controversy, thesis and antithesis, along corridors and up and down stairs. After years of practice, Rist and Zesen were at it again — two purifiers of the language, wrangling over spelling, accent, the naturalization of foreign words, neologisms. Theological entanglements soon developed. For they were all religious. Every form of Protestant opinionatedness was put forward. Every man among them thought himself nearer to God. None permitted doubt to test the fabric of his faith. Only Logau, in whom a freethinker lurked (unavowed), infuriated Lutherans and Calvinists alike with his obnoxious irony. All you had to do, he cried out, was listen a while to the Old German and New Evangelical scholasticism, and you'd be tempted to turn Papist then and there. A good thing that Paul Gerhardt was already asleep. And better still that old Weckherlin reminded the gentlemen of their deferred project, the German poets' appeal for peace.

The final script, cried the publishers, must deplore the economic situation of the printing houses. And of the writers, Schneuber demanded. They should at last be enabled to write poems celebrating the marriages, baptisms, and funerals of common citizens, not just those of the upper classes. True peace, said Moscherosch, required such justice for every Christian man and woman. He even wanted the manifesto to include a price scale for commissioned poems, graduated according to class and fortune. So that not only the noble and patrician burgher should be dispatched on his last journey with rhymes, but the poor man as well.

And so Moscherosch, Rist, and Harsdörffer sat down at a table in Hofmannswaldau and Gryphius's room, while the others, after leaving elaborate instructions, went to bed. Hesitantly, peace crept into a house full of restless guests. Not far from the four drafters, Gryphius slept stormily, as though wrestling with the angel; actually he should have been numbered among the authors of the manifesto, for his head, even in sleep teeming with words, cast its shadow on the manuscript.

When the drafters decided they were satisfied, not, to be sure, with the newly framed text but with the effort they had contributed, and each for himself (with a head full of several-times-rejected sentences) collapsed into bed, only Harsdörffer remained sleepless, tormented, as he lay across from the deeply breathing Endter, and not only by the moon in the window. Time and again he made a decision and rejected it. He wanted to count sheep but instead counted the gold buttons on Gelnhausen's doublet. He wanted to get up, but stayed in bed. He longed to go out, along corridors, down steps, and across the courtyard, and hadn't the strength to throw off his eiderdown. One force tugged at him, another held him still. He wanted to go out to Gelnhausen, but couldn't have said exactly what he wanted of Gelnhausen. At one moment it was anger, at another it was a brotherly feeling toward Stoffel that tried to pull him out of bed and across the courtyard. In the end Harsdörffer took to hoping that Gelnhausen would come to him, so they might weep together — about their wretched lot, about the wheel of fortune, about the delusion beneath the glitter, about the wretchedness of the world....

But Gelnhausen was shedding his tears with landlady Libuschka. She, an old woman, to him forever young, his bottomless barrel and bucket to pour himself out into, his wet nurse, his bed of sloth, his leech, held him close and listened her fill. Once again everything had gone wrong. Nothing he attempted turned out right. Again he had blundered. Yet he had only wanted to do a bit of trading in Coesfeld, where his acquaintance with the nuns of the Marienbrink convent extended under their habits, and not to forage as was customary in those parts. One of the eleven devils must have driven the Swedes within range of their muskets. He was good and sick of soldiering. He was going to cut his ties with Mars once and for all and content himself from then on with small, peaceful gains. Maybe as an innkeeper. Just as she, the restless Courage, had settled down as landlady Libuschka. He already knew of a good place for sale. Near Offenburg. The Silver Star, it was called. If Courage could do it, so could he. All it took was gumption. And only a little while ago, the great Schütz, who had every reason to be hard on him, had advised him — good, fatherly advice — to settle down. When he, Stoffel, had wanted to go down on his knees to Schütz and beg forgiveness, the world-famous man had spoken kindly, told him about his childhood in Weissenfels on the Saale, and how ably his father had managed his spacious inn, At the Sign of the Archer.* And how under the great bay window there had been a stone statue of an ass playing the bagpipes. Stoffel, Schütz had said laughing, had just such an ass inside him, and he proceeded to call him Simplex. Whereupon he had asked the worthy gentleman whether he thought Simplex and the bagpipe-playing ass capable of operating a spacious inn. Of that and far more, had been the kindly gentleman's reply.

But since landlady Libuschka from Bragoditz in Bohemia, whom Stoffel never wearied of calling (sometimes affectionately, sometimes disparagingly) Courage, had no confidence in his ability to run an inn, and only scoffed at him — with his "far more," she suggested, Maestro Sagittario must have been referring to the volume of his debts and accruing interest — and went on to deliver herself of the opinion that, apart from the ability to sit still, what he lacked to become a successful innkeeper was the subtle art of distinguishing between good customers and those who evaporated without paying, Gelnhausen, who had thus far listened in silence,

---

*German *Schütze* = "archer" or "marksman." — *Trans.*

went livid with rage. Old sow! Gallowsbird! Whore! Cesspit! he cried. He called her a witch, whose entire fortune had been made by whoring. Ever since she had fallen in with Mansfeld's cavalry in the Bohemian Forest, Courage had laid herself open to all comers. Whole regiments had ridden through. You had only to scratch her French face paint to see the whore underneath. She, the barren thistle, who could never bear a child, had tried to palm a brat off on him. But one thing was sure! He'd get even. Word for word. As soon as he got clear of the army and his future inn began to prosper, he would cut himself the finest pens. Yes indeed! And in his finely spun, crudely wrought manuscript he would depict the life that had come his way. And, along with the fun and the horror, the venal splendor of Courage's body. He'd known her checkered history ever since the whisperings at the spa: the rake-offs she had taken, the ill-gotten gains she had stashed away. And what Courage had then kept secret from him, his crony Harum-Scarum had told him down to the smallest detail: how she had plied her trade in the camp outside Mantua, what magic she had kept in little bottles, how many Brunswickers had passed over her... everything! He would put the whoring and thieving of close to thirty years on paper — in accordance with all the rules of art — and make them live forever.

That handed landlady Libuschka a laugh. The mere idea made her shake. Her laughter drove first Gelnhausen, then herself out of bed. Did he, Stoffel, the simple-minded regimental secretary, think he could compete with the art of the learned gentlemen now gathered in her house? Did he, whose mouth overflowed with foolishness, hope to keep pace with Master Gryphius's verbal cascade, with the eloquent wisdom of Johann Rist? No, really, did he think he could rival the daring, lavishly ornamented wit of Masters Harsdörffer and Moscherosch? Had he, whom no magister had taught how to put a sentence together or count feet, the gall to measure his metric skill with that of the acute Master Logau? Did he, who didn't even know what religion he believed in, suppose he could drown out Master Gerhardt's pious hymns? Did he, who had started life as a wagoner and stableboy, then turned common soldier, and only lately risen to the rank of regimental secretary, he who had never learned anything but murder, robbing corpses, highway robbery, and perhaps in a pinch the art of keeping regimental records, aspire to make his way with hymns and sonnets, with witty and entertaining satires, odes, and elegies? Why, while he was about it, wouldn't he pen deep-thinking treatises for the instruction of others? Did he, Stoffel, really imagine that he could become a poet?

The landlady didn't laugh long. Opposition caught up with her in mid-sentence. She was still scoffing — how she would just love to see the flyspecks this Stoffel would put on paper about her, Libuschka, of noble Bohemian family! — when Gelnhausen struck. With his fist. It hit her left eye. She fell, pulled herself to her feet, staggered around the cluttered storeroom that served as her bedchamber, tumbled over saddles and boots, groped, and found a wooden pestle of the kind used for pounding dried peas. With one eye, for the blow had shut the other, she looked for the maggot-shitter, the peeping Tom, the redbeard, the pockmarked devil, but all she could find was junk. She struck pitifully at thin air.

Gelnhausen was already outside. Across the moon-bright courtyard and through alder bushes, he ran to the outer Ems, where, weeping, he met the weeping Harsdörffer, who, sleepless with misery, hadn't been able to stay in bed for long. Off to one side, on the weir of the fulling mill, Greflinger might have been seen fishing. But Harsdörffer saw nothing, and beside him Gelnhausen was also sightless.

The two of them sat on the steep embankment until morning. They didn't say much to each other. Even their unhappiness had no need of being exchanged. Not a word of reproof or repentance. How beautifully the river embedded itself in their vale of tears. A nightingale gave answer to their gloom. Perhaps the experienced Harsdörffer told Stoffel how to make a name for oneself as a poet. Perhaps Stoffel was eager even then to know if he should try to emulate the Spanish storytellers. Perhaps that night on the bank of the Ems supplied the poet with that first line — "Come, balm of night, O nightingale" — which was later to open the song of the Spessart Mountain hermit. Perhaps Harsdörffer already warned his young colleague against pirated editions and publishers' greed. And perhaps the two friends ended by sleeping side by side.

Not until voices and slamming doors from the Bridge Tavern announced the coming of day were they jolted awake. Where the Ems divided before separating Emshagen Island from the town wall on one side and from Tecklenburg territory on the other, crested grebes were rocking in the water. Looking toward the fulling mill, I saw that Greflinger had pulled in his net and lines.

Speaking into the sun behind the birches on the opposite shore, Harsdörffer said the congress might pronounce a sentence. Gelnhausen said: I've been there before.

Chapter 18

Much used as were the three maids who served it, pathetically swollen (as though one-eyed) as was landlady Libuschka's face as she looked on, the morning soup did not lack strength. And no one would have dreamed of complaining, for the tasty brew had obviously been boiled down from the goose giblets, the pigs' kidneys, and the (crowned, then uncrowned) sheep's head left over from the night before. In their weakened state, as the gentlemen came creeping from their rooms, their need for piping-hot sustenance was greater than their by no means negligible spiritual hangover, which, however, did not express itself until they all, from Albert and Dach to Weckherlin and Zesen, had spooned up their soup.

First—while Birken and others were still bending over their seconds — new trouble was aired. Weckherlin had been robbed. A leather purse full of silver shillings had vanished from his room. Though the old man dismissed Lauremberg's prompt assumption that it must have been Greflinger, the suspicion that the vagabond had snatched the purse was reinforced by Schneuber's report that he had seen him playing dice with the musketeers. And a further mark against Greflinger was the fact — which no one could overlook — that he was still absent. He was lying in the bushes on the riverbank, beside dead or still-quivering fishes, sleeping off the weariness of his night's exertions.

After Dach, visibly worn by the accumulated unpleasantness, had promised that the theft would soon be cleared up and gone so far as to vouch for Greflinger, the wretchedness of the previous day repeated on them: What were they to do with this horror? Could they go on reading from manuscripts as if nothing had happened? Wouldn't all poetry sound flat after that butcher's feast?

Were the assembled poets still entitled, after such dreadful revelations — possibly a thief in their midst! — to look upon themselves as honorable men, let alone to issue a morally motivated appeal for peace?

Birken asked: had they not, in gobbling up that bandit's food, entangled themselves in complicity? No satire, Lauremberg complained, could accommodate so much bestiality. As though the sacramental wine were still at work within him, Gryphius's imposing frame disgorged bundles of words. And Weckherlin declared that such a feast would make even gluttonous London, that veritable Moloch, vomit. Whereupon Zesen, Rist, and Gerhardt outdid themselves in images of guilt, repentance, and atonement.

(What was not expressed were the private troubles underlying this cosmic nausea: Gerhardt's worry, for example, that he might never be gratified with a parsonage; Moscherosch's bitter fear that his friends might stop believing in his Moorish descent and, on the mere strength of his name, start calling him a Jew to his face, stoning him with words; or Weckherlin's grief over the recent death of his wife, which stayed with him through all his jests. And the old man also dreaded his return to London, the loneliness in Gardiner's Lane, where he had been living for years but remained a foreigner. Soon he would be pensioned, his place taken by Milton, another poet but a partisan of Cromwell. And other fears...)

And yet, for all his tribulations, Simon Dach seemed to have gathered strength overnight. Pulling himself up to stalwart middle height, he observed that each and every one of them had a lifetime ahead in which to dwell on his recent increment of sin. They had all enjoyed their morning soup, and there was no need of further lamentations. Since he did not see Gelnhausen at table and since it was hardly to be expected that his contrition would allow him to attend additional readings, there seemed to be no point in trying him, especially since such a trial would seem presumptuous and pharisaical. Feeling sure that friend Rist, not only as a poet but still more as a clergyman, agreed with him, and gleaning from Gerhardt's silence that even so pious and rigorous a Christian was of the same mind, he would now — if Lauremberg would finally stop chattering with the maids — announce the program for the day and once again commend the meeting — what remained of it — to God's inexhaustible goodness.

After taking his Albert aside and bidding him look for the still regrettably absent Greflinger, Dach read the names of those who had yet to read: Czepko, Hofmannswaldau, Weckherlin, Schneuber. When calls rang out begging him finally, for the delectation of all, to read his lament for the lost cucumber bower, Dach tried to get out of it by invoking the shortage of time. But when Schneuber (at the suggestion of Moscherosch) undertook to forgo his contribution, it was agreed that Dach would conclude the session with a reading of his poem; for Dach wished to devote a special session, apart from the poetry reading, to the final drafting of the appeal for peace, demanded by Rist and others, in the form of a political manifesto — two new versions had meanwhile been submitted. "Therefore," he said, "we will not let the discussion of war and peace obtrude into our Muses' grove, the cultivation of which must be ever on our minds. For, undeterred by fences, a frost might nip our shady cucumber vine, causing it to wither, as, so the Scriptures tell us, befell Jonah."

His concern was shared. It was decided that the appeal for peace would be discussed in detail and completed between the last reading and the simple (as unanimously demanded) noonday meal. After the meal — the landlady promised to make it "honest," that is, meager — the assembled poets would disperse, each in his own direction.

At length order was put into chaos. Thanks to Simon Dach's protective interpretation of his name,* we were all of good heart and witty in groups. Some of us were even growing frolicsome — young Birken wanted to crown Dach with a garland — when Lauremberg's shouted question — against what bedpost had the landlady blackened her eye? — revived the misery of the day before.

After holding it in for much too long, Libuschka spoke out: it wasn't the work of a bedpost but of Gelnhausen's manly vigor. Apparently, she said, it hadn't yet dawned on the gentlemen what a foul trick that peasant lout had played on them. Everything that crossed the fellow's lips was a tissue of lies and fabulation, and that included his confession to Sagittario. Gelnhausen's horsemen and musketeers had not commandeered those provisions from any Swedes, no, they themselves had taken them, professional raiders,

---

Dach = roof. — *Trans.*

that's what they were, that smooth-talking bandit had lived up to his reputation. His green doublet was feared from Soest to Vechta. Any virgin pleading with him for mercy would be wasting her breath. His methods could make the mute talk. And incidentally, the church silver, altar cloths, and sacramental wine had been hornswoggled out of the whores' convent in Coesfeld. The Hessian guard was no help, a weasel like Gelnhausen could always get through. No loyalty to either camp. He swore only by his own flag. And if Master Harsdörffer still believed that the papal nuncio himself had given Stoffel the little volume of the playful *Conversation Pieces for Women* to have it dedicated by the author, she would have to cut the cords of his vanity: Gelnhausen had bribed one of the nuncio's servants to steal it from the cardinal's library. The pages hadn't even been cut. That was how finely Gelnhausen spun his web of lies. For years the fellow had been hoodwinking the finest gentlemen no less effectively. No devil could hold a candle to him. She knew it to her sorrow.

With difficulty Dach succeeded in relieving the general consternation and his own — a little. Harsdörffer drooped. Anger darkened the usually even-tempered Czepko. If Logau had not remarked appeasingly that birds of a feather flock together, another long argument could have been feared. Gratefully Dach clapped his hands. Enough now! He would look into these accusations. One lie had a way of leading to another. He hoped they would all close their ears to this new hubbub. From then on the poets should concentrate on their own calling; if not, their art would fail them.

Consequently Dach's first impulse was one of anger when his Albert suddenly led Greflinger into the taproom. He was already beginning to shower the long-haired young fellow with reproaches — what had got into him? Where had he been? Had he made off with Weckherlin's purse? — when, like all the others, he saw what Greflinger had brought back in two buckets: barbels, roaches, and other fish. Draped in the net and hung with fishing lines — which he had borrowed the day before from the widow of the Telgte town fisherman — the young man stood there like a portrait. He had fished all night. Not even the Danube could boast better barbels. Fried crisp, even the bony roach would prove tasty. The whole lot could be served up for their noonday meal. And if anyone called him a thief, he'd tell him what for.

No one was inclined to challenge Greflinger's fists. All looked forward to the honest fish. Behind Dach, the company moved into the great hall, where their symbol, the thistle, stood beside the unoccupied footstool.

Chapter 19

No one hesitated. All, including even Gerhardt, stood up for their literary undertaking, prepared to fight for it. The war had taught them to live with adversity. Dach was not alone; no one was willing to be put off. Not Zesen or Rist, much as those two purists and purifiers of the language might quarrel between themselves; neither the commoners nor the nobles, still less since under Dach's chairmanship the classes had spontaneously shaken off their structure. No one wanted the meeting to break up — not the unknown Scheffler, not the vagrant, always suspect Greflinger, not even Schneuber, who, on instructions from the uninvited Magister Rompler, kept looking for ways of fomenting trouble; and definitely not the older men, Buchner and Weckherlin, who had never been deeply interested in anything but poetry; even Gryphius, easy as he found it to repudiate all work in progress as vain delusion, stood firm. No one was willing to give up merely because reality had once again put in an objection and cast mud at art.

Accordingly, all those who had gathered in the semicircle remained seated on their chairs, stools, and barrels when Gelnhausen — the instant Czepko had taken his place between the thistle and Simon Dach and prepared to read — climbed from the garden into the great hall through an open window. With his red beard he sat down on the window seat and had nothing but summer behind him. Since the company showed no sign of restlessness, since a paralysis born of determination held them still, Dach felt justified in giving Czepko the sign. Having poems to read, the Silesian took a deep breath.

But then — before he could utter so much as a line — Gelnhausen spoke in a voice that purported to be modest but carried an overtone of mockery. He was glad, he said, that in spite of the trickery that Master Schütz had so sternly censured, but then like a true Christian forgiven, the illustrious and widely famed gentlemen who were forgathered under Apollo's aegis, now and for all time, had readmitted him, the peasant lout escaped from the Spessart Mountains, to the end that he, the simple-minded Stoffel, might continue his education until such time as he, too, might learn to create order out of everything he had read, which lay helter-skelter in his mind. Thus instructed, he hoped to climb into art as he had just climbed through the window and — should the Muses be propitious — become a poet.

Only then did pent-up rage explode. If he had sat still — all right. If by quietly sitting there he had helped them to show magnanimity — better yet. But the pretension to be their equal was too much for the far-traveled members of the Fruit-bearing, Upright, Pegnitz, and German-minded societies. They unburdened themselves with cries of "Murdering scoundrel! Liar!" Rist shouted, "Popish agent!" Someone (Gerhardt?) went so far as to cry out, "Get thee hence, Satan!"

They jumped up, shook their fists, and would probably, Lauremberg in the lead, have dealt blows, if Dach had not grasped the situation and reacted to a sign from Harsdörffer. With his voice, which even in earnest took an easy, casual tone and always seemed to say, "It's all right; don't take yourselves so seriously," he pacified the company and then asked The Playful One to explain himself.

Addressing Gelnhausen as a friend, Harsdörffer asked him rather gently whether he confessed to the crimes that landlady Libuschka had added to his account. He listed all her accusations, concluding with what was most galling to him personally, the lie about the copy of his *Conversation Pieces for Women* stolen from the nuncio's library.

Now predominantly self-assured, Gelnhausen replied that he no longer had any wish to defend himself. Yes and by all means yes. He and his horsemen and musketeers had acted in the spirit of the times, just as the gentlemen here assembled were constrained to act in the spirit of the times when they wrote poems in praise of princes to whom murder and arson came as naturally as their daily prayers, whose robberies, out of all proportion to the bit of food he had made off with, were blessed by the priests, who switched loyalties as easily as they changed their shirts, and whose repentance lasted no longer than a paternoster. He, on the other

hand, the accused Stoffel, had long repented and would long continue to repent of having helped so unworldly a company to find
lodgings, of having protected them from bandits with his horsemen and musketeers, and, to top it all, of having sullied himself
by supplying them with three kinds of roast meat, delectable wine,
white bread, and spicy condiments. All that, as was now evident,
without advantage to himself and purely out of gratitude for certain lessons received. Yes, it was true, he had wished to give the
learned poets pleasure with his fantasy about the massed greetings from the princely, royal, and imperial ambassadors assembled
at the Münster chapter house. Similarly, he had wished to please
Harsdörffer, who had thus far been so well disposed to him and
whom he loved like his own Heartsbrother,* with a mild deception; wherein he had been successful, for the Nuremberger had
taken unfeigned delight in the papal nuncio's request for a dedication. What did it really matter whether Chigi actually wanted the
dedication, whether he could or should have wanted it, or whether
the whole story was no more than a pleasant fantasy sprung from
the brain of the here accused Stoffel? If because they were without
power the gentlemen were also without standing in their country — and that was the truth! — a credible show must be made
of their nonexistent standing. Since when were poets so intent on
dry, flat truth? What made their left hands so dull when their
right hands were so practiced in exalting their rhymed truths to
the realm of the incredible? Must poetic lies be printed and published before they could be ranked as truth? Or, in other terms,
was the bargaining in land and people now entering its fourth
year in Münster more authentic, not to say more honorable, than
the commerce with accented and unaccented syllables, with words
and spoken sounds and images, being conducted here at Telgte's
Ems Gate?

At first the company had listened to Gelnhausen with reserve,
then here and there with repressed laughter, thoughtful head-
shaking, cool attentiveness, or like Hofmannswaldau, with visible
relish — but the dominant reaction was one of amazement. Dach
gave frequent signs of amusement at the consternation gathered
around him. There was challenge in the look that he trained

---

*A character in Grimmelshausen's novel *Simplicissimus*.

on the silent circle: was no one going to refute the man's insolent wit?

After stopping to quote Herodotus and Plautus in Latin, Buchner concluded with a quotation from Stoffel himself: That is the
truth! Whereupon Logau suggested that they let the matter rest.
At last, he said, they knew who they were; only jesters could hold
up such accurate mirrors.

That didn't satisfy Greflinger. No, he cried, it was not a jester,
but the common people, who were not present at this meeting,
who had told him the truth. Stoffel was his, Greflinger's, kinsman.
He, too, the vagrant peasant boy, had been tossed about by life before he had a chance to sniff at books. If anyone spoke of throwing
Stoffel out, he, too, would go.

At length Harsdörffer declared that after thus being made a fool
of he knew what to write about vanity. Brother Gelnhausen should
kindly stay and regale them with further unpalatable truths.

But already Stoffel was standing in the window opening, ready
to take his leave. No. Mars was putting him back in harness.
The Münster chapter house had entrusted him with a message to
take to Cologne and beyond: The chapter would have to pay nine
hundred thousand talers in indemnities if the Hessians were to
evacuate Coesfeld, the Swedes Vechta, and the Dutch Bevergern.
This war gave promise of costing money for a long time to come.
He, however, would depart with a promise that cost nothing, the
promise that they would hear from him again. True, years and
years might pass before he had refurbished his knowledge, bathed
in Harsdörffer's sources, studied Moscherosch's craft, gleaned rules
from this and that treatise, but then he would be present: as lively
as you please, though tucked away in countless printed pages.
But let no one expect mincing pastorals, conventional obituaries,
complicated figure poems, sensitive soul-blubber, or well-behaved
rhymes for church congregations. No, he would let every foul smell
out of the bag; a chronicler, he would bring back the long war
as a word-butchery, let loose gruesome laughter, and give the language license to be what it is: crude and soft-spoken, whole and
stricken, here Frenchified, there melancolicky, but always drawn
from the casks of life. Yes, he would write! By Jupiter, Mercury,
and Apollo, he would!

With that Gelnhausen removed himself from the window. But, both feet in the garden, he turned back with an ultimate home truth. From his breeches pocket he drew a purse and tossed it up twice in his hand, so making its silvery contents known. He laughed briefly and, before throwing the purse through the window to land just short of the thistle, said that it still remained for him to deposit this small thing he had found. For one of the gentlemen had left his purse in Courage's bed. Enjoyable as it was to visit the landlady of the Bridge Tavern, no one should be overcharged for his brief pleasure.

Only then was he really and truly gone. Gelnhausen left the assembled poets alone among themselves. Already we missed him. From outside there was no other sound than the hoarse braying of the mules. Well rounded, the leather purse lay beside the thistle. Old Weckherlin arose, took a few steps with dignity, picked up the purse, and returned calmly to his chair. No one laughed. Gelnhausen's speech still held power, which no one wanted to break. Finally Dach said without transition: Now that everything had been found and cleared up, there was to be zealous reading. Otherwise the morning would escape them with Stoffel.

Chapter 20

I, too, was sorry to see Christoffel Gelnhausen, once more in his green doublet and leathered hat, leave with his imperial horsemen and musketeers. Not a single gold button was missing from his doublet. In spite of all that had happened, he had suffered no harm.

That was one more reason why no word of reconciliation could fall between him and landlady Libuschka. Unmoved, she looked on from the tavern door as his little company saddled horses, harnessed one of the covered wagons requisitioned in Oesede, and (taking the child-size bronze Apollo with them) left the Bridge Tavern — Gelnhausen in the lead.

Since I now know more than Libuschka, gray with hatred, could have suspected in the tavern doorway, I will speak for Stoffel. His *Courasche* — published in Nuremberg under the pen name Philarchus Grossus von Trommenheim roughly a quarter century after his silent parting from the landlady of the Bridge Tavern, under the long title *Defiance to Simplex or Detailed and Most Strange Description of the Arch-Trickster, Trollop, and Most Notorious Rogue Courage,* and distributed by Felssecker, his publisher — was the late fulfillment of his vows of vengeance. Since the author of *Simplicissimus,* which had appeared two years before, lets his Courage speak with her own voice and settle accounts with herself, his book is a paper monument to a sturdy and unstable, childless yet inventive, vulnerable and embattled woman, man-mad in skirts, manly in breeches, making the most of her beauty, a woman both pitiful and lovable, all the more so since the author of all subsequent "Simpliciads," who occasionally called himself Hans Christoffel von Grimmelshausen, granted his "Courage" paper on which to mete out powerful blows to Simplex, his very own self; for what stirred Gelnhausen and Libuschka together like milk and vinegar was an excess of love, or call it hate.

Not until the regimental secretary and his men were crossing the outer Ems bridge on their way to Warendorf (and thence to Cologne) and out of the landlady's sight did her right hand attempt a motion that might have been taken for waving good-bye. I, too, would have liked to wave good-bye to Stoffel, but thought it more important to attend the last readings of the assembled poets in the great hall, where the thistle stood significantly. Having been there from the very beginning, I also wanted to witness the end. For fear of missing something.

There were no further interruptions. Daniel von Czepko, a Silesian jurist and counselor to the dukes of Brieg, in whom, since his period of study, in Strassburg, the God-and-man-fusing mysticism fired by the shoemaker Böhme had flickered beneath a show of indifference, that reserved, little-noticed man whose friend I should have liked to be, read several epigrams, the form of which (alexandrine couplets) was also congenial to Gryphius and Logau. Young Scheffler had attempted something similar, though his efforts were still crude, the antitheses not yet carried to their ultimate clarity. Possibly because in the ensuing discussion period the Breslau medical student seemed (though startled) to understand Czepko's "beginning in the end, end in the beginning," and because on the day before Czepko had been the only one (apart from Schütz) to grasp the overall meaning of the student's confused offering, they conceived a friendship that remained possible even after Scheffler became the Catholic Angelus Silesius and published his *Cherubinic Wanderer,* whereas Czepko's chief work, his collected epigrams, found no publisher — unless perhaps the author held them back.

In keeping with their subsequent lack of success, Czepko's couplets caught the attention of few of the assembled poets. Who had ears for so much silence? Only one poem, a political piece that Czepko referred to as a fragment — "The fatherland is where freedom and justice are. It knows us not and we know not that distant star" — met with wider approval. After Moscherosch and Rist it was again the diminutive Magister Buchner who threw out his chest and interpreted Czepko's lines into a chaotic world hungering for harmony, in the process quoting Augustine, Erasmus, and time and time again himself. In the end, the magister's speech aroused more applause than Czepko's marginally praised poem. (Buchner was still extemporizing after the author had relinquished the stool beside the thistle.)

Next the seat up front was taken by a gaunt, long-limbed man who didn't know what to do with his legs. The surprise was general when Hofmann von Hofmannswaldau, who had failed thus far to distinguish himself with any published work and was regarded as a mere literary dilettante, expressed his readiness to read. Even Gryphius, who had known the wealthy nobleman since their student days together in Danzig and Leiden — he had encouraged the rather passive aesthete to write — seemed surprised and even a bit appalled when Hofmannswaldau insisted on reading.

Cleverly exaggerating his embarrassment, Hofmannswaldau apologized for his presumption in wishing to sit between Dach and the thistle, but owned that he was itching to submit his efforts to criticism. He then astonished the company with a genre deriving from Ovid, new to Germany, and cultivated only in foreign parts, for his selection consisted of so-called "heroes' letters," which he introduced with a tale, "The Life and Love of Peter Abelard and Helisse."

This is the story of an ambitious young scholar in Paris who is occasionally driven by academic intrigues to take refuge in the provinces. Back in Paris, he outshines even the famous theologian Anselme, and becomes a universal favorite. Finally a certain Folbert employs him to give his niece private instruction, but instead of confining himself to Latin, Abelard falls madly in love with his pupil, who falls madly in love with her teacher. "In short, their scholarship suffers from a different sort of assiduity...." But their lessons continue and the consequence is a "learned wantoning," which takes root. The teacher removes his pregnant pupil to the home of his sister in Brittany, and there she is delivered of a boy. Although the young mother has no desire to marry and protests vehemently "that it would please her more to be called his mistress than his wedded wife," the teacher insists on a simple marriage ceremony, which is performed in Paris, while the child stays in Brittany with Abelard's sister. But since Uncle Folbert is hostile to the marriage, Abelard hides his pupil and wife in a convent near Paris; whereupon Folbert, infuriated by his niece's flight, bribes Abelard's servant "to unlock his master's bedchamber at night and castrate him with the help of some likewise bribed ruffians," which is irrevocably done.

The loss of Abelard's wantoning equipment is the subject of the two ensuing letters written in alternately rhymed alexandrines and periphrasing unspeakable horror in a courtly refinement of the Opitzian manner: "I thought the fire of passion was no such grievous thing; No bramblebush, thought I, will bar my chosen way; On thinnest ice I thought to go a-wantoning. But now, alas, I find a knife hath spoiled my play...."

Since form was everything to Hofmannswaldau, he had asked leave before starting to read to call Abelard's pupil "Helisse" for the sake of the rhyme: Helisse now tries, in her letter to Abelard, to overbalance the loss of his equipment with higher love: "And though your sweetsome lips moved me too carnally, Built a lubricious house with roses all entwined, My passion never stripped my intellect from me, And every kiss I gave was leveled at your mind...."

Little as the assembled poets found to criticize in Hofmannswaldau's art — Buchner declared that it far outdid Opitz and even Fleming! — the morality of the story stuck bittersweet in several of their craws. The first to speak was Rist with his eternal: Where does it lead? What good can come of it? Then indignation poured from Gerhardt, who had heard nothing but gilded sin in all that "vain feast of words." When, after Lauremberg's grumbling about "artificial rhymes," young Birken took umbrage at those horrible goings-on, Greflinger asked him if he had forgotten what instrument he had recently used on the maids in the straw. No, Birken replied, he had no objection to the implement either before or after the cutting, what he minded was the smooth and slippery manner. A pity that Gelnhausen was gone. He would have shown the bloody butchery and Helisse's forced continence naked and screaming.

When many (but not Gryphius) then asked leave to speak, wishing to carp at Abelard's genitals, Simon Dach said he had heard enough about the ill-reputed but useful implement. The tale, he owned, had moved him. But, he went on, let no one forget the touching end, which at long last unites the lovers in one grave, where their bones are at pains to intertwine. On hearing that, he said, the tears had come to his eyes.

As though all this criticism had been known to him in advance, Hofmannswaldau took the flood of words with a smile. Originally suggested by Dach, it had since become the rule that the reader should not speak in his own defense. For this same reason Weckherlin submitted unresisting to the excess cleverness that filled the air after the reading of his ode entitled "A Kiss."

The old man had written this poem — and all his other literary work, for that matter — when still young, almost thirty years before. Then, because there was nothing to hold him in Stuttgart, he had become an agent in the service of the Elector Palatine and finally, hoping to make himself more useful to the Palatinate, gone to work for the English government. Since then he had written nothing worth mentioning, only hundreds of subversive secret-agent's letters to Opitz, Niclassius, Oxenstierna, and others.... And yet Weckherlin's playful, sometimes amateurish little poems, written years before the appearance of Opitz's book on German poetics, had retained their freshness, all the more so because, thanks to his Swabian tongue, the old man managed to use his delivery to help his frivolous verses and sometimes dreary rhymes — "honeyed lips" /"soul's eclipse" — over the rough spots.

Weckherlin had let it be known at the outset that, since his duties as traveling undersecretary of state left him sufficient leisure, he was planning to rework (handling the rise and fall, the accented and unaccented syllables, more proficiently) the rhymed sins of his youth, most of which had been modeled on French originals and dated from the old prewar days, and have them reprinted. He knew, he said, that the young men thought him a fossil. In his opinion only the late lamented Bober Swan and the worthy Augustus Buchner had published anything helpful about German prosody, and that was since his time.

In the discussion period he was applauded. Because he was still around. We younger men had thought the old fellow dead. We were surprised to see the precursor of our young art alive and kicking; he had even climbed into Libuschka's bed like a man still capable of light-footed odes.

Though Rist abominated all bawdy verse, he nevertheless, though an Opitzian, came out in favor of Weckherlin. Buchner, plunging deep into the past, made common cause with Zesen and Gerhardt, who had been his students in Wittenberg, in sending the rest of the company back to versification school. Logau was as silent as before.

Then Simon Dach had to change chairs and asked old Weckherlin to guard the armchair in which he seemed to have taken root. Dach's long "Lament on the Ultimate Decline and Fall of the Musical Cucumber Bower and Garden" is an attempt at an epicedium to console his friend Albert for the loss of his garden, destroyed by mud and roadbuilder's rubble on Lomse Island in the river Pregel. In spacious alexandrines it relates the laying out of the garden, in which Albert was assisted by his tippling and now spade-wielding organ-blower, the friends' literary and musical entertainments and idyllic pleasures — their happily discovered harmony. Far away the war is sowing hunger plague desolation; closer at hand burghers are wrangling, preachers quarreling. Just as Jonah under his biblical gourd threatened sinful Nineveh with God's wrath, so Dach admonishes his tripartite Königsberg. His lament over the destruction of Magdeburg (where he had studied as a young man) leads to generalized lamentation over Germany's self-dismemberment. A condemnation of war — "So prompt are men to draw the sword of war and death, So pitifully slow to return it to its sheath" — is followed by the yearning for a just peace: "Oh, if the pain and loss of others made us wise, We surely then would find grace in our Maker's eyes." But, adjuring himself and his Albert to do what they can and make the best of the times —

"To counter their duress however hard they press" — Dach concludes with the lofty demands of poetry, which will outlive their cucumber bower: "Provided life and spirit inspire our poetry, Each line will give us part in immortality."

That appealed to us. Spoken from the hearts of all there assembled. Though at present they had no power and little glory, since the present was dominated by war and land grabbing, religious oppression and short-term greed, they aspired with the help of poetry to gain future power and secure eternal glory. This slight, rather ridiculous power helped them to well-paid commissions. Wealthy burghers and a sprinkling of princes, suspecting themselves to be more mortal than poets, hoped that verses, for the most part hastily written, commemorating their marriages, deaths, and illustrious deeds, would carry them into eternity, name and all.

Even more than any of the others, Simon Dach earned supplementals with commissioned poems. Whenever fees were compared at meetings with his colleagues, he had his bitter joke ready: "At Marriages and Deaths, they hire me as their mummer, Just as they might engage a baker or a plumber." Dach even owed his Kneiphof professorship to certain encomiums that he had tossed off in the late thirties, when the elector made his entrance into the city.

Consequently, after the company had richly complimented the lament for the cucumber bower, Gryphius's ambiguous demur — "You pen three hundred verses before my three I write, A laurel tree grows slowly, a cucumber overnight" — was taken as a malicious allusion to Dach's forced prolixity. When, soon thereafter, Rist first praised the moral content of the lament, but then took umbrage at the mythological allusions — the comparison, for example, of gutted Magdeburg with Thebes, Corinth, Carthage — and at the invocation of the Muse Melpomene, Buchner was prepared for rebuttal even before Zesen. No foreign influence, he declared, desecrated this poem. The whole of it flowed from a German mouth. Needed for contrast, the few witnesses from antiquity were an integral part of the magnificent edifice, which was beyond compare.

From Dach's armchair old Weckherlin said: A finer conclusion could not have been found. And Harsdörffer cried out: Oh, if only we had a cucumber bower big enough for us all, to shelter us from these evil times!

There was no need to say more. Gryphius's insult had been buried beneath sufficient praise. Laughing (and as though relieved), Simon Dach stood up from the stool beside the thistle. He embraced Weckherlin and led him back to his chair. Several times he paced back and forth from his armchair to the unoccupied stool and the thistle in the flowerpot. Then he said that was the end. He was glad the meeting had proceeded peaceably after all. For that he gave thanks to the Heavenly Father in the name of all there assembled. Amen. And yes, he wished to add, he had enjoyed the sessions in spite of certain vexations. At the noonday meal, before they dispersed in all directions, he would have a few more things to say. At the moment nothing occurred to him. But now — he could see that Rist and Moscherosch were restless — he would have to let politics in, that tiresome manifesto.

Thereupon Dach sat down again, bade the authors of the appeal for peace come forward, and, when Logau's objection provoked disorder, cautioned his charges: But no fighting, children.

Chapter 21

No! he cried several times. No, before we had reentered the great hall; no, when we all sat gathered around Dach and the thistle. And when Rist and Moscherosch finished reading the drafts of the manifesto, Logau was still shouting: No! Before and after. Absolutely: No!

He termed everything wretched. Rist's thund'rous words, the bourgeois niggling of the Strassburgers, the flowery phrases in which Hofmannswaldau stifled every conflict, Harsdörffer's Nuremberg-style maneuvering, the use of "German" or "Germany" as expletives in every half-sentence. Pitiful, hypocritical, cried Logau, who, relinquishing expressive brevity, casting off the irony that makes for succinctness, was angry enough to make a long speech aimed at stripping sentence after sentence of its verbal trumpery....

The rather frail-looking man stood in the background, distinctly apart, and spoke cuttingly over the heads of the seated gathering. Swaggering cowards, they had catered to all the parties. In one passage they wished the Swedes far away, in another they implored them to stay and help. In one sentence the Palatinate was to be restored, the next wanted to secure the favor of Bavaria through an offer of the electoral dignity. With their right hand the authors invoked the old Estate system, with their left they abjured the injustice that went with it. Only a forked tongue could in one sentence advocate freedom for every religion and in the next threaten all sects with banishment. True, the authors invoked Germany as often as a Papist invoked the Virgin Mary, but nowhere did they refer to more than a part of the whole. Loyalty industry honesty were named as German virtues, but those who were treated in truly German wise, like beasts, the peasants throughout the country, were nowhere mentioned. The authors spoke contentiously of peace, intolerantly of tolerance, and penny-pinchingly of God. And after all this talk about Germany, their praise of the fatherland stank of local interest: of Nuremberg's self-seeking, Saxony's caution, Silesian fear, Strassburgian arrogance. The whole thing was stupid and pathetic, because it hadn't been thought out.

Logau's speech inspired gloom rather than disorder. The two drafts, which differed only stylistically, passed from hand to hand, barely glanced at. Once again the poets were certain only of their impotence and their inadequate knowledge of political forces. For when (unexpectedly) old Weckherlin rose to speak, they were addressed by the one man in the entire gathering who had gained political awareness — participated in the play of forces, tasted power, shifted the weights a little, and worn himself out in the process.

The old man's tone was not at all didactic; he spoke jovially, making light of his thirty years of experience. As he talked, he strode back and forth, as though strolling from decade to decade. Sometimes he turned to Dach, sometimes he spoke out the window, as though wishing the two tethered mules to hear him, and, now rambling, now framing his thought succinctly, he pulled out the stopper. Actually the vessel was empty. Or full of rubbish. His hard work for nothing. His collected defeats. How, like the late lamented Opitz, he had been the diplomat of every conceivable party. How as a Swabian he had become an English agent and in the English service worked for the Palatinate, and how, because nothing could prosper without the Swedes, he had ended by turning double agent. And how with all his intriguing he had never achieved what had always been the aim of his slippery arts: to gain the military support of England for the Protestant cause. With all but toothless laughter Weckherlin cursed the English Civil War and the always sprightly Palatine court, Oxenstierna's harsh coldness and the Saxon betrayal, the Germans in general, but especially and repeatedly the Swabians: their greed, their narrowness, their mania for cleanliness, and their sanctimonious prevarication. Terrifying how young the old man's hatred of everything Swabian had remained, how bitter the German quality in the Swabians and the Swabian quality in the increasing cult of Germanism rose in his gullet.

In his indictment he did not acquit himself, but called all irenicists hairsplitting fools who, to forestall the worst, had consistently prolonged the national disaster. Just as he had tried, persistently though in vain, to bring English regiments into the German war of religion, the universally honored Opitz had striven, almost to the day he died of the plague, to involve Catholic Poland in the German butchery. As though, Weckherlin cried, there had not, what with the Swedes and the French, the Spaniards and the Walloons, been butchers enough at work in the German slaughterhouse. All his and Opitz's efforts had only made matters worse!

In the end the old man had to sit down. He had run out of laughter. Drained, he could no longer participate when the others, Rist and Moscherosch in the lead, converted their hatred of everything foreign into German self-hatred. All spilled their guts. Cataclysmically they spewed their fury. Self-nourishing agitation lifted the assemblage off chairs, stools, and barrels. They beat their breasts. They wrung their hands. Where, they shouted at one another, was the so often invoked fatherland? Where had it hidden? Was there any such thing, and if so what was it like?

By the time Gerhardt, as though to console the questioners, expressed his certainty that they could count on no earthly, but only on a heavenly fatherland, Andreas Gryphius had already disengaged himself from the knot and gone looking for something. Standing beside the unoccupied stool and in front of the decomposed semicircle, he grabbed hold of the pot with the transplanted thistle and thrust the emblem and symbol of their era against the timbered ceiling. In that menacing posture he grew to mighty proportions. A giant, a savage, a groaning Moses, whose tongue was in his way until the torrent of words broke loose: barren, prickly, strewn by the wind, food for the ass, noxious weed, plague of the peasant, sent by the angry God, this thing, the thistle, was the flower and fatherland of them all! Whereupon Gryphius dropped the thistle that was Germany, dashed it to the floor in our midst.

No one could have done better. That fitted in with our mood. The fatherland had never been put before us more graphically. We seemed almost happy, glad as only Germans can be, to see our misery imaged so forcefully. Moreover, the thistle lay unharmed amid the shards and scattered soil. Behold, cried Zesen, how the fatherland emerges unscathed from the severest fall!

All saw the miracle. And only then, after childlike joy over the unharmed thistle had spread, after young Birken had heaped up earth over the bared roots and Lauremberg had run for water — only after the company had thus recovered its innocence but before the usual chatter had time to start up did Simon Dach, beside whom Daniel Czepko had stationed himself, speak. During the widening, increasingly active search for the lost or no longer recognizable or totally weed-ridden fatherland, the two had been busy, here deleting, there adding, on a manuscript that, while Czepko was writing out a fair copy, Dach identified as the final version of the manifesto and read aloud.

The new text managed without any of Rist's thund'rous words. No ultimate truth was proclaimed. In plain, simple language the assembled poets entreated all parties desirous of peace not to scorn the preoccupations of the poets, who, though powerless, had acquired a claim to eternity. Without denouncing the Swedes or the French as land grabbers, without condemning the Bavarians for their haggling over territory, without so much as naming any of the warring religions, they looked into the future and pointed to some of the possible dangers and burdens implicit in the forthcoming peace: that pretexts for future wars might creep into the longed-for peace treaty; that for want of tolerance the so passionately longed-for religious peace might merely lead to further denominational strife; that the restoration of the old order, desirable as were its blessings, might — God forbid! — be accompanied by a restoration of the old, accustomed injustice; and finally, the overriding preoccupation of the assembled poets, speaking as patriots: that the empire was so threatened by dismemberment that no one could recognize in it what had once been his German fatherland.

This final version of the appeal for peace concluded with a prayer for God's blessing. As soon as the fair copy was available, it was signed without further dispute, first by Dach and Czepko, then by the others, including Logau. Whereupon the gentlemen, as though their plea had already been granted, embraced one another, some joyfully, others on the verge of tears. At last we were sure of having done something. Since the appeal lacked any grandiose gesture, Rist compensated by calling the place, day, and hour momentous.

An occasion for bell ringing. But the hand bell affixed to the door of the great hall was rung for a lesser reason. This time it was not the landlady who summoned the company to the noonday meal. Under the supervision of Greflinger, who was last to sign the manifesto, his last night's catch had been fried.

When the assembled poets poured from the great hall into the taproom, no one paid attention to the thistle that had remained unscathed amid shards. No one was interested in anything but fish. The smell led us and we followed.

Simon Dach, who was holding the momentous manuscript, was obliged to adjust his parting words to the fish that awaited us.

Chapter 22

Never has a meal been more peaceful. The fish made for gentle words around the long table. We all spoke to and about one another in soft, contented voices. And the poets listened to one another; they did not interrupt.

In the grace, which Dach assigned at the last moment to Albert, the Kneiphof cathedral organist set the tone by citing fishing-related Bible passages. After that it was easy to praise the crisp skin of the barbels and the white flesh beneath it, which fell so gently off the backbone; but then again, no one grumbled at the humbler, bony roaches. Now it could be seen how many of them — in addition to tench, perch, and one young pike — had swum into Greflinger's net or bitten at his hooks during the night. The maids brought in more and more on shallow platters, while the landlady stood with face averted at the window.

Greflinger's fish seemed to multiply miraculously. The Nurembergers, Birken in the lead, were soon obliging with pastoral rhymes. Everyone was eager to praise fish in verse, if not immediately, then at some propitious hour. And the water in the pitcher! cried Lauremberg, who along with the others — never again! Moscherosch proclaimed — had lost his taste for brown beer. They remembered legends and old wives' tales about enchanted fishes who promised happiness: the tale of the talking flounder, who fulfilled a fisherman's greedy wife's every wish, all except the very last. The gentlemen became more and more fond of one another. How delightful that Rist should please to invite his friend Zesen to be his guest soon in Wedel. (I heard Buchner praising the absent Schottel's industriously compiled collection of words.) In a small bowl, the merchant Schlegel collected copper and silver coins to show the company's gratitude to the maids; and everyone, even the pious Gerhardt, gave something. When old Weckherlin, wishing, after and in spite of all that had happened, to do the landlady honor, bade her in courtly phrases leave the window and sit down at the table, we saw that Libuschka was wrapped in her horse blanket as though summer gave her the shivers. She did not hear him. She stood there absently, with rounded shoulders. Someone suggested that her thoughts were running after Stoffel.

Then there was talk of him and his green doublet. Since the poets were given to similes, the solitary young pike was likened to Gelnhausen and then allotted to his sponsor Harsdörffer. Several confided plans. It wasn't only the publishers — Mülbe and Endter in the lead — who wanted to get a few books out of the peace; the authors, too, had peace pageants or plays in the process of being written or rattling merrily around in their heads. Birken was planning an allegory in many parts for production in Nuremberg. Rist was intending to follow up his "Germany Yearning for Peace" with a "Germany Jubilant over the Peace." Harsdörffer felt sure that the court in Wolfenbüttel would welcome texts for ballets and operas. (Would Schütz be inclined to contribute great music?).

Still the landlady was showing her narrow back, humped under her blanket. But after Buchner had given it a try, not even Dach succeeded in persuading Libuschka or Courage or the obscurely begotten daughter of the Bohemian Count Thurn — or whoever else she might be — to join the poets at the long table. It was not until one of the maids (Elsabe?) spouted news while serving the last of the fried fish — seemed that a troop of gypsies had camped on the Klatenberg and the Ems Gate had been locked — that I saw Libuschka start and prick up her ears. But when, in his farewell to all, Simon Dach gave thanks to the landlady, her thoughts were again elsewhere.

He stood smiling, surveyed the long table, saw the bare fishbones heaped up between head and tail, and held the rolled and now sealed manifesto in his left hand. At the start of his speech there was something of a lump in his throat. But then, when he had devoted sufficient hard-found melancholy words to leavetaking, to the necessity of parting, and to the enduring ties of friendship, he spoke casually, freed from a burden, almost as though wishing to belittle the importance of the meeting, to patter away its weight. It cheered him, he said, to see that Greflinger's fish had made them all honest again. Whether the whole affair should be repeated at some auspicious time, he did not, or not yet, know, eagerly as he was being urged to set a place and time. Yes, he reflected, there had been vexations. Almost too many to count. But all in all the effort had proved worthwhile. After this, none of them would feel quite so isolated. And anyone who at home might feel constrained by narrow-mindedness, overwhelmed by new misery, deceived by false glitter, and in danger of losing the fatherland, was advised to remember the unscathed thistle at the Bridge Tavern hard by Telgte's Ems Gate, where the language had given promise of scope, supplied glitter, taken the place of the fatherland, and yielded names for all the misery of this world. No prince could equal them. Their riches could not be bought or sold. And even if they should be stoned and buried in hatred, a hand with a pen would rise out of the stone pile. They alone had the power to preserve for all time whatever truly deserved the name of German: "For, my dear and esteemed friends, brief as may be the time granted us to remain on earth, each one of our rhymes, provided our spirit has fashioned it from life, will mingle with eternity...."

Then, cutting into Dach's speech, which soared to incorporate the assembled poets into eternity, cutting into his sentence about immortal poesy (during which he lifted up the rolled appeal for

peace and likewise dedicated it to immortality), came the landlady's word from the window, not uttered loudly but sharpened
to a cry: "Fire!"

Then the maids came running in with their screams. And only
then — Simon Dach was still standing as though wanting in spite
of it all to complete his speech — did we all smell smoke.

Chapter 23

From the rear gable, whose damaged thatched roof frayed down
over the windows of the great hall, the smolder had eaten into the
drafty attic, where, drawing breath, it seized upon bales of straw,
straw spread out for sleeping, litter, bundles of fagots, and forgotten lumber, burst into running flames that leapt up to the rafters,
pierced the thatched roof on both sides, consumed the floorboards,
tumbled with burning joists and planks into the great hall, invaded
the front gable, and raced down the attic stairs and through the
hallways, attacking the hastily evacuated open-doored rooms, so
that sheaves of flame soon burst into the open from all the bed-
room windows and, rising skyward at one with the flaming roof,
gave the conflagration ultimate beauty.

That was how I saw it: the overwrought Zesen, the diabolical
Gryf, all saw it differently — all those who had barely managed
to escape into the courtyard with their luggage and had previously seen Glogau, Wittenberg, or Magdeburg in flames. No bolt
held firm. From the vestibule the blaze burst into the taproom,
the kitchen, the landlady's alcove and the remaining downstairs
rooms. The Bridge Tavern had one other guest than fire; the lime
trees planted on the weather side burned like torches. Despite the
absence of wind, sparks flew. Greflinger had barely time, with the
help of Lauremberg and Moscherosch, to lead the horses across
the courtyard, push the remaining covered wagons into the outer
gateway, and harness the terrified beasts; then the stable went up
in flames. Lauremberg was kicked by a black horse, and from then
on he limped on his right side. No one heard his lamentations.
All were concerned with themselves. I alone saw the three maids
load one mule with bundles and cooking pots. On the other mule

sat Libuschka, her back to the fire, but still wrapped in her horse blanket, as calm as if nothing had happened, the dogs whimpering at her feet.

Birken lamented because his industriously filled journal had been left in the attic with the young men's luggage. The publisher Endter deplored the loss of a stack of books he had been planning to sell in Brunswick. The manifesto! cried Rist. Where? Who? Dach stood empty-handed. The German poet's appeal for peace had been forgotten among the fishbones on the long table. In defiance of all reason, Logau wanted to run back into the taproom: to save the screed. Czepko had to hold him. And so, what would in any case not have been heard, remained unsaid.

When the roof of the Bridge Tavern collapsed and spark-spewing beams tumbled in the courtyard with chunks of thatch, the assembled poets and publishers gathered up their luggage and fled to the covered wagons. Schneuber looked after Lauremberg. Harsdörffer helped old Weckherlin. Gryphius and Zesen, who were still standing there enthralled by the fire, had to be called and shoved, and the praying Paul Gerhardt had to be wrenched out of his devotions.

Off to one side, Marthe Elsabe Marie prodded the pack mule and Libuschka's mount. The maid Marie told the student Scheffler that they were going to the Klatenberg. It almost looked as though the future Silesius were going with them to the gypsies. He leapt from the wagon, and Marie fobbed him off with a Catholic chain to which was attached the Telgte Madonna, stamped in silver. Without a word or gesture or backward glance, Libuschka rode off with her maids in the direction of the Outer Ems. The tavern dogs — four in number, as we now could see — followed them.

But the poets wanted to get home. In three covered wagons they arrived unharmed in Osnabrück, where they separated. Singly or in groups, as they had come, they started on the return journey. Lauremberg recovered from the horse's kick at Rist's parsonage. As far as Berlin, Gerhardt traveled with Dach and Albert. Without incurring serious danger, the Silesians reached home. Undeterred by the detour, the Nurembergers stopped off at Wolfenbüttel to report on the meeting. Buchner stopped in Köthen. Once again Weckherlin took ship in Bremen. Greflinger went to Hamburg, where he was planning to settle down. And Moscherosch? And Zesen?

None of us got lost. We all arrived. But during that century no one assembled us again in Telgte or anywhere else. I know how much further meetings would have meant to us. I know who I was then. I know even more. But who set the Bridge Tavern on fire I don't know, I don't know....

Translated by Ralph Manheim

Afterword by Leonard Forster

Grass sets his meeting in Telgte, in Westphalia, in May of 1647. The negotiations leading up to the treaties of Westphalia, which brought the Thirty Years' War to an end, were well under way. In England the Civil War had reached its most critical phase; Cromwell had by now realized that there could be no accommodation with the king. "Old Weckherlin" (not so old by present-day standards — he was only sixty-three) in London was busier than he had ever been in his life as secretary of the Committee of Both Kingdoms (a sort of Anglo-Scottish war cabinet): not too busy to prepare a collected edition of his German poetry, which was published at Amsterdam the following year, but much too busy to take ship to Bremen in order to attend a meeting of German poets — he had too many meetings already. In America the four colonies of Massachusetts, Connecticut, New Haven, and Plymouth were maintaining their recently formed, uneasy confederation. In Germany everyone — the various German powers, the Swedes, the French — was jockeying for position and making secret deals about the transfer of German territory. Only England was no longer in a position to pursue the Stewart dynastic aim — the restitution of the palatinate. On the surface the great division between Catholic and Protestant determined the confrontations, but vested interests of all kinds undermined this simple pattern, as indeed they had all along. The negotiations were held at the two cities of Osnabrück and Münster, thirty miles apart, one uneasily Protestant, the other firmly Catholic; emissaries posted hastily back and forth between the two. And between the two Grass situates his German poets, who had hoped to find accommodation at Oesede, close to Osnabrück, but who then had to settle for Telgte, close to Münster, a place of pilgrimage, whose miracle-working Madonna plays a part in the story and still draws thousands to the town. There they meet and feel themselves to represent German intellectual and literary life; in a fragmented and exhausted Germany, a rallying point for men of good will; a third force. To this end Grass brings them together in a meeting that never took place, that never could have taken place; indeed, it can be shown that none of the participants could have been in that place at that time — like Weckherlin.

Grass dedicates his book to Hans Werner Richter, and in the opening paragraph he makes it plain that he senses a parallel between events in 1647 and 1947. In 1947 Hans Werner Richter had gathered a number of German writers around him and formed a loose association of authors, critics, and publishers which provided a forum for reading and discussing new work. It met every year until 1967 and during those twenty years exerted a considerable influence on literature in West Germany. Grass himself first attended in 1955, and he was awarded the Prize of the Group 47 (as it came to be called) in 1958 for *The Tin Drum*. In his new book he has turned a kind of backward somersault and projected the twentieth-century group back into the seventeenth; he has put the question: What could we have done if we had been alive then? (In much the same way he has tried, in a more recent book, to envisage what he himself would have been like if he had been born ten years earlier and had thus been twenty-eight in 1945 instead of eighteen, with enlightening results; these imaginative gymnastics are more than just parlor tricks.)

German readers were quick to see the parallels, and critics looked eagerly for portraits (especially of themselves) as though Grass had written a *roman à clef* — but that is not the way the book works. There are some correspondences in detail between the two groups — readings of unpublished work, immediate criticism and comment to which the reader may not reply, the special seat in which the reader sits (known in the Group 47 as the "electric chair"), the presence of publishers and professors, and so on — enough to make it clear that a parallel is intended, but no more.

The parallel in the general situation of the two groups is clear. In 1647 the negotiations for peace after the most destructive war Germany had ever known were taking their mysterious and largely uncomprehended course; in 1947 negotiations for a peace treaty were being halfheartedly pursued and fronts were developing over the heads of the baffled and exhausted Germans after the most destructive war Germany has ever known. In an atmosphere of incomprehension and frustration people take recourse to art as something that can transcend political divisions. Grass's dustjacket design (drawn, as always, by himself), the hand with the frail quill pen emerging from a pile of rubble, points in the same direction; it is perhaps inspired by a baroque emblem showing a standard bearing an uplifted hand with a motto enjoining unity and confidence. In a similar spirit, Hugo von Hofmannsthal spoke in 1927 of literature as the intellectual living space of the nation.

In 1647 Germany was divided between Catholics and Protestants; in 1947 the division between the three Western zones of occupation on the one hand and the Soviet zone on the other was hardening; it later gave rise to the divided Germany we now know. The writers who came together in 1947 were from the Western zones (where an intellectual journal planned by Hans Werner Richter had been banned by American censorship); they were as critical of developments in the capitalist West as of those in the socialist East, and tried to maintain what in 1647 would have been called an "irenic" position. It is not for nothing that the poets Grass assembles in Telgte continually refer to men who represented what we would call now an "ecumenical" stand transcending denominational divisions. And just as in 1947 the group was firmly rooted in the West and despite all criticism in detail was oriented to Western thinking, so the poets in Telgte are firmly Protestant — indeed, Lutheran — in their thinking. German literature in 1647 was in fact almost exclusively Lutheran; the language of literature was the language of Luther's Bible. The purification of the German language in 1647 meant the elimination of foreign words (mostly Latin and French); in 1947 it meant the avoidance of Nazi terminology and Nazi-tainted concepts: in both cases the creation of a new idiom.

The meeting in Telgte was not a success; the voice of the third force went unheard because circumstances — fire and chance —

were too strong. So why lay this account of a failure at the feet of a respected colleague? Because he had achieved what Simon Dach and his friends could not: his achievement is seen afresh in the light of what might have been attempted three hundred years before but could not possibly have succeeded. The pen rising triumphant out of the rubble of the destroyed cities was Richter's achievement, not Dach's.

Dramatis Personae

HEINRICH ALBERT (1604–51): Composer and poet. He and SIMON DACH were the leading figures of the Königsberg circle of poets. He set his friends' verses to music in four parts and published them together with his settings.

JAKOB BALDE (1604–68): Jesuit Latin poet with a European reputation, admired by ANDREAS GRYPHIUS, who translated some of his lyric poems.

CORNELIUS BECKER (1561–1604): The author of metrical psalms for church use, set to familiar German tunes, a Lutheran counter to the German version of the Calvinist Huguenot metrical psalter by AMBROSIUS LOBWASSER, which was set to French tunes.

MATHIAS BERNEGGER (1582–1640): Professor in Strasbourg and an important figure in the intellectual life of the city. Himself a Protestant refugee from Austria, he stood for a liberal humanism transcending denominational barriers and maintained an extensive and influential correspondence with scholars in other countries.

SIEGMUND VON BIRKEN (1620–81): A Protestant refugee from Bohemia brought up in Nuremberg, where he became a leading figure in the local literary society, the PEGNITZ SHEPHERDS, and an extremely prolific writer. Contemporary portraits confirm his handsome face and curly hair, mentioned by Grass.

GEORG BLUM (d. 1648): A Prussian official and friend of DACH, ALBERT, and ROBERTHIN.

JAKOB BÖHME (1575–1624): A mystical shoemaker, often called *Philosophus teutonicus,* who sought to restore into a harmony the dualities of which men were aware. His writings were extremely influential, especially among his fellow Silesians, notably ABRAHAM VON FRANCKENBERG, JOHANN SCHEFFLER, and DANIEL VON CZEPKO, but also in England and America, where they influenced George Fox and the early Quakers.

AUGUST BUCHNER (1591–1661): A friend of MARTIN OPITZ and professor of poetry at Wittenberg. His views on the theory and practice of poetry were greatly respected during his lifetime, though they did not appear in print until after his death, compiled from students' lecture notes. His advocacy of dactyls and anapests went beyond Opitz's restriction of German verse to iambics and trochees and extended the resources of German poetry considerably, especially in the hands of HARSDÖRFFER and BIRKEN; among his pupils were KLAJ, ZESEN, and GERHARDT. The rivalry between Buchner and SCHOTTEL, who also was one of his pupils, seems to have been invented by Grass.

DANIEL VON CZEPKO UND REIGERSFELD (1591–1661): Silesian religious poet. He studied in Strasbourg under BERNEGGER and became a lawyer. In 1647 he was living on his estates as a country gentleman. His works circulated mainly in manuscript; his mystical epigrams were an important source of inspiration for JOHANN SCHEFFLER.

SIMON DACH (1605–59): Professor of poetry in Königsberg and the most important figure in the Königsberg circle of poets (see also ALBERT, BLUM, ROBERTHIN) following OPITZ. Much of his lyric poetry appeared in the musical publications of his friend ALBERT, but more of it consisted of occasional pieces written to order. His great poem on the destruction of the cucumber bower, referred to by Grass, was not published until 1936. The poem "Annie of Tharaw," translated by Longfellow and referred to by Grass, is now generally thought to be by ALBERT.

LUDWIG ELZEVIHR [LODEWIJK ELSEVIER] (1604–70): A member of the important Dutch publishing dynasty of Elsevier or Elzevir, the namesake and grandson of the founder of the firm. He established the Amsterdam branch and published many of the works of PHILIPP VON ZESEN.

WOLFGANG ENDTER (1593–1659): An important publisher in Nuremberg, specializing in Lutheran devotional literature and the works of members of the PEGNITZ SHEPHERDS (especially

HARSDÖRFFER and KLAJ). He did in fact publish the work by JOHANN RIST on the conclusion of peace, referred to by Grass.

ALEXANDER ERSKEIN (1598–1656): Swedish general of German-Scottish antecedents. Despite his cavalier treatment of the poets in this book, he was in fact a member of the FRUIT-BEARING SOCIETY, though there is no other evidence of his interest in literature.

PAUL FLEMING (1609–40): One of the major figures in German seventeenth-century literature. He took part in an embassy from the Duke of Holstein-Gottorp to Russia and Persia, in the course of which he spent a year in Reval and became engaged to Elsabe Niehus, the daughter of a city councilor. On his return he found she had married another, and he became engaged to her sister Anna. He went to Leiden to complete his medical studies but died suddenly before he could practice. His poetry, mainly lyrical, was highly thought of at the time, and still is. Some of his hymns have passed into church use in Germany, and a few in England as well.

ABRAHAM VON FRANCKENBERG (1593–1652): Silesian nobleman and mystical writer influenced by JAKOB BÖHME, whose biography he wrote. He was a friend of CZEPKO and SCHEFFLER and lived for a time in Danzig.

GIOVANNI GABRIELI (d. 1613): Venetian composer who had many contacts with Germany, the teacher of HEINRICH SCHÜTZ.

CHRISTOFFEL GELNHAUSEN: See GRIMMELSHAUSEN.

PAUL GERHARDT (1607–76): As an orthodox Lutheran pastor under a Calvinist prince, he experienced in his own person the dissensions among Protestants. He is the greatest German hymn-writer; twenty-seven of his hymns have been translated into English, and sixteen of them are in English church use, including "I know that my Redeemer liveth" and "O sacred Head, surrounded"; the original of "Now all the woods are sleeping," referred to by Grass, was not actually in print in 1647.

GEORG GREFLINGER (c. 1620–67): After a checkered career, he settled down in Hamburg in 1676 as a notary public and produced many translations. From 1665 on he published the *Nordischer Mercurius,* one of the best newspapers of the century.

JOHANN JAKOB CHRISTOFFEL VON GRIMMELSHAUSEN (1621–76): Appears here under the name of Christoffel Gelnhausen (after his birthplace, Gelnhausen, in Hesse). He wrote the picaresque and largely autobiographical novel *Simplicissimus* (1668), which is one of the great works of German literature. It deals with the author's variegated career in the Thirty Years' War and was continued and complemented in a number of further writings, which together make up a wide-ranging cycle. Grass's Gelnhausen has many traits in common with Simplicissimus, whose female counterpart is the heroine of one of these novels, with the name of Courasche; she appears in her own person in Grass's book as Libuschka. There are English translations of *Simplicissimus* by A .T .S. Goodrick (1912) and George Schulz-Behrendt (1965), of *Courasche* by Walter Wallich (1965) and Hans Speier (1964).

HUGO GROTIUS (1583–1645): Dutch humanist, diplomat, and international lawyer, universally respected in his day as a scholar and still a key figure in legal history. He was important in the irenic movement in the seventeenth century and was in contact with OPITZ, BERNEGGER, and LINGELSHEIM.

ANDREAS GRYPHIUS (1616–64): With OPITZ, FLEMING, SCHEFFLER, and GRIMMELSHAUSEN, a major figure in German seventeenth-century literature, both as a lyric poet and as a dramatist. Grass incorporated a memorable scene between the young Gryphius and the middle-aged Opitz in *The Flounder.* Some of Gryphius's religious poems have been translated for English church use. Besides his literary activity, which began early, he was a scholarly polymath who refused chairs at Uppsala and Heidelberg in order to enter the public service in Silesia.

GIAMBATTISTA GUARINI (1538–1612): Italian court poet. He wrote the classic pastoral play *Il pastor fido* (1580), which had a European vogue and was translated into German by HOFMANNS-WALDAU. Many of his poems were set to music.

GEORG PHILIPP HARSDÖRFFER (1607–58): The central figure of literary life in seventeenth-century Nuremberg. Together with JO-HANN KLAJ he founded the literary society of the PEGNITZ SHEP-HERDS, to which BIRKEN also belonged, in 1644. He studied at Strasbourg under BERNEGGER and eagerly adopted the metrical theories of BUCHNER. Besides being active in public life as a councilor of the city-state of Nuremberg, he was a prolific writer and a popularizer of contemporary science, philosophy, and literature.

CHRISTIAN HOFMANN VON HOFMANNSWALDAU (1616–79): Silesian nobleman and man of affairs. He wrote technically accomplished poetry comparable to that of the Restoration poets in England, but whereas they really were rakes, he really was not. His poems circulated widely in manuscript and set the tone for poetic production in Germany throughout the second half of the century, as OPITZ's had for the first half. They were not collected until after his death.

JOHANN KLAJ (1616–56): With HARSDÖRFFER, the moving spirit of the Nuremberg literary society of the PEGNITZ SHEPHERDS.

BERNHARD KNIPPERDOLLING (d. 1536): In 1534 a revolutionary group of Anabaptists led by Bernd Rottmann, Jan Beuckelson van Leiden, and Bernhard Knipperdolling took over the city of Mün-ster and established a theocratic state. They abolished Sundays and holy days, instituted love feasts, practiced polygamy, executed hostile citizens, and did away with all books except the Bible.

JOHANN LAUREMBERG (1590–1658): Professor of poetry at Rostock, his native town, later professor of mathematics at Sorø in Denmark. He wrote satires in Low German expressing a sturdy conservatism, one of which he reads in this book. They were, however, not actually in print at the time and did not appear until 1652.

LIBUSCHKA: See GRIMMELSHAUSEN.

GEORG MICHAEL LINGELSHEIM (1556–1636): Humanist and states-man in the service of the Palatinate, the principal figure of a literary circle in Heidelberg, in the early years of the century, to which ZINCGREF and the young OPITZ belonged. He maintained an extensive irenic and scholarly correspondence, especially with MATHIAS BERNEGGER.

AMBROSIUS LOBWASSER (1515–85): In 1573 he translated the Hu-guenot metrical psalms (by Clement Marot and Théodore de Bèze) into German, retaining the original meters. This translation, though Calvinist (see also BECKER), was influential in Lutheran circles and continued in use until the eighteenth century.

FRIEDRICH VON LOGAU (1604–55): Silesian nobleman and official, author of epigrams, two hundred of which appeared in 1638; the final collection, which appeared in 1653, comprised three thousand. They embody social and political satire in pregnant form.

LUDWIG, PRINCE OF ANHALT-KÖTHEN (1579–1650): Head of the FRUIT-BEARING SOCIETY.

GIAMBATTISTA MARINO (1569–1625): Italian poet in the high ba-roque style, greatly admired by HOFMANNSWALDAU. His poems were often set to music.

CLAUDIO MONTEVERDI (1567–1643): Italian composer who wrote the first operatic masterpiece, *Orfeo* (1607).

JOHANN MICHAEL MOSCHEROSCH (1601–69): Novelist and satirist of remote Spanish (apparently Marrano) antecedents, whose de-scriptions of life at the time of the Thirty Years' War (1642) were inspired by the *Sueños* (*Dreams*) of the Spanish author Francisco de Quevedo. Grass's allusions to his presumed Jewishness refer to his Marrano ancestry.

JOHANN PHILIPP MÜLBE (1625–67): Strasbourg publisher who brought out the works of MOSCHEROSCH and SCHNEUBER, among others.

JOHANN NAUMANN (1627–68): Hamburg publisher who issued works by RIST and ZESEN, but not, as Grass seems to imply, by MOSCHEROSCH.

GEORG NEUMARK (1621–81): He studied law in Königsberg, where he had contacts with DACH and other members of his circle. By 1647 he had only published one pastoral novel. He later became librarian and archivist in Weimar and kept the archives of the FRUIT-BEARING SOCIETY.

MARTIN OPITZ (1597–1639): By his reform of versification, reducing metrics to an easily grasped regular alternation of stressed and unstressed syllables (iambics and trochaics), he brought German poetry into line with what was being written elsewhere in Europe. He himself provided specimen models of the most important literary genres, either by translation or by original composition. Throughout the century he was regarded as the "father of German poetry." See also GRYPHIUS.

OTTAVIO RINUCCINI (1552–1621): Italian poet and author of libretti for the first operas, including the *Arianna* (1608), of MONTEVERDI. OPITZ translated his libretto *Dafne* for music by Heinrich Schütz (now lost).

JOHANN RIST (1607–67): A learned country parson, author of works of popular science and theology. He was a faithful follower of OPITZ in his numerous works of poetry. Seventeen of his religious poems have been translated into English for church use, including "Eternity, thou word of fear." He founded the ORDER OF ELBE SWANS in 1658. His feud with ZESEN, referred to by Grass, did not break out until 1648, though their relations were strained before that.

ROBERT ROBERTHIN (1600–1648): Prussian official, a friend of DASH and ALBERT and pupil of BERNEGGER.

JESAIAS ROMPLER VON LÖWENHALT (1628–58): Together with SCHNEUBER, he founded the UPRIGHT SOCIETY OF THE PINE TREE in Strasbourg in 1633.

JOHANN SCHEFFLER (1630–77): Silesian medical student in contact with the mystical circle around ABRAHAM VON FRANCKENBERG and CZEPKO. He was converted to Catholicism in 1652 and assumed the name of Angelus Silesius; he took orders in 1661 and became the moving spirit of the Counter-Reformation in Silesia. By virtue of his religious pastoral poems and his mystical epigrams, many written before his conversion, he is one of the great names in German literature. Some thirty of his poems have been translated for English church use, including "O Love who formedst me to wear." At the time of the meeting at Telgte he was in fact studying medicine in Italy. There is an English translation of his epigrams by J. E. C. Flitch (1932).

JOHANN MATHIAS SCHNEUBER (1614–65): Professor of poetry in Strasbourg, member of the PINE TREE SOCIETY and a friend of ROMPLER VON LÖWENHALT and MOSCHEROSCH.

JUSTUS GEORG SCHOTTEL (1612–76): The leading linguistic theorist of seventeenth-century Germany; his work of normative and systematic linguistics of the German language is still important. He was an official of the court of Brunswick-Wolfenbüttel for most of his life. His rivalry with BUCHNER seems to have been invented by Grass.

HEINRICH SCHÜTZ (1585–1672): One of the greatest precursors of Bach; he composed mainly religious music but also the earlier German opera, *Dafne*, to a text by OPITZ after RINUCCINI. The score is lost.

FRIEDRICH SPEE VON LANGENFELD (1591–1635): A Jesuit, the first important writer of sacred poetry in Catholic Germany in the vernacular after the Reformation. Several of his religious poems have passed into English church use. He published anonymously an attack on witch hunting to which Grass refers, based on his experience as chaplain in Würzburg. This was the only work of his to appear in his lifetime.

TORQUATO TASSO (1544–95): Italian lyric and epic poet. The combat between Tancredi and Clorinda from the twelfth book of his epic *Gerusalemme liberata* (1576) was frequently set to music.

ANDREAS TSCHERNING (1611–59): Professor of poetry in Rostock and a pupil and friend of BUCHNER.

GEORG RUDOLF WECKHERLIN (1584–1653): Lyric poet and civil servant. From 1619 on he lived and worked in London and was Milton's predecessor as Latin secretary under the Commonwealth. His residence in London put him out of touch with developments in Germany, but before that he was a pioneer of baroque poetry in Germany before OPITZ and continued to be respected later, especially by South German opponents of Opitz like ROMPLER and his PINE TREE SOCIETY.

PHILIPP VON ZESEN (1619–89): Poet and novelist who lived largely by his pen at Amsterdam (one of the first German authors to do so). He founded a literary society, the GERMAN-MINDED ASSOCIATION, in Hamburg in 1642. He followed the metrical theories of BUCHNER, whose pupil he was, and he was in touch with the Nuremberg group, especially HARSDÖRFFER. His feud with RIST is referred to by Grass.

JULIUS WILHELM ZINCGREF (1591–1635): Palatine diplomat and official, and a prominent member of the Heidelberg circle around LINGELSHEIM. He published the first collected volume of poetry by OPITZ in Strasbourg in 1624 and an influential collection of proverbs and apothegms in 1626.

Literary Societies

Grass mentions six. These societies were founded for the cultivation and purification of the German language after the model of the Italian academies, especially the Accademia della Crusca (Florence 1582). The main aims of all were similar: the cultivation of the German language, the worship of God, and the pursuit of virtue; in other words, they were social and moral as well as linguistic and literary. Many literary men belonged to more than one; this circumstance, as well as the similarity of aims, meant that the rivalry which Grass assumes to have existed was not important though there were differences of policy and emphasis. The Pegnitz Shepherds, for instance, admitted women on an equal footing with men; the Fruit-bearing Society discriminated against the clergy and in favor of the nobility; the Pine Tree resisted the literary hegemony of Silesia; and so on. These societies represented attempts at organizing the literary world — producers and consumers and patrons — which continued despite the vicissitudes of the Thirty Years' War; they also sponsored publications, either directly or indirectly. All the societies dealt with here were Protestant, though the Pegnitz Shepherds admitted a few Catholics. All aimed at producing grammars, dictionaries, manuals of poetics, and translations, and at providing models of the various literary genres, though not all actually did so. In all societies the members received special names, emblems, and insignia. Business was conducted mainly by correspondence; no general meeting of any society is recorded. If there had been one, it would probably have been very much like the meeting at Telgte, though doubtless more formal.

GERMAN-MINDED ASSOCIATION (*Deutschgesinnte Genossenschaft*): Founded by ZESEN in 1642, with seat at first in Hamburg, later in Amsterdam. Members included BIRKEN, HARSDÖRFFER, KLAJ, MOSCHEROSCH, and ROMPLER; many were of noble birth.

ORDER OF ELBE SWANS (*Elbschwanenorden*): Founded by RIST in 1658, apparently as a subsidiary of the FRUIT-BEARING SOCIETY.

234 · *Günter Grass*

FRUIT-BEARING SOCIETY (*(Fruchtbringende Gesellschaft, Palmen-orden*): The first and most prestigious of the literary societies, founded in 1617 under the presidency of Prince Ludwig of Anhalt-Köthen, who was already a member of the Accademia della Crusca. By 1652 it had 527 members, most of whom were of noble birth and relatively few of whom were greatly concerned with literature. Nonetheless the influence of the society was important, thanks to the consistent critical work put in by its first president; its tendency was irenic. Among its members were BIRKEN, BUCHNER, GRYPHIUS, HARSDÖRFFER, LOGAU, MOSCHEROSCH, OPITZ, SCHOTTEL, RIST, and ZESEN, though not by any means all of them at the time Grass's story takes place.

PEGNITZ SHEPHERDS (*Pegnitzschäfer, Blumenorden*): Founded by HARSDÖRFFER and KLAJ in Nuremberg in 1644, partly inspired by Sir Philip Sidney's *Arcadia*. Few members were of noble birth, but many were from the patriciate of the cities. Women were admitted as members (though very few). HARSDÖRFFER, the first president, had admitted only fourteen members by 1658; his successor BIRKEN admitted many more.

CUCUMBER LODGE (*Kürbishütte*): Not a literary society in the then accepted sense, with a constitution, officers, insignia, etc., but an informal group of friends meeting at intervals, usually in HEINRICH ALBERT's garden in Königsberg in a bower overgrown with cucumbers (cp. Isaiah 1:8), where they used to sing their own songs set to music by him. Among the members were DACH, ALBERT, BLUM, and ROBERTHIN; OPITZ once paid them a visit.

UPRIGHT SOCIETY OF THE PINE TREE (*Aufrichtige Tannengesell-schaft*): Founded in Strasbourg in 1633 by ROMPLER, as a rallying point for South German opponents of OPITZ. MOSCHEROSCH and WECKHERLIN may have been members. SCHNEUBER was a co-founder.

Part Three

THE BALLERINA

In the apartment of a restauranteur, I found some prints that illustrated scenes in the manner of the commedia dell'arte, pantomimic performances, all kinds of allegorical stage magic. One of these pictures is the subject of this discourse.

Small, accomplished etchings, arrayed intricately one above the other deep in the room, in the open darkness of the window, a long-legged rumpled bed — as though an insomniac had abandoned it — in the background a narrow wardrobe, a bookshelf half-imagined. Sketched first and foremost with a bold hand, carefully retaining the shade of the paper, the most exciting scene unfolds: The poet is sitting on his cheap chair, dressed carelessly in shirt, shawl, and trousers. He has leaned back, lets his head droop with the pen, has seized the blank page in his left hand. Thus, still incredulous, he catches sight of the ballerina. Wearing pointed shoes, she is standing on his table. The crossed ribbons above her ankles can be seen, then a lavish, weightless skirt billows up, her breast breathes under pearls and an openwork flounce. Slender from her waist up, with arms raised she stretches to the ends of her fingers. Under the faint pain in the lines of her brow she scarcely smiles and looks at the observer of the print as though she were dancing for him and not for the poet. The quiet contour of these positions make us believe that a series of well-chosen movements conclude like this. Perhaps, however, she will begin anew, now will also fill this room, almost obstructed by wardrobe, table, chair, and rumpled bed, with pirouettes or, in a fragile arabesque, like a pair of scales, she will signify harmony. But perhaps a leap, a slow leap distinct to the very end, will carry her in an ascending line through the open window into the night sky and leave the empty table behind. He, paper and pen in his hands, will try to grab her, will want to keep what cannot be kept, least of all by one who grabs with filled hands. Then he will find his way back to his chair, will sit for a long time, the hand with the pen drooping, in his left the quickly grasped paper, will look for the place on the table where everything happened, and will find a scratch — stupid like all scratches. And then the poet in that etching will write.

We may smile while observing this naive picture and with a finger seek and find the places that, much too distressing to us, resemble the dusty porcelain flourishes in grandmotherly glass cabinets. We will banish the intimacy of this encounter between poet and muse to the garden bower and not permit that kind of unasked-for offering on the surface of our desk. And still, it could be that today, when we exchange garden statuary and fragile shepherd idylls for Bakelite ashtrays and glass cabinets for kidney-shaped tables — a questionable profit — the poet with his typewriter needs this specific event. Even today no poem comes into being without one of the muses bending down to help.

Should the poet be moved to describe the ballerina — her dance gave him reason enough, the primly indifferent space traced by her movement — he will wish to step closer, to look beyond it, to penetrate the illusion. He resembles the stamp collector who, scrutinizing it, holds a small, coveted quadrangle to the light in order to have a clear view of the perforations and the watermark. The crown and smile of the colorful queen, no matter how successful the miniature, will never influence the discriminating eye.

Let us return to our etching. A moment of the most artful performance left the poet with only the trace of a ballet shoe on the desk surface. He will write about that. The performance will become a vision, the scratch a sign. But the ballerina? He will speak of the window through which she entered and departed, and should a fine poet have been sitting at the table — we cannot judge from the picture — he will refrain from calling the ballerina's eyes golden, her features winsome, and her tiny feet dainty. Such observations about eyes, face, and feet are not practicable in such vague moments. For that he would require permission to stand behind the scene, to peer into the dressing room.

Her Body, Her Accouterment

Any tenor, when his voice demands it, will reach around for the back of a chair — and a chair or something he can hold onto will always be standing nearby — with this grip he will give his voice new power, he will accomplish his aria more superlatively. But not the ballerina. She does not have much liberty. Her body, this excrescence of tortured, outwardly twisting beauty close to faintly hysterical weeping, as soon as she leaves the wings with tiny *pas de courus,* remains her only accouterment. Alone she draws her figures, and between the third and fourth pirouette achieves that degree of isolation that even the most German minor poet does not achieve. Will this place of banishment be occupied with every single whirl, if it is only spirited enough? Is it just like that when little Irma whirls in a waltz tempo and blissfully closes her eyes the while? We will see that with the pirouette, with this spiraling, affected abstraction, the last possible whirl seems to be accomplished, that the artistic feat is here revealed. Artistic because it is no longer nature, because here the paper rose — we know it from shooting galleries — is ahead of all garden growth and will never wither. And artistic, too, because force, the renunciation of foolish, limited limbs, trivial polishing on an empty form, suffices here and always for a weightless loveliness without first or last name.

It remains then for the dressing room to call this sweating, twenty-seven-year-old creature a Vera or a Tascha, to shelter a body marked by hard work, which lisps and no longer has an appendix. Now it becomes apparent how innocuously and banal the pause between two gracefully strenuous masterly performances can be spent. The ballerina knits woolen socks for her little brother, the ballerina talks nonsense, the ballerina recently became engaged, though it is not impossible that she will soon again break the engagement. The ballerina puts on glasses, she is somewhat nearsighted, and leafs through the illustrated until she finds the crossword puzzle and solves half of it. Now the ballerina weeps a bit. She had a bad balance today, she "blurred the arabesque" and during the third pirouette "thudded from the point" — and that's not allowed.

Seeking help, the tenor may reach for the back of the chair when he is only singing. Little Irma may even stagger a bit in the middle of the waltz and determine pensively that everything is whirling. No one will be mad at her for that. But when the ballerina "thuds from the point," then the parquet freezes, then it turns hot in the balconies, the stage stretches bright as day and dispassionately, programs are folded, unfolded, and all the whispering means that the ballerina is already twenty-seven, lisps, and no longer has an appendix.

On Dancing Barefoot

The enemy and deadly serious opposite of the ballerina is the modern dancer. While the ballerina moves her body according to firm rules and smiles the while, as though irrelevance had been painted in the corners of her mouth, the modern dancer dances with her troubled soul and moves her limbs as though her own personal and moreover bent knee were reason enough to rivet an eighth of the parquet and the half-filled balconies for two long hours. The ballerina lives with her mother, does not smoke, eats yogurt and bananas, feeds a little dog, and before and after practicing feels tired, just tired.

The modern dancer is educated. She can recite "The Lay of Life and Death" by heart and has seen Cocteau's "Orphée" five times already. In her furnished room hangs an African mask, a reproduction of a picture by Paul Klee, and the photograph of a Siamese temple dancer. She makes all her own clothes herself and never goes to the hairdresser with her long, marvelous hair. Since the ballerina goes to bed early, any nightlife for her, except for a few movies, is regulated in a fairly innocuous way. The modern dancer has a friend who plays the piano. Both live in constant fear of having a child but want a child, she even wants *children,* motherhood. Now, as though to compensate, with flowing hair — thus her aversion to the hairdresser — in a sack-like robe, she dances lullabies, expectations, deliverance — her last creation was called: Weeping Embryo.

The modern dancer dances barefoot, so she could be called a barefoot dancer, too. The practice of the ballerina is like a monotonous, Prussian regimen. Tortured, squeezed flesh hides in white, red, even silver ballet shoes. The feet of the ballerina may be called ugly. Flayed, open toes, an oversized instep. They seem to be the true victims of all this effectively displayed beauty. Here below is collected what harmonious gesture and mellow smile conceal above. The proportions of these shoes are still determined by the Middle Ages and the Inquisition. So we may appraise the desirable thirty-two fouettês as a confession, and nothing — no barefoot dance — will be able to replace this confession, this pain.

Asceticism before the Mirror

Like a nun, exposed to every kind of seduction, the ballerina lives in a condition of the most rigorous asceticism. This comparison should not be surprising, since all art that has come down to us was always the result of consistent restraint and never of genial excess. Even when at times outbursts into the illicit made it, and makes it, seem that art was permitted anything, even the most versatile spirit always devised rules, fences, forbidden rooms. So the space of our ballerina is also limited, visible at a glance and permits alterations only within the floor space that is available. The exigencies of time will again and again demand of the ballerina a new face, will wish to hold up exotic and pseudo-exotic masks before her. She will go along with this decorative little game, knowing that every fashion looks good on her. The true revolution will, however, have to take place in her own palace.

How similar it is with painting. How senseless do all attempts seem, to perceive fundamental discoveries in the invention of new materials, in the exchange of oil painting for a spray-paint procedure on aluminum. Dilettantism, easily recognized by its mannerisms, will never be able to oust the tenacious métier, conservative even in a revolution.

Through the ballerina the mirror becomes an unrelenting tool of asceticism. She trains before its surface wide awake. Her dance is not a dance with closed eyes. The mirror is to her nothing more than a glass that reflects everything, ultrabluntly, a merciless moralist, faith in whom becomes commandment to her. The things the poet inflicts on a mirror! What mystic, illegible postcards does he stick in its baroque frame. To him it is exit, entrance, like young, still ignorant cats he looks behind the pane and there finds, at best, a small broken box filled with assorted buttons, a bundle of old letters that he never expected to find again, and a comb full of hair. Only at moments of definite transformation, when our body seems enriched or impoverished, do we — like she — stand with wide-open eyes before a mirror. It shows girls their puberty, no pregnancy escapes it, no missing tooth — in the event a laugh provokes it. Perhaps the hairdresser, the taxi driver, the tailor, the painter at work on a self-portrait, the prostitute who has furnished her small room with a number of such plain-spoken shards, have something in common with the ballerina. It is the careworn look of the artisan, of the human being who works with his body, it is the examination in the confessional mirror of conscience.

Applause and Curtains

Applause is the small change of the ballerina. She counts it very carefully, and if these coins — like other hard cash — had the property of being able to be stuffed into a stocking, she would save them for later, for times when hands will be wanting, when no one will clap anymore, when clapping could hurt, when the man who controls the curtain will no longer have a reason to make marks on a blackboard till it says: Sixteen curtains today, two more than yesterday.

The same thoroughness and care with which we count the calls of the cuckoo during a Sunday stroll in the municipal woods is shown by the ballerina, when it is a matter of inferring the potential number of curtains from the length and intensity of applause. She counts and would like to tempt the parquet and the balconies with her precise and charming curtsies, like we tempt the cuckoo who calls out the years left to us. — Then, after the last curtain, the ballerina collapses like a house of cards suddenly exposed to a draft. Each of her otherwise poised limbs slips into whatever. The order of her face, in that plateful of cosmetic fare, gives way. Her eyes are capable of no glance; overstrained they slip away and widen horribly. The same with her mouth. At all times ready to break out into hysteria, a smile — meant harmlessly — strains so much that a cramp sits in its corners. Why this constant wrinkling of the brow, this raising of the eyebrows? Every piece of the exhibition arranged with much effort and ability leaves its place. The ballerina seems completely out of hand.

The Dot

She raises her arm in effortless flexion. The hand rises above, a superfluously many-membered projection. All of that without significance, merely nice to look at, not even a greeting or an invitation to step nearer. Halfway to becoming an ornament it only wishes to show what is there, that an arm bends and subdivides the background, that there where the little finger points is a dot that all beauty obeys — and so too does the ballerina. The thought would never occur to her that she could flex her arm differently, flex it so that it could signify only strength, desperation, or even, horribly bent, mean an accident. Never would she send her finger toward any dot other than that which is absurd as a goldfish and still so spacious, so insatiable, that all our ballast could be lost in it. For were we to say to our ballerina: "Oh, dance the atom bomb for us!" she would spin seven pirouettes and afterwards come smiling to a standstill. And were someone to come and wish to see the traffic problem or reunification danced, she would at once show him that combination of aesthetic figures at the end of which then an arabesque would complete the reunification and solve the traffic problem, as she points to the dot.

Accompanying all these demonstrations sounds the "Turkish March" or a piece of the "Nutcracker Suite," it does not matter, the ballerina cannot be called especially musical. She lets the pianist set the tempo, define it, and count it out, and surrenders herself in exquisite devotion to the ballet master, so that he determines the number and sequence of the attitudes, figures, relevés, and altogether formulates her appearance.

It may also be the "Radetsky March," whose inescapable sounds accompany her way onto the stage in bewildering irrelevancy, if only at the end, with the last chord and drum beat, the finger again points at the dot, then it is all right.

Nature and Art

Back to the picture again. The ballerina, in stiff, lightly crumpled fabrics, was dancing on the table. The open window presaged that her entrance and exit required no door. The room, table, and window can easily be exchanged for a stage, a platform, wings. The poet, narrow-chested in the etching, is likewise transformed, becomes a leaping, dancing troubadour. The tale takes its further development with a pas de deux. Love, separation, temptation, jealousy, and death. This action is simple, just a pretext to show the ballerina in her difficult existence, dancing on tiptoes. Here is fulfilled in the richest decor what the daily drill to the sounds of a piano out of tune prescribes for the body and only the body.

Who forces the ballerina, this sensitive creature, almost insipid in daily life, to take her position at the barre and under the supervision of an elderly, often somewhat cynical ballet mistress to train year after year? Is it only ambition, only the drive for success? — Reluctantly she enters the rehearsal hall, locates her position. Reluctantly she performs her first movements. And then it seizes her. Suddenly this battle against her body is as fascinating to her as a deadly serious marching review in goose-step is to a pacifist.

After all, if it is just a pedestrian joke to give the poet on his way the all-too-well-meant advice always to write naturally, how much more intolerable to the practiced eye would be the dancer who dared — always following some unknown impulse — to hop about the stage naturally, that is, without any sort of decorum, babbling, and extravagant as the vegetation of a primeval forest or even a greenhouse.

It has become matter-of-course for us not to gobble up a piece of mutton barbarically in a raw, still bloody state. No, we fry, boil, or stew it, always add a spice to the pot, say finally that it is done and tasty, eat it politely with knife and fork, tie a napkin around our neck. The other arts ought, in the final analysis, to be treated like the art of cooking and — if now and then voices make themselves heard and want to pronounce classical ballet dead — it ought to be declared with admiration that up to now this art, even more than the arts of cooking and of painting, may be called one of the most unnatural and thus most perfected in form of all arts.

Only when all the experiments — and until now only experiments have been shown — have succeeded in crystalizing equally strong formulas of choreographic movement, which like ballet lacks all fortuitousness, will the ballerina bow for the last time.

Perhaps then the immense wholly artificial doll will be revealed. In his little treatise about the marionette theater Kleist refers to her. Kokoschka had such an insensitive girl tailored for himself. In Schelmmer's triadic ballet boldly sketched figures took the first, important step. Perhaps the two will become compatible and enter upon a marriage — the marionette and the ballerina.

Translated by A. Leslie Willson

Part Four

SELECTED POEMS

Hochwasser

Wir warten den Regen ab,
obgleich wir uns daran gewöhnt haben
hinter der Gardine zu stehen, unsichtbar zu sein.
Löffel ist Sieb geworden, niemand wagt mehr
die Hand auszustrecken.
Es schwimmt jetzt Vieles in den Straßen,
das man während der trockenen Zeit sorgfältig verbarg.
Wie peinlich des Nachbarn verbrauchte Betten zu sehen.
Oft stehen wir vor dem Pegel
und vergleichen unsere Besorgnis wie Uhren.
Manches läßt sich regulieren.
Doch wenn die Behälter überlaufen, das ererbte Maß voll ist,
werden wir beten müssen.
Der Keller steht unter Wasser,
wir haben die Kisten hochgetragen
und prüfen den Inhalt mit der Liste.
Noch ist nichts verloren gegangen. —
Weil das Wasser jetzt sicher bald fällt,
haben wir begonnen Sonnenschirmchen zu nähen.
Es wird sehr schwer sein wieder über den Platz zu gehen,
deutlich, mit bleischwerem Schatten.
Wir werden den Vorhang am Anfang vermissen
und oft in den Keller steigen,
um den Strich zu betrachten,
den das Wasser uns hinterließ.

The Flood

We are waiting for the rain to stop,
although we have got accustomed
to standing behind the curtain, being invisible.
Spoons have become sieves, nobody dares now
to stretch a hand out.
Many things are floating in the streets,
things people carefully hid in the dry time.
How awkward to see your neighbor's stale old beds.
Often we stand by the water gauge
and compare our worries like watches.
Some things can be regulated.
But when the containers overflow, the inherited cup fills,
we shall have to pray.
The cellar is submerged, we brought the crates up
and are checking their contents against the list.
So far nothing has been lost.
Because the water is now certain to drop soon,
we have begun to sew parasols.
It will be difficult to cross the square once more,
distinct, with a shadow heavy as lead.
We shall miss the curtain at first,
and go into the cellar often
to consider the mark
that the water bequeathed us.

Translated by Christopher Middleton

Nächtliches Stadion

Langsam ging der Fußball am Himmel auf.
Nun sah man, daß die Tribüne besetzt war.
Einsam stand der Dichter im Tor,
doch der Schiedsrichter pfiff: Abseits.

Familiär

In unserem Museum, — wir besuchen es jeden Sonntag, —
hat man eine neue Abteilung eröffnet.
Unsere abgetriebenen Kinder, blasse, ernsthafte Embryos,
sitzen dort in schlichten Gläsern
und sorgen sich um die Zukunft ihrer Eltern.

Stadium at Night

Slowly the football rose in the sky.
Now one could see that the stands were packed.
Alone the poet stood at the goal
but the referee whistled: offside.

Translated by Michael Hamburger

Family Matters

In our museum — we always go there on Sundays —
they have opened up a new department.
Our aborted children, pale, serious embryos,
sit there in plain glass jars
and worry about their parents' future.

Translated by Michael Hamburger

Die Bösen Schuhe

Die Schönheit sieht —
und oben im Applaus
gerinnt das Lächeln, Milch
in bloßen Schalen,
Gewittern ausgesetzt und der Zitrone,
zerdrückt mit Schwermut, fünf verbrauchten Fingern,
doch ohne Absicht, Aussicht auf Erfolg.

Ein Ausflug junger Mädchen im April,
mit Hälsen, die an Zugluft leiden.
Nun abgeschnitten diese Köpfe,
nur Säulen bleiben, die Akropolis.
Geflüchtet sind die Hüte, Kapitäle,
ein abgestanden Bier, — die Schönheit dauert
in spitzen Schuhen, relevé.

So langsam springt das Glück,
den Sonntagsjägern deutlich.
Mit weißen Händen, so zerbrochnen Blumen,
daß man die Mühe, Kolophonium riecht.
Und Schweiß aus unendeckten Höhlen,
und Tränen, Hysterie vorm Spiegel, —
danach, in der gemütlichen Garderobe.

Nein, unerträglich ohne dich, Tabak,
ist dieser Blick in die gestellte Szene.
Denn was sich beugt und ausläuft, eine Uhr,
sich dreht und oben wimmeln Augen,
doch leergelöffelt, ohne Freundlichkeit,
den Vorglanz Nachher und die Hoffnung auf: Bis gleich.
Nur wieder Stand, die angewärmte Geste,
die erst bei dreißig Grad zum port de bras gefriert.

Wer löst denn diese Haltung ab
und bricht der Venus unerlaubte,
der Arktis nachgelaßne Beine?

The Wicked Shoes

The Beauty looks —
aloft in the applause
the smile is trickling, milk
in lidless dishes,
exposed to thundershowers and to lemons,
expressed with melancholy, five used fingers,
without intent or prospect of success.

An outing of young girls in April,
with throats that suffer from the drafts.
These heads are now decapitated,
but columns now remain, Acropolis.
The hats have fled, capitals,
a beer left standing — beauty endures
in pointed shoes, relevé.

So slowly does good fortune leap,
quite plain to weekend hunters.
With white hand, such crushed flowers,
that one can smell the effort, resin.
And sweat from undiscovered hollows,
and tears, hysteria before the mirror —
afterwards, in the pleasant dressing room.

Without you quite unbearable, tobacco,
is this glance in the scene set up.
Because what bows and trickles out, a clock,
what twirls and eyes aquiver above,
but spooned out empty, and not friendly,
the ante-brilliance After, and the hope for: Soon.
Just the pose again, the warmed-up gesture,
which freezes to a port de bras at 90 degrees.

But then who can resolve this stance
and break forbidden legs of Venus,
the legs bequeathed by the Arctic!

Wer nimmt den krustig alten Füßen
die bösen, spitzen Schuhe ab
und sagt zum Arabesk vorm Sterben:
O sei doch barfuß, nackt und tot.

Who will take the wicked, pointed shoes
off of the callused, aged feet
and say to the perishing arabesque:
O do be barefoot, naked, dead.

Translated by A. Leslie Willson

Blechmusik

Damals schliefen wir in einer Trompete.
Es war sehr still dort,
wir träumten von keinem Signal,
lagen, wie zum Beweis,
mit offenem Mund in der Schlucht, —
damals, ehe wir ausgestoßen.

War es ein Kind, auf dem Kopf
einen Helm aus gelesener Zeitung,
war es ein irrer Husar,
der auf Befehl aus dem Bild trat,
war es schon damals der Tod,
der so seinen Stempel behauchte?

Heute, ich weiß nicht, wer uns geweckt hat,
vermummt als Blumen in Vasen
oder in Zuckerdosen,
von jedem bedroht, der Kaffee trinkt
und sein Gewissen befragt:
Ein oder zwei Stuckchen oder gar drei.

Nun fliehen wir und mit uns unser Gepäck.
Alle halbleeren Tüten, jeden Trichter im Bier,
kaum verlassene Mäntel, stehengebliebene Uhren,
Gräber, die andre bezahlten
und Frauen, die sehr wenig Zeit haben,
füllen wir kurzfristig aus.

In Schubladen voller Wäsche und Liebe,
in einem Ofen, der Nein sagt
und nur seinen Standpunkt erwärmt,
in einem Telefon blieben unsere Ohren zurück
und hören, nun schon versöhnlich,
dem neuen Zeichen Besetzt zu.

Music for Brass

Those days we slept in a trumpet.
It was very quiet in there,
we never dreamed it would sound,
lay, as if to prove it,
open-mouthed in the gorge —
those days, before we were blown out.

Was it a child, on his head
a helmet of studied newspaper,
was it a scatterbrained hussar
who walked at a command out of the picture,
was it even in those days death
who breathed that way on his rubber stamp?

Today, I don't know who woke us,
disguised as flowers in vases,
or else in sugar bowls,
threatened by anyone who drinks coffee
and questions his conscience:
one lump or two, or even three.

Now we're on the run and our luggage with us.
All half-empty paper bags, every crater in our beer,
cast-off coats, clocks that have stopped,
graves paid for by other people,
and women very short of time,
for awhile we fill them.

In drawers full of linen and love,
in a stove that says No
and warms its own standpoint only,
in a telephone our ears have stayed behind
and listen, already appeasing,
to the new tone for busy.

Damals schliefen wir in einer Trompete.
Hin und zurück träumten wir,
Alleen gleichmäßig bepflanzt.
Auf ruhigem, endlosem Rücken
lagen wir jenem Gewölbe an
und träumten von keinem Signal.

Those days we slept in a trumpet.
Backward and forward we dreamed,
avenues, symmetrically planted.
On a tranquil unending back
we lay against that bell,
and never dreamed it would sound.

Translated by
Christopher Middleton

Im Ei

Wir leben im Ei.
Die Innenseite der Schale
haben wir mit unanständigen Zeichnungen
und den Vornamen unserer Feinde bekritzelt.
Wir werden gebrütet.

Wer uns auch brütet,
unseren Bleistift brütet er mit.
Ausgeschlüpft eines Tages,
werden wir uns sofort
ein Bildnis des Brütenden machen.

Wir nehmen an, daß wir gebrütet werden.
Wir stellen uns ein gutmütiges Geflügel vor
und schreiben Schulaufsätze
über Farbe und Rasse
der uns brütenden Henne.

Wann schlüpfen wir aus?
Unsere Propheten im Ei
streiten sich für mittelmäßige Bezahlung
über die Dauer der Brutzeit.
Sie nehmen einen Tag X an.

Aus Langeweile und echtem Bedürfnis
haben wir Brutkästen erfunden.
Wir sorgen uns sehr um unseren Nachwuchs im Ei.
Gerne würden wir jener, die über uns wacht,
unser Patent empfehlen.

Wir aber haben ein Dach überm Kopf.
Senile Küken,
Embryos mit Sprachkenntnissen
reden den ganzen Tag
und besprechen noch ihre Träume.

In the Egg

We live in the egg.
We have covered the inside wall
of the shell with dirty drawings
and the Christian names of our enemies.
We are being hatched.

Whoever is hatching us
is hatching our pencils as well.
Set free from the egg one day,
at once we shall draw a picture
of whoever is hatching us.

We assume that we're being hatched.
We imagine some good-natured fowl
and write school essays
about the color and breed
of the hen that is hatching us.

When shall we break the shell?
Our prophets inside the egg
for a middling salary argue
about the period of incubation.
They posit a day called X.

Out of boredom and genuine need
we have invented incubators.
We are much concerned about our offspring inside the egg.
We should be glad to recommend our patent
to her who looks after us.

But we have a roof over our heads.
Senile chicks,
polyglot embryos
chatter all day
and even discuss their dreams.

Und wenn wir nun nicht gebrütet werden?
Wenn diese Schale niemals ein Loch bekommt?
Wenn unser Horizont nur der Horizont
unserer Kritzeleien ist und auch bleiben wird?
Wir hoffen, daß wir gebrütet werden.

Wenn wir auch nur noch vom Brüten reden,
bleibt doch zu befürchten, daß jemand,
außerhalb unserer Schale, Hunger verspürt,
uns in die Pfanne haut und mit Salz bestreut. —
Was machen wir dann, ihr Brüder im Ei?

And what if we're not being hatched?
If this shell will never break?
If our horizon is only that
of our scribbles, and always will be?
We hope that we're being hatched.

Even if we only talk of hatching
there remains the fear that someone
outside our shell will feel hungry
and crack us into the frying pan with a pinch of salt.
What shall we do then, my brethren inside the egg?

Translated by Michael Hamburger

Die Vogelscheuchen

Ich weiß nicht, ob man Erde kaufen kann,
ob es genügt, wenn man vier Pfähle,
mit etwas Rost dazwischen und Gestrüpp
im Sand verscharrt und Garten dazu sagt.

Ich weiß nicht, was die Stare denken.
Sie flattern manchmal auf, zerstäuben,
besprenkeln meinen Nachmittag,
tun so, als könnte man sie scheuchen,
als seien Vogelscheuchen Vogelscheuchen
und Luftgewehre hinter den Gardinen
und Katzen in der Bohnensaat.

Ich weiß nicht, was die alten Jacken
und Hosentaschen von uns wissen.
Ich weiß nicht, was in Hüten brütet,
welchen Gedanken was entschlüpft
und flügge wird und läßt sich nicht verscheuchen;
von Vogelscheuchen werden wir behütet.

Sind Vogelscheuchen Säugetiere?
Es sieht so aus, als ob sie sich vermehren,
indem sie nachts die Hüte tauschen:
schon stehn in meinem Garten drei,
verneigen sich und winken höflich
und drehen sich und zwinkern mit der Sonne
und reden, reden zum Salat.

Ich weiß nicht, ob mein Gartenzaun
mich einsperren, mich aussperren will.
Ich weiß nicht, was das Unkraut will,
weiß nicht, was jene Blattlaus will bedeuten,
weiß nicht, ob alte Jacken, alte Hosen,
wenn sie mit Löffeln in den Dosen
rostig und blechern windwärts läuten,
zur Vesper, ob zum Ave läuten,
zum Aufstand aller Vogelscheuchen läuten.

The Scarecrows

I don't know if you can buy ground,
if it's enough to bury four posts,
with just rust in between and underbrush,
into the sand and call it garden.

I don't know what the starlings think.
Sometimes they flutter up, disperse,
besprinkle then my afternoon,
and act as though they could be scared,
as though scarecrows all were scarecrows
and B-B-guns behind the drapes
and cats among the tendrilous beans.

I don't know what old jackets
and panted pockets know of us.
I don't know what broods in hats,
what thoughts slip out of what,
take wing and won't be frightened off,
ever are we watched by scarecrows.

Are all scarecrows mammalian?
It looks as though they reproduce,
by changing all their hats at night:
Already three stand in my garden,
bow to each other and wave politely
and turn and twinkle with the sun
and talk, talk to lettuce.

I don't know whether my garden fence
wants to shut me in, exclude me.
I don't know what the weeds may have in mind,
don't know what the leaf louse intends,
don't know whether old jackets, old pants,
when they tinkle spoons in cans
rusty and tinnily windward,
tinkle for vespers, or for Angelus,
tinkle for the revolt of all the scarecrows.

Translated by A. Leslie Willson

Schreiben

In Wirklichkeit
    war das Glas nur hüfthoch gefüllt.
        Vollschlank geneigt. Im Bodensatz liegt.
Silben stechen.
Neben dem Müllschlucker wohnen
und zwischen Gestank und Geruch ermitteln.
Dem Kuchen die Springform nehmen.
Bücher,
    in ihren Gestellen,
        können nicht umfallen.
Das, oft unterbrochen, sind meine Gedanken.
Wann wird die Milch komisch?
Im Krebsgang den Fortschritt messen.
Abwarten, bis das Metall ermüdet.
Die Brücke langsam,
    zum Mitschreiben,
        einstürzen lassen.
Vorher den Schrottwert errechnen.
Sätze verabschieden Sätze.
Wenn Politik
    dem Wetter
        zur Aussage wird:
Ein Hoch über Rußland.
Zuhause
    verreist sein; auf Reisen
        zuhause bleiben.
Wir wechseln das Klima nicht.
Nur Einfalt
    will etwas beleben,
        für tot erklären.
Dumm sein, immer neu anfangen wollen.
Erinnere mich bitte, sobald ich Heuschnupfen
oder der Blumenkorso in Zoppot sage.
Rückblickend aus dem Fenster schauen.
Reime auf Schnepfendreck.

Writing

In reality
        the glass was filled only hip high.
                Inclined to stoutness. In the dregs lies.
Quibble.
Live next to the garbage disposal
and mediate between stench and aroma.
Take the springform off the cake.
Books,
        in the racks,
                cannot fall down.
Those, often interrupted, are my thoughts.
When will milk become funny?
Measure progress with a crab walk.
Wait until the metal grows fatigued.
Let the bridge,
        so I can write along,
                collapse slowly.
Before that calculate the scrap value.
Sentences legislate sentences.
When politics
        predicates
                the weather:
A high over Russia.
At home
        be traveling; on trips
                stay at home.
We don't change the climate.
Only simplicity
        will vitalize something,
                declare it dead.
Be stupid, always want to start over.
Remind me, please, whenever I say hay fever
or the Parade of Flowers in Zoppot.
Look out of the window to the rear.
Rhyme with roast giblets.

Jeden Unsinn laut mitsprechen.
Urbin, ich hab's! — Urbin, ich hab's!
Das Ungenaue genau treffen.
Die Taschen
    sind voller alter Eintrittskarten.
        Wo ist der Zündschlüssel?
Den Zündschlüssel streichen.
Mitleid mit Verben.
An den Radiergummi glauben.
Im Fundbüro einen Schirm beschwören.
Mit der Teigrolle den Augenblick walzen.
Und die Zusammenhänge wieder auftrennen.
    Weil...wegen...als...damit...um...
        Vergleiche und ähnliche Alleskleber.
Diese Geschichte muß aufhoren.
Mit einem Doppelpunkt schließen:
Ich komme wieder. Ich komme wieder.
Im Vakuum heiter bleiben.
Nur Eigenes stehlen.
Das Chaos
    in verbesserter Ausführung.
        Nicht schmücken — schreiben:

Loudly join in with any nonsense.
Urbin, I've got it! — Urbin, I've got it!
Hit the inexact exactly.
My pockets
     are full of old admission tickets.
            Where is the key to the ignition?
Caress the key to the ignition?
Compassion for verbs.
Believe in the eraser.
Conjure up an umbrella in the lost-and-found.
Waltz with a roll of dough for a moment.
Undo the correlatives again.
     Since... because of... when... so that... in order to...
        Similes and similar omnipastes.
This story has to stop.
Finish with a colon:
I'll be back. I'll be back.
Stay cheerful in a vacuum.
Steal only your own stuff.
Chaos
     in an improved model.
        Don't embellish — write:

Translated by A. Leslie Willson

Bei Tisch

Damit niemand sich erschreckt
und dem Zählzwang verlobt:
Neunaugen auspunkten.
Vorbehalten bleibt Irrtum.
Die Schwierigkeiten beim Töten,
weil sich Nachleben in der Pfanne:
Gott lebt! Gott lebt!
und krümmt sich kategorisch:
Acht sind es. Acht.

Also den Kopf zur Öse geschlitzt,
eingefädelt den Schwanz.
Denn Legenden und Dill überwintern,
Essig verwischt überschreit.

Allenfalls fragen Kinder:
Neun, sind es neun?
Aber der Lehrer sagt: Saugt sich und nährt sich.
Schaut, welche Unzahl fleißig die Luft küßt.
Schaut, wieviel Glaube ihnen das Wasser ersetzt.

Luft zählt nicht.
Wasser tauft nicht.
Dies und das schmeckt uns,
macht uns gesprächig bei Tisch:
Wie heißt dieser schmackhafte Fisch?

At Table

So that no one will become alarmed
and betroth himself to compulsory counting:
count off the nine-eyed points of the lamprey.
Keeping in reserve is a mistake.
The difficulties of killing
because of afterlife in the skillet:
God lives! God lives!
and crumples categorically.
There are eight. Eight.

So, the head slit to the eyelet,
the tail threaded in.
For legends and dill keep through the winter,
vinegar rubs out, shouts down.

In any case, children ask:
Nine, are there nine?
But the teacher says: It sucks and takes nourishment.
Look what a countless number kisses the air diligently.
Look how much faith the water restores to them.

Air doesn't count.
Water doesn't baptize.
This and that tastes good to us,
makes us loquacious with each dish:
What's the name of this delicious fish?

Translated by A. Leslie Willson

Irgendwas Machen

Da können wir doch nicht zusehen.
Wenn wir auch nichts verhindern,
wir müssen uns deutlich machen.
(Mach doch was. Mach doch was.)
Zorn, Ärger und Wut suchten sich ihre Adjektive.
Der Zorn nannte sich gerecht.
Bald sprach man vom alltäglichen Ärger.
Die Wut fiel in Ohnmacht: ohnmächtige Wut.
Ich spreche vom Protestgedicht
und gegen das Protestgedicht.
(Einmal sah ich Rekruten beim Eid
mit Kreuzfingern hinterrücks abschwören.)
Ohnmächtig protestiere ich gegen ohnmächtige Proteste.
Es handelt sich um Oster-, Schweige- und Friedensmärsche.
Es handelt sich um die hundert guten Namen
unter sieben richtigen Sätzen.
Es handelt sich um Guitarren und ähnliche
die Schallplatte fördernde Protestinstrumente.
Ich rede vom hölzernen Schwert und vom fehlenden Zahn,
vom Protestgedicht.

Wie Stahl seine Konjunktur hat, hat Lyrik ihre Konjunktur.
Aufrüstung öffnet Märkte für Antikriegsgedichte.
Die Herstellungskosten sind gering.
Man nehme: ein Achtel gerechten Zorn,
zwei Achtel alltäglichen Ärger
und fünf Achtel, damit sie vorschmeckt, ohnmächtige Wut.
Denn mittelgroße Gefühle gegen den Krieg
sind billig zu haben
und seit Troja schon Ladenhüter.
(Mach doch was. Mach doch was.)
Man macht sich Luft: schon verraucht der gerechte Zorn.
Der kleine alltägliche Ärger läßt die Ventile zischen.
Ohnmächtige Wut entlädt sich, füllt einen Luftballon,
der steigt und steigt, wird kleiner und kleiner, ist weg.

Do Anything

We can't just look on here.
Even if we prevent nothing,
we have to make ourselves clear.
(Do something. Do something. Anything. Do something.)
Fury, anger, and rage look for their adjectives.
Fury called itself righteous.
Soon people were talking about everyday anger.
Rage fell impotent: impotent rage.
I speak of the protest poem
and against the protest poem.
(Once I saw recruits taking their oath
abjuring it with crossed fingers behind their backs.)
Impotently I protested against impotent protests.
It had to do with Easter, silent, and peace marches.
It had to do with a hundred good names
among seven correct sentences.
It had to do with guitars and similar
protest instruments promoting records.
I speak of wooden swords and the missing tooth,
of the protest poem.

Just as steel has its boom, Lyrics have their boom.
Armament opens markets for anti-war poems.
Production costs are small.
Just take: an eighth of righteous fury,
two eighths of everyday anger
and five eighths, so it has a good foretaste, of impotent rage.
For medium-sized feelings against war
are cheap to get
and since Troy drugs on the market.
(Do something. Do something. Anything. Do something.)
You're airing your wrath: already righteous fury is fuming.
Little everyday anger lets its vents hiss.
Impotent rage bursts forth, fills a balloon
that rises and rises, gets smaller and smaller, is gone.

Sind Gedichte Atemübungen?
Wenn sie diesen Zweck erfüllen, — und ich frage,
prosaisch wie mein Großvater, nach dem Zweck, —
dann ist Lyrik Therapie.
Ist das Gedicht eine Waffe?
Manche, überarmiert, können kaum laufen.
Sie müssen das Unbehagen an Zuständen
als Vehikel benutzen:
sie kommen ans Ziel, sie kommen ans Ziel:
zuerst ins Feuilleton und dann in die Anthologie:
Die Napalm-Metapher und ihre Abwandlungen
im Protestgedicht der sechziger Jahre.
Es handelt sich um Traktatgedichte.
Gerechter Zorn zählt Elend und Terror auf.
Alltäglicher Ärger findet den Reim auf fehlendes Brot.
Ohnmächtige Wut macht atemlos von sich reden.
(Mach doch was. Mach doch was)
Dabei gibt es Hebelgesetze.
Sie aber kreiden ihm aus, dem Stein,
er wolle sich nicht bewegen.
Tags drauf ködert der hilflose Stil berechtiger Proteste
den treffsicheren Stil glatter Dementis.
Weil sie in der Sache zwar jeweils recht haben,
sich im Detail aber allzu leicht irren,
distanzieren sich die Unterzeichner
halblaut von den Verfassern und ihren Protesten.
(Nicht nur Diebe kaufen sich Handschuhe.)
Was übrig bleibt: zählebige Mißverständnisse
zitieren einander. Fehlerhafte Berichtigungen
lernen vom Meerschweinchen
und vermehren sich unübersichtlich.

Da erbarmt sich der Stein und tut so,
als habe man ihn verrückt:
während Zorn, Ärger und Wut einander ins Wort fallen,
treten die Spezialisten der Macht
lächelnd vor Publikum auf. Sie halten fundierte Vorträge
über den Preis, den die Freiheit fordert;
über Napalm und seine abschreckende Wirkung;

Are poems breathing exercises?
If they serve that purpose — and I ask,
prosaically as my grandfather, about purpose —
then Lyric is therapy.
Is the poem a weapon?
Some, overarmed, can hardly walk.
They have to use their uneasiness at conditions
as a vehicle:
they approach the goal, they approach the goal:
first in the Sunday news and then in the anthology:
The napalm metaphors and their variations
in the protest poem of the '60s.
It has to do with tractate poems.
Righteous fury recites misery and terror.
Everyday anger finds a rhyme on want of bread.
Impotent rage is talked about breathlessly.
(Do something. Do something...)
And then there are laws of leverage.
But they chalk the stone up
to not wanting to move.
The following day helpless style of righteous protests
entices the unerring style of smooth denials.
Since they occasionally are right in the matter,
but all-too-easily err in detail,
those signing on distance themselves
in an undertone from the writers and their protests.
(Not only thieves buy themselves gloves.)
What remains left over: tenacious misunderstandings
quote one another. Error-prone justifications
learn from the guinea pigs
and reproduce unintelligibly.

Thereupon the stone takes pity and acts
as though it had been moved:
while fury, anger, and rage interrupt one another,
the specialists of power step up
before the audience with a smile. They give endowed lectures
about the price that freedom demands;
about napalm and its terrifying effect;

über berechtigte Proteste und die erklärliche Wut.
Das alles ist erlaubt.
Da die Macht nur die Macht achtet,
darf solange ohnmächtig protestiert werden,
bis nicht mehr, weil der Lärm stört,
protestiert werden darf. —
Wir aber verachten die Macht.
Wir sind nicht mächtig, beteuern wir uns.
Ohne Macht gefallen wir uns in Ohnmacht.
Wir wollen die Macht nicht; sie aber hat uns. —
Nun fühlt sich der gerechte Zorn mißverstanden.
Der alltägliche Ärger mündet in Schweigemärsche,
die zuvor angemeldet und genehmigt wurden.
Im Kreis läuft die ohnmächtige Wut.
Das fördert den gleichfalls gerechten Zorn
verärgerter Polizisten:
ohnmächtige Wut wird handgreiflich.
Die Faust wächst sich zum Kopf aus
und denkt in Tiefeschlägen Leberhaken knöchelhart.
(Mach doch was. Mach doch was...)
Das alles macht Schule und wird von der Macht
gestreichelt geschlagen subventioniert.
Schon setzt der Stein, der bewegt werden wollte,
unbewegt Moos an.
Geht das so weiter? — Im Kreis schon.
Was sollen wir machen? — Nicht irgendwas.
Wohin mit der Wut? — Ich weiß ein Rezept:

Schlagt in die Schallmauer Nägel.
Köpft Pusteblumen und Kerzen.
Setzt auf dem Sofa euch durch.
   Wir haben immer noch Wut.
   Schon sind wir überall heiser.
   Wir sind gegen alles umsonst.
   Was sollen wir jetzt noch machen?
   Wo sollen wir hin mit der Wut?
Mach doch was. Mach doch was.
Wir müssen irgendwas,
mach doch was, machen.

about righteous protests and inexplicable rage.
All of that is allowed.
Since power respects only power
then impotent protests may take place until,
because the noise is bothersome,
they may no longer take place. —
But we have contempt for power.
We're not powerful, we vow to ourselves.
Impotent we fancy our impotence.
We don't want power; but it has us. —
Not righteous fury feels misunderstood.
Everyday anger ends in silent marches
that were applied for and approved ahead of time.
Impotent rage runs in a circle.
That challenges the likewise righteous rage
of angry policemen:
impotent fury becomes manifest.
The fist grows into a head
and thinks in hard-knuckled low blows to the liver.
(Do something. Do something...)
All of that finds followers and is
petted slapped supported by power.
Already the stone, that was to be moved,
begins to grow moss unmoved.
Will that continue? — In the circle, sure.
What ought we to do? — Not anything.
Where do we take our fury? — I know a recipe:

Drive nails into the sound barrier.
Behead dandelions and candles.
Hold your own on the sofa.
      We still have rage.
      We're hoarse everywhere.
      We're opposed to everything in vain.
      What shall we do now?
      Where shall we take our rage?
Do something. Do something.
We must do,
do something, something.

Los, protestieren wir schnell.
Der will nicht mitprotestieren.
Los, unterschreib schon und schnell.
Du warst doch immer dagegen.
Wer nicht unterschreibt, ist dafür.
Schön ist die Wut im Gehge,
bevor sie gefüttert wird.
Lang lief die Ohnmacht im Regen,
die Strümpfe trocknet sie jetzt.
Wut und Ventile, darüber Gesang;
Ohnmacht, dein Nadelöhr ist der Gesang:
    Weil ich nichts machen kann,
    weil ich nichts machen kann,
    hab ich die Wut, hab ich die Wut.
    Mach doch was. Mach doch was.
    Irgendwas. Mach doch was.
    Wir müssen irgendwas,
    hilft doch nix, hilft doch nix,
    wir müssen Irgendwas,
    mach doch was, machen.
Lauf schweigend Protest.
Lief ich schon. Lief ich schon.
Schreib ein Gedicht.
Hab ich schon. Hab ich schon.
Koch eine Sülze. Schweinekopfsülze:
die Ohnmacht geliere, die Wut zittre nach.
Ich weiß ein Rezept; wer kocht es mir nach?

Come on, let's protest quick.
He doesn't want to protest with us.
Come on, sign it and quick.
You were always against it.
Anyone who doesn't sign is for it.
Rage is always nice in its pen
before it gets fed.
Impotence ran for a long time in the rain,
now it's drying its socks.
Rage and vents, and song over it all;
impotence, your needle's eye is song:

> Because I can't do anything,
> because I can't do anything,
> I'm enraged, I'm enraged.
> Do something. Do something.
> Anything. Do something.
> We've gotta do something,
> it won't help, it won't help,
> we must do,
> do something, something.

Run a protest silently.
I ran already. I ran already.
Write a poem.
I did already. I did already.
Cook jellied meat. Pig's head jellied meat:
Make jelly of impotence, let rage quiver like that.
I know a recipe; who will cook it after me?

Translated by A. Leslie Willson

Part Five

SPEECHES

On Writers as Court Jesters and on Nonexistent Courts

Address delivered April 1966 at the Princeton Conference on the occasion of the meeting of the German literary Group 47 at Princeton University.

They seldom meet, and then as strangers: I am referring to our over-tired politicians and our uncertain writers with their quickly formulated demands which always cry out for immediate fulfillment. Where is the calendar that would permit the mighty of our day to hold court, to seek utopian advice, or to cleanse themselves from the compromises of everyday life by listening to expositions of preposterous utopias? True, there has been the already legendary Kennedy era; and to this day an overworked Willy Brandt listens with close attention when writers tot up his past errors or darkly prophesy future defeats. Both examples are meager; at the very most they prove that there are no courts and hence no advisers to princes, or court jesters. But let's assume for the fun of it that there is such a thing as a literary court jester who would like to be an adviser at court or in some foreign ministry; and let's assume at the same time that there is no such thing, that the literary court jester is only the invention of a serious and slow-working writer who, merely because he has given his mayor a few bits of advice that were not taken, fears in social gatherings to be mistaken for a court jester. If then we assume both that he exists and that he does not, then he exists as a fiction, hence in reality. But the question is: Is the literary court jester worth talking about?

When I consider the fools of Shakespeare and Velásquez, or let us say the dwarfish power components of the Baroque age — for there is a connection between fools and power, though seldom between writers and power — I wish the literary court jester existed; and as we shall see, I know a number of writers who are well-fitted for this political service. Except that they are far too touchy. Just as a "housekeeper" dislikes to be called a "cleaning woman," they object to being called fools. "Fool" is not enough. They just want to be known to the Bureau of Internal Revenue as "writers"; nor do they wish to be ennobled by the title of "poet." This self-chosen middle — or middle-class — position enables them to turn up their noses at the disreputable, asocial element, the fools and poets. Whenever society demands fools and poets — and society knows what it needs and likes — whenever, in Germany for example, a writer of verse or a storyteller is addressed by an old lady or a young man as a "poet," the writer of verse or storyteller — including the present speaker — hastens to make it clear that he wishes to be known as a writer. This modesty, this humility, is underlined by short, embarrassed sentences: "I practice my trade like any shoemaker," or "I work seven hours a day with language just as other self-respecting citizens lay bricks for seven hours a day." Or differing only in tone of voice and Eastern or Western ideology: "I take my place in socialist society" or "I stand foursquare behind the pluralistic society and pay my taxes as a citizen among citizens."

Probably this well-bred attitude, this gesture of self-belittlement, is in part a reaction to the genius cult of the nineteenth century, which in Germany continued to produce its pungent-smelling house plants down to the period of Expressionism. Who wants to be a Stefan George running around with fiery-eyed disciples? Who wants to disregard his doctor's advice and live the concentrated life of a Rimbaud, without life insurance? Who does not shy away from the prospect of climbing the steps of Olympus every morning, who does not shun the gymnastics to which Gerhart Hauptmann still subjected himself or the tour de force which even Thomas Mann — if only by way of irony — performed as long as he lived?

Today we have adapted ourselves to modern life. You won't find a Rilke doing handstands in front of the mirror; Narcissus has discovered sociology. There is no genius, and to be a fool is inadmissible because a fool is genius in reverse. So there he sits, the domesticated writer, deathly afraid of Muses and laurel wreaths.

His fears are legion. The already-mentioned fear of being called a poet. The fear of being misunderstood. The fear of not being taken seriously. The fear of entertaining, that is, of giving enjoyment: the fear, invented in Germany but since then thriving in other countries, of producing something Lucullan. For though a writer is intent to the point of fear and trembling on being a part of society, he still wants very much to mold this society according to his fiction but chronically distrusts fiction as something smacking of the poet and fool; from the "Nouveau Roman" to "socialist realism," writers, sustained by choruses of lettered teenagers, are earnestly striving to offer more than mere fiction. The writer who does not wish to be a poet distrusts his own artifices. And clowns who disavow their circus are not very funny.

Is a horse whiter because we call it white? And is a writer who says he is "committed" a white horse? We are all familiar with the writer who, far removed from the poet and the fool, but not satisfied with the naked designation of his trade, appends an adjective, calling himself and encouraging others to call him a "committed" writer, which always — forgive me — reminds me of titles such as "court pastry cook" or "Catholic bicycle rider." From the start, before even inserting his paper into the typewriter, the committed writer writes, not novels, poems, or comedies, but "committed literature." When a body of literature is thus plainly stamped, the obvious implication is that all other literature is "uncommitted." Everything else, which takes in a good deal, is disparaged as art for art's sake. Insincere applause from the Right calls forth insincere applause from the Left, and fear of applause from the wrong camp calls forth anemic hopes of applause from the right camp. Such complex and anguished working conditions engender manifestoes, and the sweat of anguish is replaced by professions of faith. When, for instance, Peter Weiss, who after all did write *The Shadow of the Coachman's Body,* suddenly discovers that he is a "humanist writer," when a writer and poet versed in all the secrets of language fails to recognize that even in Stalin's day this adjective had already become an empty expletive, the farce of the committed humanist writer becomes truly theatrical. It would be better if he were the fool he is.

You will observe that I confine myself, in utter provincialism, to German affairs, to the smog in which I am myself at home.

286 · *Günter Grass*

However, I trust that the United States of America has committed and humanist writers and poets as well as those others who are so readily defamed, and possibly also literary fools; because it is here in this country that this topic was proposed to me: Special adviser or court jester.

The *or* means no doubt that a court jester can never be a special adviser and that a special adviser must under no circumstances regard himself as a court jester, but rather perhaps as a committed writer. He is the great sage; to him financial reform is no Chinese puzzle; and it is he, hovering high above the strife of parties and factions, who in every instance pronounces the final word of counsel. After centuries of hostility the fictitious antitheses are reconciled. Mind and power walk hand in hand. Something like this: After many sleepless nights the Chancellor summons the writer Heinrich Böll to his bungalow. At first the committed writer listens in silence to the Chancellor's troubles. Then, when the Chancellor sinks back into his chair, the writer delivers himself of succinct, irresistible counsel. Relieved of his cares, the Chancellor springs from his chair eager to embrace the committed writer; but the writer takes an attitude of aloofness, he does not wish to become a court jester. He admonishes the Chancellor to convert writer's word into Chancellor's deed. The next day an amazed world learns that Chancellor Erhard has resolved to demobilize the army, to recognize the German democratic Republic and the Oder-Neisse line, and to expropriate all capitalists.

Encouraged by this feat, the humanist author Peter Weiss journeys from Sweden to the recently recognized German Democratic Republic and leaves his card at the office of Waiter Ulbricht, Chairman of the Council of State. Like Erhard at a loss for good advice, Ulbricht receives the humanist writer at once. Advice is given, embrace rejected, word converted into deed; and the next day an amazed world learns that the Chairman of the Council of State has countermanded the order to fire on those attempting to cross the borders of his state in either direction and transformed the political sections of all prisons and penitentiaries into people's kindergartens. Thus counseled, the Chairman of the Council of State apologizes to Wolf Biermann, the poet and ballad singer and asks him to sing away his — Ulbricht's — Stalinist past with bright and mordant rhymes.

Of course court jesters, should there be any, cannot hope to compete with such accomplishments. Have I exaggerated? Of course I have exaggerated. But when I think of the wishes, often stated in an undertone, of committed and humanist writers, I don't think I have exaggerated so very much. And in my weaker moments I find it easy to see myself acting in just such a well-intentioned, or rather, committed and humanist, manner: After losing the parliamentary elections the opposition candidate for the Chancellorship sends, in his perplexity, for the writer here addressing you, who listens, gives advice, and does not allow himself to be embraced; and the next day an amazed world learns that the Social Democrats have discarded the Godesberg Program and replaced it with a sharp, sparkling and once again revolutionary manifesto encouraging the workers to discard hats for caps. No, no revolution breaks out, because for all its sharpness this manifesto is so much to the point that neither capital nor Church can resist its arguments. Without a blow the government is handed over to the Social Democrats, etc. The United States of America, I should think, offers similar possibilities. Why, for example, shouldn't President Johnson call on the preceding speaker, Allen Ginsberg, for advice?

These short-winded utopias remain — utopias. Reality speaks a different language. We have no special advisers or court jesters. All I see — and here I am including myself — is bewildered writers and poets who doubt the value of their own trade and avail themselves fully, partially or not at all, of their infinitesimal possibilities of playing a part in the events of our time — not with advice but with action. It is meaningless to generalize about "the writer" and his position in society; writers are highly diversified individuals, shaken in varying degree by ambition, neuroses and marital crises. Court jester or special adviser, both are disembodied little men — five, six lines and a circle — such as the members of a discussion panel draw in their notebooks when they get bored. Nevertheless they have given rise to a cult which, especially in Germany, is assuming an almost religious character. Students, young trade unionists, young Protestants, high school boys and Boy Scouts, dueling and nondueling fraternities — all of these and more never weary of organizing discussions revolving around questions like: "Ought a writer to be committed?" or "Is the writer the conscience of the nation?" Even men with critical minds and a genuine love of literature, such as Marcel Reich-Ranicki, who will speak to us in a little while, persist in calling upon writers to deliver protests, declarations, and professions of faith. I don't mean that anyone asks them to take a partisan attitude toward political parties, to come out for or against the Social Democrats, for example; no, the idea is that speaking as writers, as a kind of shame-faced elite, they should protest, condemn war, praise peace, and display noble sentiments. Yet anyone who knows anything about writers is well aware that even if they band together at congresses they remain eccentric individuals. True, I know a good many who cling with touching devotion to their revolutionary heirlooms, who make use of Communism, that burgundy-colored plush sofa with its well-worn springs, for afternoon reveries. But even these conservative "progressives" are split into one-man factions, each of which reads Marx in his own way. Others in turn are briefly mobilized by their daily glance at the paper and wax indignant at the breakfast table: "Something ought to be done, something ought to be done!" When helplessness lacks wit it begins to snivel. And yet there is a great deal to do, more than can be expressed in manifestoes and protests. But there are also a great many writers, known and unknown, who, far from presuming to be the "conscience of the nation," occasionally bolt from their desks and busy themselves with the trivia of democracy. Which implies a readiness to compromise. Something we must get through our head is this: a poem knows no compromise, but men live by compromise. The individual who can stand up under this contradiction and act is a fool and will change the world.

Translated by Ralph Manheim

Cloud Clenched in a Fist above Forest

An Obituary

From the summer of eighty-eight into the winter of eighty-nine, I drew dead trees, interrupted only by stated "facts" in current affairs. A decade was ending at the start of which I had written my warnings in *Headbirths — or The Germans Are Dying Out;* but what has now turned up as the result after doing accounts is no longer a headbirth: beech trees visibly downed, pines no longer proudly upright, birches robbed of their beauty, and oak trees marked by mortality. And, striving to emphasize this evidence of forest work, hurricanes in short succession occurred at the beginning of the decade, five in number, willing to play pick-up-sticks with yet standing trees.

It was like a looting of corpses. Looking and recording, documenting. Frequently photographed and exhibited in color or black and white, it nevertheless remained incredible what was to illustrate statistics and official forest condition reports. Anyone can take pictures. Who's to trust photos!

So I drew, on location — in mixed forest in Denmark, in the Upper Harz region, in the Erzgebirge, right behind the house where the forest is dense, and the evergreens have given up. In the beginning, I wanted to do sketches only and record in writing the nitty-gritty that is not visible, gets tabled in meetings, talked to death in assessments and counter-assessments, or lost in the general hubbub, just as I had recorded other matters, most recently daily life in Calcutta.

But about the forest and its dying, everything has been said and written. About causes and culprits. How fast or how slowly it is passing away on hilltops or flatland, and what of. What might save it, overall or partially. New words, such as panic-blossom or anxiety-shoots are becoming known. Blight of seeds. Everyday corruption is as accepted and boring as a count with his cane. And always, whenever the forest damage assessments are punctually delivered in the fall, editorials and commentaries arrive, which begin deeply concerned but end in daring hopes shortly before the final full stop. Everything is being said, also that the hand remains at five before twelve. Nothing has to be kept quiet. We live in a land of roomy freedom; all citizens have *all clear ahead* from childhood on.

Taciturn, I drew on location. A subtitle here and there, more shorter than longer ones, is all that came up. Trees showing their roots make you speechless. What's left to say, except Amen? About Grimm's forests and how Hansel and Gretel got lost in the dead forest I have written. I might have called up Goethe and Heine in the Upper Harz, near the Three-Cornered Pole that formerly served as the corner stone between duchies and counties. We got to talking, but the two, in spite of their wit, stuck to their own contemporary cares. They left me alone with the dead woods. Or did I turn them off by taking too literally and discussing too extensively the present statistics on damage? Patterns of mortality of the silver fir. Blight of the fine roots of beeches. What all makes acid rain: Cloud clenched in a fist above forests.

So I concentrated on looking at it. In lying flat, the dead woods inspired more than sketches can tell. Further drawings were followed by more drawings tolerating no distraction and conjuring up blackness in the light. I drew with Siberian drawing coal, a wood product. For brush and for pen drawings I used natural brew from fresh cuttlefish ink. While drawing, I smoked — too much, as usual.

Looking, looking, again consulting the sketch. Don't just be abstract. You are the eye witness. Nobody else is here. What's cracking is no longer alive. Bark beetles at most, living off dead wood, like you. What remains of birches: shame. Firs that had wanted to emigrate did not get far. These beeches here, actually strewn crisscross, would have broken your grandfather's, the master joiner's, calculating heart. What else comes to mind for you to sound again the silence. *Tannhäuser.* The Waldheim Affair. Buchenwald. To shout, in the dead forest: "Waldeslust! Waldeslust!"

Or seeing the familiar as a mirror image. How the artist approaches his subject. Often he avoids it for days. By avoiding it, he just postpones it. He looks past it. He hopes it might disappear, become a matter of indifference to him. For example, these fir trees at the edge of the forest, next to the heath, firs whose roots have rotted away and that therefore during the last northwest gale ... Windstorm breakage, the forest administration calls it. Now they are done, upright format from my perspective. Just as if they wanted to bring to light the word *radical:* roots pointing skyward. The artist brings to paper what makes him speechless: A stand of birches, frozen in time as if on order — trunks broken off midway, drawn several times broadside. Now the artist is temporarily satisfied.

Clear-cut in our heads. What makes man cause forests to die? Regretfully, sure, but yet shrugging his shoulders as if the forest had lived on beyond itself, a fossil. Someone pretending to think in large concepts says: Nature will know how to help itself. Also, the forest in our times has been able to conserve itself: in countless poems, in German song, in pictures hanging in air-conditioned museums, in our fairy tales... Here, exactly here, Rumpelstiltskin tore off his leg.

When I was there, drawing between horsetails and rushes, the GDR still existed in its self-secure, absolute power; yet compulsions began to relax: retardation of material supply. Just like once when the painter Caspar David Friedrich wanted to draw pious fir trees, we traveled down from Rügen via Dresden. From there a strategically important road leads through the Erzgebirge directly to Prague. Twice in this century, German troops with a clear mission had followed it; Czechs do remember.

Then day by day the state power of the German Democratic Republic crumbled, while I, of necessity, drew sheet after sheet of pictures of dead woods. That reflected on subtitles. If you stand in the Upper Harz, looking from Germany to Germany, you see dying forests resembling each other like relatives, and the reunification is already complete. Begin with glasnost in the forests.

When in Leipzig, Dresden, and Berlin the crowds shouted: *We are the people!*, one of the banners read: *Cut down the bigwigs! Save the trees!* Even if the bigwigs of only one state were meant, I would know of plenty to add from the other, and on both sides trees in need of being saved; but there are no people shouting *We are the people!* any longer.

Long before Leipzig: From one Monday to the next they bend, crack, and crash, shamelessly showing their roots that died off long since. Each tree in falling insists on coming to rest in a different position. The artist is grateful for so much decrepitude. Those yet standing, because they are dying from the top down, often shortened to stubble, are also capable of various gestures. This tree accuses, that one is dying of shame; another, a torso, still tells of its erstwhile wide-branched beauty; and this one is convinced of my sympathy. All of them, the artist insists, are crying for mercy.

But it's too late for that. We cannot afford sentimentalism. We have to hurry, or the Japanese, the Koreans, Asians in general will overtake us. We might deliver some thoughtful comfort as Band-

Aids: Die and be born again. Introspection for the reaping of the poet Handke for healing words.

When I was drawing in the Upper Harz at the beginning of April and in the Erzgebirge at the end of July, the weather was changeable. After short clearing — long enough for a sketch — rain mixed with snow fell in the Harz, and strong rains surprised us in the Erzgebirge, where we sheltered in Goeschel's mice-infested hut. Low-hanging, threatening clouds, stopping at no state border, moved in from a north-northwesterly direction and had enriched themselves underway, were sated, brought duty-free cargo. Last spills: dividends. Cloud clenched in a fist above forests.

It is said: With the forests, the people will die out. I do not believe it. They are tougher and can take more than they do to themselves. After short- or long-term scares (last time, after Chernobyl), they emerged unchanged — you really couldn't tell anything from their appearance — and proceeded to their daily business agenda, happy because the familiar constraints had remained intact. Only when the dying seals in the North Sea kept easy-reading material lively for weeks, the newest mood in the West was something close to pre-revolutionary. Later, when other scares had their season, this was said: They had not been poisoned by a foul environment, rather, a kind of flu had gotten the cute barkers.

The artist selects. Here it is the beginning of brown needles, at best noticed by specialists. A symbol of illness that saturates statistics when calculated in percentages. There it looks relatively mild, in spite of fir trees deteriorating in shape to resemble storks' nests rather than the initially conceived Gothic design, compared to hilltops that make you speechless, and only await the artist. He wants it clear and conspicuous. As soon as the victors have left, he is attracted to the battlefield. His place is where devastation reigns. It makes him happy in a furious way to be able to record damage and loss with his creaking wood product. Here, for example, on Sun Mountain, which in its baldness offers more view.

Then at home there was the owl in the fireplace. We had forgotten to cover the chimney with a grate against crows. Outwardly unhurt, without a particular smell, its owl's gaze reduced to a narrow line, its talons bedded in the light-colored fluff of its underside, thus it presented itself. I drew it from all sides, in lead pencil, in smelly cuttlefish ink, in charcoal. Then the artist placed it between and in front of dead trees. He let it become the cloud that rains down over dead tree trunks (between horsetails and rushes). The owl as a fist clenched above forests.

And everywhere the disappearance of syllables, decay of sound, because this rain that we call acid hits us, too. Write off the losses. Do the accounts. During the last year (rich in events) Romania plus Panama equaled Christmas. It's a crying shame. But because it's a crying shame, gradually the brave little smile called grin-and-bear-it wins out. After all, there's some disarmament going on at the fringes. Economically we are doing fine. And everything else is wide open, since the wall is falling. Those over there just have to imitate us, and they will be doing fine soon, too, just like us. And they have to get away from their brown coal. And finally learn that only achievement counts. And get rid of their homophobia — we won't bite. And if it weren't for that spoilsport the ozone hole, which after all gave us an almost unending summer, and if those down in the Amazon would finally turn off their chain saws — many of them German products and very good — and stop cutting, simply cutting down their tropical forests, which are also our tropical forests, and if in India (and elsewhere) they would finally understand that one cannot, like rabbits … and on top of that cows, far too many cows, no, not just billions of spray cans, but cows, also cows, which make our ozone hole bigger and bigger, and if a miracle doesn't finally happen. . . .

The artist hesitates. The forests on white paper turn out so transparent, soon glasslike, dry and fragile (to be knocked over by the next wind). Always standing up straight, well mannered. This is the state of affairs. Put away your utensils.

Translated by Irmgard Elsner Hunt

Acknowledgments

Every reasonable effort has been made to locate the owners of rights to previously published works and the translations printed here. We gratefully acknowledge permission to reprint the following material:

Foreword by John Irving, introduction to a reading by Günter Grass on December 14, 1992, at the 92nd Street Y in New York City. Printed with the permission of John Irving.

The Meeting at Telgte by Günter Grass. Copyright © 1979 by Hermann Luchterhand Verlag GmbH KG, Neuwied und Darmstadt. English translation copyright © 1981 by Harcourt Brace Jovanovich, Inc. Published by arrangement with Harcourt Brace Jovanovich, Inc.

Cat and Mouse. Copyright © 1961 by Hermann Luchterhand Verlag GmbH. English translation copyright © 1963 by Harcourt Brace Jovanovich, Inc., and Martin Secker & Warburg Limited. Published by arrangement with Harcourt Brace Jovanovich, Inc.

"The Ballerina"; "Hochwasser" ("The Flood"); "Nächtliches Stadion" ("Stadium at Night"); "Familiär" ("Family Matters"); "Die Bösen Schuhe" ("The Wicked Shoes"); "Blechmusik" ("Music for Brass"); "Im Ei" ("In the Egg"); "Die Vogelscheuchen" ("The Scarecrows"); "Schreiben" ("Writing"); "Bei Tisch" ("At Table"); "Irgendwas Machen" ("Do Anything"); "On Writers as Court Jesters and on Nonexistent Courts"; "Cloud Clenched in a Fist above Forest." By arrangement with Steidl Verlag. All rights reserved.

THE GERMAN LIBRARY
in 100 Volumes

Wolfram von Eschenbach
Parzival
Edited by André Lefevere

Gottfried von Strassburg
Tristran and Isolde
Edited and Revised by
Francis G. Gentry
Foreword by C. Stephen Jaeger

German Medieval Tales
Edited by Francis G. Gentry
Foreword by Thomas Berger

German Mystical Writings
Edited by Karen J. Campbell
Foreword by Carol Zaleski

Seventeenth Century German Prose
Edited by Lynne Tatlock
Foreword by Günter Grass

German Humanism and Reformation
Edited by Reinhard P. Becker
Foreword by Roland Bainton

German Theater before 1750
Edited by Gerald Gillespie
Foreword by Martin Esslin

Eighteenth Century German Prose
Edited by Ellis Shookman
Foreword by Dennis F. Mahoney

Eighteenth Century German Criticism
Edited by Timothy J. Chamberlain

Sturm und Drang
Edited by Alan C. Leidner

Immanuel Kant
Philosophical Writings
Edited by Ernst Behler
Foreword by René Wellek

Friedrich Schiller
*Plays: Intrigue and Love
and Don Carlos*
Edited by Walter Hinderer
Foreword by Gordon Craig

Friedrich Schiller
Wallenstein and Mary Stuart
Edited by Walter Hinderer

Friedrich Schiller
Essays
Edited by Walter Hinderer
and Daniel O. Dahlstrom

Johann Wolfgang von Goethe
*The Sufferings of Young Werther
and Elective Affinities*
Edited by Victor Lange
Forewords by Thomas Mann

Johann Wolfgang von Goethe
*Plays: Egmont, Iphigenia in Tauris,
Torquato Tasso*
Edited by Frank G. Ryder

German Romantic Criticism
Edited by A. Leslie Willson
Foreword by Ernst Behler

Friedrich Hölderlin
Hyperion and Selected Poems
Edited by Eric L. Santner

Philosophy of German Idealism
Edited by Ernst Behler

G. W. F. Hegel
*Encyclopedia of the Philosophical
Sciences in Outline and Critical
Writings*
Edited by Ernst Behler

Heinrich von Kleist
Plays
Edited by Walter Hinderer
Foreword by E. L. Doctorow

E. T. A. Hoffman
Tales
Edited by Victor Lange

Georg Büchner
Complete Works and Letters
Edited by Walter Hinderer and
Henry J. Schmidt

German Fairy Tales
Edited by Helmut Brackert and
  Volkmar Sander
Foreword by Bruno Bettelheim

German Literary Fairy Tales
Edited by Frank G. Ryder and
  Robert M. Browning
Introduction by Gordon Birrell
Foreword by John Gardner

F. Grillparzer, J. H. Nestroy,
  F. Hebbel
Nineteenth Century German Plays
Edited by Egon Schwarz in
  collaboration with
  Hannelore M. Spence

Heinrich Heine
Poetry and Prose
Edited by Jost Hermand and
  Robert C. Holub
Foreword by Alfred Kazin

Heinrich Heine
The Romantic School and other Essays
Edited by Jost Hermand and
  Robert C. Holub

Heinrich von Kleist and Jean Paul
German Romantic Novellas
Edited by Frank G. Ryder and
  Robert M. Browning
Foreword by John Simon

German Romantic Stories
Edited by Frank Ryder
Introduction by Gordon Birrell

German Poetry from 1750 to 1900
Edited by Robert M. Browning
Foreword by Michael Hamburger

Karl Marx, Friedrich Engels, August
  Bebel, and Others
German Essays on Socialism in the
  Nineteenth Century
Edited by Frank Mecklenburg and
  Manfred Stassen

Gottfried Keller
Stories
Edited by Frank G. Ryder
Foreword by Max Frisch

Wilhelm Raabe
Novels
Edited by Volkmar Sander
Foreword by Joel Agee

Theodor Fontane
Short Novels and Other Writings
Edited by Peter Demetz
Foreword by Peter Gay

Theodor Fontane
Delusions, Confusions and The
  Poggenpuhl Family
Edited by Peter Demetz
Foreword by J. P. Stern
Introduction by William L. Zwiebel

Wilhelm Busch and Others
German Satirical Writings
Edited by Dieter P. Lotze and
  Volkmar Sander
Foreword by John Simon

Writings of German Composers
Edited by Jost Hermand and
  James Steakley

German Lieder
Edited by Philip Lieson Miller
Foreword by Hermann Hesse

German Essays on History
Edited by Roll Sältzer
Foreword by James J. Schechan

Arthur Schnitzler
Plays and Stories
Edited by Egon Schwarz
Foreword by Stanley Elkin

Rainer Maria Rilke
Prose and Poetry
Edited by Egon Schwarz
Foreword by Howard Nemerov

Robert Musil
Selected Writings
Edited by Burton Pike
Foreword by Joel Agee

Essays on German Theater
Edited by Margaret Herzfeld-Sander
Foreword by Martin Esslin

All volumes available in hardcover and paperback editions at your bookstore or from the publisher. For more information on The German Library write to: The Continuum Publishing Company, 370 Lexington Avenue, New York, NY 10017.